The Best
AMERICAN MYSTERY & SUSPENSE 2022

GUEST EDITORS OF
THE BEST AMERICAN MYSTERY AND
SUSPENSE

The Best
AMERICAN
MYSTERY &
SUSPENSE™
2022

Edited and with an Introduction
by JESS WALTER
STEPH CHA, Series Editor

MARINER BOOKS
New York   Boston

HarperCollins books may be purchased for educational, business, or sales promotional use. For information, please email the Special Markets Department at SPsales@harpercollins.com.

FIRST EDITION

ISSN 2768-1920
ISBN 978-0-06-326448-9

22 23 24 25 26   LSC   10 9 8 7 6 5 4 3 2 1

Contents

Foreword

IT'S APRIL OF 2022, and this Tuesday my son, born in the first weeks of COVID-19 lockdown, celebrated his second birthday. If all goes well, I will have a second son by the time you read this in November; if all goes well, this life-defining pandemic will finally be over. These last two years have been difficult for many of us—exhausting, repetitive, full of illness and death.

We hoped 2021 would prove easier than 2020. Instead, we started the year with a lethal attack on the U.S. Capitol. We saw an increase in violent crime—and homicide in particular—accompanied by public anxiety and bitter political division. And of course people kept dying of COVID. We lost over 400,000 lives in the United States alone, surpassing the nightmarish toll of 2020.

How to make sense of all this? The misery, the gloom, the relentless tragedy that pervades daily life, even here in beautiful America, one of the richest countries and largest democracies in the world?

For some of us, the answer is the same as it's always been: we read. I imagine that you, reading the foreword to this year's *Best American Mystery and Suspense* anthology, are a bit like me: you draw some particular, necessary nourishment from crime fiction. I've been a professional crime writer for many years, so I've had occasion to examine what attracts us to this genre. I think we read to get educated and feel connected, as well as to escape and forget. But I developed my taste for dark, mysterious stories long before I thought to ask why. Animals don't know why they eat tree bark. Scientists have studied them and determined that the bark helps them produce an enzyme that catalyzes the digestion of starch. But ask a beaver, capybara, or squirrel, and it's liable to ignore you and keep munching.

Whatever the mechanism, and whether or not we ask, fiction helps us make sense of life, the universe, everything. Maybe what we mystery fiends get from crime fiction is a way to metabolize the horrors and uncertainties of a violent world. Crime writers translate the mystery and suspense of everyday living, and we take these stories and make them part of ourselves.

This is what I've found, anyway, in my years of reading and writing in this rich, expansive genre, and especially in the two eventful years since I started editing *The Best American Mystery and Suspense.* I'm proud to be part of this essential series, now published by Mariner Books, and grateful for the opportunity to curate these stories for your consumption. Since its inception as *The Best American Mystery Stories* in 1997, this anthology has published short fiction by many of your favorite writers at different points in their careers. It also boasts an illustrious roster of guest editors: Robert B. Parker, Sue Grafton, Ed McBain, Donald E. Westlake, Lawrence Block, James Ellroy, Michael Connelly, Nelson DeMille, Joyce Carol Oates, Scott Turow, Carl Hiaasen, George Pelecanos, Jeffery Deaver, Lee Child, Harlan Coben, Robert Crais, Lisa Scottoline, Laura Lippman, James Patterson, Elizabeth George, John Sandford, Louise Penny, Jonathan Lethem, C. J. Box, and Alafair Burke, who was the first guest editor under my tenure.

For *Best American Mystery and Suspense 2022,* I had the pleasure of working with Jess Walter, a writer I have long admired. (I have a distinct memory of spotting him at a hotel restaurant in Seattle during the Association of Writers and Writing Programs conference in 2014; I was far too intimidated to approach him.) While his most famous book is probably *Beautiful Ruins*—an incredible literary novel as well as a publishing phenomenon—he is also a crime fiction luminary. His first two novels were wonderfully written thrillers featuring Spokane police detective Caroline Mabry; his third, *Citizen Vince,* won the Edgar Allan Poe Award for Best Novel in 2006. Like many of my favorite authors, Jess slips in and out of the genre, telling the stories he wants to tell in the way he wants to tell them. He is a four-time contributor to the *Best American* series, with three appearances in *Best American Short Stories* and one in *Best American Nonrequired Reading.* His most recent novel, 2020's *The Cold Millions,* is a breathtaking historical work about the haves and have-nots in early-twentieth-century Spokane. It also features a drunken hit man and a fugitive outlaw, in addition to the crime that always accompanies stories of deep social inequality: corrupt millionaires, a thuggish police force, and desperate people in an existential struggle against a broken government.

Early on in the selection process, Jess asked me what he called "the old unanswerable question": How does one define a mystery or suspense story? I have found, after these two years of reading, that enforcing strict genre boundaries would bring me little satisfaction. The short form is inherently restrictive. It's hard to deliver all the joys of a 300-page crime novel in a spare few thousand words. The traditional mystery structure—in which questions are asked and answered, the promises of the genre fulfilled—can eat up a lot of space in a shorter work, leaving less room for scene setting and character development, or any of the other colorful, interesting, sometimes extraneous elements that make a story memorable. One of the best parts of this job is seeing the many brilliant ways in which writers incorporate crime into a broad range of stories. Some are whodunits, some are thrillers, some are just about people in bad circumstances trying to get through their day. They all bring mystery or suspense in one form or another.

I sought out stories from a variety of sources, though I did start with the usual suspects. I read through every issue of *Ellery Queen Mystery Magazine* and *Alfred Hitchcock's Mystery Magazine* as well as Akashic Books' collections of noir and genre stories. I tracked down all the crime anthologies published in 2021 and kept tabs on the various mystery publications, both in print and online. I also hit up editors of literary journals I thought might have a few stories that would fit comfortably under the crime umbrella. I sifted through all these stories and picked around fifty of the best (or more accurately, my favorites), which I passed on to Jess. He read them closely, taking thoughtful notes, and we discussed their merits at length and with great enthusiasm (another amazing part of this job: the two-person book club with authors like Alafair Burke and Jess Walter). I gave him my input, and he narrowed down the list, making increasingly painful cuts, until he selected the twenty in this volume. You can find the remaining thirty candidates in the honorable mentions at the back of this book. All the writers and stories on that list are worth seeking out. In fact, two of this year's contributors received honorable mentions last year.

With two anthologies under my belt, I feel like I have some idea of what I'm doing as I start in on *The Best American Mystery and Suspense 2023*. That said, I still worry about missing eligible stories, so authors and editors, please do send me your work. To qualify, stories must be originally written in English (or translated by the original authors) by writers born or permanently residing in the United States. They need to be independent stories (not excerpts) published in the calendar year 2021 in an American publication, either print or online. I have a strong preference for web submissions, which you can send in any reasonable format to bestamericanmysterysuspense@gmail.com. If you would like to send printed materials, you can email me for a mailing address. The submissions deadline is December 31, and when possible, several months earlier. I promise to look at every story sent to me before that deadline. Afterward, you're relying on the personal generosity of the mother of two children under the age of three.

Thank you for writing. Thank you for reading. Now enjoy these killer stories.

STEPH CHA

Introduction

I SAW MY FIRST DEAD BODY before I was old enough to drink. A rookie newspaper reporter, I chased scanner traffic one night to a dark downtown alley. There, on the other side of yellow police tape, lay the crumpled body of a man who had fallen (or jumped, or was pushed) from a fourth-floor window.

I remember the eerie quiet, and the way flashlight beams lit a narrow slick of blood. I remember a handful of onlookers coming out of a nearby tavern to crane their necks, to see if it was someone they knew. Most of all, I remember thinking, *Wait, that man is* not *getting up.* The finality of it took my breath away.

Over the next few years, I wrote news stories about Mafia witnesses, serial killers, a doomsday cult, and a shoot-out between federal agents and a white separatist family. I covered murders committed over drugs and greed and jealousy and who knows why. Two killers confessed to me, one of whom had already been acquitted of the crime. (After I was dragged into court to testify in one case, I decided to give up on jailhouse interviews.)

When I became a fiction writer, I had no shortage of such material, and some of those experiences provided inspiration for my first few novels.

But I knew from the beginning that I didn't want crime to be the *only* subject I wrote about. I wanted to write stories with suspense, but I wanted romance too. And humor! I wanted to write coming-of-age and social satire, domestic farce and paranoid fever dreams. Hell, sometimes I might even want to use footnotes.*

I wanted to write the way I read: all over the place, expansively, without the artificial limitations of genre, bounding puppylike from philosophy to politics, from sentiment to snark, from darkness to absurdity, often on the same page.

I am also an inveterate journal-keeper, and I find myself drawn to the journals and diaries of other writers.

When the stories that make up this anthology began raining down on my computer desktop, I happened to be reading *Patricia Highsmith: Her Diaries and Notebooks, 1941–1995,* a fascinating collection of entries from the great suspense writer's eight thousand pages of diaries and journals.†

Here we encounter the young Pat in 1949, just finished with her first novel, *Strangers on a Train* (soon to be adapted by Alfred Hitchcock into the classic film). She was also working on a very different novel at the time, *The Price of Salt.*‡ This was a book she would ultimately publish under a pseudonym, out of fear that her career would be endangered by its lesbian themes and her refusal to "punish" the book's female lovers—a literary requirement of the time.

It is both sad and thrilling to watch the young Highsmith try to reconcile these seemingly divergent literary ambitions, to battle both her deep self-doubt and the strict cultural biases of the time, all while defining for herself a creative ethos that could contain such an expansive talent.

"I am curious as to that part of the mind which psychology (which denies the soul) cannot find, or help, or assuage, much less banish—namely the soul," Highsmith wrote in June of 1949. "It is this I want to write about next." Later that month, she added: "There must be violence, to satisfy me, and therefore drama & suspense. These are my principles."

It was something I had to ask myself once the great young writer

---

* For instance, this pointless footnote, placed here simply to show that I can do this if I want to. So . . . actually, now that I think about it, I guess it does have a point.

† All excerpts below are from *Patricia Highsmith: Her Diaries and Notebooks, 1941–1995,* edited by Anna von Planta (New York: W. W. Norton, 2021).

‡ A terrific film version was released in 2015 under the title *Carol,* directed by Todd Haynes and starring Cate Blanchett.

and unflappable editor of this series, Steph Cha, began emailing me dozens of mystery and suspense stories. What would be *my* principles?

Several years ago, around the time of my seventh book, a clerk at that 1.6-acre temple of a bookstore, Powell's in Portland, Oregon, paid me the highest compliment: "Fiction, nonfiction, literary, crime, short stories, I'm never sure where to put you. Maybe you should have your own room."

Even now, the thought makes me a little giddy. A room of one's own* at Powell's? This would be book *nerd-vana.*

It is also a useful way to think of an anthology like this—as a well-designed, well-apportioned room. As with any room, you'd want plenty of style and panache, but you'd want utility and comfort too, a full range of furniture and art, materials and intentions, perspectives and effects. You'd want pieces that fit together, that complement the whole, but that stand on their own too.

You certainly wouldn't want a room with six couches. Or nine lamps.

This is one reason, gentle reader,† you should take an especially close look at the list of thirty honorable mention stories at the end of this anthology. There are some marvelous couches and lamps on that list. Wonderful ottomans and credenzas.

Choosing the best anything is an act of subjectivity. Choosing the best short stories in any given year is a festival of the subjective. Any one of those honorable mentions might have made the cut.

The choices only got harder as we got closer to a final table of contents. Eventually, I got the fifty-some stories that Steph sent narrowed down to twenty-some, but the last few decisions were so agonizing that I kept trying to get her to make them.‡

So, what are the Highsmithian principles I used to assemble the pieces of this particular room? Well, you can't argue with a master:

---

* Not to be mistaken for the "Room of One's Own" that Virginia Woolf longed for and wrote about in her classic 1928 essay on the financial and creative obstacles blocking the path of women writers.

† I have always wanted to write that phrase, "gentle reader," although maybe *The Best American Mystery and Suspense* isn't the place to break it out. "Devious reader"? "Twisted reader"? "Voracious reader who too often stays up until four in the morning"?

‡ She would not.

we started with drama and suspense, some violence and psychology, and a fair amount of what Pat called "soul."

"How little does plot matter," Highsmith wrote in May of 1953. "The joy and the art is how it is handled." Joy and art, check and check. Highsmith at another point: "One cannot write, however well, and leave out the heart." Heart, check again. Still later, "The main thing in any book, for me, is the momentum, the enthusiasm, the narrative rush." Momentum, enthusiasm, and narrative rush. Check, check, and check.

In addition to these qualities, I have a soft spot for humor in short stories, especially of the dark and unflinching variety, and for writing that is imagistic and inventive. I like settings that I've never seen in fiction before, and characters that display a full range of human experience. And fair warning: I don't mind a quality that (at least according to my emails) drives a few readers crazy—ambiguity.*

Finally, there is something that I have trouble defining, but which I think of as *snap*. I like stories that, at some point in the writing, or in the plot, or maybe even in the conception, shift or pop or crack like a whip.

This can take the form of a drastic turn of action, or a surprising revelation of character. It can be a ramping up of stakes or a burst of wonderful writing that makes you wish you'd been the one to compose it. It can be dialogue that crackles, beginnings that cause you to sit up, or endings that make you slap your head.

And what *snapped* in the stories that make up this collection?

- The vivid collision of unlikely narrative elements—*lucha libre* wrestling and an adult webcam girl in Hector Acosta's "La Chingona" ("'*¡Que tal cabrones!* How you all doin' over *en el cyberspacio?*'")
- The perverse joy of having a solid life lesson delivered by a sociopath in Tracy Clark's "Lucky Thirteen" ("How many people got a chance to relive their glory days? To pick up again what they'd loved and been forced to put down?")
- S. A. Cosby's marvelously rendered setting in "An Ache So Divine," a southern juke joint that comes so fully to life you're

---

* For instance, I never found out how the poor man ended up in that alley, whether he fell or was pushed or jumped. Far from making this an unsatisfying story, I find it more compelling and more haunting to *not* know. Not all endings are clean, and not all mysteries move toward a solution. Some of the most interesting ones end in dissolution.

practically sweating ("The heat inside the building jumped from uncomfortable to unimaginable before the band was halfway through their first song.")

- The one-two punch of the irresistible opening line to Alex Espinoza's fuguelike political allegory "Detainment" ("The child returned to me by the border patrol isn't my son. My Ariel is still missing.")
- The patient and clever *Strangers on a Train* symmetry of Jacqueline Freimor's "Here's to New Friends" ("I've been watching him watch her for almost fifteen minutes, and I know he'll make his move as soon as the train pulls out of the station.")
- Everything about the hilarious low-rent grifting singer in Tod Goldberg's "A Career Spent Disappointing People" ("On the dance floor, a woman was setting up for karaoke, and for reasons Shane could not fathom, there was a guy dressed as a clown sitting at the bar.")
- The inventive blend of crime and time travel (*crime travel?*) in Juliet Grames's "The Very Last Time" ("Francis had been gone five days before the police came. In retrospect, perhaps I should have pretended I wasn't expecting them.")
- The masterful way that Lauren Groff uses the distance of a story passed down as family lore in "The Wind" to create an almost unbearable narrative tension ("Mama? Ralphie said again, louder. It's him, he's here.")
- James D. F. Hannah's irreverent hardboiled poetry in the real estate noir, "No Man's Land" ("Except Hauerback's once impeccable features are now most definitely peccable. His face resembles mashed potatoes—if mashed potatoes could bleed.")
- The keen understanding of mechanics, both in jukeboxes and in narrative plots, in Gar Anthony Haywood's terrific "Return to Sender" ("Eight days after the robbery, Binny looked up to see Peoria sitting at her favorite booth, waiting for him to come around to take her order. He hadn't seen her come in and was in no fucking mood. Business was in the toilet, the Sheriff's Department was no closer to finding his father's jukebox than they were the remains of Jimmy Hoffa, and the last thing he needed was his ex-wife dropping in just to twist the knife.")
- The relatable, perfectly drawn character who starts a marijuana grow-op in Leslie Jones's well-crafted "Harriet Point" ("I know some people think my first mistake was going into business with my husband, but between retirement savings, mortgages, negotiating child care against workload and respective salaries—aren't we all in business with our husbands? I won't be faulted for having the strength of my ambitions.")

- The creative structure of LaToya Jovena's "Stingers," with its unreliable bartender, I mean, narrator, who shows us the importance of having substitute ingredients for recipes ("Life is a chemical process. If the correct compounds are present, a chemical reaction will occur. This can happen by accident, or it can happen by design.")
- The impressive way that Elaine Kagan's comic dialogue and layered characters in "God Bless America" find mystery in domestic life ("Someone didn't like mayonnaise, but she couldn't remember who it was. Joe's Aunt Margaret? She sighed. You had to keep everyone happy.")
- The devious series of expert twists in the classic antiquarian book world of Dennis Lehane's "A Bostonian (in Cambridge)" ("Truth be told, Nathaniel wasn't as interested in books these days as he was in his ever-growing collection of letters. Rejection letters, in the truest sense. Goodbye letters, stay-away letters, I-don't-love-you-anymore letters.")
- The ingenious way Kristen Lepionka brings her indelible characters together for a perfect Elmore Leonard setup-and-spike in "Remediation" ("Without her bangs in her face, she looked like her father, if her father had been a semi-recovered junkie flyer-deliverer instead of an abusive carpet salesman.")
- The surreal and inventive writing in Megan Pillow's rhythmic "Long Live the Girl Detective," a wry and canny story that is also a pointed commentary on the commodification of women in crime stories ("The Girl Detective reads about her death on Twitter. She is surprised.")
- The lively voice and characters that propel Raquel V. Reyes's "Mata Hambre," a tale of a wild Miami sandwich-making competition dripping with sexual intrigue and violence ("With black marker eyebrows, hair pulled back so tight it looked like guitar strings about to pop, big gold hoops, and a push-up bra on display from the low scooped neck of a tight tank top, my cousin was sex and intimidation stuffed into a pair of butt-lifting skinny jeans.")
- David Heska Wanbli Weiden's wonderful use of deadpan humor to heighten the suspense in his portrayal of a reservation enforcer caught between family, friends, and tradition in "Turning Heart" ("The dog was at full attention now, staring and growling . . . I could see that the dog's face was scarred and its ears were mangled. Diesel was a fighting dog. Chunky must be one of the shitbags who entered their dogs in these matches.")
- The hypnotic way that Brendan Williams-Childs braids faith,

family, and a missing body into the philosophical mystery "Lycia" ("How did my father find God? After years of personal atheism and public devotion, did he simply turn over the pillow on which he kneeled and discover God, resting amidst the fabric—a coin, a whisker, a surprise to delight?")

- The comic realism of Matthew Wilson's "Thank You for Your Service" and its keen understanding of the narrative possibility of a scheme *not* going according to plan ("Stolen valor. It was a crime. Put the videos up on YouTube, that was a public service, and if YouTube paid you money when you hit a million views, well, nothing wrong with that. But taking Odell's money, that was something different.")

So, that's what you'll find in this room we've put together. My deepest appreciation to Steph Cha and Nicole Angeloro and everyone at HarperCollins for helping to furnish and decorate it.

A big thanks, too, to the editors of the magazines, journals, and anthologies who first published these pieces and whose work highlights short fiction. These publications give young writers their first breaks and established authors a place to tell tight, coiled stories that might not fit elsewhere.

For almost forty years, I have written two or three (or sometimes five) short stories a year. When I was starting out, in the late 1980s, these were my only introduction to the literary world—a one-sided introduction, as it turned out. I had no agent, didn't know any editors, and didn't even have a creative writing degree.

Back then, you had to mail a copy of your story in a manila envelope with another self-addressed stamped manila envelope tucked inside. Not only did editors expect to reject you; they expected *you* to pay for it.

I sent out these manila boomerangs for years, until finally, in the mid-1990s, I got a letter back saying that a story of mine had been chosen from seven thousand entries and was a finalist in a short fiction contest. My prize for finishing in twenty-fifth place: a check for $25.

No novel advance has ever felt better than that first check, which I stuck to my bulletin board with a thumbtack. "Look at that," I recorded in my writing journal. "Now I'm a pro."

I hope that after you finish this book, you will continue to seek out the work of the pros in this anthology, and of those in the honorable mention section too. There will be names you recognize, veteran authors, and there will be others at the beginning of their careers, names you are encountering for the first time.

All of them are on journeys that are worth following.

Tellingly, those words, "journey" and "journal," have the same root, the French word *jour,* or "day." One is the record of a day's travails and triumphs (I'm in the *Best American Mystery and Suspense!*); the other records the distance traveled.

You see both in the diaries of Patricia Highsmith: the drudgery of daily work, and the small victories that come from it.

"Absolutely nothing happens," she wrote about a book she was struggling to write in 1953. "I try to think intensely about the suspense novel. It will not jell." During that same month, she noted simply that her publisher didn't want "another gay book."

But at other times she would write: "I produced 9 good pages," and, "A splendid morning of sunshine . . . Came home and finished part one well."

But what really emerges from her journals is that sense of a writer on a longer journey, a quest, over all those pages, to cohere her ambition and talent, her subject and style, into work that might one day transcend.

In 1952, Highsmith was in Positano, Italy, when she stepped onto her hotel balcony and spotted a man on the beach in shorts and sandals, a towel over his shoulder. He was "lost in thought . . . something enigmatic and captivating about him."

That vision would become the character Tom Ripley, the antihero of her classic novel *The Talented Mr. Ripley,* and its four sequels. In May of 1954, Highsmith was well into the first Ripley book when she wrote: "I have never felt so sure . . . The sentences of this book go down on paper like nails. It is a wonderful feeling."

Amazingly, these were the last words she wrote in her journal for seven years, until, in 1961, she suddenly began the practice again.

I am fascinated by this seven-year gap, and by the fact that her final diary entry is about the writing going well. I imagine that gap as the place where the writer finally finds someone outside the self to speak to—namely, the reader.

And how lucky that we as readers get to be the ones to encounter those wonderful Highsmith sentences, which, "like nails," were used to construct rooms where we can be thrilled and disturbed, entertained and edified, where we can lose ourselves for a few hours, or days, or weeks.

It is, for reader and writer alike, "a wonderful feeling."

Here's hoping that, as I did, you find some of that feeling in the twenty stories that follow.

JESS WALTER

The Best
AMERICAN MYSTERY & SUSPENSE 2022

La Chingona

FROM *The Eviction of Hope*

THE CHURCH STOOD across the street and flipped God off.

Peering out of her bedroom window, Veronica noticed the old building, its crumbling brick spire poking through the fog like a middle finger directed at the deity throwing down the barrage of rain they had been experiencing in Spokane all week. Inspired by the sight, Veronica joined in flipping God, or at least her upstairs neighbors, off. Rain hammered her bedroom window just as a crack of thunder sent the lights in her room flickering. Upstairs, her neighbors started arguing again, their voices and plodding footsteps crashing down atop Veronica. She'd never met the couple, didn't even know if they really were a couple, just assumed so based on how much they fought. It's something she always meant to ask Dorothy, the Hope's on-site manager, but had never gotten around to. Now, with everyone getting evicted, Veronica figured it didn't really matter.

The memory of the eviction notice she found tacked on the door jumped at her like a wolf at the throat of a felled deer. Developers had been buying entire city blocks all around Spokane, signs around the city advertising redeveloped complexes with names like The Cooper George, The Madison, and The West End Lofts. For the longest time, she believed a developer's fingers would never reach the Hope Apartments. The building was almost a hundred years old, an *institution* Dorothy called it once, and the city would never tear down an institution, right?

Turns out they would, likely swayed not only by whatever money the developers were offering but also by the Hope's reputation as a place which drew criminals and violence to it.

Waves of panic crashed against her, threatening to pull her under to the place filled with empty bottles, fast-food wrappers, and slipping time. Gripping the mask lying on her lap, the world went dark as she slipped it over her head, the familiar smell of the sweat-stained cloth becoming a pier to stand on. Split vertically into green, white, and red sections, the colors of the mask invoked the Mexican flag, the design having caught her eyes when she came across it online. The price was more than she usually paid, but she clicked the order button anyway.

Picking up a plastic bottle from the floor, she gave it a couple of shakes and took a sip. The orange and vodka skewed more toward the OJ side of things, but Veronica didn't feel like getting up to refill it. Screwing the cap back on, she threw the bottle on her bed and scooted closer to the desk which took up most of one side of the bedroom. She reached up to the webcam perched atop her computer monitor like a gawking bird and ensured it embraced her in the center of its lens while hiding most of her small and messy bedroom from sight.

Disappointment stabbed her gut when she logged into her online account and saw only a dozen viewers waiting for her. Not for the first time, Veronica wondered how much easier all of this would be if rather than the brown-skinned, slightly chubby, masked woman her webcam captured, she could display a thinner, whiter, and blonder version of herself, features all the top female streamers, the ones with hundreds of thousands of followers and millions of views, had in common.

She had started streaming six months ago, right after she lost her grocery job, and came across an online article about how much money people—especially women—were making by putting themselves in front of a camera. You didn't even have to take your clothes off. All you had to do was play some video games and maybe talk about your day. And seeing how she was already doing the video games part, Veronica decided to go for it. If nothing else, it had to beat being constantly rejected for minimum wage jobs because she didn't have a bachelor's degree. Purchasing a web camera with her one and only credit card, Veronica sprung for the best Internet package her cable company offered and signed up with the website almost everyone used to stream out of, telling herself she would recoup the costs in a couple of weeks. A month max.

Clicking through her inbox, Veronica scrolled through her

messages, responding to the ones which included money—or *donations*, as the website encouraged her to call them. The funds would already be making their way to her bank account, minus the percentage the site took. The donations never amounted to much, barely enough to cover a night at the value menu, but she responded to everyone who sent her money, having learned early on the men (she always assumed they were men) liked to be acknowledged.

She'd finished typing up her last reply just as a digital timer popped up in the middle of her screen, a reminder her stream started soon. Veronica's finger rolled the click wheel on her mouse, as above her the neighbors continued to argue. Wishing she'd gotten up to refill her drink, Veronica shifted in her seat and watched the numbers on the timer bleed away. When it reached zero, she hit the blue Live button on the corner of the screen.

"*¡Que tal cabrones!* How you all doin' over *en el cyber-spacio?*" she asked, looking directly at the camera. Her words were drenched in a loud, overstylized accent, and she was thankful for the mask as her cheeks reddened, the heat spreading all over her face. "La Chingona sees we got Goku Did It 35 Minutes Ago on here already. How you doing, *esé?*" She waited for Goku to reply in the chat window before moving on to greet some of the other viewers.

Early on, Veronica had tried to stream sans masks, but those shows had been disasters. She fumbled with her words, got flustered easily, and had a hard time splitting her attention between the video game she was supposed to be playing and the viewers she needed to interact with. Worst of all, she never knew what to talk about, leading to long moments of silence. Determined to improve, Veronica spent time watching the more popular streamers on the site, and it didn't take long for her to discover something they all shared in common. Whether it be the girl wearing cat ears who was *really* into Japanese animation, the guy who wore a fake mustache and made dad jokes, or an entire subsection of female streamers who pushed the no-nudity rules on the site by wearing tight, almost painted on clothing, the best streamers all had defined personas. And as "woman with a nonexistent saving account, crippling debt, and no real options" wasn't a character which viewers were flocking to, Veronica set out to find something new to present to the camera.

La Chingona came to her one Sunday afternoon as she was

curled up in bed, eating Hot Cheetos, drinking a beer, and stewing over yet another poorly attended streaming session. She was flipping through the television channels and wishing she hadn't canceled the cable when she came across a movie playing on the local Spanish network. It featured a masked wrestler so famous even Veronica, who never had any interest in wrestling, knew about him. Watching the man strut around the screen in his silver mask and impeccable suit sparked an idea, and before long, she was online searching for a mask to buy and watching videos of wrestlers talking directly to the camera—cutting promos—she learned they called it. She spent days in front of the mirror attempting to emulate their speech pattern, the way confidence hung from their words like icicles from a roof.

"*Órale pues*, let's get started, *sí?* You guys requested I play some *Call of Duty*, which *no sé porqué*—I don't know why—La Chingona sucks at first-person shooters. But a deal's a deal." The character of La Chingona would have never worked without the mask. It shielded her from her fears and worries, allowing her to be someone else.

Though she did wish she hadn't gone so broad with the accent.

She was in the middle of answering a question about what her favorite movie was when shouting from upstairs cut through her explanation as to why the much-maligned Ben Affleck superhero movie was better than people thought.

"*¡Qué relajo!*" she said in La Chingona's voice. "My neighbors, they make all the noise. That's why La Chingona is trying to move." She'd mentioned an upcoming move before in hopes it would garner more donations from people, but she always left the reason as to why out. It felt too pathetic, even with her behind a mask. Today, though, she found she was too tired to lie.

"*Saben que?* That's not the only reason why La Chingona is moving," Veronica said, pausing the game midlevel. "The real reason, *la verdad verdad,* is that La Chingona is getting evicted. *Pinche* city is tearing my building down. That's why I need your *ayuda*. Anything you can do or give to La Chingona will mean a lot."

Her chat window filled with well wishes and emoji prayer hands, and she was notified by a pinging noise of people sending her money, but when she checked her account, she found the amounts to be only a couple of dollars. Nothing which would make a difference. Veronica wanted to cry, wanted to scream about how hard she worked, and how she just needed a hand to pull her from this sinkhole. But she'd seen those types of public freak-outs, how they got spread through social media, the women getting labeled Karens, and the men pussies. They got made fun of, abused, and then forgotten.

She wouldn't let that be her.

Taking a deep breath, Veronica was about to get back into the game when a message popped into the corner of the screen. It was a direct message, meaning only she could see it, and it came from an account she didn't recognize.

I CAN HELP.

The building wasn't all glass, Veronica decided, stepping inside the elevator. *Only about 80 percent glass,* the stainless-steel (because of course, they would be stainless-steel) doors closing the moment her finger pushed the silver button with its inlaid black number. Veronica's stomach tightened as the elevators started its ascent to the twenty-seventh floor, a sour taste clawing its way up her throat.

She'd spent hours going through her closet, trying to pick an outfit which wouldn't give people the wrong impression. In the end, she decided none of her outfits would hide the fact she was several neighborhoods and tax brackets away from belonging in the type of building she was walking into. So she went with a pair of faded blue jeans and a long-sleeve shirt for the cold weather. Her black hair she tied back in a ponytail, and she applied just enough makeup to look presentable. With the elevator pinging the twentieth floor, she turned to look at herself in one of the mirrored walls and not for the first time, wondered if she should put on the mask currently bulging in her front right jean pocket.

The message told her to bring the mask but hadn't been specific on whether she needed to show up wearing it or not. In fact, it hadn't been specific about much. Just that he'd been watching the stream for a while now, liked what he saw, and if she were open to it, he might be able to help her situation. The message was signed ZERO_MIERDA.

He liked what he saw, Veronica thought, checking one of the multitudes of reflections the elevator's mirrored walls surrounded her with and running a hand through her hair. She wasn't dumb, she knew the possible implications of an Internet stranger asking to meet in his apartment and had been ready to decline the invitation—especially once Zero shot down her suggestion of meeting somewhere public—when she received a notification that $1,000 had been deposited into her account.

To show I'm serious, read Zero's second message.

She tried googling his username but found very little information and nothing concrete about the person she was on her way up to meet. Same with checking his account on the streaming site. All that told her was the account had been created recently and that, per the brief analytics the site gave Veronica, hers was the only stream he'd watched in the last few weeks.

I'm only here to listen, she told herself, the doors to the elevator opening and revealing a long, white hallway with a black door at the end of it. Veronica thought of the Hope's own hallways, of the crumbling art deco style no one bothered to ever update, of the broken tiles and scrawled graffiti adorning almost every inch of the walls. If there were any arguing couples on the twenty-seventh floor, Veronica was positive the walls would block out their arguments. The urge to slip on the mask rose with every step she took, and by the time Veronica reached the end of the hallway, a piece of it was between her fingers. Rubbing the cloth helped to steady her beating heart as Veronica studied the door in front of her.

I'll be fine, she thought. *I'm La Chingona, remember?*

Stuffing the mask back in her pocket, she took a breath and knocked on the door, the sound dull and weak. She waited.

The faces stared at Veronica from the wall, empty eye sockets and slacked mouths reminding her of the painting of sad clowns which people with little taste bought at art fairs.

"Which one is your favorite?" Zero—Trevor, Veronica corrected herself—asked, handing her a can of Coke. Veronica glanced down to it and confirmed he hadn't opened it for her. Then she looked back to the wall and its countless pinned faces.

Well, not actually faces. Wrestling masks.

They lined the wall of Trevor's living room, a sea of colored and stitched fabric extending from the floor all the way up to the ceiling, the masks all arranged ten to a row. Some featured simple, one-color designs, while others included multiple layers of fabric in all sorts of colors and shapes to make them stand out from each other. Somewhere in the mix, she thought she saw the mask of the wrestler which inspired La Chingona, and because it was one of the few masks she recognized, pointed to it.

"See, that's why I wanted to meet you," said Trevor, apparently pleased with her answer. "You're old school, I dig that. You have no idea how many people come here and immediately splooge over my Jushin Liger one." He pointed to a red and white mask with multiple horns coming from its side which hung on the corner of the wall, before continuing, "I mean, yeah, it's the one he wore for the Tokyo Dome show, and was a bitch to verify, but there's history, and then there's history history, right?"

Veronica nodded, though in reality, she understood almost nothing of what Trevor said. Which, from the short time they'd been speaking, was becoming a worrying trend.

The man who opened the door had held a game controller in one hand and looked to be in his early twenties. He wore a plain black shirt, cargo shorts, and flip-flops. Pushing away the shaggy, uncut hair from his face, he grinned when he saw Veronica and said, "La Chingona in the flesh." With an awkward flourish, he stepped to the side and invited her in, introducing himself as "Zero Mierda, but you can call me Trevor" in the same breath. He didn't ask for her name.

"I need to pee," she told him once inside the apartment.

Leading her to a bathroom the size of her own bedroom, Veronica locked the door behind her and did her business. Afterward, as she washed her hands, she looked in the mirror and told herself she would give this guy five minutes and then leave. *Five minutes, that's it*, she thought, rummaging through the medicine cabinet and finding a medication for asthma which confirmed Trevor's identity. When she came out of it, she found he'd disappeared, leaving her to walk around his apartment and stumble upon the wall of masks on her own.

"I wasn't sure if you were going to show up," Trevor told her, plopping down on the leather couch facing the masks. Opening his own can of soda, he took a large gulp and said, "Also, I didn't know what you would want to drink. I have other stuff if you prefer."

"This is fine," Veronica muttered, placing the can of Coke on the glass coffee table. She sat down on the couch, making sure to keep a couple of cushion lengths away.

"I don't have a lot of food in the house, but if you're hungry, I can order us something. There's a place a couple of blocks away which makes a kick-ass pizza. Or, shit, if you got, like, a taco place you want me to get you something from, go for it. I bet you know the best ones."

"I'm okay," Veronica said, looking around. "I like your place," she lied.

The apartment was gigantic, with a large open living room, a kitchen most chefs would envy, and a view of downtown Spokane. When she received the address of this place, she googled the building and spent a few minutes clicking through pictures of the apartments inside, all mocked up to look their absolute best, with understated artwork and furniture, mood lighting, and classic style. Trevor's apartment was nothing like that. To Veronica, it looked more like a frat house, beer and soda cans spread everywhere, an obscenely big television sitting on the floor, wires running from it to multiple consoles, and a large desktop computer. Clothes were flung everywhere, and if Trevor cleaned up for her, Veronica couldn't tell. The masks weren't the only memorabilia on the wall, as Veronica spotted a signed Cowboys jersey, framed baseball cards, and a gold, oversized Championship belt. Taking it all in, Veronica was 100 percent certain that somewhere in the apartment, there was a Scarface poster.

"This isn't all my collection," Trevor said, noticing her looking at the wall, "just what I managed to move from my old house in Texas. Cool, right?"

"You're new to Washington?" Veronica asked and reached for her Coke. She wished she could add some Jack to it, but even though Trevor seemed harmless so far, she wasn't about to ask for him to pour her anything.

Nodding, Trevor spent the next few minutes explaining how he moved from Texas to Washington not too long ago, "right after the Bitcoin market exploded," which is how he'd made all his money. Once again, Veronica understood almost nothing from Trevor's rapid talk and wasn't even sure if anything he said was true. The whole mining for a coin which wasn't *really* a coin, seemed like a fantasy story. But fantasy or not, she was currently in an apartment with a monthly rent which likely was more than what she paid the Hope in a year. And the man in front of her had given her $1,000 yesterday, just to prove he could.

"Thank you for the do—money," she told Trevor, having to stop herself from calling it a donation. Stupid website.

Trevor finished his soda and crushed the can. "Nothing to it. Your story really touched me, you know?"

Veronica fought not to cringe at the words "touched me." Setting her still unopened Coke can down, she remembered her promise—*five minutes, that's it*—and while she didn't have a watch, she imagined those minutes were ticking down. "You, uh, you said you could help me."

"Totally," Trevor said, moving closer to Veronica. "But I gotta ask, did you bring it?"

For a second, Veronica was unsure what he meant, and it wasn't until she caught his eyes darting to the walls of masks, and then to her, that she understood. Reaching into her pocket, she pulled out the mask. *If he asks me to put it on, I'm out of here.*

"Can . . . can I see it?"

The tone of the question was all pleading reverence, and Veronica tried not to cringe at the words. Looking at Trevor, she found his own eyes locked not on her but on the mask held in her hands. He remained two cushions away, far enough for Veronica to react if he suddenly tried anything. Still, the question and the way he was acting set off a set of alarms in her head, and she almost stood up and left. But where would she go? Back to Hope and an apartment which would be yanked away from her at the end of the month?

Still keeping an eye on Trevor, she laid the mask down on one of the cushions between them. For a second, neither spoke, both looking down at the tricolored mask.

"Where did you get it?" whispered Trevor, picking up the mask in both hands, like a priest cradling a baby during baptism.

"Online."

Trevor laughed, a giggling, nervous thing which went for too long and showed Veronica a chipped front tooth. "Online. That's insane." Turning the mask over, he ran his fingers across the laces and asked her if she'd changed them out. "Shame," he said when she told him she did. "Still, I guess it's not a big deal," he added, though his voice said that yes, it was indeed a very big deal. Flipping the mask back around, he brought it closer to his face, stretching the fabric in his fingers and wrinkling his nose as if he and only he could detect an aroma emanating from it. "Some of

the stitching is off, but that's to be expected," he said, glancing up
to Veronica, who'd been watching this whole time, and said, "You
said you got it online."

"Off eBay."

"How much you paid for it?"

Alarms rang in Veronica's head again, but this time they were
different. Tilting her head, she gave him what she hoped was a
warm smile and said, "Oh, I can't remember."

Trevor laughed. "I bet you can't." Placing the mask back down
on the cushion between them, he stood and stretched. Walking
over to a bar cart by the kitchen, he poured himself a drink and
spoke, "I love your gimmick, by the way. The whole Spanglish, the
mask, the third person. Reminds me of El Generico in lots of ways,
but you know, less problematic seeing as you're, umm," he turned
and motioned up and down, "you know. You. No one is going to
accuse you of appropriating a culture."

"Thanks, I think," Veronica said, the can of Coke he'd given her
remaining untouched and gathering condensation on the table.

"Oh, it's a compliment. Seriously, you pull the whole thing off
awesomely. When someone clued me into your channel, I wasn't
expecting much, no offense, but the whole act is really well put
together."

"Someone told you about my channel?"

"I got a couple of people who sometimes let me know when
they find something they think I'll be interested in," Trevor said
and shrugged. "And there's always message boards, and Twitter
too. When they started telling me about you and sharing videos, I
knew I had to meet you."

"Lucky you and I live in the same city then."

Trevor turned from the bar cart and grinned. "Weren't you listening? I told you I moved here from Texas."

It took a beat for Veronica to register what Trevor was saying,
and even then, she found herself repeating the words out loud just
to be sure. "You moved here just for me?"

"No!" Trevor giggled again, a sound which tightened the smile
on Veronica's face and tensed her body. "That'd be creepy. I was
bored of Texas. It's hot down there, did you know that? Plus full
of dumbass yee-haw cowboys who don't get what I do. I needed a
change. So I moved."

So I moved. He said it so simply, as if it wasn't anything to him.

And looking at the man in front of her, Veronica imagined that it wasn't, not for him and his kind.

Walking back to the couch, he threw himself on his side and motioned to the mask. "And of course, there's this. You know what you got here, don't you?"

"I think I have something you want," Veronica said. A few minutes ago, she would have been worried Trevor might get the wrong idea at those words, but after watching the way he treated her mask and finding out about his move, Veronica thought she had a good idea of why Trevor asked her over.

"Maybe, maybe," he said, though the way his eyes kept returning to the mask betrayed him.

"You do." Leaning forward, Veronica's hand grazed the mask. "Tell me why, though."

Trevor frowned. "You know whose mask this is, don't you?"

Veronica shook her head.

"That's, umm, okay. Wow. I thought you did." Pushing the hair out of his face, Trevor looked up at Veronica and studied her, and she got the feeling it was as if he was seeing Veronica for the first time, and not La Chingona, or the idea of La Chingona he had in his mind. "This," he pointed to the mask, "belongs, or belonged, to Gladiador Sagrado." He paused and looked at her expectantly, as if the information he just dropped had some weight to it. After a second, he continued, "He's a *luchador*—" he coughed and added, "wrestler," which was kind of insulting to Veronica as she got his meaning the first time around, "who came up in the late seventies, early eighties. Never made it big, I think he maybe had a couple of tag matches with El Hijo del Santo, but that's about it, which is a shame because he was ahead of his time in terms of what he could do in the ring." Trevor's voice sped up as he talked about Gladiador Sagrado, his hands gesturing as well. "But the thing which makes him special, at least to folks like me, is that the dude disappeared after a couple of years of going from promotion to promotion. There was no big send-off, no retirement announcement, and no comeback tour years later. That's frickin' rare. *Everyone comes back.*"

"What happened to him?"

Trevor shrugged. "Who knows. Some say he just switched masks, but none of the wrestlers of that era match up to what he could do. Others say, you know," Trevor motioned to his throat with a finger, "offed himself. Couldn't handle the pressure or was sad about his status, but I don't believe it."

"Why?'

Another shrug. "Just a feeling. You watch his old matches, and like, you can tell the guy was having a blast. The love of wrestling just shined through, and I don't see anyone who has that to be throwing themselves off a bridge or eating a gun."

Veronica could have told him differently. Could have told him how sometimes a job was a job, and no matter how much you might enjoy it, at some point, it beats you down. That when your options begin to trickle down, you start to wonder what the bottom is and whether you want to wait to reach it.

"Truth is, I was kinda hoping you were, like, related to him. That you'd come here and tell me he was your *abuelito* or something."

Veronica laughed. She'd only ever met her grandfather on her mother's side, but she couldn't imagine the frail, old man whose faculties were already leaving him by the time she was born to ever have been inside a ring.

"What's so funny?"

"Nothing, nothing," Veronica said and reached for her Coke can. She played with the tab on its top, not quite opening but pulling it enough to feel the tension in it. "I'm sorry, Trevor, but no, I'm not related to any *luchadores*. Like I said, I saw this mask online and bought it 'cause I liked the design."

Trevor's shoulders slumped, his pose resembling one of the drooping masks on the wall. "That sucks."

"I'm sorry, but I can still sell you the mask."

"Why would I want to buy the mask?" Trevor asked.

Veronica blinked. "The way you were handling it a few minutes ago like it was a sacred work of art, I—"

"That's when I thought it belonged to GS, that he'd handed it down to his granddaughter."

"I told you I bought it online."

"I figured that was a line you were feeding me, 'cause you didn't want to reveal all your cards. But if you're not related to him, then I guess you did buy it online. And that means this thing is worthless to me." As if to prove his point, Trevor swept his hand on the couch, knocking the mask to the floor. "I get you're not a real fan—which by the way, is super shitty that you lied to everyone that—so I'll explain it to you. Those masks over there? Those aren't cheap replicas. Each of those have been worn by the actual *luchadores*." He rolled the *r* in the same overexaggerated manner La Chingona did. "That one you pointed to when you got here? That one alone is worth ten thousand dollars. Because. It is. Real. Not something bought online." With a sigh, he reached over and picked up a game controller off the floor and turned on the television.

"You told me you could help me," Veronica said, bending down to pick up the mask. Her mask.

"Huh?" Trevor said, already starting up a game. Without looking away from the television, he said, "Why would I help a liar?"

"I never lied," Veronica said. Something cold lapped at her ankles, but when she looked down, she found they were dry.

"Lie by omission is still a big old lie. You're out there in your webcam, showing off your tits and pretending like you're actually a wrestling fan." Pausing the game, Trevor said, "Tell you what, if you can name three wrestlers off that wall," he pointed to the masks again, "I'll transfer ten thousand dollars into your account right now."

"Fuck you," Veronica said and rose off the couch.

"No, really, ten thousand right into your bank account." Digging into his pocket, Trevor pulled out his phone and, after a couple of swipes, showed her his screen. He was logged into the streaming account phone app, and he'd already typed in the amount in the proper section, along with her account in the "to" section.

"Tell you what, *Chingona,* I'll make it easier. Just give me the name of who wore that mask over there, and the money is yours," Trevor said, pointing to the mask she told him was her favorite when she first arrived. The mask belonging to the wrestler who she'd seen on television not so long ago, who had inspired her to start wearing her own mask.

"I'll give you ten seconds."

Stepping closer to the wall, Veronica focused on the silver mask. Her heart raced as the two empty sockets stared back at her. That cold feeling she'd felt a second ago was back again, and this time it reached all the way up to her knees. She gripped the mask in her hand and searched for her memories. The name was there, she knew it. She just had to retrieve it.

"Four seconds."

Fragments of the movie replayed in her head as she waded

deeper into her mind, the cold waves of panic surrounding her.
She resisted drowning in them, focusing instead on the wrestling
movie, on the announcer who kept mentioning the title every time
they cut to commercials.

"Two seconds."

She almost had it. It was there. The Priest? No. But something
like that. Closing her eyes, Veronica gripped the mask tighter,
pulled and twisted it in both hands, the laces becoming entangled
in her fingers. The name came to her just as a ripping sound filled
her ears, her hand tearing the laces and some of the fabric of the
mask.

"Santo!" she shouted and turned around to look at Trevor. "His
name is Santo."

The two stared at each other, Veronica holding the two halves
of the mask in each hand, Trevor holding his phone in one hand,
the television controller in the other.

"Oooh, it's *El* Santo. So close, but I'm sorry, the judges won't
accept your answer."

"I got the name right."

Trevor shook his head. "You *almost* got the name right. If you
were a true wrestling fan, you would have gotten it right. And it
wouldn't have taken you ten whole seconds."

"I got the name right," Veronica said again. In her mind, the
waves of panic had become still, stiller than they'd ever been even
when she put on the mask. "You said if I got the name right, you'd
give me the money."

"I say a lot of things. Now, if you'll excuse me, I gotta beat this
level. You can either show yourself out, or I can call security, and
they'll show you out." Throwing his phone on the couch next to
him, he picked up his game controller and sat down.

The masks were all looking at her. She felt their weight against
her back, the way they judged her for being here, for having
been so dumb to hope someone like Trevor could help her. They
laughed at her with the black voids they had for mouths, at the
fact she couldn't even name the mask which inspired La Chingona, at the accent she used whenever she slipped her own mask
on, at the persona she draped on herself for what? For a couple
of dollars and nothing more. Glancing down to her hands, she
watched as her fingers loosened and the torn mask dropped to the
floor. Looking up, she focused on two things, on the phone next

to Trevor, the way it landed face up, and showed he was still logged into his streaming account. The second thing she focused on was the unopened can of Coke still sitting on the coffee table.

The ocean inside her mind was perfectly still as she approached Trevor and picked up the can. Trevor didn't even glance at her, his attention still on the television. La Chingona smiled and swung.

Lucky Thirteen

FROM *Midnight Hour*

HENRY PEARSE MADE HIS WAY up the quiet street, a bag of groceries light but cumbersome in his arms. He walked slowly, mindful of the icy sidewalk and the slush beneath his feet. He was of a certain age now, not as sure-footed. Caution was the ticket. He wasn't infirm, by any means. He got around just fine for a man of sixty-two. Still to himself, as the old folks liked to say. But sixty-two was not twenty-two, and ice was ice.

He stopped a few feet from his cracked front stoop and glowered up at the old frame house, then turned to scan the raggedy block, his eyes narrowing, his look accusatory. He would have to say, if asked, that he could just about smell its despair, its cowardly resignation. It had died years ago but hadn't the good sense to lie down and toss the dirt.

The town had had a thriving factory once and jobs that paid decent wages, but the factory folded and snatched the jobs away. Now the town was as close to nothing as nothing could get. The left-behinds, the ones caught sleeping by change and innovation, now stumbled like zombies after an outbreak. Aimless. Henry hated them. They hated him right back.

He made his way up the cracked walk, wanting to get inside and settled before the fools came out. They always did on New Year's Eve, as though clowning it up at the appointed hour would make their lives any less of a waste, any less insignificant. Shooting off cheap pistols and even cheaper firecrackers like it was the Fourth of July was nothing more than meaningless noise, Henry thought. Childish.

If they knew anything, they'd know how important New Year's Eve was, especially midnight. The stroke of twelve was a gift, a sparkling moment of transformation from old to new—a new day, a new year. It was a renaissance.

Henry looked up at his mother's house and scoffed. Robin's-egg blue. It had been that color for as long as he'd known the place. As though the lightness of the paint could cancel out the darkness inside.

"Gone now, you old cow. And good riddance."

The woman had never understood him. Tried to remake him, hadn't she? Turn him away from his passion. Stuff him in a box like everyone else. What kind of mother did that?

He'd known early what he was meant to become, and he had considered that certainty heaven sent. Henry had had a calling, a talent, drive. All behind him now, though he missed the thrill of it, the sense of accomplishment. But a man had to know when to hang up his cleats, when to take his bow and leave the field.

Henry climbed the front steps, opened the door, and pushed inside, damp mustiness smacking him in the face as violently as the snap of a wet towel. He drew in a sharp breath, held it, until he could ease into the stench of his mother's rotting belongings and the ghostly remnants of her disapproval. The stink seemed to seep up through the floor cracks, slither out of the heating vents, bleed out of the walls.

Straighten up and fly right, Henry boy, she'd say. *You got to learn to get along in this world.* And later when she saw she couldn't change him, *You're the devil, Henry Pearse. The devil come straight from hell.*

Henry smiled, remembering. She hadn't known anything. But it was always the ones who knew the least that never shut up about a damn thing, wasn't it?

Whistling his favorite tune, Henry walked the bag back to the kitchen, past the worn couch and end chairs with those infernal doilies on the arms. His mother had made them one after the other like it was an obsession. *Crazy bat.* He trailed a finger along the length of the dining room table as he passed it, making sure not to disturb the single neat place setting at the table.

He'd left a simmering pot of mulligan stew on the greasy stove, and he checked it now to make sure it wasn't sticking to the bottom. He loved stew. All kinds. Stew was efficient, offering several things all at once, no need for a second pot. He'd learned to make it a while back. Another useful skill he'd acquired along the way. He'd had such a productive life, really. He had few regrets.

The kitchen was small, outdated, painted white, but the paint had long since yellowed with grease and gunk singed into the many coats. The old woman hadn't even noticed, he bet. Just kept cooking her tasteless gruel in this grimy, dark witch's kitchen, never caring how it might look to the outside world. To him. And on the yellowed walls more of those damned doilies, like sooty butterflies spread wide and matted for display. God, he hated this house.

He hadn't planned on coming back here, ever, but there'd been unfinished business, and Henry hated leaving anything undone. Maybe he'd sell it, move on. There was nothing tying him here, really.

The doorbell rang. Henry turned, stared down the long hall, then took a deep breath. He peeled off his jacket on his way to answer it, stopping at a chair to fold the coat neatly and place it over the back. When he got to the door, he stood for a time, his hand on the knob, watching the obscured figure of a man through the glass.

He looked back over his shoulder, scanning the front room, past the threadbare couch, the scarred coffee table, his eyes landing on the mantel over the neglected fireplace where he'd lined up his treasures. Clocks. All the same.

They were no more than a few inches tall, small, the kind folks used to travel with back in the day, before cell phones made that unnecessary. Each clock had little silver hands, the second hands no wider than a hair. He'd placed them side by side like a stilled phalanx of minutemen waiting for a call to battle. Twelve of them. Henry counted them again now, taking great pride. The bell rang again. He opened the door.

The man on the doorstep was in his twenties, average in every way, Henry thought. A man most people would walk right by without noticing. Not dark or light, short or tall, thin or not thin, just unremarkable, like a mailbox or a light pole. The man held a clipboard and wore a bomber jacket with the left pocket ripped. Henry's keen eyes took him in, unimpressed. He kept his face blank. "Help you?"

The man consulted the clipboard, a little nervous, Henry would have to say, unsure. "Yeah, this is forty-three thirty-nine, right?"

He had beady eyes, Henry noted, and if he had to describe the man's hair, he'd have to say it was darkish, not blond, not quite black, ashy maybe? Whatever it was, it came to a point in a prominent widow's peak. The eyes made him look ratlike. They were shifty too, making him appear no-account, his mother would have said. "Not interested in whatever you're selling, son."

The clipboard came swinging toward Henry's face fast as anything and clocked him on the chin, tumbling him back. The blow was followed by a violent shove that sent him crashing to the gappy, ratty carpet, all of it, the hit, the shove, happening so quick Henry barely had time to register surprise.

On the floor, Henry squeezed his eyes shut to quiet the ringing in his ears as the man slammed the door closed and locked it behind him. Henry lay there, the wind knocked out of him, dazed. He raised a trembling hand to his chin and drew back bloody fingers, the sight of his own blood a fascination. He looked up at his assailant. "*I'm* bleeding."

Bomber Jacket grinned, revealing yellow, crooked teeth, then reached down and dragged Henry by the back of his shirt into the living room, depositing him next to his mother's whiskey-stained lounger. It smelled of hooch and of her. Henry held his breath, not wanting to take it in.

"If you don't do what I tell you, old man, you'll get a lot worse."

Henry struggled to get up but faltered on the cheap carpet, worn thin by years of his mother's hateful pacing. "You've made a mistake. You need to leave."

Bomber laughed. It was a deep, sour, soulless sound, full of menace. "Shut up. I'll leave when I'm ready. First, you're going to tell me where you keep it." He pulled a .22 from his pocket, aimed it at Henry's head. "Or I'll end you right here."

"What are you talking about?"

He kicked Henry hard in the side, grinning as though he enjoyed the pain he caused. But Henry denied the young man even a groan, which earned him a second kick. Still he made no sound.

"So you're tough, huh, old man?" Bomber leaned down, pressed the gun to Henry's stomach. "Well, I'm tougher. Now you're going to get your old ass up off that floor, and you're going to give me everything you got in here that's worth anything." He pulled Henry up by his shirtfront and pushed him onto the couch. He sneered, glancing around the place, taking it in, finding it wanting. "What a shithole."

Henry massaged his wrists, rotated them to make sure he hadn't broken or sprained them. He'd fallen hard. His eyes held the man's. "Ask yourself, then. If I'm living here, what could I possibly have that you'd want?"

"You think this is some random hit? I been watching you. Coming and going. An old lady used to live here. I don't see her anymore, so I'm guessing she kicked off." He pointed the gun at Henry's head. "I'm betting she left a little something behind when she did."

Henry shook his head. "All I've got is what you see."

Bomber scanned the living room with its mantel full of clocks. An even dozen. All frozen at the same time. Midnight. He chuckled. "You're so far gone, man, you don't even know what time it is." He shook his head, watched Henry sitting there helpless. "But what does it matter, right? You with practically one foot in the grave." He sniffed, his eyes following his nose toward the kitchen. "What's cooking?"

"My dinner."

Bomber tucked the gun in his waistband, hovered over Henry. His breath rancid, foul. "*My* dinner now. Get it dished up." He pulled Henry up, took hold of his collar, and thrust him toward the pot. "I got time enough to eat, then deal with you." He leaned over, whispered in Henry's ear. "Because you're just a lonely old fool, aren't you? Nobody ever visits. Nobody comes. Not even the mailman."

He watched closely as Henry scooped the stew out of the pot, making sure the old man came nowhere near the knives in the drawer. Then he made Henry dish up a bowl for himself. At the table, Bomber sat with the gun in his lap, Henry across from him eating slowly as the thief ate like a man who hadn't touched a meal in days. He noticed Henry.

"Don't like your own cooking?"

Henry stared back at him. He could feel the blood drying on his chin. "I like it fine."

The thief put his spoon down, his eyes hardened. "Then fucking eat it."

Henry dipped the spoon into the bowl and slid stew into his mouth.

"More like it." Bomber ate half the bowl before he spoke again. "Don't you ever use salt?"

"It's bad for you." Henry slid in another mouthful. He figured it was going to be a long night. Best to be fortified.

The thief chuckled. "Just like an old grandpa. No salt. Nothing crunchy because you don't have teeth. What good are any of you?"

"You don't like the stew, don't eat it."

The man's eyes fired. He raised the gun from his lap and showed it to Henry, in case he'd forgotten who was in charge. "You're going to want to cut that crap out right now, you get me?"

Henry flicked a look at the saltshaker between them. "There's the salt. Add it yourself."

Bomber put the gun back in his lap, grabbed for the shaker, and sprinkled salt generously over the stew before digging in again. After one taste, he smiled, finding the improvement satisfactory. "More like it." He sprinkled a little more, then winked at Henry playfully. "When I'm done, we'll do business."

Henry let his stew go and sat with his hands clasped on the table. His side ached from the kicks, but he'd get over that in due time. He'd always been a patient man. He'd had to be in his line of work. The breaks didn't always go his way. Sometimes when he went out, he didn't get anything, and he'd have to wait for another try. Like fishing. Fishermen weren't guaranteed a catch, were they? Sometimes they had a good haul, sometimes the nets came up empty. Henry had learned to deal with disappointment, to delay gratification.

Henry moved the shaker back to its original spot, next to the pepper shaker, touching, perfectly aligned. "Three days this week. Two the week before," he said, his voice placid as a summer lake.

The spoon stopped halfway to Bomber's mouth. "What?"

"That's how long you've been watching. You stood across the street, down two houses, behind that big elm." Henry smiled. "Nothing wrong with my sight or my hearing."

Bomber registered a slight confusion but not worry. He was a man with a gun in an old man's house. He smirked and went back to the stew. "Good for you, then. When I finish this, you'll do what I need you to do, and then I'll be out of here."

Henry pushed his bowl toward the center of the table, checked his watch. "Okay." He ran a hand along the tabletop. Not a scratch on the dark, polished wood. It had been his mother's pride and joy, a big, heavy table, a lace runner down the middle. Handed down by some dead relative, it was the only thing of real value she'd had to her name, other than the house.

Bomber looked up, frowned. "What the hell are you doing?"

"Admiring the table. It's worth something. You want it?"

"What the hell am I going to do with some old table?"

"Sell it."

Bomber leaned back, taking the old man in, slightly amused. "Listen up. I'm here for money, and that's all. You got that?"

Henry's eyes met his. "Sure."

Bomber looked around the room, his eyes landing in the corner where a chair sat covered in a paint-splotched drop cloth. "What the hell's all that?"

"It's a chair."

"I see that. Why's it covered up?"

Henry sighed. "You cover furniture if you're not going to use it for a while."

Bomber blinked, dullness in his eyes. "And, what? You don't use *that* chair?"

"Haven't in a while."

Bomber shook his head. "That's dumb as hell. You even have plastic under it, like it makes a difference if this jacked-up carpet gets any dirtier."

Henry let a few moments pass. "How old are you, son?"

"Not your son, gramps."

"I need to call you something. What's your name?"

Bomber pushed the bowl away, clattering the spoon. He leaned back again in the high-back chair, his stomach full, certain of how this was all going to go. "You can call me the man who's going to break you, right here, right now."

"On New Year's Eve, no less," Henry said. "A special day. Will you wait for midnight or no?"

"Midnight? Man, I'm going to be gone way before then. I got plans with my lady tonight—and I'll be using your scratch to show her a real good time." He shoved up from the table. "Now get up and go get my money. I want all of it."

Henry stood, smoothed down his shirt, straightened his belt. "It's upstairs. In my bedroom. I have a safe."

"That's more like it. Let's go, then." Bomber took a step, blinked, a stunned look on his face, like he'd seen a ghost or been put into a trance. "Hey."

Henry said nothing, just watched.

Bomber shook his head as though trying to clear it, then began to sway, his eyes glassy. Sweat formed on his forehead right below the widow's peak. He began to cough. "Get me . . . some . . . water. That stew's sticking . . . in my throat."

Henry didn't move. He didn't have to.

"You hear? . . . Old . . . man?"

Bomber's face paled, then his eyes fluttered. Henry calmly reached over and took the gun from him and waited for the man to fall unconscious to the floor. He grinned then. "Night-night, *son.*"

The gun was nothing special. You could buy one just like it in any dark alley for fifty bucks. He set it on the table, then swept the bowls and spoons up and walked them to the kitchen sink, where he set them in soapy water to soak. Henry hummed as he opened the refrigerator and pulled out a pitcher of ice water, then poured himself a glass. Again he checked his watch. An hour to midnight.

"All the time in the world."

Bomber's eyes flew open to find the room dark except for a single lamp shining in the corner. The drapes had been drawn. The place cold. He couldn't move his arms and looked down to find they'd been strapped to armrests by nylon zip ties. He was sitting in a high-back chair, his legs bound to the legs. He flicked a look into the corner. The chair under the cloth was gone, the plastic too. Realization dawned. He was sitting in the chair, the plastic now under his feet.

"Hey. What the hell?"

Henry walked calmly out of the shadows, leaned in, a leather apron covering his clothes, plastic goggles hanging from a strap around his neck, exam gloves on his hands. "Wakey, wakey, *Albert.* That is your name, isn't it? I checked your wallet. According to your driver's license, you're Albert Grant. Twenty-six." Henry offered a playful pout. "But not an organ donor. You selfish bastard."

Albert fought the restraints. "Let me out of this chair, you crazy fool!"

Henry turned his back to the chair, walked over to the corner. "I will. Eventually I'll have to." He shot Albert a sly look. "You had forty dollars in your wallet. What say I take that off your hands?

Funny, isn't it, how tables turn? You came here to rob me, but I end up robbing you instead."

Albert struggled to free himself but made not a single bit of progress. The ties weren't budging. "I said let me go, you son of a bitch."

Henry laughed. "You've got that right. It's too bad you never met my mother. She was quite something."

Albert bucked in the chair, desperate to free himself. "Call the police, then. Let them take me in, but when I get out, I swear, I'm going to mess you up. Count on it."

Henry pulled a rolling cart from the corner and moved it close to the chair. He looked over at Albert, who had no idea what kind of trouble he was in. "No police. It'll just be you and me tonight." His eyes held Albert's. "And you won't be coming back."

Sweat trickled down Albert's face, his eyes wild with rage, frustration, fear. He was prey caught in a trap, and he was just now getting it. "I'll kill you! I'm going to gut you like a fish." He issued his threats through clenched teeth, each one as toothless, as impotent, as the one before it. "I'll make you *bleed.*"

Henry nodded, adjusted his gloves. "Funny we should have such similar plans for the evening, isn't it?" He drew the covering off the cart to reveal rows of silver scalpels, drills, saws, knives, needles— all polished to a brilliant gleam.

Albert's breath caught. "What's all that? What're you going to do?"

Henry stood captivated by the display. He'd taken good care of his tools since he'd used them last. He'd put them away, he'd thought for the last time. Who knew he'd get another chance? "I used to be the best." He picked up a scalpel, felt the point. "Funny how I was watching you as you were watching me, isn't it? Your mistake was assuming I was too old to notice. How could I not? You wore the same clothes every time. Rookie mistake."

"Hey, c'mon. I'm apologize for busting in on you, okay? Just let me go. I didn't take anything. We call it even, how's that?"

"Apology accepted, Albert." Henry drew a small clock out of his apron pocket, showed it to Albert, and set it on the cart next to a small hand drill. Albert stared at the clock, then turned to look at the ones over the fireplace. It was the same.

"What's that?" His voice shook, fear having stolen whatever bravado he'd come in with. "What's it for?"

Henry winked. "That's you, Albert. Lucky thirteen."

"*What?*"

"I had a long career. I earned a bit of a reputation. Newspapers always like to give you a catchy name. It sells copies, I guess, but it doesn't really mean much otherwise."

"What the hell are you talking about!"

Henry swept his hand over his tools, reverently, as though he were almost afraid to touch them. "Doesn't matter. I knew you'd pick tonight." There was a twinkle in his eyes. "It's the perfect night to get up to mischief. The perfect time to steal what isn't yours . . . money . . . other things."

Albert's lips were dry; he licked them. "Please, Henry, *sir*. You don't want to do this. You can't be serious. Just untie me."

Henry readied his tools, the small saw just perfect for fingers and toes. The hand drill for the eyes and ears. His blood raced through his veins in anticipation. How many people got a chance to relive their glory days? To pick up again what they'd loved and been forced to put down? He breathed in, his eyes closed, lost for a moment in remembrance. Henry twanged the saw. It was music to his ears.

Albert screamed. "Help! Somebody!"

Henry placed the saw back on the cart, picked up the drill and revved it. "No one's listening, Albert. New Year's Eve, remember? They're all either out for the evening or shit-faced drunk." He scanned the room. "And everything here is locked up tight." A quick glance at his watch. Just minutes till midnight now. He winked at Albert. "Soon."

He eyed Albert's wrists. The man had worn them raw by struggling. He came closer, holding the drill, plotting his first strike. It was always the most important one, Henry felt. How it went determined how everything after it would go.

"Don't come near me with that!"

Henry chuckled. They always did that. Forbid him, as though *they* had the power. "I will come near you, Albert. I'll come very near." He leaned over, whispered in the young man's ear. "Remember when you knocked me down, dragged me around, then kicked me?" He pointed to his bruised side. "Right here. Twice."

The sound that came out of Albert's mouth was a pathetic whimper. "I'm sorry. Sorry-sorry-sorry. *Please.*"

Henry straightened. "You were quite the big man with that gun."

"I got dizzy. You took it. I blacked out. The stew." Albert glared up at Henry, tears in his eyes. "But you ate it too. I made you."

Henry moved around the chair, still plotting. "I did. I like stew. I learned to make that particular variety in a prison kitchen. But I didn't touch the salt."

"The salt?" Albert's brow furrowed. "You roofied the *salt?* You . . ."

Henry laughed. "I'm having such a good time. Aren't you, Albert?"

"You're crazy. You're sick! Psycho freak!"

Henry turned his back to the chair again. "Well, now you sound just like Mother." He picked up the clock from the cart. Its hands frozen straight up at twelve.

"What *is* that?"

Henry smiled, happy to talk about it. "A clock. One for each of my special projects. There are twelve on the mantel now. This one's for you. I had thought I'd have to leave my job undone, but then you chose *me*, Albert. I couldn't believe my luck. Lucky thirteen."

"Help!" Albert screamed, fighting the chair, the ties. "Help. *Help.*"

Henry padded back over to the cart and grabbed a roll of duct tape from a drawer. It was almost time. He peeled off a stretch of it and slapped it across Albert's mouth. "A man is lucky to find his true calling, Albert. To do what he must do." Albert's muffled screams went nowhere. "'The Midnight Killer.'" Henry shrugged. "That's what they called me. Not the name I would have chosen, but what're you going to do, right?" He looked the room over. "Maybe I'll stay put. Wait for someone else to wander by." He grinned at Albert. "A Venus flytrap waiting patiently for . . . someone." Henry exhaled deeply, mindful of the time. "I'm waiting for the countdown to start the drill. You will go out with the old year. It's quite an honor, young man."

Albert's body was drenched in sweat; fatigue and terror had weakened him. How could he have known? Henry was an old man. Just an old man. Now he was going to die. He slumped in the chair, little fight left in him. *Just an old man.*

Henry's smile was so serene, so content. He revved the drill, having decided gleefully where he'd strike first. The fates had delivered him the world's best belated Christmas gift.

"Old man, you said. Shithole. You ate my stew as though I'd made it just for you—which, I guess you could say, I did. You, Albert Grant, were expected."

Henry checked his cart. He checked his tools. All present and accounted for. Thirteen. A baker's dozen. "Almost time," Henry announced. "Just one more thing."

He walked over to the turntable against the wall. It was ancient by today's standards, but it still worked. His mother had rarely used it; didn't know how, Henry suspected. He dug into the pile of old LPs and found the one he needed, the one that had always spoken to him and spurred him on to greatness. Unconventional choice, maybe, but okay by him.

The album cover was near pristine, the plastic film over it just a little ragged. He slid the record out and put it on the turntable. Before the music even started, Henry began to hum the tune, then sing it with great feeling.

"*I'm gonna wait till the midnight hour . . .*" He turned, smiling devilishly at Albert, who'd come to steal and got stolen instead. "*When there's no one else around . . .*"

Henry whistled along to the song, happy. "Wilson Pickett," he told Albert, who appeared to give less than a shit. Right at the moment, he had other concerns. "Before your time, of course. I like it because I also wait until midnight. It's just how I'm wired, I guess. And, of course, there's no one around but you and me, Albert. See how it all fits?"

He stood by his tools, checked for time. Less than two minutes now. Albert's struggling had ceased. He was too exhausted to go on. Still, even in his weakened state, Henry could see in his eyes he wasn't keen on dying.

"I get it, Albert. It's human nature. We fight to the last, even if it's futile. Self-preservation. It's instinctual." He palmed the drill, caressed it. Albert's eyes pleaded for mercy but found none. "Eyes first?" Albert wailed behind the tape, then wept. "Maybe you're right. One minute." The song replayed on the player. Henry sang his favorite part.

Henry walked over to the window and cracked it, though it was winter and cold. He could hear the revelry from his neighbor's house next door as the countdown approached. He knew for a fact everyone over there was likely too drunk to hear a bomb go off. He inhaled deeply, let the breath out slow. The old year was dying, a new one coming. A cleansing, Henry thought, a blank page.

Ten, nine, eight . . .

Henry revved the drill. "I had thought eyes, but now . . . temple?"

Six, five, four . . .

"I'll only have a few seconds, though; then I'll move on to the rest."

Three, two, one . . . HAPPY NEW YEAR!

The drill punched a hole in Albert's skull and burrowed its way through his brain. There wasn't much blood, and what noise Albert had managed to make never made it above the roar next door. Henry savored the moment Albert's life drained away, then calmly padded over to the window and closed it. He turned off the player.

He stood for a moment watching what he'd done, anticipating his next steps. He moved back, breathed easy, plucked the clock off the cart, and walked it over to the mantel. He placed it next to the others, then stepped back to admire its placement, making sure it lined up just so.

"Right next to Mother, Albert. How's that?"

He began to hum. He was happy. He had all night to play.

"Not bad for an old man, is it, Lucky Thirteen?"

An Ache So Divine

FROM *Jukes & Tonks*

HATTIE MAE SAW the sun bouncing off the hood of the Plymouth Fury as it pulled into the gravel-covered parking lot of The Sweet Spot. The light spilled across the red surface like melting candle wax. Hattie Mae kept wiping down the bar between glances at her night-school workbook. This week there was a test for accounts receivable. She saw a slim brother climb out of the backseat of the Fury carrying a pair of drumsticks that he beat against the air to a rhythm known only to himself. A heavyset brother climbed out of the passenger seat. A handkerchief appeared in his hand like magic as he mopped at his brow and wiped his neck.

Hattie Mae moved to the end of the bar and gave the front window her full attention.

A tall, broad-shouldered brother climbed out of the driver's side of the Fury. His coal-black hair was conked and swept back from his forehead with a flourish. He wore a silver blazer like his bandmates but there was something in the way he carried himself that made his jacket seem to glow. A thin sheen of sweat covered his tawny skin. Hattie Mae thought it made him look like a movie star. Chester walked the way you expected a lead singer and guitarist to walk.

She watched as they grabbed their instruments from the Fury's cavernous trunk. They laughed, shimmied, and shook their way up to the front door of The Sweet Spot.

"That bar ain't gonna wipe itself, Little Girl." Her daddy's voice boomed as he came out of the kitchen. Otis Jones nudged Hattie Mae as he walked by on his way to the front door.

"You turn your head any harder to peep out that window, it gonna pop off," Otis said.

Hattie Mae felt her cheeks get hot.

"The East Side Playboys!" Otis said as he opened the door. The trio lugged their equipment through the door.

"Shit, Otis, it's hotter in here than it is outside," Ellis said. He was the heavyset one.

Otis laughed. "It's hotter than this in Hell and I'll send you there if you keep running that mouth, son!"

Ellis chuckled and held out his hand. Otis shook it, pumping it up and down. Chester pulled out a cigarette and lit it with a gold Zippo.

"That fine-ass Sally still working here, Otis?" he said after taking a long drag.

"You mean Susie," Hattie Mae said. Chester took a drag off his smoke, then exhaled through his nostrils. Hattie Mae could feel his eyes on her through the smoke.

"She got married and moved out of Red Hill up to Richmond," Otis said.

Hattie Mae noticed how her daddy's shoulders stiffened.

"That's too bad. She had some pretty eyes. Make-a-man-think-about-settling-down kinda eyes," Chester said.

"Well, somebody did settle down with her. A good man," Otis said. He let the words hang in the air between them for longer than was comfortable.

"Uh . . . can we get some Cokes before we set up? We been driving for about four hours and my throat so dry I could spit dust," Fred said as he tapped his sticks together in a staccato rhythm.

Otis relaxed. "Sure. Hattie Mae, get Fred and the boys some sodas."

"With ice please," Fred said.

"Make mine with Jack, baby girl," Chester said. Hattie Mae glanced at him. He was looking at her but not the way she remembered him looking at Susie. Hattie Mae didn't respond but set about pouring their drinks.

By the time the band had finished setting up, the sun had set, and folks were trickling in like sand in an hourglass. Hattie Mae put away her workbook. She set about making sure the few booths and tables had napkins and ashtrays while Otis fired up the stove in the kitchen. The menu of The Sweet Spot was pretty simple because no one who stepped through the door had come there for the food. Fried chicken sandwiches on two pieces of bread and still on the bone. Pickled pigs' feet that sat in a big glass pickle jar at the end of the bar. Macaroni and cheese that Otis made with his mama's secret recipe.

Hattie Mae's mother had gone on to glory four years earlier, the day Hattie Mae turned seventeen. The cancer had eaten away at her in big monstrous bites. One day she was there with her big beautiful smile and sassy hips, then the next she was a wisp of flesh and bones in a bed that smelled like the sour mash her daddy used to make his corn liquor.

"Take care . . . of your daddy." Those were the last words Ardelia Jones ever spoke on this side of the veil.

Hattie Mae returned to the bar and leaned against the cash register. When she was little, she had been afraid of it. She'd gotten it into her head that it was going to bite off one of her fingers. Her daddy had choked on his drink when she'd told him.

"Girl, the only thing that cash register eat is money from fools that don't know when they done had enough," he'd said.

Couples started to pile into the place. The men walked across the pitted wood floor in cheap shoes shined to perfection. The women clicked and clacked their way toward the tables and booths in high heels they'd bought down at the Sears in the bargain bin. Tight Saturday night dresses that would lead to Sunday morning prayers of forgiveness. The Sweet Spot was the only place in Red Hill where black folks could go without worrying about ending the night with a white man's boot on their neck because they'd had the temerity to exist. A place where you could go at the end of the week and spend what you could spare to forget the world for a while. A world that never let you forget for one minute where you stood.

A few boys Hattie Mae's age came through the door, but Press Williams stopped one of them. Press was the bouncer, janitor, and assistant cook for The Sweet Spot. Hattie Mae hadn't noticed him come in but that was par for the course. For such a big man, Press moved like a ghost.

Otis had given him a job last summer when he'd gotten out of Coldwater Penitentiary. Hattie Mae knew the fact that he was her cousin and her mama's nephew was the only reason her daddy had deigned to hire the man. He walked around like he had a cord of wood on his shoulder instead of a chip. His dark skin rippled with rough-hewn muscle wrapped around his arms and chest like rigging rope.

"You ain't allowed back in yet, George. Otis say you got another week," Press said. His voice was deep and dark like the river that ran through the county.

"Aw, come on, Press, I said I was sorry," George whined.

"Ain't about being sorry. You need to learn how to handle you liquor. Another week oughta do it," Press said.

George didn't move.

"If I gotta get off this stool it's gonna be longer than a week," Press said.

George had balled up his fists, but he unfurled his fingers one by one.

"Come on, let's over to Mathews," George said.

"Shit, you can go. Me and Royal going inside. Them Playboys 'bout to make this place jump," Mack Chasen said. He gave Press his money and headed for the bar.

"Sorry, George," Royal Thomas said.

"Fuck this ol' rat hole," George said before stomping out the door.

Hattie Mae chuckled to herself.

"What you laughing at?" Mack asked. He was smirking at her with a light dancing in his brown eyes.

"Nothing. You gone let George sit outside all night?" Hattie Mae asked.

"He ain't come with us. Ain't my fault he got fighting, got his ass kicked, then threw up all over the dance floor. Fool was looking like a water fountain," Mack said before blowing air over his lips and imitating said water fountain.

Hattie Mae shook her head. "What you want, boy?" she asked.

"Let me get two tastes of your daddy's special brew and a dance later," Mack said.

"Drinks the only thing you getting, Mack. My daddy might wring your neck, he see you dancing with me," Hattie Mae said.

"Girl, you daddy love me. I always give him an extra half pound when I cut his meat at the store. He'd love to have me as a son-in-law," Mack said.

"How he gonna have you as a son-in-law when I ain't marrying you?" Hattie Mae asked.

"Ha, she got a point, boy," Royal said.

Mack shrugged.

"My mama say a closed mouth don't get fed. That's all I'm say-ing about that. Think about that dance, girl," Mack said as Hattie Mae handed him two shot glasses filled to the brim with moon-shine. He and Royal threw them back and headed over to one of the booths.

But not before Mack gave Hattie Mae a wink. Hattie Mae didn't have the heart to tell him he was wasting his winks. Her eyes were on somebody else.

"Good evening, ladies and gentlemen. We are The East Side Playboys, and we are so glad to be here at The Sweet Spot tonight! Now we just come up from Surry County and them folks down there know how to. . . ." Chester paused before strumming his guitar.

"Twist and Shout!" He sang into the mic. The band launched into a bluesy rendition of the down-home classic. Bodies filled the modest dance floor as Otis turned the regular lights down and turned up the two lights with red cellophane over their clear shades. The magenta hue gave Chester a devilish appearance. Hat-tie Mae thought he was what ol' Lucifer would look like if he ever popped up behind her and tried to tempt her to throw away her virtue. Handsome and dangerous in equal measure.

The heat inside the building jumped from uncomfortable to unimaginable before the band was halfway through their first song. Press got up off the stool and opened the front door. He went to each of the casement windows and cranked them open. Her daddy went to the end of the bar and flicked a switch and two large green metal fans he had bolted to the ceiling came to life. They clattered and shook in time with Fred's frenetic movements on his sparse drum kit.

Chester had jumped down off the stage and was playing the gui-tar with his tongue. Right before he put the strings to his mouth, he'd locked eyes with Hattie Mae. She shivered. The crowd was moving in unison like some great amorphous beast. Dark faces soaked in sweat and split by wide smiles nodded in time with the beat.

"Looks like we gonna be able to eat for another week," Otis said as he nudged Hattie Mae with his elbow.

*

They were on their fourth song when the white girl showed up. She strode through the door with her chin up and her long black hair spilling down her back. Her eyes were hidden behind big frameless sunglasses that were less than useless inside the shadowy confines of The Sweet Spot. The music didn't screech to a halt like someone had bumped a record player, but Hattie Mae felt a change in the atmosphere. Hedonism was replaced by caution. Joy was replaced with suspicion. The men appraised her warily but with a hint of desire. The women glared at her like they had seen a cockroach in their ice cream. The girl didn't seem to notice. She took a seat at the table where Mack and Royal sat. Her white leather go-go boots were in sharp contrast to their Buster Browns. Mack leaned forward and whispered in her ear. Royal's face was screwed up in a knot.

Hattie Mae thought, not for the first time, how the road between the black side and white side of town was a one-way street. The girl wasn't the first white woman to find her way across Route 14 and she wouldn't be the last. White boys wandered in from time to time as well, drawn by the fantasy of the forbidden and made bold by the freedom their skin color afforded them. Mack came to the bar.

"Hey, let me get three chicken sandwiches and three shots."

"You sure you wanna be buying shots for Betty Anderson?" Hattie Mae asked.

Mack grinned like a jack-o'-lantern. "What, you jealous? You can still get that dance."

"Ain't nobody jealous of your skinny ass, Mack. But Jimmy Anderson ain't gonna let you get nowhere near all that Sears and Roebuck money," Hattie Mae said.

Mack threw his head back and howled.

"You laughing but the way I hear it he got more white sheets in his closet than he got on the shelves at the store," Hattie Mae said.

"Ain't nobody worrying about Big Jim," Mack said.

"You should be," Otis said. He'd popped up behind Hattie Mae like a phantom. Her daddy was almost as quiet as Press.

Mack stood up straight. "I ain't mean no harm, sir," he stammered. He grabbed his drinks and stiff-leg-walked back to the table.

Otis shook his head and clucked his tongue. "He don't need no part of that girl," Otis said. He wiped his wide hands on his apron.

"Huh," Hattie Mae said.

"What?" Otis asked.

"Nothing. Just, he said you liked him. I thought he was lying," Hattie Mae said.

"Just because he cuts me an extra half pound of meat don't mean we running buddies, but I don't want to see him hanging from a tree. Jim Anderson is about as mean a son of bitch you ever gonna meet, Little Girl. If it was up to me, I'd tell Miss Betty there to swing her hot hips on out the door," Otis said.

"Ain't her fault she's pretty," Hattie Mae said.

Otis snorted. "It's her fault what she do with it."

"I tell you what, the last time we was in Red Hill I don't think we had the right crowd cuz y'all know how to get it cracking. Now, if you don't mind, we gonna slow it down for a few. Here's a song we wrote, and we sure hope you like it," Chester said. He'd nearly sweated out his conk. His hair was laying across his forehead like a peacock's tail in repose.

He sat down his guitar and grabbed the mic. Ellis picked it up as Fred began a slow languid rhythm. Chester stepped off the stage again and put the mic to his lips.

> To have a love so fine
> Even if it's only from time to time
> Oh girl, it's an ache so so divine

His voice soared to a falsetto on the last note of "divine." Ellis strummed the guitar, then abruptly stopped as Chester slid across the floor on his knees until he came to a stop in front of Betty Anderson. He sang the opening lyric again a cappella until the last note, where Ellis came back in with a vengeance.

Hattie Mae felt a fetid thing awaken in her chest. It opened its green eyes and spread its fibrous wings until they enveloped her heart. Of course, he'd focus on her. Not only was she the only snowflake in a sea of chocolate, but she was gorgeous. He was gorgeous. They were like magnets. It was natural for them to be drawn to each other. How could she be mad about that? That's just the way it was. Might as well be mad at a fish for swimming or a bird for flying.

Hattie Mae poked her head into the kitchen. "Daddy, I need a break."

"All right. Give me a minute to finish—"

She didn't wait for him to finish anything. She slipped from behind the bar and slid along the wall toward the exit. They didn't call it the front door because it was the only door. She tried not to pay attention to the couples pressed together, slow dancing to Chester's mournful baritone.

The air outside was so much cooler it made her skin pop up with gooseflesh. The moon hung in the sky like a sand dollar tossed in the air by John Henry in some forgotten tall tale. Hattie Mae bounced from one foot to the other as she smoothed her hair against her skull.

Don't be so damn dumb. What you getting mad for? Don't nobody own nobody, she thought. Cars zipped by like dragonflies made of iron.

She clapped her hands together and went back inside.

Her breath caught in her throat.

The dance floor had emptied except for one couple.

Chester had one arm around Betty's narrow waist. The other hand still held the microphone. He was touching her. His free hand was just above the small of her back. Her hips moved in time with his. Her head swayed, making her hair undulate like endless waves against an imaginary shore. When the song ended, he did something that made Hattie Mae's stomach clench.

He kissed Betty Anderson right on her milky cheek.

The men hooted and hollered as Chester took a little bow. Many of the women clapped but the sound was hollow. Betty performed a little curtsy before stumbling toward the bathroom in the back of the building. Hattie Mae pushed her way through the crowd as the band launched into "The Blues Is Alright."

Betty was leaning over the sink. Hattie caught a sliver of her own reflection in the mirror above Betty's. Betty's face was bright red. An acrid scent wafted up from the sink.

"You're drunk. You can't handle that moonshine, can you?" Hattie Mae asked. Betty took off her sunglasses, ran the faucet, and splashed some water in her face.

"I'm okay," she slurred.

"Why are you here? Why'd you come here tonight?" Hattie Mae asked.

Betty pushed an errant lock of hair out of her face. "When I was in San Fran, I used to go to blues clubs all the time."

"Red Hill is not San Fran," Hattie Mae said.

"You telling me," Betty said.

"You sitting with Mack, you dancing with Chester. Are you trying to get them killed?" Hattie Mae said.

"What are you going on about?" Betty asked.

"You, here in my daddy's place sitting with colored boys when we both know your daddy is the grand wizard of what passes for the Klan around here," Hattie Mae said.

"Who's here gonna tell him?" Betty asked and Hattie Mae had to admit she had a point.

"Don't matter who tell him. It only matters if he finds out," Hattie Mae said.

"It's cool. You worry too much," Betty said.

"Why you dancing with Chester anyway? Mack I can maybe understand, but not Chester. He ain't shit."

"I don't know, he's a hep cat. Kinda cute, ya know?" Betty said. Her voice had an upward lilt at the end of every sentence.

"Yeah, he real cute. He so cute last year he came through and got Susie Cunningham pregnant. She almost died having the baby. He ain't nothing but a low-down dog who thinks the world begins and ends at the tip of his dick." Hattie Mae spat the words out like they were soaked in arsenic.

"Hey, can you cool it? What's wrong with you?" Betty asked. Hattie Mae stepped closer to her. Betty turned to face her. Their noses were less than an inch apart.

"He ain't nothing. Man like that don't care about nothing. He ain't gonna care about you," Hattie Mae whispered.

She took a deep breath and inhaled Betty's scent. The shampoo in her hair. The soap she used. A special kind her daddy ordered for her through his Sears account. The Wrigley's she had just popped into her mouth. The heat from that mouth created tendrils that caressed her own lips. When Betty had come back home from San Francisco last January, she was not just different from the girl who had hung around her Daddy's leg while he tried to sell a washing machine. She was different from anybody who walked the dusty, dreary roads of Red Hill County.

They'd met in night school. Hattie Mae was taking bookkeeping; Betty was taking secretarial science. She swore it was only until she could persuade her daddy to smooth over the people at the college in San Francisco and make them readmit her. Even though the night-school classes were segregated, Betty had stopped her in the hall. She'd seen Hattie Mae's copy of *On the Road* on top of her stack of books.

"Jack is such a bore. But Allen, if he liked girls, he'd be the bee's knees. He is so groovy," Betty had said.

"You . . . you met them?" Hattie Mae had asked. Betty had flashed those dimples at her as she nodded her head.

Soon they were making time to talk before and after class. She had talked to Betty about being torn between helping her daddy and finding her own road to travel. Betty had talked about wanting to get back to Haight-Ashbury. One night after class Betty had asked her if she wanted to go somewhere and hang.

"I know this place near where my grandparents used to live. We can hang for a bit. Talk some more. Do you smoke grass?" Betty had asked.

"No, I don't mess with that kind of stuff," Hattie Mae had said.

"You mean not yet you don't," Betty had said with a sly grin.

"Hey, look, you're a really swell kid but ya know I'm all about living in the moment, man. Ya know, going with the flow," Betty said. The music from out front beat at the walls and thrummed up from the floor.

"What does that mean?" Hattie Mae asked even though she knew damn well what it meant. She felt her face get hot. Her eyes began to sting.

"I mean we had some fun, got our kicks. I'm all about free love but that's it, ya know?" Betty said. Hattie Mae thought if Betty said "ya know" one more time she might just scream.

"I thought you wanted to go back out west. I thought we were going to go together?" Hattie Mae asked.

Betty moved a lock of hair out of her face. "I never told you that."

"I know but I thought . . . I mean we . . ."

"We had fun, Hattie. We had fun," Betty said. The lock of hair fell in her face again. Hattie Mae reached out to move it, but Betty tossed her head back and the lock fell to the side.

Hattie Mae studied Betty's face. The flawless lines and the heart-shaped lips were still there, but it was as if a caul had been pulled from Hattie Mae's eyes, and she saw Betty for what she really was—a spoiled little rich white girl who didn't care about anything or anyone but herself, a selfish brat who could press Hattie Mae against the hood of her MGB convertible with kisses as hot as fresh asphalt one night and slow grind on Chester Harris the next. Betty had probably never even seen Jack Kerouac, let alone met him.

"You leaving with him? Gonna take him out there to the mulberry grove?" Hattie Mae whispered.

"He says he got some killer grass," Betty said as if that explained everything.

"He ain't the kind of guy to take 'no' for an answer." Hattie Mae grasped her left hand with her right. It was the only way she could keep herself from grabbing Betty and shaking her until she shook some sense into her. The things they had done to each other didn't fill her with shame. It was exactly the opposite. But she had known they couldn't be what they wanted to be if they stayed in Red Hill. California had been the dream but now she realized she had been the only one dreaming it.

"Who says I'm gonna say no?" Betty said. She smiled and stumbled back, hitting her butt on the sink. Hattie Mae felt tears fill her eyes. Betty touched her cheek.

"Hey, don't make this so heavy, okay?" she said.

Before Hattie Mae could respond, a woman barged into the bathroom. Betty and Hattie Mae moved away from each other as much as they could in the tiny room.

"I gotta pee!" the woman said as she tumbled through the door.

Betty deftly moved around the woman and out the door. Hattie Mae swallowed hard. Her throat felt like it was coated in glass.

"That white girl think her shit don't stink," the woman slurred from her seat on the toilet.

Hattie Mae got back to the floor just in time to see Mack take a swing at Chester. The taller man sidestepped the punch and reciprocated with one of his own. It caught Mack under his left eye. Press was off his stool and positioned between the two of them before Mack hit the floor. Royal grabbed his friend.

"Take him on out of here, Royal, or I'm gonna have to do it and trust me, he don't want that," Press said.

"Come on, Mack," Royal said. He half-carried, half-dragged his friend out the door. Mack and Hattie Mae exchanged a glance. They both saw regret in the eyes of the other but for different reasons.

As the night wound down and midnight became a fading memory, Otis turned on the overhead lights and the East Side Playboys finished their last song for a smattering of applause. Most of the folks had gone home or had migrated out to the parking lot. A few couples were still inside, cuddled up despite the heat.

Betty was still there too. She stayed as the band packed up their instruments. She stayed as Otis paid the Playboys and gave them a mason jar of his special blend for the road. She stayed as Fred and Ellis looped arms with the Marshall sisters.

"I'll meet y'all back up here in the morning," Chester said.

Betty crossed her legs as she sat all by her lonesome at a table behind him. Ellis peered over Chester's shoulder.

"Hey, be careful. This ain't Harlem," Ellis said. Chester gave him a grin.

"See you in the morning, Ace," Chester said.

Ellis nodded and went out the door with Fred and the Marshall sisters.

Chester turned to Betty. "You gonna be okay?" he said.

She stood and rolled her shoulders so that her hair fell down her back like a waterfall made of darkness.

"I'll be just fine," she said. She walked out the door with a strut and an extra twist.

"See ya next time, Otis," Chester said.

Otis didn't respond.

Hattie Mae heard Betty's MGB convertible roar to life. A few moments later the Plymouth Fury's engine joined the convertible's choir. Hattie Mae went to the door. She watched as they raced off into the night, their taillights winking at her like the eyes of demons sent to taunt her.

"I'm gonna help Press clear the parking lot. You start sweeping the floor, Little Girl," Otis said.

"I'm twenty-one," Hattie Mae murmured.

"What ya say there?" Otis asked.

"Nothing," Hattie Mae said.

Minutes later she heard her daddy telling the stragglers they didn't have to go home but they had to get the hell out of the parking lot. Hattie went in the back and grabbed the broom and the dustpan. She passed the phone on her way to the pantry. It hung on the wall away from the prying eyes of their customers. Most people in Red Hill had a party line. The Sweet Spot had its own private line. The novelty of it had proven irresistible, so her daddy had moved it from the bar to this dreary alcove.

Hattie Mae leaned the broom against the wall. Susie had told her how rough Chester had been.

"Girl, he barely gave me time to get my drawers off before he was all up in my guts," Susie had said. She'd arched her eyebrows when she'd said it, but the idea had sickened Hattie Mae. Betty didn't know what she was getting into. She had no idea what kinda man Chester was.

Before she could stop herself, before the gentle angels of her better nature could intervene, she grabbed the phone and dialed the sheriff's number.

A tired voice answered. "Red Hill Sheriff."

"There's a white girl, Betty Anderson, down on Cricket Hill Lane parked under them mulberry trees across from the old Carter place getting run through by a colored boy in a bright red Plymouth Fury. You might wanna get out there before Big Jim Anderson find himself with a half-breed grandchild," Hattie Mae said. She slammed the phone back in the cradle.

Hattie Mae went back out front and began to sweep the floor. She thought it was way past time for her to get out of Red Hill. Out of Virginia. Out of the past where the promises she had made to her mama held her tight and the memory of who her daddy thought she was held her down.

"An ache so divine," she sang to herself as the sounds of sirens screamed through the night.

Detainment

FROM *Speculative Los Angeles*

THE CHILD RETURNED to me by the border patrol isn't my son. My Ariel is still missing. Maybe he was left in those overcrowded detention centers. What I am certain of, though, is that this boy, the one I have, he's an impostor.

He's wrong.

I want *my* son back.

He looks just like him, right down to the birthmark he has on the back of his left arm. He even has the cluster of three little moles on the side of his neck.

"Máma," he said the moment he laid eyes on me, tugging at the arm of the social worker who'd traveled with him. "Máma."

"*Sí*," I said, sobbing, "*soy yo*. Máma!" I stood in the airport terminal with my cousin Licha, her boyfriend Juan, and the attorney named Grace Lopez-Hull. I gripped the teddy bear I'd bought him—a large brown thing wearing a bright red bow tie with yellow polka dots.

"That's your mother," I heard the social worker state. "Mercedes."

"Máma. Mercedes," his voice echoed.

He even lisped the way my Ariel did, pronouncing my name Mer*th*edes like he always had.

Grace shouted at the reporters and the police and the airport security in their puffy jackets and dark boots to move aside, to give me some room. Let the woman go to her son, she implored. They've been separated long enough. The photographers and the reporters smiled and snapped pictures of me as I made my way to him. Then I hugged my boy and I pulled his black hair back and brought his face to mine and said, "Look at me, Ariel. Look at me. It's your mother. Do you remember?"

He nodded, rubbed a few tears from his eyes, and said, "Yes. You are my *máma.*" He pressed his finger against my collarbone, and I felt the jab penetrating my skin, warming my blood because here was my son again. There were more pictures, and a handful of the reporters sighed and gripped their microphones and I could hear one saying into a camera positioned near us, "We're reporting live at LAX where five-year-old Ariel Tomás Garza has been reunited with his mother. The two were separated for months after being detained by ICE. They were part of the second wave of asylum seekers stopped at the border."

"A tearful reunion after a harrowing separation," I heard another reporter say.

A woman speaking into a tiny tape recorder said, "I'm witnessing Mercedes Garza and her young son finally together. As I stand here in an unassuming LAX terminal this cold and rainy evening, I am reminded of the bond between a mother and her child, how strong and yet fragile this bond is. Who knows how many other mothers out there are missing their children? The current administration's policies are literally ripping families apart. We have no idea what the psychological ramifications of a traumatic experience like this could have on these individuals."

There were questions, so many questions, and my head was spinning, and all I could do was grip Ariel with the same force I had exerted when the officers tore him away from me. Grace Lopez-Hull answered the inquiries in English, and I could only make out a few phrases: ". . . not for six months," she replied to one reporter. "If you have kids, imagine not knowing about your child for six long months."

"I feel like a piece of me has been recovered," I told another reporter from a Spanish-language newspaper. "We gave up everything to come here. We were only seeking asylum. We just wanted to be safe." My hands shook, and Ariel looked away. "At the border, they questioned us. They separated me from my boy. I have not seen him until now. I didn't know where he was, if he was alive. Nothing."

Grace, Licha, and Juan led us out as the reporters followed, a

long mass of people trailing behind. It was like a pageant. Exciting
and terrifying at the same time. All I heard was the consistent snap
of pictures, the endless murmuring of questions, and Grace shouting at them to stop, urging them to leave us alone. There would
be more time, she promised, but now we needed some peace, my
son and me. Because we were going home.

In the car, I kissed his head and cheeks and each eye. I felt his
hands, checked his arms and legs for bruises or injuries. It wasn't
until Licha turned the car light on that I was able to notice that
he looked taller, his limbs dangling down the seat bench like limp
tree branches. He was wearing different clothing—a red jacket
with a hood, a striped undershirt, tan trousers, and brand-new
shoes with different-colored laces.

"You're safe," I said. "*Seguro*," I said, again and again.

Licha maneuvered the car out of the airport, and we started on
the freeway toward their apartment.

"Let's get you some food, yes?" Juan said from the passenger
seat. "Hamburgers and fries."

"Does that sound good?" Licha asked. After switching lanes,
she reached around and squeezed his foot. "Your mother said you
asked about me before the migra took . . ." Her voice trailed off.
"Anyway, aren't you happy to see me?"

He hardly said a word, though. He just stared out the window,
the teddy bear resting on his lap. I thought, *Shock*. That's likely
what it was. *Shock*. After all, this was a lot for a child to endure.

Licha and Juan cracked jokes, tried engaging him, but Ariel
was so aloof and distant. Not like him at all, they whispered. He
would talk and talk for hours. He had always been so curious, my
boy. This child was silent, almost brooding. The whole car took on
an air of unease. It was immediate. What had they done to him in
there? I wondered. How long would it take for my Ariel to be himself again? I had to be patient, to love and reassure him. But when
I reached out across the car seat to hold his hand, he recoiled.

He then turned and asked, "Why are you doing that?"

"What do you mean?" I said, my voice meek. "I haven't seen
you in months. You are my son, and I'm so happy to be with you
again."

He placed his hand out and said, "Go ahead then."

His skin no longer felt like his skin. It wasn't soft like I remembered. It felt like holding a doll, plastic and hard.

Was I losing my mind?

We'd been through a lot, I thought, as we continued on toward the apartment. Here we were. Finally. After everything. After all the walking and the sleeping in muddy ditches and on the cold steps of the few churches that offered us clemency, us looking like a band of marauders with plastic bags draped over our shoulders to protect us from the torrential rains.

I sighed. Things were fine. We were the lucky ones. We got out of that infernal country, and now we were here. We would start over. In Los Angeles.

In a neighborhood named for peace and serenity.

El Sereno.

At the apartment, I watched him pick up his french fries, take tiny bites of his hamburger, then rub his nose and eyes. He must be tired. Licha and Juan had retired to her bedroom. I took the sheets and pillows from the hall closet and made up the couch.

"Here is where I've been sleeping," I told Ariel.

He looked around at the small living room—its oversize television and mismatched chairs, the broken tiles of the entryway, and into the kitchen where the crumpled fast-food bag sat, bloated and empty. I bathed him, using an old margarine tub to splash water over his head and body. I rubbed soap over his distended belly and across the small crevices along his back. I felt the bones of his spine, little lumps connected, one after the other, like smooth river stones. He stood in the middle of the bathroom, shivering. I pulled strands of his wet hair back, wiped his face, his body, and dressed him in the pajamas I had brought with us from home.

I wanted to ask where he'd been. Where they'd kept him. Had anybody hurt him? Was he afraid? Did he know I had spent the weeks after I was released racked with guilt and anger? That I blamed myself for this? That I thought it would have been better had we stayed put, never trying to make the journey to the United States? There was danger back home, of course. He was getting older. It was only a matter of time before the gang would come into town again, rounding him up like they did so many others, and take him into the jungle, never to be seen again.

There was so much I wanted to know. Instead I picked him up, cradled him in my arms, and walked him down the short hallway and back out to the living room. He was already asleep; I could hear the familiar whistling of his breath as it passed through those small nostrils. *Not even an ant could wiggle through them,* my mother would say before she died.

Tomorrow, I told myself. There will be time for questions tomorrow.

I undid my braid, let my long hair tumble down my back and across my chest. I held my son tightly against me, rocked him even though I knew he was fast asleep, even though no amount of my moving would ever rouse him. This is what a mother yearns for. To be with her child like this. In the serenity. No bullets piercing the night sky, rattling the trees, disrupting the movements and rhythms of the spirits they say roam the darkness.

Tomorrow there would be an opportunity for questions.

Between the gangs, the drug cartels, the corrupt military and politicians, where could someone like me turn? I watched whole communities burn to the ground, saw countless men and women and children slaughtered, their bodies tortured and disfigured, left to rot and fester in mass graves. It was the stuff of nightmares. I need no proof of the existence of hell; I have lived there. Hell is where I came from. Hell is what I was determined to leave behind. For the safety and well-being of my son.

The handful of us that were left cowered in fear whenever we saw the trucks. We watched as they took turns on us—soldiers one day, drug kings the next, then the *pandilleros.* They would descend into town, gather us in the main square, and make us watch the public executions or tortures. We watched as they hauled the young girls away, raped them, then returned them to us, shattered, their eyes vacant, their mouths quivering.

One of those was my *comadre* Amparo's daughter, Venacia. I remember the day. How could anyone forget something like that? I stood with Amparo under the shade of a guava tree washing clothes and hanging them out to dry on a string we'd tied across the front of my house. It was weeks since Venacia had gone missing, taken by a group of soldiers. She was destroyed. Her skirt was torn, her legs scratched and bruised. She only wore her green sweater, the school's crest over the right side of her chest frayed. There were leaves and bugs in her hair. But it was her face that made us both gasp, that caused us to turn away. She'd been beaten badly, and her nose had been fractured. Her eyes were swollen and there was a large gash running down the side of her cheek. She screamed when we tried touching her, when we tried getting her out of the filthy rags she was wearing. There was dried blood caked on her underwear, inside her thighs, and along her back. Bite marks and cigarette burns dotted her breasts. This is what happened to our children. They would come back broken, forever changed.

I loved Ariel's father very much. He read books and believed in the ability of people to rise up and change things. Daniel wanted to fight. He wanted to take back the country and overthrow the crooked politicians and mercenaries, the drug lords and gang members. He thought democracy could one day return to the country, that we would live to see the moment when everything would be restored once more.

"A utopia," he once said to me.

"A what?" I asked. This was in the days when we'd just discovered that I was pregnant with Ariel.

"A utopia," he repeated. "A place where people live communally, where everything is shared, and where everyone has a purpose."

He saw hope in everything. That's what I loved so much about him, my Daniel. His courage, his faith that was endless, a faith that indeed made me believe that things would change someday. But, in fact, they got worse.

After Venacia returned—and was never again in her right mind—and once Ariel was born, more factories closed down, more people lost their jobs, and everything was teetering toward complete collapse. Paper money lost all value; a few street vendors started stitching together shirts and jackets out of bills. It was a sight to see a purse made of hundreds and hundreds of thousand-peso notes selling for less than a pack of cigarettes. The supermarkets ran out of food. Teachers went on strike, hospitals closed down, and the police simply stopped caring. My husband grew more and more desperate and angry. He took to pacing back and forth. He cursed the wealthy and those who supported the president and his crooked administration. I tried calming him down, but it was useless. He was frightened. He had me and Ariel to worry about. What kind of future would there be for our son?

The protest happened on a warm Saturday afternoon. First it was a few campesinos. Then somebody showed up with a bullhorn. Then more people came out. A hunger strike was called. Some of the men, including Daniel, sat down, linked their arms together, and demanded justice. Then we heard a loud rumble, a slow groan coming deep from the bowels of the earth. People scattered when they saw the tear gas canisters fly through the air and hit the ground. Daniel and the others held firm, though. They didn't budge. They wrapped handkerchiefs over their mouths and noses and remained there, even when the gunfire began. I heard fast, sharp whizzes, smelled smoke; one of the buildings was on fire now.

I watched the soldiers descend on the square. A woman gripped my arm. Daniel shot me a look, those wide eyes of his cutting through the smoke and bullets. *Go,* he was telling me. So I ran, following the stream of women shouting and crying, all of us scattering like torn strips of paper. There was no Daniel. No Horacio. No Miguel. No Antonio. No Justo. No Mario. All our men were gone. We waited a few days. A body turned up, splayed across a pile of boulders beside the river with a note attached to his chest. It was a warning. I had no time to mourn him, no time to remember my beautiful man. Soon they would come for the rest of us. There was only one thought: *Leave.* So, we gathered our things, those of us who were left—the women, the children, the homosexuals, the elderly, the sick and disabled—and we formed a caravan. We walked for days, addled by the heat and hunger. Some of us died or got lost along the way.

"May God be with them," we said, erecting crosses along the roadside.

We arrived. Somehow. We arrived. We declared ourselves at the border, told the agents we sought asylum. This was when they separated me from Ariel. They took him and the rest of the children. We were sent into a giant room with green cots lined up along a cinder-block wall. There was one bathroom, a handful of tables, and a television. All of this was enclosed behind a metal fence, and guards with guns paced back and forth along the outside perimeter.

I don't know how long I was there. I was allowed only one call. Thank goodness Licha was home. It took them a few days, but she showed up with Juan and the lawyer, Grace, who argued and argued with the government officials, and I was released.

"She's a real *chingona,*" Licha said.

Juan nodded. "Don't mess with Grace."

I told her about Ariel. I pleaded, said I would not leave the facility without him. We had come too far, I explained. We had lost so much.

"The children were sent to another facility," she told us. "And I don't know where that is, but I promise you I'm going to find out."

"She owes us a solid," Juan said. "Isn't that right, Gracie?"

She balled up her fist and gave him a soft punch in the arm. "Yes. Anything for Licha. She's like family." Grace glared at Juan. "You, on the other hand—"

"Stop joking," Licha said. "This is serious. How do we know the boy will be okay?"

"Because he has to be," Grace said. "I promise you that we will find your Ariel and get him back."

Weeks went by. There were phone calls. There were forms that needed to be filed. There were meetings and interviews. An endless parade of men and women in suits and ties who scrutinized me, who asked me why I would risk so much, why I would take such a dangerous trip with my young son. Wasn't I afraid that something terrible would happen to him along the way?

"Yes," I said. "But I was also afraid that something terrible would happen to him if we stayed back there."

Weeks became months. I cried a lot. Licha and Juan tried to distract me. They took me places on the weekends. The beach. The mountains. We saw celebrities' houses, large structures as ornate as birthday cakes. The weekdays were the hardest, though. There was no one to keep me company. I found myself wandering up and down the street. I went to the El Sereno Park just a short walk from the apartment. I sat there for hours watching the children play. My heart longed only to see them jump and laugh and run around. I imagined my Ariel there, among them.

More time. More waiting. Nothing.

It was agony.

Then the call came. Grace had located him. He was on his way, from where we weren't told, only that he was safe.

I cried. Licha and Juan clapped and shouted.

He was coming back to me. At long last. The only piece of home I had left. A reminder of my husband. I would feel complete again.

Hot dogs sliced into little pink circles and cooked with eggs. To drink, a glass of chocolate milk. That was his favorite meal. Always.

Without fail. Only, the next morning, when I cooked this and offered it to him, he refused it. He sat at the table and stared and stared at the food.

"What's wrong?" I asked.

He shook his head. "I'm not hungry."

"Try," I implored him.

He played with the food for an hour. He moved the hot dog circles to one side of the plate, stabbed the eggs with his fork, and tapped his finger against the glass of chocolate milk. I sensed an unease in him, a restlessness.

A few hours later, as I was in the kitchen cleaning up, my back to him, I heard a sound. Movement. Like furniture being dragged across the floor. I turned the water off and found him standing in front of the television. Just staring at it.

It was turned off. His eyes were vacant, his mouth wide open, like he'd seen something awful and was about to scream. I tapped him on the shoulder, but there was no response. I shook him. Nothing. I snapped my fingers right in front of his face. Still nothing. I picked him up, carried him to the couch, and shouted his name, over and over. It was only a few seconds, but it felt like an eternity before I saw movement in his eyes and his face.

"Ariel," I said, "what happened?"

He paused, opened his mouth, and recited a string of numbers in Spanish: "186543379-675-344547."

"What?" I asked. "I don't understand."

Then he looked at me and said, in a voice that was clear and very stern, "I'm fine now. You can return to what you were doing."

"But, Ariel—"

"I'm fine."

Water, he said. He needed water. I poured him a glass, and I watched as he gulped the entire thing down in a matter of seconds. He demanded another. Then another. In total, he finished four large glasses, then sat on the couch and smoothed out the wrinkles on his shirt from where I'd grabbed him.

"What is there to do here?" he said.

He didn't talk like my son. His words were elevated, clear, almost like they'd been rehearsed. "What do you mean?" I asked.

He tilted his head to one side, squinted his eyes, and repeated it: "What is there to do here?"

I pointed out the window. "There's a park."

He rose slowly off the couch, zipped up his jacket, and said, "Let us go there then."

I put the dishes away, grabbed my sweater, and we headed out.

Fresh air will be good, I thought as we made our way down the steps and toward the street. *He probably wasn't allowed outside where they kept him and the others. Poor children. They need air and grass and trees.*

Still, I tried convincing myself that the feelings of unease and dread cascading down and around me were just figments of my imagination. At the park, instead of playing, instead of running around or climbing on the playground equipment, he sat down on a bench and just watched them, watched the other children. When I asked him if he wanted to walk over, maybe talk with some of the other kids, he said he was fine.

"Do you just want to sit here?" I asked.

"Yes," he replied. "It suits me fine."

The sun was warm; a bright white light bathed everything. I looked out across the street, watched ravens circle in the sky over the railroad tracks running parallel to Valley Boulevard. We just . . . sat there. I was on one end of the bench and he was on the other. He perched at the edge, starting intently like an animal stalking its prey. He flinched when I reached out and tapped him on the shoulder. It was getting cold, and the clouds were gathering. I was afraid it would rain.

"I don't mind the rain," he said. I noticed a few drops fall on his jacket.

"You'll get soaked," I explained. "I didn't bring an umbrella."

He didn't budge, though.

I stood, stretched my legs. Nervousness had settled in my stomach. I took a few steps away from the bench, turned around for just one second, and then he was gone. I called his name, but there was nothing. My eyes scanned the playground, the trash can near the bathrooms. No Ariel. Where was he? Then I caught a sense that someone was watching me. Standing in front of a cluster of low bushes was my son. At first, I thought the light was playing tricks on me, and I approached slowly. The few drops of rain turned to drizzle as I bent down toward him. I couldn't see that it was a dead raven at first; all I could make out through the drizzle clouding my eyes was a clump of black feathers, oily and slick as tar. The bird's beak was ash gray, dusted with a white film that looked like chalk.

Its yellow eyes were still, bulging out of their sockets, as if the poor creature had been startled or choked.

"He was making too much noise," Ariel said, holding the animal's limp body. "He needed to be quiet. He needed to obey. If you break the rules, you get punished severely."

I looked on in horror. "Put that down," I finally said. "Please, Ariel. Put it down now."

He said nothing to me, though. He simply tossed the dead bird on the ground; it landed with a light thud on a muddy patch between our feet.

The rain was falling harder now. I reached out to scoop him up in my arms. I gripped him, and I ran down the street, past the tire shop and the liquor store, across the parking lots riddled with empty bags of chips. A man with stringy blond hair holding a dog on a leash was coming out of the coffee shop. I almost knocked him over, and I apologized in my best English.

He nodded, said, "It's okay. *No hay problema.*"

The dog wore a silly pink knitted sweater. Those big, moist eyes looked up at us, but the animal concentrated its stare on Ariel. Then it growled and barked, baring its teeth, its nostrils flaring. When the man reached out to pet the dog, speaking to it in a soothing voice, the animal lunged forward, biting his arm. It broke skin, and I saw fat sores starting to form, then bleed across his hand as he dropped his coffee and yelled, "Rufus! What the fuck?"

On I ran. Past the run-down motel with its coral-blue walls and rusted iron gate, past the little shop with the purple doors selling nopalitos in glazed pots. The puddles on the sidewalk widened and grew deeper. The drops falling on the roofs of the houses and the shops sounded like bullets. My breathing became ragged. I couldn't see very well; strands of damp hair fell over my eyes. But I held onto my Ariel, and we ran and ran and my skirt was soaking wet and so was my sweater and my feet and my arms were sore and my legs were trembling and by the time we reached the front of the apartment door, I was heaving and crying and I was wet and angry and I couldn't figure out why. And my son, there in my arms, he felt light as air. It seemed the tighter I held him, the thinner he became.

Inside, I took off his wet shoes and hurried him into the bathroom. I grabbed towels and placed him inside the tub and told him to remove his wet clothing. First his jacket and his shirt, then his pants and underwear and socks. I noticed a strange patch of raised skin across his waistline as I reached over to pull a pair of freshly washed pants on him. A cluster of perfectly round bumps. I touched them and asked if they itched.

He shook his head. "No," he said.

"Do they hurt?"

"No, it's fine. You don't need to worry."

The raised bumps didn't go away. They never spread. He never complained about them. If I asked him to let me see them, he'd raise his little shirt. I'd push the elastic band of his pants down, and there they'd be. Always the same. I rubbed ointments and lotion on, but they never went away. They never worsened. They just were. I was confused. Were they an inoculation? Maybe someone had hurt him in there. How long would they last? Would they ever go away?

Then one night, I was awakened by a strange voice. It sounded like a man speaking. Through the haze of half sleep, I rubbed my eyes and focused. Yes, it was a man, I was sure of it. The voice was gruff and deep. At first, I thought maybe it was Juan; he was spending the night so he wouldn't have to drive back home to Fontana after his long shift at the factory.

The voice speaking, though, was closer. It wasn't coming from the bedroom. I turned my head. Through the light of the streetlamps outside, I could make out Ariel's profile. I could trace the dark outline of his forehead, the small ridge of his eyebrow, his nose, and then his lips. They seemed to be moving, like he was talking in his sleep. It was his voice that I was hearing. Low and sinister. It wasn't my son. That wasn't his voice. And the words he was speaking. It was like he was talking in another language. An endless string of words I couldn't figure out. But he only knew Spanish and a little English. Finally, after about thirty minutes, he stopped. He just . . . stopped talking.

The next morning, as Licha and Juan got ready to leave, Licha turned to me and asked what I'd been watching the night before.

"Me?" I looked at her confused. "Nothing."

"I heard the television on. Voices."

"Me too," Juan said. "Like a conversation."

"Oh," I said. "It was just . . . I couldn't sleep."

I lied. I also said nothing about the strange marks on his body and the dead bird.

I didn't want them to think I was crazy. It would all pass, I thought. Little by little.

We walked to the library up on Huntington Boulevard. There, we gathered a stack of picture books, and I asked Ariel to sit by me and look at them as I turned the computer on. I didn't know exactly what I was looking for, but there had to be something to explain all these odd things. It took a while, but slowly certain similarities began emerging. A mother in Texas reported that her daughter had grown very depressed and moody ever since she'd been returned. The girl refused to go outside and spent all day in her bedroom, the curtains drawn. She turned very pale, and her hair started to fall out in clumps. Another woman reported that her son had become increasingly violent, harming himself and others; he had beaten up a classmate and pushed him down a flight of stairs. Another mother from Arizona was so sure her daughter had been replaced by a robot that she began cutting the little girl's arms and legs to see if she bled. The little girl nearly died before the mother was arrested and her daughter placed in a foster home.

All of these children had been separated from their parents after crossing the border. Just like me and Ariel. None of it made sense. I watched Ariel flipping through a book on dinosaurs. He was so unfamiliar to me now, so distant and far away. No matter what I did, I couldn't break through to him.

I remember my mother and grandmother telling us stories about *duendes,* small creatures that lived in the forests and caves around the village. They'd roam the countryside at night and steal laundry and food, vandalize the barns, and rouse the chickens and roosters.

"I saw one once," my grandmother told me when I was a girl. "A little thing. It looked like a child scurrying a few feet ahead of me as I was coming back from the *río* one evening. In the moonlight, I could see that it walked funny. As I approached, it turned to look at me. Its eyes glowed bright green. And when it grinned, I saw a set of sharp yellow teeth. It had long fingernails, and its skin was covered in hair."

The truly sinister ones, though, did more things, awful things. They butchered animals for food, skinned their hides to wear.

They disguised themselves and walked into houses, caused mischief; some even reportedly lit a woman's home on fire as she slept.

They would also steal babies and children, replacing them with look-alikes in order to trick the parents and cause more mischief. When I asked why they did this, my grandmother sighed and shook her head.

"They're just bad," my mother replied. "They only do it because they are evil. There's no other reason. They are bitter and foul things with hate in their souls."

Maybe politicians are *duendes* disguised as people. I don't know who this child is, but he is not mine. I am not crazy. Even after all that I've been through, I've remained fully intact, fully aware of myself. I am of sound mind, as the Americans say. I look at this boy now, this mysterious little life lying next to me, sleeping. The rash on his waist has changed now. After the blisters broke, scabs formed that scarred, leaving a series of marks on his skin, dark lines like those found on the backs of packages with tiny letters and numbers.

Grace took notes in her pad and snapped a few pictures. She said she'd get to the bottom of this, though I have little faith now. Things are getting worse. They say on the news that more caravans of migrants are on their way. It seems governments everywhere are unraveling, and the only choice people have is to leave. Such is the will to live. Part of me wishes I could tell those mothers I see on television not to come here. To stay where they are, that the lives of their children aren't worth it. That this process changes them, that they will forever be plagued by irrevocable damage, that our babies will be lost to us.

But I can't stop them. And even if I could, I wouldn't. Because at least we are alive.

My child is out there somewhere. I'll find him.

I'm a mother and, like all mothers, this is what we do.

Here's to New Friends

FROM *When a Stranger Comes to Town*

I'VE BEEN WATCHING HIM watch her for almost fifteen minutes, and I know he'll make his move as soon as the train pulls out of the station. He: late thirties, big head with glossy black hair; she: maybe twenty, a rabbity strawberry blonde.

As for me, I'm in my midfifties, tanned and quite bald, but I'm not in this story yet; I'm an observer, as both my profession and my avocation have trained me to be.

Sure enough, as soon as we start moving, he rises from his window seat, squeezes past my knees and heads to the aisle. The first red flag.

"Excuse me?" he says, his voice deep and smooth. She's sitting in our row at the window on the other side of the train, hunched down, attached to her phone by earbuds. There's an open book in her lap. Her body language clearly states *Leave me alone*, but he's decided to ignore it.

Red flag #2.

"Excuse me?" he says again. "Miss?"

She looks up warily and plucks out the earbuds. "Yes?"

His form-fitting tank top and thin jogging pants show well-defined arm muscles and a lean physique. He bounces a little on the balls of his feet like a boxer and points to the aisle seat next to her. "Do you mind if I sit here? I'm at the window there"—he gestures vaguely—"and it's making me claustrophobic."

Red flags #3, too much information, and #4, false information. Claustrophobic at the window? Not likely.

The train from Union Station to Newport News this evening

has a number of empty seats. And yet he's chosen the one next to her—red flag #5.

Honestly, how many warnings does she need? But she has no doubt been brought up to be polite, which is another way of saying she's been trained to be prey. If I were her father, I would have made sure she understood the possible consequences of that kind of passivity.

"No problem," she says, but she shrinks into herself even further. She puts her earbuds back in and looks down at her book.

He pulls his phone from his pocket and sits, manspreading into the aisle on one side and into her space on the other. A tattooed tiger snarls on his biceps.

He stares at his screen, pretending to read, then scrolls down with a spatulate thumb and grins. He chuckles. "Aw," he says and then repeats himself: "Aw." He angles his body toward her. "Sorry to interrupt, but do you like animal videos? You have to see this."

Completely fatuous. Who doesn't like watching a half-drowned baby squirrel being nursed back to health? A one-armed spider monkey befriended by a cat? You'd have to be a sociopath not to respond.

Reluctantly, she detaches her earbuds once more, lips compressed into a thin smile that looks more like a grimace. I can see her entire body sigh. So can he, I know. He just doesn't care.

"Sure. I like them," she says flatly.

He holds up his phone and leans toward her. Whatever they're watching is engrossing. They both laugh, and little by little, she leans toward him too. She's softening. She closes her book and puts it in the mesh pocket of the seatback in front of her.

I'm impressed. He's a quick worker, having accomplished steps one through five of the Request Assistance Scenario—identify the target, enlist her help, invade her space, establish a common interest, and get her to mirror you—in record time.

After that, he's got her. He introduces himself—Tony, like Tony the Tiger, ha, ha, ha—and quickly establishes that her name is Megan, she's a student at George Washington University, and she's joining friends in Virginia Beach for spring break. They don't know she's coming. She didn't have enough money for the trip, but her parents surprised her with cash for her birthday, which was just last week.

I keep listening and watch them out of the corner of my eye.

Here's his opening. "Hey, happy birthday!" Tony says. "Let me buy you a drink."

Megan reddens. "No, no, you don't have to."

"I know I don't have to. I want to."

"No, that's okay. Really."

"Come on. We have to celebrate."

He stands and crooks his finger, and after a moment, she stands too, grabs her backpack, and hoists it over her shoulder. Slick. He's established a pattern in which his wishes override her objections.

Tony steps into the aisle and retreats a foot or two, gesturing for Megan to precede him.

After a moment's reflection, I find that I too have developed a powerful thirst and, grabbing my newspaper, follow him following her as we lurch toward the café car.

Once we arrive, we line up at the counter—Tony tall, broad, meaty; Megan short, thin, insubstantial. Now that I'm close to her, I see she has pale orange eyelashes and a charming overbite. She's wearing black leggings and a too-big GWU sweatshirt into which, I can tell, she likes to disappear.

"May I help you, sir?" says the blue-aproned attendant, whose nameplate identifies her as Trisha.

Tony points first to himself and then to Megan. "Champagne for two."

The attendant says, "I'm sorry, we don't carry Champagne. But we do have a lovely California Chardonnay."

"That's fine," Tony says without consulting Megan. It's clear from the look on her face that she's never had Chardonnay. Maybe she doesn't even know what it is.

Trisha says, "I'll have to see the young woman's ID."

In full blush now, Megan fumbles in her backpack and pulls out a card. Trisha gives it a cursory glance. "Thank you."

When Trisha turns her back and does a deep-knee bend to retrieve the wine from the half-size refrigerator, Tony glances at Megan's ID, and, heads together, they laugh softly. They keep their voices down, so I'm only guessing they're murmuring about Megan's fake ID, which she may even have procured specifically for this spring break. Now the two of them share a secret. They're Bonnie and Clyde, bucking an unfair system. Next on the checklist: he's going to get her drunk.

It never ceases to amaze me how unsuspecting young women can be, despite daily reminders of the world's dangers. In any city you visit in the United States, you'll see flyers headlined MISSING taped to storefronts and telephone poles. Even in Town Center, near my home in Virginia Beach, a few still broadcast the search for an Old Dominion student who disappeared eight years ago. Hasn't Megan seen flyers like these? Or does she think nothing like that could ever happen to her?

Involving myself in this kind of scenario was not on my agenda when I boarded the train, but now I think I'm going to tell Megan Tony's not the good person he's pretending to be. I'll take the opportunity when—if—he goes to the lavatory. Until then, I can only wait.

Trisha sets a half bottle of wine and two plastic glasses on the counter, deftly peels the foil, inserts a corkscrew, and pops out the cork. As she pours, Tony pulls cash—of course—from his pocket, licks his thumb, and counts out the bills. "Keep the change."

"Thank you, sir. Enjoy."

"Thank you," he says. Megan nods.

Tony picks up the glasses and slides onto the blue vinyl seat of the nearest booth. Megan sits across the table from him. He hands her a glass and lifts his in a toast. "Here's to you. Happy birthday."

She clicks her cup against his. "Thank you."

"And here's to new friends."

"To new friends," she echoes.

Over the next sixty minutes, I sit in the booth across from theirs, sipping ginger ale and pretending to read my newspaper. The café is doing a brisk business in beverages, sandwiches, and microwavable pizza, and a steady stream of people pass. They provide cover for me while I track the progress Tony is making with Megan.

Both are now leaning their backs on the window, their legs on the seats. His are outstretched in front of him, crossed at hairy ankles; hers are bent at the knee, sneakers flat on the vinyl.

From this angle, I can see him only in profile, as he's looking straight at her and making her the focus of all his attention. She looks mostly at him and occasionally turns her head to stare into space—in my direction, but without seeing me.

One half bottle of wine has turned into two, and Megan's doing most of the drinking, especially since Tony's also bought pretzels to make her thirsty. Tony himself takes small sips and keeps topping up her glass.

I can hear snatches of their conversation whenever the flow of passengers thins. I learn she's from Roanoke and majoring in art history at GW, and he lives in Newport News, where he's a software developer. This is almost certainly a lie. Had she said she was studying computer science, he would have said he owned an art gallery or was a Realtor. They make small talk about movies and TV shows and what they like to do in their spare time, etc. I turn the page of my paper and wait, sensing a shift in the atmosphere.

Tony ostentatiously clears his throat. "So, first spring break, huh?" he says. "Excited?"

"Yes!" she says.

"You're going to have a great time. But you know this train doesn't go all the way to Virginia Beach, right? You have to transfer to a bus at Newport News."

"I know." But she sounds uncertain.

He laughs. "Don't worry. I'll make sure you get on the bus."

She picks up a pretzel and nibbles on it. "Thank you. That's so nice of you."

Here it is. He's going in for the kill.

"Wait a minute," Tony says, and actually smacks himself on the forehead. "My car's at the station in Newport News. I can give you a lift."

Her eyes widen. "To Virginia Beach? But isn't that, like, two hours from there?"

He shrugs. "Nah. It's an hour fifteen. An hour, if you drive like me." He grins.

She shakes her head. "I can't ask you to do that. It'd be totally out of your way."

He shrugs again. "Not really. Plus, my girlfriend lives at the Beach. It'll be great to go meet her for a drink."

"But—"

He lifts a finger to shush her and picks up his phone. "I won't take no for an answer." He stabs at the screen, scrolls down, and taps a number. He lifts the cell to his ear and winks at Megan. She smiles faintly.

"Hey, baby," Tony says. "How you doin'?" He waits a beat. "Great. Yeah, listen. I'm going to be out your way tonight. Want to—?" He laughs. "That's what I was going to say. How about"—he looks at his watch—"11:00?" He waits. "You got it. See you then."

He hangs up and smiles at Megan. "See? It's all good. I'll drop you at your friends' house and go meet my honey after."

She hesitates, then gulps her wine. "I guess that'd be okay. I mean, as long as you don't mind."

He raises his glass to her. "Not at all. Anything for a friend."

She heard what he wanted her to hear. He's already taken. He has no designs on her.

They're just friends.

Nicely done, Tony. Very nicely done.

I give them a few minutes to return to their seats before following suit. When I sit down, they're talking quietly, apparently about Tony's nonexistent girlfriend. I put my newspaper in my briefcase, then lean back and close my eyes. If I'd had lingering doubts about Tony's plans for Megan, they're long gone. It's time for me to step in.

My chance arrives when Tony finally stops prattling and says, "Excuse me for a minute. I have to use the facilities."

"Sure," Megan says. I hope she doesn't take the opportunity to visit the restroom herself.

I hold my breath. I hear the sound of soft footfalls and feel a slight whoosh of air as he moves past me. I wait a beat, open my eyes, and turn my head to see Tony hesitate at the lavatory—it must be occupied—and then open the connecting door between cars. When it slides shut with a bang, I hurry into Tony's seat, warmed by his body.

Megan rears back in alarm. "What—?"

"I'm sorry to frighten you," I say in a low voice, "but this is important. I'm a psychologist, and I've been listening to your conversation with this man. I feel obliged to warn you. His intentions toward you are not good. He's not going to drive you to Virginia

Beach. He's going to abduct you and . . . force himself on you. I'm sorry," I say again. "I know it's a lot to take in."

Her eyes are wide with shock and fear, her freckles standing out against her white skin. "What? What are you talking about?"

I scan the car for Tony. I hope there's a long line for the lavatory.

Quickly, I repeat what I've just said and pull a business card from my wallet. "Here. I have a practice in Virginia Beach. I specialize in sexual deviance."

She takes the card and stares at it—James McIntyre, PsyD, and my office address—and then at me. She's trembling.

"When we stop at Newport News," I continue, "get on the bus to Virginia Beach. You can't miss it. It'll be waiting at the station. Whatever you do, do *not* get into a car with Tony. Do you understand?"

She nods mutely. Then, in a small voice, "How do you know—?"

"I have patients with this paraphilia who have described exactly this scenario. There's no time to explain."

"Paraphilia?"

"It's—never mind. I know you have no reason to believe me, but please. Don't get in the car."

Quickly, I stand up and reclaim my seat across the aisle. Just in time. The sliding door opens, and Tony saunters in. I glance at Megan and see her stuff my business card into the front pocket of her backpack, pull the hood of her sweatshirt up and curl up against the window, her face mostly hidden.

"So listen, I—" Tony says when he reaches our row. He stops when he sees Megan. She murmurs something unintelligible, as though half-asleep.

"Whoops! Sorry," Tony whispers. He takes out his phone and gently eases himself into his seat. He gives Megan a long, hard look and then turns to his screen. She's fooled him; he thinks she's sleeping.

Good girl.

The remainder of the trip is uneventful. Megan sleeps, or at least pretends to, and Tony also nods off. I feel the need to stay alert, even though there's nothing else I can do. The rest is up to Megan.

The conductor announces we'll be arriving at Newport News in just a few minutes. Passengers traveling through to Virginia Beach must transfer to the Amtrak Thruway Motorcoach waiting at the station.

Tony awakens, yawns hugely, and nudges Megan. "Hey, Sleeping Beauty," he says. "We're almost there."

She starts and sits up. "What? Oh." She turns her head to look at me, then past me and back at Tony. There's a large red mark on her cheek where it was mashed against the window.

"Are you okay?" he says.

"Mm-hmm. Just tired. And my head hurts. You got me drunk." She says this with just enough flirtatiousness for him to think she's teasing, but I can see a flicker of anger in her eyes. Again she looks at me and then away.

"Guilty." He laughs. "But that's spring break, right?"

"Uh-huh."

With a shriek of the hydraulic brakes, the train pulls into Newport News, and the gathering of belongings obviates further conversation. A pulse beats in my throat, and I realize I'm nervous. I think I know what Megan's going to do, but will she be strong enough to go through with it?

Tony and Megan detrain first and stop midway between the tracks and the bus idling in front of the station house. The night air is chilly, blustery, bracing, and as I walk past them, I see Megan's long red hair blown into wild shapes that look like the flames of a bonfire. I take a seat on the bus and watch their silent interaction under the bluish glare of the parking lot lights. Is she refusing his offer?

She's refusing, all right. At first, her body language is submissive—crossed arms and legs, slumping to make herself even smaller than she is—and his is puzzled, then cajoling. He's pleading with her, arms outstretched, palms up, but as she gradually unwinds herself and stands her ground, his posture becomes more aggressive and threatening. He spreads his feet apart and puts his hands on his hips. Then he reaches out and grabs her wrist. Even through the thick window glass, I can hear her scream, and she tries to yank her arm away. He won't let go. Then, before I or any of the other men around can intervene, he sneers and shoves her backward, releasing her. She staggers but doesn't fall. She races around him toward the bus.

"You're not *that* hot, bitch," he bellows after her, so loudly that I can hear every word. "Fuck it! Fuck you! Fuck YOU!"

"Hey!" says the burly bus driver, lurching from his seat and lumbering down the steps and onto the pavement. "What's going on?"

I watch from the window. "I have to get on the bus," I hear Megan say through the open door. "Please. I have a ticket."

The bus driver points to Tony, who's now backing away with his hands raised. "Is this guy giving you any trouble?"

"I'm okay."

"Go ahead, honey," he says, and moves to let her pass.

Tony's still retreating. "Sorry," I hear him call out. "Sorry."

The bus driver shakes his head in disgust. "Get outta here before I call the police."

Tony doesn't need another warning. He turns, hurries into the darkest recesses of the parking lot, and disappears.

When I turn away from the window, I see Megan making her way down the aisle, rubbing her wrist. When she sees me, she drops into the seat next to mine. She's shaking.

"So you were right," she says. The corners of her mouth are turning down as though she's going to cry and, sure enough, one tear drops, then two.

I reach into my pocket and pull out a package of Kleenex. "Here."

"Thanks." She plucks out a tissue and hands the package back. She scrubs at her face, and when she looks up again, she's gotten herself under control. "I mean, I tried to be nice about it. I just told him I changed my mind and wanted to take the bus. I didn't mention you or tell him what you said"—good—"but it didn't matter. He went crazy anyway."

I take a deep breath. "If he really was a nice guy offering to help you, your turning down a ride wouldn't have set him off. That little display"—I nod at the window—"shows you he cared too much about the outcome."

"I guess," she says dully.

"Look," I say kindly, "you've had a shock. But Tony's gone. He can't hurt you. And we'll be in Virginia Beach before you know it."

"Okay." She gives me a watery smile. "Thanks."

We spend the short trip chatting. I'm happy to see Megan relax as we increase the distance between her and the train station. By tacit agreement, we don't discuss what happened. Megan seems to want to put it all behind her as quickly as possible. Which is fine with me.

By the time the bus deposits us at the small shelter at Nineteenth and Pacific, it's almost 10:00, and it's even colder by the ocean than it was in Newport News. The other passengers are either being picked up or walking to their cars. As usual, there are no cabs. Megan sets her backpack on the pavement and looks around anxiously.

It's crucial I get this part right.

"Well, good night, Megan," I say casually. "Despite everything, I enjoyed talking to you. I hope you have a lovely vacation."

Her voice wobbles. "Thank you. I enjoyed talking to you too."

I start to walk away. I go ten steps, then twenty, with bated breath. Can it be that I've misread her?

"Dr. McIntyre?"

I exhale. No, I haven't. I stop and turn. "Yes?"

She huddles inside her sweatshirt. "Do you know where I can get a taxi?"

I act taken aback. "You don't have anyone meeting you?"

She shakes her head. "My friends don't know I'm coming. It's a surprise."

I let a note of impatience creep into my voice. "Well, can't you call and ask them to pick you up?"

"They don't have a car." She bites her lip.

I walk back toward her. "What's the address?"

She picks up her backpack and unzips the front pocket. She pulls out a piece of paper and shows it to me. Her friends' house is five blocks from where we're standing.

I furrow my brow. "Hmm. That's a good two, three miles away. You can't walk it. You'll freeze."

She gazes at the deserted streets and looks forlorn. "Oh, no." This is it. It's important that it be her idea.

I look at my watch. "I hate to leave you here all by yourself, but I have to get home. My wife is expecting me."

The words "all by yourself" and "wife" do the trick. Megan puts her hand on my arm. "Please, Dr. McIntyre. Is your car around here? Could you give me a lift?"

I pretend to ponder this, then say, "Sure. I'm just around the corner."

Relief washes over her face. She slings her backpack on her shoulder. The unzipped front pocket gapes, and I see my business card. I make a mental note to retrieve it. Afterward.

"Thank you so much," Megan says, when we're snug and warm inside my car. "I hope this isn't taking you out of your way."

Having successfully activated the Provide Assistance Scenario, I now activate the automatic door locks and smile. "Not at all. What are friends for?"

A Career Spent Disappointing People

FROM *Palm Springs Noir*

THREE HOURS OUT of the hospital, his left foot too swollen for a shoe, Shane's car breaks down. It's July, a trillion degrees outside, Interstate 10 a gray ribbon of shit unspooling east out of Palm Springs toward Arizona. Not exactly where he wanted to go, but who the fuck wants to go to Arizona? It's what was on the other side of Arizona that mattered to Shane, the chance that there might be another life in that direction. He never liked being on the coast. The one time he ever even tried to swim in the Pacific— back when he came out on vacation with his dad, so, over twenty years ago, half his lifetime now—he was gripped with the ungodly realization that unlike a pool, there were no sides. You were always in the deep end out there.

It was a feeling that stuck with him, even when he was in one of those towns in the San Fernando Valley that sounded like an escape route from an old western: North Hills . . . West Hills . . . Hidden Hills . . .

The Honda was the one damn thing Shane thought he could depend on. But as soon as he pulled out of the parking lot at Centinela Hospital in Inglewood, the CHECK ENGINE light flashed on. A hundred thousand miles he put on that fucking car and not a single problem, and the one time he really needed it, it was telling him it couldn't comply. He didn't have the time—or the money—to swing by the mechanic, considering he'd left the hospital before the nurse had filled out the paperwork for the cops, which was a problem. Not as big a problem as staying would have been. It wasn't the kind of thing that would have the cops trawling the city for him, especially since the wound did look self-inflected, since it was. Someone else holding his fucking hand while he shot himself with his own damn gun.

Shane couldn't remember if he still had AAA, but he called anyway.

"Looks like you canceled your account six months ago," the customer service agent said.

Rachel must have done it after she moved out. Like how she canceled their shared credit cards. Or how she took their dog Manny to get his teeth cleaned on the same morning she kicked him out of the house, knowing full well Shane wouldn't have the cash to pick the dog back up.

God, he loved that dog. Probably more than he loved Rachel. No *probably*. *Actually*. If he got out of this fucked-up situation, he was going to buy another dog that looked like Manny and name him Manny too.

"How much is it to re-up?" Shane asked.

"It's sixty-eight dollars, which gets you seven miles of towing service."

"What if I need to go farther?" Shane asked, thinking, *What the hell, maybe I'll have AAA tow me to Arizona, give me someone to talk to.* Or maybe he'd just steal the tow truck. He could do that. He was capable of anything now.

"You'd need the premier membership for that," the customer service agent said, and then began to tell Shane the particulars of how amazing the premier membership was. He had $274 in cash in his pocket—Gold Mike, the fucker who shot him in the foot, that's what he gave Shane as a parting gift after he'd asked him to stop by their storage unit over by the Forum; Shane thinking it was to plan the night's job, Gold Mike with other ideas.

"It's not working out," Gold Mike told him. The storage unit was half-empty already, Gold Mike's van filled with their deejay and karaoke equipment, all their locksmith materials, plus their three industrial-sized lockboxes filled with pills. They'd been coming up light lately, but for a while it was a good living. Black-tie weddings in the Palisades, bar mitzvahs in Calabasas, retirement parties in Bel-Air. How it worked, one of them would be inside at the wedding, singing or deejaying, the other guy parking cars and collecting addresses. Three-hour wedding meant they could get as many keys made as they wanted. Spend the next couple days casing a house, go in and steal all the pills, which wasn't a crime any cop gave a shit about, particularly when there was no evidence of breaking and entering. Plus, it was a victimless crime, Shane not feeling too bad about taking a cancer patient's Klonopin, knowing full well CVS would hook them back up in thirty minutes, maybe less. They didn't steal jewelry or TVs or cars or any of that shit. Just pills.

Then this whole opiate crisis started getting on the news right when weed got legalized, so people in California started loading up on edibles and vape pens instead of Percocet and benzos.

"It's just an ebb," Shane said.

"I'm moving my operating base," Gold Mike said. "Got a friend in Reno. Says everyone's hooked on something. He can get me into the hotels. That's next-level."

"Cool," Shane said. "I'm down to relocate." His only steady, legal gigs were running karaoke at Forrest's Bar in Culver City and a honky-tonk in Thousand Oaks called Denim & Diamonds.

"You're not hearing me," Gold Mike said. "You can't hit the high notes anymore. If you can't sing, this whole operation is moot." *Moot.* Where the fuck had he learned that word? "Jessie's Girl"? "Don't make it weird, all right? Ten years is a good run."

"Who needs a high note? You think Mick can hit a high note?"

"Bro," Gold Mike said, "I don't even like music."

"So that's it? No severance?"

"You think you're getting COBRA up in this bitch? Come on, man."

"Manny's chemo put me back ten grand," Shane said. Manny had a tumor on his ear that turned out to be a treatable cancer, in the sense that the dog could get treatment and still die, but he hadn't yet, as far as Shane knew. "I've been upside down ever since."

"That was like eighteen months ago." Gold Mike took out his wallet, thumbed out a few fifties, put them on an empty shelf next to a broken turntable.

"Couple hundred bucks?" Shane said. "How about you give me 50 percent of everything or I walk into a police station. How about that?" And then Shane pulled out his gun, which had actually been a gift from Gold Mike. A little .22. He'd given it to Shane after a robbery went sideways, a Vietnam War vet came home and found Shane in his bathroom, beat the fucking shit out of him with a golf club, Gold Mike coming in at the last minute and knocking the fucker out with a Taser.

You pull out your gun, mentally, you gotta be ready to kill a guy right then, no talking shit, no cool catchphrase, no *freeze*, no *hands up*, nothing, just *pop pop pop*. That's what cops are always saying, it's what Gold Mike had taught Shane too. Which is how he also had all of Gold Mike's credit cards and his driver's license, in addition to $274.

"Seven miles is fine," Shane said to the customer service agent, and gave him his location on the 10. "I need a place with a kara-oke bar, if possible." He had a hustle he liked to do where he'd bet people that he could make them cry and then he'd bust out "Brick" by Ben Folds Five and every girl who ever had an abortion would be in a puddle. It didn't make him proud, but he had bills to pay.

"Let's see what we have here." The agent made a whistling sound. "Well, the Royal Californian is 6.7 miles from where you are. They have a sports bar with karaoke. If that works, shall I charge it to your existing credit card and get the truck to you?"

"How about I give the driver cash," Shane said. He needed as little paper trail as possible.

"I'll need to check with my manager," the agent said, and put Shane on hold.

He was parked beneath a billboard that advertised THE WON-DER OF WATERFRONT LIVING IN THE DESERT! and showed a happy couple of indeterminate race walking into what appeared to be an Italian lakeside villa surrounded by palm trees. He looked to the west and could make out the obvious signs of civilization: the billboard for a Starbucks, an RV park called the Long Run, a billboard touting an upcoming concert by Rick Springfield at the Fantasy Springs Casino. That fucking guy. Twice in the same day. Had to be a harbinger.

"Cash is just fine. We'll have a tow truck to you in about twenty minutes," the agent said.

It was nearly four o'clock. He was supposed to be singing "Come On Eileen" in a couple hours, always his first song over at Forrest's, everyone always losing their shit when he did that "*Toora loora toora loo rye aye*" bit, like it was 1982 and they were thirteen and it was the eighth grade dance.

That fucking song.

More trouble than it was worth, that was for sure.

He couldn't think about that now.

He needed to get Gold Mike's body out of the trunk.

Or, well . . . choice cuts of Gold Mike's body.

2009 and Shane's working the Black Angus in Northridge. They've got something they call the "Fun Bar," a relic from disco years, lit-up floor, big dark booths, great sound system, but no one dancing. Just frat boys over from the college drinking vodka and cranberry like they all have UTIs. At first, he's just doing karaoke like anybody does karaoke, stand up there, let some drunk come up and sing "American Pie," help him out when he realizes the song is eight minutes long and he doesn't have the wind. Flirt with the bartender, maybe get a hand job in the dry storage. Woman or man. Hand job was a hand job, Shane believed in equal opportunity back then, because of all the coke and a profound lack of giving a fuck. Love is love, friction is friction.

Maybe a little guilt now, thinking about it, thinking about how he did Rachel wrong, staring at the ceiling fan twirling in his room at the Royal Californian, eleven P.M., still a hundred degrees outside, giant flying roaches committing suicide against his window every couple minutes, Shane dying for a fucking Percocet, a million of them still in Gold Mike's van, Shane could hit himself for being so stupid, not thinking this all through, his foot throbbing, sweat sticking his shirt to his chest.

His own fault. Rachel, that is. A lot of lying. *Fuck it* had been his point of view back when he worked at the Angus. Go home with a hundred bucks for the night and an empty load? *Fuck it.* Problem was, he'd kept that point of view long into his relationship with Rachel and she was not a *Fuck it* kind of person, so he pretended it was just how performers were, though by the time Rachel came along, he wasn't a performer anymore, he just performed.

"Baby," he'd tell her, "you gotta just say *Fuck it* when you're in this business, otherwise, every night would crush your spirit."

And Rachel, she'd say, "Then you should get another way to earn a living."

And so he had.

Kind of.

Thing was, Shane could really sing. All this other shit was ephemeral. His talent, man, that was in his genetic code. His dad played in the Catskills back in the day, singing in cover bands, even came out to California one time and brought Shane with him, doing a night at Melvyn's in Palm Springs, which was the last time Shane had been anywhere near here. Typically, his dad would come back home the first week of September with a roll of cash, and for a month everything would be good between him and Shane's mom. Dinners out. New clothes. Shane's mom falling in love all over again, talking about how maybe this year they'd get married, maybe she'd go to college, then maybe law school, Shane's mother always talking about how she was going to be a lawyer, but by the time she died, she'd spent twenty-five years as the lunch lady at Rensselaer Point Elementary down in Troy. She'd had Shane when she was fifteen. Dead by fifty-one. Got diagnosed with early onset Alzheimer's and put a fucking noose around her neck two hours later. Shane's dad saying, *Maybe she didn't really have the old-timers, because wouldn't she have forgotten?* His dad was still alive, that was the irony, doing what Shane thought of as the Dead Man's Tour: Buddy Holly and Elvis tribute shows at Native American casinos in Connecticut, Shane keeping track of him on the Internet, that fucker doing pretty well.

But the Angus.

In comes Gold Mike. Sits at a table right by Shane's kit, nurses a Diet Coke. Really gets into it when Shane sings. Tapping his foot. Bobbing his head. When Shane busts out "Come On Eileen" and hits his full register, Gold Mike stands up and whoops.

When he goes on break fifteen minutes later, Gold Mike follows him outside, where Shane is having a smoke and watching the traffic on Corbin Avenue.

"You got a nice presence," Gold Mike says.

"Thanks, man," Shane says.

"Wasting it out here, if you want my opinion," Gold Mike says.

"Just waiting to be discovered."

"That's not ever gonna happen," Gold Mike says, like he knows. He's maybe twenty-seven, but he's one of those guys who talks like he's been around the world fifty times. Gold Mike fingers a diamond-encrusted V that hangs around his neck.

"Whatever," Shane says. He takes one more drag from his cigarette, then puts it out on the bottom of his shoe, like it's a thing he does all the time, which it isn't.

"Whatever?" Gold Mike says. "I insult you and you say, *Whatever*. Passivity, man, that's an illness."

"You want me to hit you or something?"

Gold Mike laughs hard. He's one of those Armenian dudes who shaves his head just to look tough, Shane making out the outline of a full head of stubble. Shane isn't much of a fighter. He's the kind of person who will stab a guy, though.

"I been watching you," Gold Mike says.

"How long have you been watching me?"

"A couple weeks," Gold Mike says, like it's perfectly normal. "You ever do any time?"

"*You* ever do any time?"

"A couple days here and there," Gold Mike says.

"That must impress some people."

Gold Mike laughs again but doesn't respond.

"What's the V stand for?" Shane points at Gold Mike's neck.

"My last name is Voski."

"Okay."

"It means *gold* in Armenian. What's your last name mean?"

"Solomon? It means peace. From the Hebrew word *shalom*. That's what my mother said anyway."

Gold Mike leans forward, motions Shane to lean in too. "You want to make some real money, Shalom?"

Shane finally fell asleep after one A.M., woke up again at 5:47 A.M., sunrise filling his room on the second floor of the Royal Californian with orange light, his foot like an anvil at the bottom of his leg. He unwrapped the gauze and examined the wound. His foot had swollen to twice its normal size, at least, even though the wound wasn't that big. An inch around. The nurse told him yesterday that the bullet shattered two of his cuneiform bones, that he'd need surgery to stabilize his foot, a couple pins would be inserted, and then he'd be in a hard cast for six to eight weeks. But he was going to need to speak to the police before any of that happened.

That wasn't going to work.

Not with 66 percent of Gold Mike rotting in his storage unit, the other 33 percent in the Honda's trunk, Shane thinking 1 percent was probably drying on the floor, blood and viscera and whatnot. He'd chopped Gold Mike's head off using the fire hose hatchet inside the storage unit, then cut the head up into smaller pieces to make it easier to shuttle around, then took off Gold Mike's hands and feet too, because he thought that would make it harder to identify him, but with DNA, fuck, it probably didn't matter, but Shane hadn't been thinking too terribly straight.

He'd taken the battery out of Gold Mike's van and poured acid over the rest of the body, but that was really just cosmetic. For sure Shane's DNA was in the unit and the van and on Gold Mike's body, but then his DNA was all over everything regardless. They were business partners. That was easy enough to explain. Plus, he had no *legitimate* reason to kill Gold Mike. Anyone who saw them together knew they were a team. Really, the only proof that it was Shane who'd plugged him an excessive number of times was probably the hole in Shane's fucking foot and the gun itself, which Shane had tucked under his mattress.

Well, and Gold Mike's head and all that, which was now in his hotel room's safe, zipped up inside a Whole Foods freezer bag filled with ice.

Shane stepped out onto his second-story balcony—which was just wide enough to hurl yourself over—and lit up his second-to-last cigarette. He'd given up smoking when Manny got cancer, truth be known he sort of blamed himself for that whole thing, but it was the only drug he had on his person and he needed about ten minutes of mental clarity to figure out how he was going to get himself out of this situation.

He needed to get rid of Gold Mike's body parts.

He needed to get rid of the gun.

He needed to get himself an alibi . . . or he needed to change his entire identity, which didn't seem like a plausible turn of events, though he was open to whatever reality presented itself to him.

He needed to go across the street to the Circle K and get some disposable phones.

He also was in a fuck-ton of pain and under normal circumstances might go find a dispensary and get some edibles, but he wasn't showing anyone his ID. He'd get some ice and soak his foot in the tub; that would bring down the swelling. He'd get some bleach from housecleaning, put a couple drops in the water, maybe that would disinfect the wound? Then he needed to get a new car.

The Royal Californian sat on a stretch of Highway 111 in Indio that could have been Carson City or Bakersfield or Van Nuys
or anywhere else where someone had the wise idea to plant a
palm tree and then surround it with cement. This wasn't the part
of greater Palm Springs where people came to actually visit—it
was nowhere near the leafy garden hotel he'd stayed in with his
dad, the Ingleside Inn—unless they were going to court or bail-
ing someone out, since the hotel was a block west of the county
courthouse and jail. He hadn't realized it at first, not until he was
checking in and the clerk gave him a brochure of local amenities.
Page 1 had all the dining options. Page 2 was local entertainment
and information about how to get to the polo fields a mile south.
And then page 3 was all bail bonds, attorneys, and AA meetings.

Made sense, then, when the clerk didn't seem bothered by his
bloody foot and that he didn't have ID when he gave him Gold
Mike's Visa to check in.

He'd given the AAA driver an extra fifteen dollars to park his
car just down the block, in a neighborhood of taupe houses called
the Sandpiper Estates, the word "estate" apparently one of those
words whose meaning had been lost to insincerity, since all Shane
saw were a lot of children standing by themselves on front lawns
made of rock, staring into their phones. Shane left the keys in the
ignition and the doors unlocked. If he was lucky, the car would
be stripped clean in a few days, best-case scenario. Worst case, it
would get towed to some county yard and there it would stay, forever.

Now, Shane counted seven cars in the Royal Californian's
parking lot. A van with a SAVE MONO LAKE sticker faded on the
bumper. A white pickup truck missing the tailgate. Two Hondas
that looked just like his dead Accord. A red Buick Regal, probably
a rental, no one bought fucking Buicks. An SUV. Another SUV. He
tried to imagine who owned each car, and what their favorite song
might be, Shane always interested if people picked a sad song or a
happy one. Gave you a sense of how people viewed their own lives.
Real or imagined.

Rachel's favorite song was "American Girl" by Tom Petty. His
mom's favorite song was "Suspicious Minds" by Elvis. Shane? He
didn't have a favorite. Not anymore. Songs had stopped having
meaning for him. He'd prefer absolute silence, forever.

A man of about seventy walked out of his ground-floor room

and into the parking lot, wearing blue boxer shorts, a white V-neck undershirt, and a pair of black sandals, keys in his hand. *A Sinatra guy,* Shane thought. Probably "My Way" or "Come Fly with Me." Shane made him for the red Buick Regal. It was backed into a space, always the sign of an asshole. Instead, the old man looked up and down the block, which was stone empty, then crossed the street to a one-story office building with storefront-style signs advertising a law office—TERRY KALES, CRIMINAL   DEFENSE-DUI-DIVORCE-IMMIGRATION—accounting offices, a Mexican bakery, a notary, and a place where you could get your cell phone fixed.

Not Sinatra.

Neil Diamond.

He went inside the law office, came back out a few minutes later holding a manila envelope, unlocked a silver Mercedes using his key fob, the lights blinking twice, disappeared inside, started it up, rolled back across the street to the parking lot. A woman came walking out of the old man's hotel room then—she looked young, maybe sixteen—met the old guy in the parking lot, got in the passenger side of the car, pulled away. Five minutes later, the Benz was parked in the Royal Californian's lot and the old man was headed back into the hotel, which is when he spotted Shane up on his perch.

"You always stand around at dawn watching people?"

"Just having a smoke," Shane said, "while I contemplate which car to steal."

"Why not just get an Uber?"

Shane pointed at the man's Benz. "German engineering has always appealed to me, but as a Jew, it feels shameful. So you're safe." Shane telling him he was a Jew to put him at ease, no one ever felt scared of Jews, but also just to see how he reacted, Kales seeming like a Jewish last name. Shane flicked his cigarette butt over the balcony. It landed, still smoking, a few feet away from the man. "You mind stepping on that for me?" Shane pointed at his own foot. "I'm down a limb."

The old man scratched his stomach absently but didn't make a move to the cigarette. "You here for a court date?"

"No," Shane said. "Not today."

"You need a lawyer, I'm right across the street, as I think you know."

"How much for a murder defense?" Shane asked, but he laughed, a big joke, two guys at dawn, bullshitting.

"Less than you'd think." Terry walked over to the butt, stepped on it, cocked his head sideways to get a better look at Shane's foot up above him. "Looks like self-defense to me."

"I'll keep that in mind," Shane said.

"I keep office hours at Cactus Pete's." He pointed at the bar attached to the Royal Californian. "Be there until at least six-thirty. I'll buy you a drink, we can talk about your case."

"I'm innocent."

"Yeah," Terry said, "that's what we'll tell 'em."

Shane couldn't tell if Cactus Pete's had a seventies kitsch design aesthetic or if it just hadn't changed since that decade. He'd never been in a bar that had shag carpeting. The VIP area, set off from the tiny dance floor and deejay booth by an actual red-velvet rope, had high-backed booths that reminded Shane fondly of the Angus, Terry Kales sitting in the biggest one, sipping on a glass of something brown, papers spread out in front of him, a cell phone to his ear, another cell phone and his car keys keeping his papers from blowing away, the overhead fans working overtime to keep the room cool. He didn't look up when Shane walked in, at least as far as Shane could tell, which was hard because Terry had on sunglasses, the bar's windows flooding the room with bright light.

It was just before three. Tomorrow at this time, he'd be in the clear. That was the hoped-for result. He'd found a 99 Cents Only store two blocks away, limped his ass over there, his foot on fire, picked up a change of clothes, some sunglasses, a Padres baseball cap. Went next door to the Circle K, got his disposable phone. He was about out of cash now, but he'd figure that out. This old man? He'd probably had a good enough life.

On the dance floor, a woman was setting up for karaoke, and for reasons Shane could not fathom, there was a guy dressed as a clown sitting at the bar. Green hair. Red nose. Striped pants. Big red shoes. Stars-and-stripes shirt and vest. Back of the vest, embroidered in rhinestones, it said HERMIETHECLOWN.COM. He had a cup of coffee and a *Desert Sun,* the local paper, reading the sports page. Shane sat down at the bar but kept a stool between himself and Hermie.

"Get you something?" the woman setting up the karaoke asked.

She was younger than Terry, older than the clown, somewhere on the plus side of fifty. She had on a tank top that showed off her shoulders—muscular, but lean—and a full sleeve of tattoos down her right arm. Shane saw two names—CHARLOTTE and RANDY—amid flowers, sunsets, and spiderwebs. She had a name tag pinned above her left breast that said GLORY.

"Was wondering what time the show was," Shane said.

"Six," Glory said. "You sing?"

"Yeah."

"We have a lot of regulars, so sign up early."

"Truth is, I was wondering if I could warm up first." When Glory didn't respond, Shane said, "I'm staying here."

"Room?"

"Two-oh-four," he said. "On account of my foot. Gotta have surgery in the morning. Just trying to have one last good night before I get the knife." He looked over at the clown. "Unless you've got first dibs."

"He don't speak," Glory said, "or sing."

The clown nodded in the affirmative.

Glory leaned over the bar and examined Shane's foot. So did the silent clown, who blew lightly on a whistle he kept around his neck, which Shane found disconcerting. He slid his flip-flop off, wiggled his toes.

"You can't be in here without a shoe on," Glory said.

"Just letting it breathe," Shane said.

Glory nodded solemnly, like they'd come to some agreement about life. "What's your song?"

"I mix it up," Shane said, and out of the corner of his eye, he saw Terry slide his sunglasses down his nose, "but mostly Neil Diamond."

Shane was midway through "Girl, You'll Be a Woman Soon" when Terry came over and stood next to the clown; Terry had tears streaming down his face. Terry and the clown swayed back and forth together, Shane digging down deep for the end, telling that girl, *sooooooooon you'll need a man,* giving it some real soul, some real pathos.

"Again," Terry said, and tossed Shane a fifty, so he did it again, Terry breaking down in full sobs this time, clearly going through some shit. When he finished, Terry said, "One more, your pick," and then went and sat back in his booth, the clown following him. Shane went with "Song Sung Blue." When he was finished, Terry motioned him over to his table.

"You really having surgery?" Terry asked once they were all comfortable in the sweaty half-moon banquette, Terry's shit spread out everywhere, Shane eyeing his car keys, his plan coming into full focus, Hermie busy on his phone, answering texts. Popular fucking clown. "I heard you talking to Glory."

"Yeah," Shane said. "At the hospital up the street." He'd seen it in the brochure. It was named for John F. Kennedy, which Shane thought was some bad presidential juju.

"Good hospital," Terry said. "All of my best clients have died there."

"Like the girl this morning?"

"That was my daughter."

"Really?" *Really.*

"Yeah," Terry said, "I've got limited visitation at the moment, so I take what I can get."

"Okay," Shane said, not sure if he believed him. "What about you, Hermie? Any kids?"

Hermie looked up from his phone, shook his head no.
Thank God.

"Can I give you some legal advice?" Terry said. "Jew to Jew."

"Mazel tov," Shane said.

"You've clearly been shot in the foot. In about two hours, when the courthouse closes? This bar is gonna fill up with off-duty cops, DAs, public defenders, judges, and expert-witness types. You should be gone by then."

"That is good advice," Shane said. "Why are you giving it to me?"

"When it all comes down," Terry pointed at a television above the bar, the sound off, running Fox News, "they'll take us both."

"Apart from that."

"You have the natural ability to make a person feel something, you know? That's special." Terry adjusted his sunglasses, Shane thinking maybe he was getting a little teary-eyed again, or maybe he just liked the Jim Jones vibe he was giving off. "Sometimes a song, sung by the right person, it'll touch you. You touched me up there just now. I don't know. Maybe I'm drunk."

Hermie nodded vigorously.

"You saw my daughter? Her mother," Terry said, "won't have me

in the house, which is why I'm in this situation over here. 'Girl,'
that was our song. Our wedding song. Seems dumb, no?"

"People pick terrible songs for their weddings," Shane said, and
then told Terry about his job working weddings, all the times he
sang "Wild Horses" for newlyweds.

"No one *listens* anymore," Terry said. "Words used to mean
something." He looked over at Hermie. "No offense."

Hermie shrugged.

"Anyway," Terry said, "you seem like a nice guy in a bad situation. So. Maybe I can help you. Do you want help?"

"I could use a friend," Shane said.

"I could be a friend." Terry reached into his back pocket and
pulled out his wallet, slid a business card over to Shane. One side
was in English, the other in Spanish, but both were for a dentist
named Marco Degolado in Los Algodones, Baja California, right
over the Mexican border, according to the thumbnail map printed
on the card.

"You got any warrants?" Terry asked.

"No," Shane said.

"That's two hours from here. Two exits before Yuma. Easy in
and out of Mexico, all the snowbirds go there for dental care
when they're down here. They're liberal with their opiates and an-
tibiotics in Mexico." Shane nodded. "Dr. Degolado knows his way
around minor surgery as well. He's a friend too." Shane nodded
again. His foot *was* killing him. "Let me make a call."

"You'd do that?"

"You walk into JFK with that," Terry said, "you won't walk
out."

Shane looked over at Hermie. He gave Shane an affirmative
nod. What the fuck went on in *that* guy's fucking mind?

"All right," Shane said. "Set it for tomorrow afternoon?"

"What's your name?"

Shane thought for a moment. "My friends," he said, "call me
Gold Mike."

"What do you want the doctor to call you?"

"Mike Voski."

Terry picked up his cell phone. "Give me five minutes," he said,
and then headed outside, which gave Shane a chance to casually
snatch up Terry's car keys from the table. He turned and looked
out the window to where Terry's Benz was parked, around the cor-

ner from where Terry stood, hit the unlock button, watched the
car's lights blink twice, set the keys back down.

Hermie the Clown didn't utter a word, so Shane said, "You a
monk or something?"

Hermie stared at Shane for a few seconds, then said, out loud,
"You ever meet a chatty clown?"

"Can't say I have."

"That's part of the game." He reached over and picked up the
car keys. Hit the button. Lights flashed again. Locked.

"How about I give you fifty dollars and we call it even?" Shane
said.

Hermie said, "How about everything you've got in your wallet?"

Shane had his gun tucked under his shirt and could have, he
supposed, shot Hermie, done him like Han Solo did Greedo, but
Shane wasn't yet the unprovoked murdering type. "Not gonna be
much more than fifty." He dug out his wallet, pulled out everything, set it on the table, sixty-seven bucks.

Hermie took it all. "Not personal, you understand."

"Just two guys doing business," Shane said.

Hermie stood up then, gathered up all his belongings, then
pulled out his own business card, everyone in this fucking place
the kings of Vista Print, apparently. It said:

HERMIE THE CLOWN
Parties. Charity Events. Private Functions.
  Restaurant & Bar PR.
NO KIDS 18+ ONLY
SEE WEBSITE FOR RATES/CELEBRITY PHOTOS
Hermietheclown.com
Phone: 760-CLOWN-69
E-mail: Hermie@Hermietheclown.com

"I'll be back in a few days," Hermie said. "If you're coming
back."

"I'm coming back."

"You'd be good in the clown game. You've got a nice presence."

"Thanks," Shane said.

"I got my teeth capped in Los Algodones. Can't have janky teeth
and be a clown. Freaks people out. Terry hooked me up." Hermie
went silent again, like he was trying to get Shane to ask him a
question.

"And then what?" Shane finally said.

"And then I have to do Terry favors, periodically. Drop things off. Take out the garbage sometimes. Clean up his room. Favors. So, if you're not willing to do that, I'd say keep moving, hoss."

There it was.

"He really Jewish?" Shane asked.

"His brother was a rabbi," Hermie said.

"Was?"

"Died."

"Natural causes?"

"I didn't ask for an autopsy."

"Out here?"

"Las Vegas," Hermie said. "Everyone here is always trying to get to Las Vegas, everyone in Las Vegas is always trying to get somewhere else, no one happy to be any one place."

"You make a lot of sense, for a clown."

"You'd be surprised what a guy can learn by staying quiet." He looked outside, where Terry was still on the phone. "My Uber is here." Hermie stood there for a moment, shifting back and forth in his big red shoes. "He doesn't have a daughter," Hermie said, then closed a giant, exaggerated zipper across his mouth, locked it, tossed away the key, and walked silently back out into the heat of the day. Hermie bumped fists with Terry, got into a waiting Prius, and drove off.

Shane unlocked the Benz again.

Terry came back in a few minutes later. "You're all set, Gold Mike," he said.

"What do I owe you?" Shane asked.

"Doctor will have a couple prescriptions for you to bring back."

"That all?"

"Well," Terry said, "you'll need to go back for a follow-up. In which case, I might have something for you to deliver. Could be you come to find you like Mexico."

"I'm gonna need wheels."

"You beam here?"

"No," Shane said. "Car broke down. It won't be fixed for at least a week."

Terry tapped a pen against his lips. "Okay," he said. "How about I have Enterprise drop off a car for you. Nothing fancy, you understand. What do you have for collateral?"

Shane pondered this for a moment, then reached under his shirt and put his gun on the table.

Shane waited until Cactus Pete's was in full swing to make his move. Terry wasn't kidding about the clientele: a steady stream of men with brush cuts and tucked-in polo shirts were followed by men and women in business suits, mostly of the off-the-rack variety, not a lot of tailored sorts doing time in Indio's courthouse. Terry came out a couple times to take phone calls, cops and attorneys greeting him as they passed by, Shane watching from his window as they all glad-handed each other.

Shane took Gold Mike's head, hands, and feet out of the safe, refilled the freezer bag with some fresh ice to help with the smell, zipped the bag back up, and headed downstairs. It was about seven, the sun still up, at least 105 degrees, and Shane saw that there were now anthill mounds rising up through the cracks in the parking lot pavement. The lot was full, a dozen Ford F-150s with American flags and 1199 Foundation stickers in the window, a couple Lexuses, a few BMWs, another five nebulous American cars, a surprising number of motorcycles, a couple Benzes. There was a Mexican kid, maybe six or seven, sitting on the tailgate of an F-150 parked next to Terry's Benz, eating a Popsicle, playing on his phone. Shane's rental, a white Ford Fiesta, was parked next to Terry's Benz.

"You staying here?" Shane asked the kid.

"On the other side of the fairgrounds." The kid pointed beyond the courthouse and jail.

Shane looked down the block. There was, in fact, a giant county fairground right next to the jail and courts. Across the street was an A-frame Wienerschnitzel cut-and-pasted from the 1970s, a fire station, an Applebee's, a used car lot. He tried to imagine what it would be like to grow up here. Figured it was like anywhere else. Either you lived in a happy home or you lived in a shitty one.

"You should go home," Shane said. "It's late."

"My dad works at the jail," the kid said.

"Oh yeah?"

"He's inside having a drink."

"What's he do there," Shane said, "at the jail?"

"Something with computers."

So probably not a cop. That's good. "You see anything weird here?"

The kid looked at Shane for a few seconds, like he couldn't be sure of his answer, then said, "I saw a clown. Like in that movie."

"What movie?"

"I didn't see it," the kid said. "But my cousin? He saw it and said it was fucked up."

Shane looked around but didn't see Hermie. "Recently? The clown I mean."

"Couple minutes, I guess."

Odd.

"You do me a favor?" Shane asked.

"I'm not supposed to talk to anyone," the kid said, "cuz my dad says the East Valley is filled with criminals and pedos and losers and that's just who he works with."

"Yeah, that's smart." Shane pointed at his foot. He'd wrapped it in a towel and then taped his flip-flop to it, so he could walk around a bit better. It looked absurd. "Could you just run over and get me a bucket of ice from the front desk?"

The kid looked at Shane's foot. "What happened?"

"Stepped on a nail."

"Must have been pretty big."

"You do this for me or not?"

The kid slid off the back of the truck and headed to the hotel's lobby, which gave Shane the chance to pop open the unlocked trunk of Terry's Benz, drop the freezer bag in, and then close it.

Shane got in the Fiesta—it smelled weird inside, like vinegar and shoe leather and wet newspapers—started it up, turned left on Highway 111 out of the hotel, so he wouldn't pass Cactus Pete's, since he'd told Terry he wasn't leaving until the morning, then kept going, driving west into the setting sun, his left foot inside a bucket of ice. He rolled past the presidents—Monroe, Madison, Jefferson—then was in La Quinta—Adams, Washington—and into Indian Wells, then Palm Desert, just another snowbird in a rental car, could be anyone, so he opened the Fiesta's moon roof, let some air in, get that weird smell out. Then he was in Rancho Mirage, passing Bob Hope Drive, then rolling by Frank Sinatra Drive, Shane starting to feel like he'd gotten away with it, so he took out his burner, called the anonymous Crime Stoppers hotline, was patched through.

"This is going to sound crazy," Shane said, now in Cathedral City, passing Monty Hall Drive, a street named for a guy who'd spent his entire career disappointing people by giving them donkeys instead of cars, "but I swear I saw a man at the Royal Californian in Indio chopping up a human head. He put it all into a bag in the trunk of his Mercedes."

By the time he finished his story, Shane was in downtown Palm Springs, rolling north down Indian Avenue. His left foot was numb, but the rest of his body felt alive, sweat pouring down his face, his shirt and pants damp, even though the AC was cranked at full blast, the moon roof just cracked. He'd go back to LA tonight, get all the pills from the storage unit, then torch it, now that he was thinking straight. Then he'd turn around and head to Mexico, get his foot operated on, since he had an appointment already, and Terry was going to be in a jail cell for a good long time, maybe forever. And then he'd just keep rolling east, until he got back to Upstate New York. Find his father at some Indian casino, see if he wanted to start a duo, figure out how to have a life together, Shane thinking, *Whoa, what? Am I high?* Shane thinking his foot was probably infected, that what he was feeling was something bad in his blood, sepsis most likely, and then he was passing the road to the Palm Springs Ariel Tramway, burning it out of town, the fields of windmills coming into view, Shane finally taking a moment to look in the rearview mirror, to make sure there weren't a hundred cop cars lined up behind him, and thinking, for just a moment, that he was really fucked up, that he was really hallucinating some shit, that he needed to get some real meds, because sitting right there in the backseat, a gun in his hand, was a fucking clown.

The Very Last Time

FROM *Ellery Queen Mystery Magazine*

FRANCIS HAD BEEN GONE five days before the police came. In retrospect, perhaps I should have pretended I wasn't expecting them. But by the time the squad car pulled up the driveway, I wasn't thinking clearly through my dread.

I met the cops—two of them, just like on TV—at my screen door. They were both young white men, I would guess in their late twenties, of similar stocky builds. If I'd met them in the street I would probably have found them indistinguishable. One officer pulled a small notebook out of his pocket and propped it on his wrist, ready to scribble. The other spoke. "Are you Susan Hatcher?"

"Yes," I answered apologetically. I was so nervous I could choke, but I still felt bad that this officer had had to climb my steep porch stairs, that he was huffing a little, and that I was going to have to lie to him. "Is something wrong?"

The lighter-haired officer—Jared Dube, according to his brassy name tag—answered gravely, "Your husband's employer has reported him missing, Mrs. Hatcher."

"He's missing, then." I heard how small my voice sounded. My poor Francis used to say it drove him crazy when my voice got whiny.

Officer Dube leaned forward. "Do you mean to say he's not missing?"

In that instant, the cloud of numbness I'd been hiding in dissipated, and I felt tears gather in my eyes. "I've just been waiting for him to come back," I said truthfully. "I keep expecting him to show up at any moment."

When my voice cracked, the officers exchanged glances, and I quickly turned my gaze to the floor so they wouldn't think I was testing their reactions. I took a step back into my foyer and fanned them into my house. "Why don't you both come inside? We can talk more comfortably."

Jared Dube and his partner, Evan Gates, sat at my kitchen table and established my identity as I filled them each a glass of tap water.

"We've been trying to reach you for two days, Mrs. Hatcher," Officer Gates said sternly. "Francis's employer, Hart Media, reported him missing on Wednesday. Apparently he has not been to work this week, and their calls to his cell phone and residence have gone unanswered. As have ours." Officer Gates eyed me, letting the unasked questions hang in the air, although he failed to wait long enough for me to implicate myself. I was still trying to figure out how I would explain why I hadn't answered the phone when he asked, "Do you have any idea where Francis could be?"

"No," I said, and then had to stop myself from saying more. I cringed at how clipped my answer sounded, how artificial.

Officer Dube asked, "Mrs. Hatcher, when was the last time you saw your husband?"

What was the correct answer to this? Five days ago? Or three centuries ago? It certainly felt as though three centuries had passed since Sunday evening, when I had arrived home—alone—from our last trip. "Well, we spent the weekend here. At home." I looked down at my hands, which were folded on the placemat. Next to the officers' purposeful young hands, mine looked swollen and sick, the fingers almost swallowing my engagement and wedding bands.

"Did Francis tell you he was going to work on Monday?" Officer Dube asked. I saw Officer Gates crane his neck to observe the two cars sitting in our driveway.

"No. He was already . . . missing by then." The officers were both watching me steadily, and I made an effort to hold one or the other's gaze. "On Sunday afternoon, he told me a friend was coming to pick him up to take him to their Sunday-night chess league." My heart skipped with sudden hope. The chess league was true; I felt both relieved and foolish that I hadn't thought of it before. "But then he never came home Sunday night." Yes, this was much better. The police would go away to follow up, and this would buy me some time to figure out how to get Francis back.

"Did you try calling him?"

"Yes, of course," I said quickly. "But he left his cell phone here." Without thinking, I pointed to the counter, where Francis's cell sat. We always left our technology at home when we went on excursions.

Officer Gates eyed the phone from his seat at the table, and for a moment I was speechless with fear that he would retrieve it and start scrolling through the call history. But the other officer, Dube, the one I had come to think of as the good cop, spoke up before things got out of hand.

"So, Mrs. Hatcher, to the best of your knowledge, the last people to see your husband would have been the folks at his Sunday-night club?"

I nodded, swallowing back my relief.

"We're going to need the names of the other members of the . . . chess group, then."

I nodded again. I was suddenly feeling much better.

"Mrs. Hatcher." Jared Dube leaned forward, as if to make this question more intimate. "Has Francis disappeared without warning like this before?"

"Only a couple of times." I knew what they heard when I answered that way, however true my words were. They heard a spirit-battered, cuckolded wife, whose husband had jetted off to some relaxing getaway with a more attractive lover, leaving her waiting at home, sadly accustomed to these abuses. My mouth twisted against tears as I thought about how they must be picturing my husband. My poor Francis, whose fate I held in my trapped hands.

When the police left, I locked myself in the bathroom and sobbed until I had used the last of the tissues. My face stiff and inflated with tears, I took the hottest shower I could stand. Steam filled the bathroom and the stuffiness, the fight for oxygen, helped my mind anchor itself. I couldn't bite back my sorrow or panic, though. The desperation of my situation almost overwhelmed me. I knew my husband was dead, and if I didn't figure something out soon, he was going to stay that way.

There were many things I could not tell the police.

I could not have told them, for example, that my husband was trapped in the late seventeenth century by a broken soup tureen, stuck in a time traveler's nightmare. I could not have said the words "time travel" at all. Any such attempt to tell the truth would have instantly driven the investigators in the direction of their most sinister suspicions, and placed me at the heart of their darkest theories. Francis would have slid from the list of *Missing* to that of *Missing and Presumed Dead,* and I from *Spouse* to *Person of Interest.* My wrists would be tied by an inevitable goose-chasing murder investigation, preventing me from solving the real problem.

If I thought they would have listened, I might have explained to the police that my husband and I were hobbyist time travelers, that we enjoyed taking weekend jaunts to different epochs in history, the fourth-dimensional transport made possible by locking ourselves in our garage with a piece of pottery I'd picked up at a yard sale last summer. I might have saved Officers Dube and Gates time on their missing-person investigation by revealing that, unless Francis had accomplished some miracle after our terrible schism, he had probably died three hundred years ago, trapped in an abandoned root cellar. That barring the destructive efforts of silt and erosion, his remains would most likely be found buried several feet under our garage.

My story was untellable, because I had no means of proving it, and to men like them, in a matter like this, proof is a requisite. I would never be able to demonstrate to the policemen how Francis and I used to be able to travel through time. The tureen, our key to the past, had been broken beyond repair in an inexplicable turbulence on Sunday evening as we returned, and when the shaking around me had stilled and coalesced into my clean twenty-first-century garage, I was alone, the fragments of only half the bowl in my bleeding hands. I could only assume the other half was trapped in colonial Massachusetts with Francis.

Well, there, in brief, is the truth. I understand how preposterous it sounds—a soup tureen, of all magical objects—but as is the case with these things, there is always a break with our familiar realities at the onset, a leap of faith.

Over the last fourteen months, since we discovered the tureen, Francis and I took a total of six excursions to different moments in Massachusetts history. I'm sure you will not be surprised to hear that I've gone out of my way to seek out time-travel literature since the first time it happened. Although the authors of these time-travel novels almost certainly had nothing like my own true-life experience to draw on, I was still eager to read what people imagined it was like, to see how close the best guessers might have come. It seems in these various authors' imaginations that the first "time travel" experience always takes the hero or heroine unaware, often against their will, such as what befalls the heroes of William Morris's *News from Nowhere* and Mark Twain's *A Connecticut Yankee in King Arthur's Court.* In some cases, the hero is dragged through time when they touch some kind of magical object or pass into some magical place—a perpetuation of the not uncommon idea that certain points in the universe are more permeable than others. I perceive how this idea is appealing, since it corresponds to so many primitive understandings of time, space, and God—one of the reasons that fantasy authors so often explore this line of transposition.

In the case of my excursions with Francis, we would touch the tureen—our port key, to borrow a term from Joanne Rowling—in the confines of our garage, and we would be transported together to the same geographical location at a different year in history. We never established how the tureen selected the year of our destination, nor learned to influence it, but after the first experience we enjoyed the element of surprise. Our house is quite old, with portions dating back to the earliest English and French colonial settlements in this part of the state. It has a long history, and could accommodate a diverse range of voyeuristic holidays. Some journeys were more stressful than others, to be sure—what else could one expect when taking the risk of time travel? Witnessing D-Day at the Springfield Armory was a highlight, however, as was visiting Bronson Alcott's transcendental commune, Fruitlands, during its only active summer of 1843, although I have to say we were both a little shocked at how dictatorial Louisa May's father turned out to be.

It was Francis who discovered the time slip, to borrow another term, this time from Kurt Vonnegut. The discovery was inadvertent, of course. I had purchased the tureen at a yard sale—I admit to being a bit of a yard-sale scavenger—but Francis, who was often difficult about my taste in knickknacks, took an inexplicable dislike to it and was adamant it not be kept in the kitchen. I decided to shelve it in the garage, what has become my Susan-space, next to other such disappointing purchases I'd made, including the his-

and-hers hiking-gear set for the safari we never ended up going on, or the love seat I thought would have done nicely in our living room. I have redone that garage space as my little lair, and was meaning to display the tureen for myself on my lilac hutch.

I can't remember now why Francis followed me into the garage that day, or how we came to grasp the tureen at the same moment—those details have been blotted away by everything that came immediately after. The first experience was unpleasant, as one might expect. When the shaking began we thought it was an earthquake, as we'd only so recently had that tremor in New Bedford; when the shaking failed to subside, our succession of fears included terrorism, meteors, the end of the world as it was choosing to take shape. When the tremors stopped, there was much disorientation, both mental and physical. I felt a heat rash creeping over my skin, for example, and Francis experienced a terrible pain in his pelvis. I won't bore you with all the specifics of how we wrapped our heads around our changed circumstances—noticing our house was the wrong color, the spit-shiny war-era Ford that sat in the incorrectly angled driveway—but suffice it to say the revelation of our predicament was traumatizing. Realizing one's reality is not what one had thought it was, well—the physiological as well as psychological repercussions can be overwhelming.

But the second response to altered circumstances, once one has absorbed them, is to try to exploit them. The reverse side of that same human-nature coin—first the trauma, then the exploitation. And so as the details started to come together, as Francis, the amateur historian, began to diagnose his surroundings, and especially as we realized that the way back to our earlier lives was not entirely closed to us, we began to calm down, and then to get excited.

Of course, I never expected anything like this to happen to me—I don't mean to sound blasé about this—but it is funny how once something unfathomable happens in one's life, something one could not earlier have imagined surviving . . . well, after that first bridge of disbelief has been crossed, even the extraordinary begins to feel mundane. I remember, for example, when Francis and I first learned we could never have children. The channels of disbelief were quite the same. It was a thought that had never fully crossed my mind until the doctor told me, point-blank, exactly what was wrong with us. I kept waiting for the disbelief to kick in, but it never did. The hurdle, once jumped, is behind us.

I said earlier that the trauma of the situation receded when we realized we would be able to return to our earlier lives. But that was a misapprehension, since there was no true way back. We couldn't time-travel to a world where we had never time-traveled, where the impulse and dangerous curiosity had never been awakened, where we would be safe from our own strange desires. It was already too late for that, and the first successful indulgences in our whimsy ruined us, lulled our sense of self-preservation, prepared us to push our power too far. I have had five days to reflect on these sins, after all. To ponder where we went wrong, and to search for a way to undo what was done.

This is why I was tortured by guilt and mourning for Francis's predicament. Even if I could rewrite my husband's fate, I cannot unwrite the fact that the door to this one horrible possibility was opened. Even if somehow I were able to bring him back to this time and place, I cannot undo the fact that in some alternate reality, he died slowly in a root cellar. He might not remember his own alternate path, but for me, those five days would always have passed.

The visit from the police made me realize that hiding in my house was not helping me deal with my situation. Once I'd taken my steaming shower, I pinned back my hair, which in its flyaway state must have struck the police officers as somewhat insane, and drove my car into Framingdale center. I needed to get away from the site of my misery, clear my mind's eye of the vision of Francis's body trapped beneath my garage.

On a Friday afternoon, there was not very much to do in Framingdale—a family-run supermarket; a barnlike craft-supply store in which to pick through knitting wool I would never use. But I didn't have the emotional energy to drive any farther, to a real town. We had chosen this rural lifestyle seventeen years ago at least in part because of the quaint peace of mind it might afford on a day like today.

Stilling my twitching nerves, I parked competently in the empty lot by Charlie's, Framingdale's railroad-car diner. Old-fashioned sleigh bells jingled as I entered. Behind the counter, Beth-Ann was grilling a row of cheese sandwiches for three middle-aged men in nearly matching flannel shirts.

"You want the usual today, sweetheart?" Beth-Ann called over the flat grill.

"Yes, please, Beth-Ann." I sat down carefully on the red-leathered stool farthest from the construction workers, or whatever they were. I confess I am not very fond of diner-style stools, which offer no sense of back protection. As I pulled my purse over my lap to cover my thighs, I couldn't help but imagine that the men were exchanging glances over me.

Feeling my neck reddening, I pressed my thumbs on the Formica counter and watched as Beth-Ann filled a six-ounce porcelain mug from the hot-chocolate machine. "Now I forget, sweetheart," she called, "do you take whipped cream?"

"No," I replied automatically, before I had given myself a chance to think about my own desires. "But you know what, maybe I will today."

She nodded, lips pinched in shrewd sympathy. She was giving me whipped cream, I realized, because she already knew something was wrong, that this was not a whipped-cream day for happy reasons.

To my great relief, the men counted their money out onto the counter and left. Beth-Ann set a griddle-crispy corn muffin by my hot chocolate and rested her heavy torso on her elbows. "Now how are you holding up, Susan?"

"Oh, I'm fine," I said. My gay voice rang so falsely off the stainless-steel utensils that both Beth-Ann and I cringed.

"Susan. You know it's already been in the Community section this morning, about Francis disappearing."

Of course it had already been in the papers. I took a bite of the muffin, but as happens in these situations, all the saliva in my mouth had evaporated, and I was left chewing raggedly, like a cow.

"Even if it hadn't made the police blotter, that Kathy Long down at the radio station can't keep her lid on anything." Beth-Ann fixed me with her caring brown eyes, and I noticed the ruptured red capillary next to one iris. "What they won't do for a little celebrity gossip. It's just dreadful to listen to. I heard her yakking away on the six-o'clock this morning. You know what she's like. I couldn't get out of my head the whole time how unfair this is to you." She shook her head. "As if you're accountable for his behavior. Really. Whenever I hear about a situation like this, I think to myself, don't these media demons think about what they're doing to the man's poor wife? As if she's not already suffering enough?"

I swallowed tightly. "I'm sorry to trouble you, Beth-Ann, but I'm going to need a glass of water."

"No problem, sweetheart." As she turned to get a glass, I noticed the dark brown stains on the leg of her jeans. Worcestershire sauce, I thought, or maybe very old paint.

"Kathy Long is a piece of work," Beth-Ann said over the rumble of the ice-cube coffin. "After everything she's already put you through. You know, I think if you had half a mind to, you could sue her. For whatsit called, defamation? I'm not sure what would stick, but you could give her a run for her money."

"Oh, I'm not going to sue anybody," I replied mechanically. "Kathy's just a bunch of hot air. She doesn't bother me."

"I don't mean to be involved in your affairs," Beth-Ann said confidentially. "I just want you to know that the ice is broken, and that you can talk to me about these things any time you want. You shouldn't feel alone in this."

I heard a loud snap inside my brain, like a popgun firing. "Alone in what?" I gripped the pearling glass of ice water she had set in front of me. "What do you mean, 'in this'?"

"Oh, sweetheart. Just wanted you to know I was on your side. When men run off with another woman, you know, people forget to reach out to the poor wives. But I'm not afraid of being awkward if it does you some good to know you have a friend."

"Francis has not *run off* with another *woman*." Saying the words filled my throat with bile. *How dare she.* My vision filled with Francis's face, that last look of abject horror as he held up the porcelain shards in his bloody hands and our two worlds ripped us apart. My poor Francis. How dare she think of him as an adulterer. I felt the way a porcupine must feel when it bristles under attack, or a dog must when its hackles rise. The skin of my exposed back rose to attention, the pores flexing with anger.

I saw Beth-Ann's eyes roll to the right, and she took a step back toward the grill. "All right, Susan. I'm sorry I overstepped. I was just trying to help."

"I think you'll find I don't need your *help*." Without meaning to, I slammed the water glass down on the counter, and it shattered, casting a puddle of ice and ice-colored glass across the Formica. I counted five dollars from my wallet, the same amount I always leave, and tucked the bills pointedly under the dripping plate. "I will take a bag for the muffin to go," I told her, my voice full of exactly what I thought of her.

"All right," she said again, her voice much more contrite now. She used a napkin to pick up the now-soggy muffin and transfer it into a white paper bag.

As the jingling strap of bells sounded my exit, I noticed I had accidentally reopened the cut on the heel of my hand that I had sustained when the tureen broke; it had only just scabbed over completely. I was so enraged that for several minutes I forgot about Francis entirely.

The second time the police came, they brought dogs.

It had been fewer than twenty-four hours since their first visit, when kind Jared Dube and ferret-eyed Evan Gates had sat civilly at my kitchen table. Today there were a total of six cops, five men and one incongruously well-made-up woman with large gold hoop earrings. I hadn't realized the municipality of Framingdale retained six police, and couldn't imagine how six salaries were paid out of our tiny tax pool.

"Hello again, Mrs. Hatcher," Officer Gates said as he reached my front door. He was out of breath and gave a small cough. "We have a warrant to search your premises. We're going to have to ask you to stand aside and let us in."

He spread an accordioned blue document for me to examine as two men led unfriendly-looking German shepherds past me into the house. The dogs nosed at the planks of my porch, my doorframe, my slippers.

I stood dumbfounded as the four unfamiliar officers began to canvass my house. "What are the dogs for?"

"These are cadaver dogs, ma'am," Officer Dube answered. "To see if they pick up any decomposition on the property." His elbows and shoulders twitched as he spoke. He was nervous this time, unlike his last visit. I understood he thought he was interviewing a murderer, and that thought made me begin to tremble too. Things like this never happened in small towns.

"What . . . what are the grounds for the search warrant?" I managed.

"It seems like you never called anyone in the chess league to see whether they had seen Mr. Hatcher," Officer Gates said. His voice was arch, openly accusatory. "Pretty suspicious, that."

Why hadn't I thought to call the chess league? My stomach seized violently. I should have known it would come to this, this search, this creeping guilt. Why had I not thought it through, placed a few empty calls? How much could I have spared myself with a little planning? "I . . . I just assumed when I woke up on Monday that he must have come home already. It didn't occur to me that . . . that this might have anything to do with anyone there."

"You lied to us, Mrs. Hatcher." Officer Gates's expression was terribly cold. "You made no outgoing phone calls, not to his place of work, not to any of his friends. It strikes us as awful funny behavior. You didn't do anything to try to figure out where your husband might have gone to."

"I . . . I wasn't in a sound frame of mind." By the last word, my voice had dropped below audibility. *Why. Why didn't you just think to call.*

"Is there anything you want to tell us now, Mrs. Hatcher?" Officer Dube said. I almost thought I could still hear the traces of warmth and understanding in his voice.

"I." I couldn't help it; I simply had nothing to say. "No."

He nodded, his dark eyes narrow. I don't know if it was in disappointment, or if he was merely squinting against the early morning sun.

The officers stood on either side of me, like bodyguards, and together we watched the search. I couldn't help but wonder about the elapsed time of these investigations. It had been a week since Francis had disappeared; if I really had been one of those crazy women who would hurt or imprison their husbands, it would almost certainly be too late for him by now. As I watched the teams sniff their way through my hallways, shedding on my newly vacuumed carpets, I realized how dangerous a small town might actually be.

I'm not sure how much time passed in our awkward silence—my entire recollection is dark and clouded—but it felt like only one long and terrifying moment before I heard a man's voice call across my yard, "The garage."

I had the right, of course, to remain silent. But we had passed the point of silence, and now I needed to explain.

"It seems like he's dead, but he is only trapped in the past," I repeated, again, for the third officer to visit me in the holding cell.

"As I've explained, Francis and I were visiting the seventeenth-century version of our house, and the Puritan family who lived there. It was a routine time-travel excursion, but it went wrong when our transport device—a soup tureen—broke in transit. So he's alive, only trapped."

"Ma'am, if he's not dead, how can you explain that his remains were exhumed from your property?"

"You're not listening." I felt the frustration of total impotence; this barrier of disbelief was one I could not break down. I remembered the ease with which Dana, the main character in Octavia Butler's *Kindred,* is able to explain her time travel to her husband, who simply believes her and helps her manage her predicament. Clearly things were not going to be so smooth for me. I was glad again, in that moment, that I had declined a lawyer, whose judgment and interference would surely have made this situation even more difficult. "Of course you found his body. In *this era,* he has been dead for three hundred years. But *in fact* he has only been *traveling* for *six days.* If you would help me find a way to reopen the connection to the past, we could retrieve him and everything would be fine."

I wasn't sure of the practicality of that last part. How could they help me, when I could not even imagine a way to help myself? But that was something we could come back to later.

"Mrs. Hatcher, how can you account for the fact that your husband was wearing modern clothing?"

"Because, *Officer Martin,* we are *modern people.*"

I did not like that this officer, a debonair mustached man I was certain was older than I, referred to me as "Mrs. Hatcher" or "ma'am." I couldn't decide whether this was patronizing false respect—I knew he thought I was crazy—or a reminder of my marriage, which he thought I had ended violently.

Officer Martin frowned. "Well, ma'am, if he's been dead for all that time, how are you accounting for the fact that Mr. Hatcher's body wasn't hardly decomposed?"

That question tripped me, not only because of its poor grammar, and I coughed in surprise. "I . . . that I'm not sure. Maybe your forensic specialists would have an answer. The soil in our region, or . . . or the climatic dryness?" I knotted my knuckles to stop their shaking. "I'm sure, though, that science will reveal I am telling the truth."

I tried not to let into my mind the idea that Francis was truly dead, dead forever. I had spent the last week fearing that idea, skirting away from it. These police officers, their intrusion into my life, forced that reality upon me. Their disbelief brooked no alternatives to their version of the story.

"Another thing I don't understand, ma'am." He paused and looked down at his yellow notepad, identical to the one Evan Gates had carried to my front door only yesterday morning. When he raised his gaze to me again, I knew he was trying to break me. "It's just that you've told me, and Officer Planter and Officer Tebo, that you time-traveled into the past and left your husband there, in a 'root cellar,' it says here." Was he mocking me? How could he be amused, if he really believed my husband was dead? I found his expression grotesque. "What I don't understand is, if your husband was stuck in the past, why would he have stayed in the root cellar? Why would he just wait there to die?"

"*Officer Martin,*" I replied, "why don't you tell me exactly what it is you think happened? Clearly you have your own vision of what took place, and my testimony here means nothing to you."

"I'm happy to share my *vision* with you," he said. "I think maybe your husband, who everybody round these parts knows from that radio show of his, well, my guess is that he hasn't always been so faithful to you, has he? Mr. Hatcher has got a bit of a reputation."

I didn't bother to address this. I was so tired of those allegations; they made me sick and exhausted.

"So maybe Mr. Hatcher cheated on you one too many times, and after years of turning a blind eye to his behavior, maybe you snapped." He shrugged with infuriating lassitude, and the brass of his name tag glimmered briefly. "Now, our team is still doing work over there on your house, but based on the forensics we've got so far, I would guess that there was an altercation"—he pronounced this word carefully, dwelling on the *r*—"in your garage, during which Mr. Hatcher got stabbed repeatedly with the large piece of broken pottery Officers Gates and Tebo recovered by the body. And *then*, Mrs. Hatcher, in the way *I* imagine it, Mr. Hatcher most likely bled out on the garage floor, since the officers think the Luminol examination will reveal that the garage has been bleached down recently. After he was dead, I think maybe his body was dragged around the back of the garage and buried pretty shallow under a flower garden." His brown eyes were flat and full of fake sympathy. "How does my vision of the whole thing compare with yours?"

My rage boiled up inside me. I didn't understand why he couldn't just believe me. If he would only make the one first small leap of faith, as I had been forced to do! Then he would be able to understand everything else I was telling him. Instead, I was going to be convicted unjustly by the disbelief of all of these small-minded small-town men, who understood nothing but the Christian God whose scriptures they slept through in Sunday school.

I crossed my arms over my blouse and turned my face toward the brick wall of the detention room. At least that way he could not try to manipulate me with his eyes. I would not let him trick me into admitting what he wanted me to.

This morning I spent several hours remembering the week Francis and I rented a cottage in Cape Cod back in 1999, when we were twenty-seven and had only been married for two years. We pulled mussels off the jetties and cracked them on the rocks, using their flesh to catch fat, grasping crabs. At sunset each night that week we walked, barefoot, on the pebbly, wild-rose-lined road, from the cottage to the ice-cream shop by the beach. Every night for a week, we split a large fudge sundae with mint chocolate chip ice cream and walnuts. In Cape Cod, the cream was always hand whipped, and the hot fudge always carried the slightly burnt aftertaste of stovetop homemade. I have plenty of time to remember now.

Here in this cell there is nothing I can do to free him. Over these long quiet weeks, as I wait for the "next steps," I have had to reconcile myself to the fact that the situation is irrevocable, that I will never have the means to free my Francis, that he is, in fact, *dead*. Can you imagine how hard it is to have to wake up every morning and realize that the close-mindedness of your own persecutors has killed someone you love? It is almost impossible to live through. And yet: like the time travel itself, once the initial bridge is crossed, the initial trauma endured, it is difficult to envision any other possible present.

What consoles me is my invulnerability. They can take away my

husband, they can take away my freedom, my house, my posses-
sions, my dignity, my personhood, my right to vote. But they cannot take away my faith. They cannot take away the brightness that
Francis and I had together. That is my eternal consolation, more
sacred to me than time or reality itself.

The Wind

FROM *The New Yorker*

PRETEND, the mother had said when she crept to her daughter's room in the night, that tomorrow is just an ordinary day.

So the daughter had risen as usual and washed and made toast and warm milk for her brothers, and while they were eating she emptied their schoolbags into the toy chest and filled them with clothes, a toothbrush, one book for comfort. The children moved silently through the black morning, put on their shoes outside on the porch. The dog thumped his tail against the doghouse in the cold yard but was old and did not get up. The children's breath hovered low and white as they walked down to the bus stop, a strange presence trailing them in the road.

When they stopped by the mailbox, the younger brother said in a very small voice, Is she dead?

The older boy hissed, Shut up, you'll wake him, and all three looked at the house hunched up on the hill in the chilly dark, the green siding half installed last summer, the broken front window covered with cardboard.

The sister touched the little one's head and said, whispering, No, no, don't worry, she's alive. I heard her go out to feed the sheep, and then she left for work. The boy leaned like a cat into her hand.

He was six, his brother was nine, and the girl was twelve. These were my uncles and my mother as children.

Much later, she would tell me the story of this day at those times when it seemed as if her limbs were too heavy to move and she stood staring into the refrigerator for long spells, unable to decide what to make for dinner. Or when the sun would cycle into one window and out the other and she would sit on her bed unable to do anything other than breathe. Then I would sit quietly beside her, and she would tell the story the same way every time, as if ripping out something that had worked its roots deep inside her.

It was bitterly cold that day and the wind was supposed to rise, but for now all was airless, waiting. After some time, the older brother said, Kids are going to make fun of you, your face all mashed up like that.

My mother touched her eye and winced at the pain there, then shrugged.

They were so far out in the country, the bus came for them first, and the ride to town was long. At last it showed itself, yellow as sunrise at the end of the road. Its slowness as it pulled up was agonizing. My mother's heart began to beat fast. She let her brothers get on before her and told them to sit in the front seats. Mrs. Palmer, the driver, was a stout lady who played the organ at church, and whose voice when she shouted at the naughty boys in the back was high like soprano singing. She looked at my mother as she shut the bus door, then said in her singsong voice, You got yourself a shiner there, Michelle.

The bus hissed up from its crouch and lumbered off.

I know, my mother said. Listen, we need your help.

And when Mrs. Palmer considered her, then nodded, my mother asked quickly if she could please drop the three of them off when she picked up the Yoder kids. Their mother would be waiting there for them. Please, she said quietly.

The boys' faces were startled, they hadn't known, then an awful acceptance moved across them.

There was a silence before Mrs. Palmer said, Oh, honey, of course, and she shuffled her eyes back to the road. And I won't mark on the sheet that you were missing, neither. So they won't get it together to call your house until second period or so, give you a little time. She looked into the mirror at the boys and said cheerfully, I got a blueberry muffin. Anyone want a blueberry muffin?

We're okay, thanks, my mother said, and sat beside her younger brother, who rested his head on her arm. The fields spun by, lightening to gray, the faintest of gold at the tops of the trees. Just before the bus slowed to meet the cluster of little Yoders, yawning, shifting from foot to foot, my mother saw the old Dodge tucked into a shallow ditch, headlights off.

Thank you, she said to Mrs. Palmer, as they got off, and Mrs. Palmer said, No thanks needed, only decent thing to do. I'll pray for you, honey. I'll pray for all of you; we're all sinners who yearn for salvation. For the first time since she rose that morning, my mother was glad, because a person as full of music as the bus driver surely had the ear of God.

The three children ran through the exhaust from the bus as it rose and roared off.

They slid into the warm car where their mother clutched the steering wheel. She was very pale, but her hair was in its familiar small bouffant. My mother thought of the pain it must have cost my grandmother to do up her hair in the mirror so early in the morning, and felt ill.

You did good, babies, my grandmother said as well as she could, her mouth as smashed as it was. She turned the car. A calf galloped beside them for a few steps in the paddock by the road, and my younger uncle laughed and pressed his hand to the glass.

This is not the time for laughing, my uncle Joseph said sternly. He would grow up to be a grave man, living in an obsessively clean, bare efficiency, teaching mathematics at a community college.

Leave him be, Joey, my mother said. She said in a lower voice to her mother, Poor Ralphie thought you were dead.

Not dead yet, my grandmother said. By the skin of my teeth. She tried to smile at the boys in the mirror.

Where we going? Ralphie said. I didn't know we were going anywhere.

To see my friend in the city, my grandmother said. We'll call when we find a phone out of town. She put a cigarette in her mouth but fumbled with the lighter in her shaky hands until my mother took it and struck the flame for her.

They were going the long way so they wouldn't have to drive past the house again, and my mother watched the minute hand of the clock on the dash, feeling each second pulling her tighter inside.

Faster, Mama, she said quietly, and her mother said without looking at her, Last thing we need's being stopped by one of his buddies. I got to pick up my pay first.

The hospital loomed on the hill beside the river, elegant in its stone facade, and my grandmother parked around back, by the dumpster. Can't risk leaving you, she said. Come with, and bring your stuff. But when she began to walk she could only mince a little at a time, and my mother moved close, so she could lean on her, and together they went faster.

They went up the steps through the back door into the kitchen. A man in a ridiculous hairnet, like a green mushroom, was carrying a basin of peeled potatoes in a bath of water. Without looking he barked, You're late, Ruby. But then the children caught his eye, and he saw the state of them, and put the potatoes down and reached out and touched my mother's face gently with his hot rough hand. Lord. She get it too? he said. She's just a kid.

My mother told herself not to cry; she always cried when strangers were tender with her.

Put herself between us. She's a good girl, my grandmother said.

I'll kill the bastard myself, the man said. I'll strangle him if you want me to. Just say the word.

No need, my grandmother said. We're going. But I got to have my check, Dougie. All we got is four dollars and half a tank of gas, and I don't know what I'm going to do if that's all we got to live on.

Can't. No way, Dougie said. Check gets sent to the house, you know this. You filled the form. You checked the box.

My grandmother looked him directly in the face, perhaps for the first time, because she was a timid woman whose voice was low, who made herself a shadow in the world. He sighed and said, See what I can manage, then he disappeared into the office.

Now through the door of the cafeteria there came two women moving fast. One was a plump pretty teenager chewing gum, the cashier, and the other was Doris, my grandmother's friend, freckled and squat and blunt. For extra money, she made exquisite cakes, with flowers like irises and delphiniums in frosting. It was hard to believe a woman as tough as she was could hold such delicacy inside her.

Oh, Ruby, Doris said. It got even worse, huh. Jesus, take a look at you.

Shoved his gun in my mouth this time, my grandmother said. She didn't bother to whisper, because the kids had been there, they had seen it. Thought I was going to be shot. But, no, he just knocked out a few teeth. My grandmother gingerly lifted her lip with a finger to show her swollen bloodied gums. When Doris stepped forward to hug her, my grandmother winced away from her touch, and Doris took the hem of her shirt and lifted it, and said, Oh, shit, when she saw the bruises marbling my grandmother's stomach and ribs.

Better go up and get looked at by a doctor, the cashier said, her damp pink mouth hanging open. That looks real ugly.

No time, my grandmother said. It's already too dangerous to show up here.

In silence, Doris took her cracked leather purse from the hook and put all the cash in her wallet in my mother's hand. The cashier blew a bubble, considering, then sighed and pulled down her own purse and did the same.

Bless you, ladies, my grandmother said. Then she took a shuddering breath and said, In a way, it was my fault. I thought I'd stay until we finished the shearing. You know he's rough with the sheep. I wanted to save them some blood.

Mama? my younger uncle said by the door.

No, don't you do that nonsense, you know that's not right, Doris said, fiercely. It's his fault. Nobody else but his.

Mama? Ralphie said again, louder. It's him, he's here. He pointed out the window, where they could see just the nose of the cruiser coming to a stop behind my grandmother's Dodge.

Get down, Doris said, and they all crouched on the tile. They heard a car door slam. Doris, moving faster than seemed possible, went to the door and locked it. Half a second later the knob was rattled, and then there was a pounding, and then my mother couldn't hear for the blood rushing in her ears.

Doris picked up the pan of potatoes and came to the window wearing a furious face. What in hell you want? she shouted. Dare to show your face here.

There was a murmuring, then Doris shouted down through the glass, Not here, up in the ER getting looked at. Quite a number you done on her. Couldn't hardly walk. She said this nastily, glowering. Then she turned her back on the window and went to the stainless-steel table in the middle of the room, where the cashier watched out the window over Doris's shoulder.

They heard an engine starting up, and at last the cashier said in a thick voice, Okay, he got in and now he's driving around. But, like, when he figures out you're not up in the ER he's gonna just come into the kitchen through the cafeteria, you know. Like, there's no lock on that door and we can't stop him.

Doris called for Dougie in a sharp voice, and Dougie hurried out of the office with an envelope, looking flushed, a little shame-faced. He had been hiding in there, my mother understood.

I won't forget your kindness, all of you, my grandmother said, but my mother had to take the paycheck because my grand-mother's hands were shaking too much.

Send us a postcard when you make it, Doris said. Get a move on.

My grandmother leaned on my mother again and they went out to the car as fast as they could, and it started, and slid the back way, down by the green bridge over the river. When they had twisted out of sight of the hospital, my grandmother stopped the car, opened her door, and vomited on the road.

She shut the door. All right, she said, wiping her mouth gin-gerly with a finger, and started the car up again.

My mother saw on the dashboard clock that it was just past eight. The teachers were doing roll call right now. Soon a girl would col-lect the sheets and take them to the office, where someone, think-ing they were doing the right thing, would notice that all three of the kids were gone, and call their absence in, first to the house, where the phone would ring and ring. But then, getting hold of nobody, they would call it in to the station, and it would be radi-oed out immediately to him. And he would know that not only was his wife gone but his kids were gone with her. They had an hour, maybe a little more, my mother calculated. An hour could maybe take them out of his jurisdiction. She told her mother this, pressing her foot on an imaginary accelerator. My grandmother did drive faster now through the back roads. Gusts of sharp wind pressed the car.

For some time, they were strung into their separate thoughts. My mother counted the cash. A hundred and twenty-three, she said with surprise.

Doris's grocery money, I bet, my grandmother said. Bless her.

Ralphie said sadly, I wish we could've brought Butch.

Yeah, just what we need, your stinky old dog, Joey said.

Can we go back someday to get him? Ralphie said, but my grandmother was silent.

My mother turned around to look at her brothers and said, bitterly, We're never going back. I hope it all burns down with him inside.

Hey, the little boy said weakly. That's not nice. He's my dad.

Mine, too, but I'd be happy if he eats rat poison, Uncle Joseph said. Then he bent forward and looked at the floor, then at the seat beside him, and said, Oh, jeez. Oh, no. Where's your knapsack, Ralphie?

Uncle Ralphie looked all around and said at last, with his eyes wide, I took it into the kitchen but I think I left it.

There was a long moment before this blow hit them all, at once.

Oh, this is bad, my mother said.

I'm so sorry, Ralphie said, starting to cry. Mama, I gotta go pee.

Surely Doris will hide it, my grandmother said.

Hold your bladder, Ralphie. But what if she doesn't find it in time? my mother said. What if she doesn't see it before he does? And he knows that you took us. And he gets on the radio for them all to keep an eye out for us. They could be looking for us now.

My grandmother cursed softly and looked at the rearview mirror. They were whipping terribly fast on the country curves now. The boys, in the back, were clutching the door handles.

My uncle Joey, in a display of self-control that made him seem like a tiny ancient man, said, It's okay, Ralphie, you didn't mean to leave your bag.

My younger uncle reached out his little hand, and Joseph, who hated all show of affection, held it. Ralphie had a fishing accident when I was a teenager, and my cold, dry uncle Joseph fell apart at the funeral, sobbing and letting snot run down his face, all twisted grotesquely in pain.

Mama, we got to get out of the state, my mother said. We'll be safer across state lines.

Shush now, I need to think, my grandmother said. Her hands had gone white on the wheel.

No, what we got to do is ditch the car, my uncle Joseph said, they'll be looking for it. Probably already are. We got to find a parking lot that's full of cars already, like a grocery store or something.

Then what do we do? my grandmother said in a strangled voice. We walk to Vermont? She laughed, a sharp sound.

No, then we take a bus, Joseph said in his hard, rational voice. We get on a bus and they can't find us then.

Okay, my mother said. Okay, yeah, Joey's right, that's a good plan. Good thinking. We're fifteen minutes out from Albany, they got a bus station, I know where it is.

It was her father who had once driven her there in his cruiser, because her middle-school choir was taking a bus down to New York City for a competition. He had stopped on the way for strawberry milkshakes. This was a good memory she had of him.

Fine, my grandmother said. Yes. I can't think of nothing else. I guess this will be our change of plans. But, for the first time since the night before, tears welled up in her eyes and began dripping down her bruised cheeks and she had to slow the car to see through them.

And then she started breathing crazily, and leaned forward until her forehead rested on the wheel, and the car stopped suddenly in the middle of the road. The wind howled around it.

Mama, we need to drive, my mother said. We need to drive now. We need to go.

I really, really have to pee, Ralphie said.

It's okay, it's okay, it's okay, my grandmother whispered. It's just that my body is not really listening to me. I can't move anything right now. I can't move my feet. Oh, God.

It's fine, my mother said softly. Don't worry. You're fine. You can take the time you need to calm down.

And at this moment my mother saw with terrible clarity that everything depended upon her. The knowledge was heavy on the nape of her neck, like a hand pressing down hard. And what came to her was the trail of bread crumbs from the fairy tale her mother used to tell her in the dark when she was tiny, and it was just the two of them in the bedroom, no brothers in this life, not yet, and the soft, kind moon was shining in the window and her father was downstairs, worlds away. So my mother said, in a soothing voice, So what we're going to do is, Mama's going to take a deep breath and we're going to drive down into Albany, over the tracks, take a right at the feed place, go down by the big brick church, and park in that lot behind it. It's only a block or two from the station. We're going to get out and walk as fast as we can and I'll go in and buy the tickets on the first bus out to wherever, and if we have time I can get us some food to eat on the bus. And we'll get on the bus, and it will slide us out of here so fast. It'll go wherever it's going, but eventually we'll get to the city. And the city is so enormous we can just hide there. And there are museums and parks and movie theaters and subways and everything in the city. And Mama will get a job and we'll go to school and we'll get an apartment and there'll be no more stupid sheep to take care of and it'll be safe. No more having to run out to the barn to sleep. Nobody can hurt us in the city, Okay, boys? We're going to have a life that will be so boring, every day it will be the same, and it is going to be wonderful. Okay?

By now my mother had pried my grandmother's hands off the steering wheel and was chafing the blood back into them. Okay? All we need is for you to take a deep breath.

You can do it, Mama, Joseph said. Ralphie covered his face with both hands. The grasses outside danced under the heavy wind, brushed flat, ruffled against the fur of the fields.

Then my mother prayed with her eyes open, her hands spread on the dash, willing the car forward, and my grandmother slowly put the car back into gear and, panting, began to drive.

This was the way my mother later told the story, down to the smallest detail, as though dreaming it into life: the forsythia budding gold on the tips of the bushes, the last snow rotten in the ditches, the faces of the houses still depressed by winter, the gray clouds that hung down heavily as her mother drove into the valley of the town, the wind picking up so that the flag's rivets on the pole snapped crisply outside the bus station, where they waited on a metal bench that seared their bottoms and they shuddered from more than the cold. The bus roaring to life, wreathed in smoke, carrying them away. She told it almost as though she believed this happier version, but behind her words I see the true story, the sudden wail and my grandmother's blanched cheeks shining in red and blue and the acrid smell of piss. How just before the door opened and she was grabbed by the hair and dragged backward, my grandmother turned to her children and tried to smile, to give them this last glimpse of her.

The three children survived. Eventually they would save themselves, struggling into lives and loves far from this place and this moment, each finding a kind of safe harbor, jobs and people and houses empty of violence. But always inside my mother there would blow a silent wind, a wind that died and gusted again, raging throughout her life, touching every moment she lived after this one. She tried her best, but she couldn't help filling me with this same wind. It seeped into me through her blood, through every bite of food she made for me, through every night she waited, shaking with fear, for me to come home by curfew, through every scolding, everything she forbade me to say or think or do or be, through all the ways she taught me how to move as a woman in the world. She was far from being the first to find it blowing through her, and of course I will not be the last. I look around and can see it in so many other women, passed down from a time beyond history, this wind that is dark and ceaseless and raging within.

JAMES D. F. HANNAH

No Man's Land

FROM *Only the Good Die Young*

BARRY WASHES the night down with a half-bottle of bourbon to balance out the cocaine, and he's dead asleep when two guys with necks like tree stumps knock the front door off its hinges. They find him in his bedroom and throw a pillowcase over his head, which rouses him to a state adjacent to consciousness.

"He don't look like no king to me," one says.

"At least he's wearing underwear," the other one says.

Barry instinctively tries to fight, but there's one of him and two of them. They meet his efforts with a blow to the base of his skull, and he's pulled under to a warm and comforting darkness.

Barry wakes with his face flush to plush cream-colored carpeting. A second later, he's kicked in the gut so hard his stomach grinds against his spine.

"Again." A man's voice. "Get his balls."

The kicker obliges. Waves of white-hot pain wash over him, and he empties the contents of his stomach—bourbon, medium-rare steak, baked potato—onto the carpet.

"Jesus Christ, Vinnie, you know what I paid a square foot for that?" A woman's voice now. Through nausea and the bite of acid at the back of his throat, Barry IDs it as Nora Anderson. He notes her concern for the carpet and not his family jewels.

Shadows shift and shapes sharpen with a few blinks. Nora, enveloped in a pink robe, orbits a thick-chested guy in a blue suit who pours a drink from a well-stocked bar.

Barry guesses this is Nora Anderson's living room. High-dollar

Long Island style, fake Grecian statuettes, paintings by artists whose names she can't pronounce, overpriced furniture arranged around a glass coffee table. A girl sobs in a chair. Honey-colored locks hide her face as she whines like kittens in a sack dangled over a river. Alicia Anderson, Nora's sixteen-year-old daughter.

Barry hears a groaning behind him. Twists around to see Scott Hauerback, an agent at Barry's office, a rising star in Long Island real estate. Except Hauerback's once impeccable features are now most definitely peccable. His face resembles mashed potatoes—if mashed potatoes could bleed—and he's buck-ass naked. Barry self-consciously tugs at his own white briefs, making sure everything's covered and tucked away.

The man in the blue suit sips his bourbon and pulls a chair around to face Barry and Hauerback.

The man's about Barry's age. The suit's expensive, and the shine on his black Gucci loafers is bright enough to shave by. He unbuttons his jacket and melts into the back of the chair.

"So you're the Real Estate King of Long Island," he says.

You see Barry Willard's face coming out of the ground like dandelions on FOR SALE signs all across the island, almost as many of them as there are Clinton/Gore placards. Ubiquitous at bus stops all the way out to Riverhead. His slogan is "Let me get you home!" His game-show-host visage is comfortable yet distant. The photo was taken after he got his teeth capped, before his hair thinned and he had to color the gray.

"NAMED LONG ISLAND'S REAL ESTATE KING SIX YEARS STRAIGHT!" the yard signs announce.

Thing is, those six years were a long time ago.

The man rattles the ice cubes in his now-empty glass. Another man takes the glass, refills it, returns it.

Nora paces, pausing every few seconds to look at the man Barry guesses must be Vinnie. The look on her face is the exasperation of a wife at her husband.

Barry says, "You the ex?"

"I'm the husband," Vinnie says.

Another Nora pause. "We're getting a fucking divorce, Vinnie!"

"I'm not talkin' about that," he says, not looking at her. "Right now, I'm talkin' to Mr. Real Estate King here."

"His name's Barry," Nora says.

You're not helping, Barry thinks.

Hauerback moans, and that draws a shattering wail from Alicia. Barry grits his teeth at the sound—a mistake, because he feels something shatter in his mouth. He spits an actual shard of enamel onto the carpet, not a porcelain cap. Goddammit.

"Let 'em go, Vinnie," Nora says. "They didn't do nothin'."

Vinnie shakes his head. "I know exactly what these assholes did." Vinnie's nostrils flare, and Barry imagines steam blowing out like the bull in a Bugs Bunny cartoon. He sips his drink, disgust settling into his face. "I can't act like it's nothin'."

They call Barry the Real Estate King of Long Island, but what's it been since his last decent close? Six months? Eight? Long enough, he's getting looks from the other agents. Not sympathy, because that doesn't exist at Hooper Realty. More like when dogs realize a weakness in the pack. Incisors bared, ready for the smell of blood.

Except at Hooper Realty it's Drakkar Noir and "Any luck out there, old man?" Mostly the razzing comes from Hauerback. Twenty-six years old, features chiseled from stone, hundred-dollar haircut gelled into place. He's been the top seller for the past year. Just bought himself a Beemer. Used, but a late model. The ride of a man on the rise.

Hauerback marks more and bigger sales on the board in the office. Every time he writes one up, he walks past Barry and says, "That's how you do it, old man."

At the bar and grill where they gather for lunch, Barry's two scotches in while the other agents nurse the same beers for the entire meal. Hauerback's there, but he doesn't drink, doesn't smoke, just sits there looking satisfied with himself.

On the TV, the news keeps talking about the chick in Massapequa who shot her boyfriend's wife over the summer. Barry wonders if there's a seventeen-year-old out there hot enough to let her fuck up your life.

He orders a third scotch as everyone else disperses back out into sunlight and the workday. Everyone except Barry and Hauerback. They trade silent stares across the table.

Barry knocks a half-inch of ash off his cigarette. "Got any game you're working?"

Hauerback shrugs, his muscles rippling beneath his suit jacket. "Pieces on the board." Sips a Clearly Canadian. "What about you, old man? You got anything going?"

"I got stuff happening," Barry says.

Hauerback pats down his jacket, removes a folded sheet of paper from an inside pocket. "All that stuff you got happening, any of it hot this afternoon, or can you make some space?"

Barry knows what the paper is: a lead slip. Information on a potential client is gold. You guard it like you'd guard your child. Maybe closer. If Hauerback's handing him a lead, Barry's got to ask himself why. Probably absolute shit, a waste of time.

But Barry's schedule is a goddamn wasteland, all he's *got* is time.

"Fill me in," he says.

The client's name is Nora Anderson, and she keeps Barry waiting twenty minutes outside the first showing. Barry's in his Park Avenue, buzzing off a fresh bump, when the Volvo pulls up across the street. Nora flashes tanned leg and short skirt as she gets out of the Swedish-made moneymobile. She fishes cigarettes from her purse, lights one. She's forties and looks it, but looks it good. Somebody wrote checks to keep her like this.

She scans the sidewalk. Thirty seconds, already impatient.

Barry wipes his nostrils, checks himself in the rearview before crossing the street.

"Mrs. Anderson," he says. "So glad—"

She exhales a plume of smoke into his face. "Been waiting on you."

Barry gives a perfunctory glance to his watch. "I believe our appointment was at two, right?"

"Shit happens." A long inhale and an up-and-down. "Where's the other guy?" Twin veins of smoke exit her nostrils. "He was nice-looking."

The showing schedule for Nora Anderson focuses on small houses in old neighborhoods. Postwar developments with well-manicured lawns and an American car in every driveway. The houses lack style and flash, and style and flash are obviously a thing for Nora Anderson.

"This all you got?" she says.

"This is the market," he says. "Low supply, high demand."

When they pull up to the next showing, Barry notices the face she makes. *Let's get this over with.*

He takes her by the wrist before her door's even open. "This ain't right for you," he says, using his neighborhood voice. Not the one he uses to sell a house, but the one he uses when he calls his mother. "I got somewhere else."

They drive to a five-bedroom in Westhampton. Sprawling front yard, green and even as pool-table felt. Been on the market for months and nothing but crickets, because who needs this much house, right?

Nora Anderson apparently does. Approval registers on her face for the first time that day. "Okay, now we're getting somewhere, Mr. Willard."

"Please, call me Barry." He adds a smile and a wink. It's like a nearly forgotten muscle memory, this sensation. This is what it feels like to be the Real Estate King of Long Island.

On the way to the next house, Nora makes a call on her mobile phone, a brick from the bottom of her purse. Calls her daughter, tells her to grab a cab and meet them.

They're checking a six-bedroom all-brick when a young woman's voice calls, "Where is everyone?"

"In the back, honey," Nora yells. To Barry she says, "That's my Alicia."

Barry has to take a breath when Alicia comes into the backyard. She might be the most perfect thing he's ever seen. Long straight hair shimmering in the late-afternoon sun. Bottlecap nose, full cheeks, lips that draw into a perfect bow. Her oversized sweatshirt denotes a Catholic school. Backpack slung over her shoulder, a field-hockey stick in hand.

Nora wraps her arm around her daughter's shoulder. "My Alicia's already getting talked up for scholarships. You should see her kick ass out there."

Alicia rolls her eyes. "He doesn't want to hear that, Mom."

"Hey, I got a right to be proud of my kid." Curls her lip. "Your father was any kind of man, he'd be proud of you too."

"Christ, Mom, I—"

A whack upside the back of her head. "Watch your mouth."

Alicia scowls and rubs where her mother struck her.

The air suddenly feels thick and tense, and Barry excuses himself. Nora says something to Alicia about how a pool would look here.

Barry finds a bathroom and knocks out two lines of coke onto the edge of the sink, stripping them straight and even across the marble. Rolls up a twenty from his wallet and inhales a line. Tendrils of electricity spiral through his synapses, snapping to life a million little pieces of himself. That initial line is always Barry's favorite. Like falling in love for the first time.

He doesn't hear the bathroom door open, doesn't notice Alicia watching him. When he does, he freezes.

She takes the rolled twenty from his hand, powers the second line of coke up her nose. She holds the sink edge, pushes her chest forward and her head back as the spasms of euphoria hit her. Goose pimples fly across her arms and her pupils turn to pinpricks as she drops her gaze onto Barry. She grabs his lapels and pulls him to her and kisses him.

Barry's lizard brain takes over, hardwired from caveman times. Biological imperative. He puts his arms around her, holds her tight, like she could float away. She tastes like pineapple lip gloss.

Alicia pushes him off. Her smile—sly and knowing, a look of secret knowledge she'll never share—returns.

"Not bad," she says. "I've had better."

She turns and walks out of the bathroom, Barry left unsure if she was judging the coke or the kiss.

Barry drives Nora and Alicia back to Nora's car. Alicia slides into the Volvo's backseat, looking like a Lolita behind heart-shaped sunglasses and a paperback of *In Cold Blood*. Barry considers similarities shared between mother and daughter: the apple hasn't fallen far from the tree, and the tree is still mighty fine. He also considers the leanness of Nora Anderson's calves and the sleekness of her thighs, and the glories and hallelujahs to which they surely lead.

"I think you might have yourself a sale with that last house," Nora says.

"Let me buy you a drink tonight," Barry says. "To celebrate."

They meet at a bar Barry knows well enough the piano player gives him a wave as they enter. Midway through her second gin and tonic, Nora mentions her ex, a prick named Vincent Anderson, who owns Anderson Shipping. Barry's seen the eighteen-wheelers on the LIE. This explains the Volvo, the perfect tits, the kid in a pricey private school.

"But after a while," she says on her third G&T, "the money wasn't worth it. I knew he'd fuck around on me, but he actually put her in an apartment. Paid her rent, Con Ed bills. I ain't standin' for that."

Nora's hand slips under the table, grabs Barry's knee. "What about you, Barry? You have your own sordid past?"

Barry looks into her gin-hazed eyes and laughs. "I don't spend much time thinking about the past. Selling real estate, you turn one person's yesterdays into someone else's tomorrows, so you got no time to worry about your own."

Nora's hand climbs higher up Barry's thigh.

"What about tonight?" she says. "Have you got time for that?"

Barry pays cash for a motel room. When the door is closed and locked and Nora's stepped out of her skirt suit, he sees she's wearing actual garters and stockings, like someone from a 1950s movie, like Marilyn Monroe or Jayne Mansfield.

Later, when Barry drops Nora back at her front door and drives off, he notices the black BMW.

Behind the wheel, a guy who looks like Hauerback.

Next to the guy who looks like Hauerback, a girl who looks like Alicia Anderson.

Barry flips a vicious U-turn. There's a chorus of horns and single-fingered salutes from the passing traffic, but he ignores them, his focus on the Beemer.

It's parked across the street from Nora Anderson's home, and Barry finds a spot several car lengths behind it. Far enough back they won't notice him, close enough to see Hauerback take Alicia Anderson's face into his hands and kiss her.

Alicia's still dressed in her school uniform when she comes out of the car. The next generation of her mother's firm, tanned legs pumping her through traffic and across the street. She stops at the sidewalk to look back at Hauerback with the blind adoration you only offer once in your life.

Barry can't do anything but laugh. "Sneaky little sonofabitch," he says.

What Barry doesn't notice is the Caddy, or the two gigantic men inside it. Watching him, watching Hauerback.

Vinnie sets his glass aside. "The name Vincent Andretti mean anything to you?"

It does. Because you do business on Long Island, you do business with the Andrettis. Shipments on the waterfront? The Andrettis get a piece. Run a card game? You pay the Andretti family. Need permits for an addition, dig a pool, put up a tree house for your kid? Yeah, the Andrettis. The Andretti family gets a cut of more Long Island business than Uncle Sam. Difference is, Uncle Sam won't carve you up and bury you in four different locations if you jerk him around.

For Uncle Vinnie, though, that is the very cornerstone of his business model.

Vinnie leans forward, rests his forearms on his knees. "Now let's talk about you fuckin' my wife."

A sharp laugh from Nora. She's made herself a gin and tonic, drinking it from her position at the bar. Her robe parts, and Barry can see that she's naked underneath.

"You mind?" Vinnie says. "We're havin' a conversation here."

"Sure, sure," she says. Folds her arms across her chest. "You boys go right on. Talk about Barry and me. Can't wait to hear."

Creases furrow Vinnie's forehead. He looks back to Nora. Wearing a smile like a homecoming crown.

"Ask him about the motel," she says.

Barry thinking, *Just fucking kill me now.*

The motel is where chemistry and biology collide, and it's a ten-car pile-up, because Barry's doing so much coke nothing works like it should. His junk lies there, shriveled up like an earthworm on the sidewalk, drying out in the sun, disinterested in the entire process.

There's uncomfortable silence and cigarette smoking, and he tells her this has never happened before. She doesn't even pretend to believe him, and all she offers is a curt goodbye when he takes her home.

Vinnie stares at Barry like he's an alien species. "So you and Nora didn't fuck?"

"We did not," Barry says.

"What's your problem? My wife not hot enough for you?"

Alicia retches loudly. "Daddy, this is so gross!" Her first actual words, pushed through a picket fence of tears.

Vinnie checks over his shoulder. "Little girl, you and me will have a conversation once all this is done."

"But I *love* him," she says.

Vinnie throws himself out of the chair and storms in his daughter's direction. He's not a big man, but he becomes huge in his movement. She balls herself up tighter and smaller into the chair.

Nora swoops from the bar and steps between them. Alicia makes such a wail, Barry has hope for a second—maybe the cops are coming—before he realizes what he hears are the mournful cries of a teenager, not sirens.

"Barry?" Hauerback whispers. His eyes, swollen and purple, open into the tiniest of slits. His muscled physique is a Pollack painting, varying shades of bruises and dried blood.

Barry can't muster pity here. "You fucking moron." Contempt drips in every syllable. "You couldn't find a piece of underaged ass *not* tied to the Mob?"

That's when it hits Barry why Hauerback gave him a client who was obviously money.

To Hauerback, Barry's nothing but a washed-up old man, someone who'll keep Nora busy with shitty properties while Hauerback bangs the daughter.

Barry stretches out, pushes himself to his feet. Body screaming, stomach swimming, world spinning—*hello, concussion*—he presses his soles hard into Nora's expensive carpet, solidifying his stance.

"Hey!" he says. His voice reverberates like a gunshot, but it gets everyone's attention and, more importantly, shuts them the fuck up.

Vinnie glares at him. "Can I fucking help you?"

"Yeah," Barry says. "You gonna kill us or what?"

"Why? You got somewhere to be?"

"Maybe I have appointments in the morning."

Vinnie laughs with an edge of surprise. It's what Barry knows is the next-to-last sound some guys ever hear, just before the gunshot that sprays their gray matter onto a wall. He tells one of his goons to take Nora and Alicia upstairs. Alicia opens up a fresh round of

screams and pounds at the goon with small fists, which is like trying to chop down a tree with a butter knife. The goon hoists the
girl over his shoulder, carries her out of the room. Nora follows
close behind, cursing Vinnie with every step. The voices dissipate
into the recesses of the house. The silence left in their wake becomes more apparent.

Vinnie walks over to Barry, lays a hand on his shoulder. Casual.
Two guys talking.

Barry swallows hard and struggles to keep his legs from collaps-
ing.

"She don't understand, is the problem," Vinnie says. "I got
a lot of stress, and sometimes I gotta take pressure off that
valve."

"I don't think she's real concerned with your . . . valves,"
Barry says. "I'd say she just doesn't want to be married anymore."

"The fuck that got to do with anything? Judge comes along,
writes his name on a piece of paper? That don't mean nothin'.
We're still married in the eyes of God."

"The eyes of God are the least of my worries right now, Mr.
Andretti."

"Vinnie." He sighs, shakes his head. "You have put me in a position, Barry. People talk. I can't have guys mouthing off about this
shit."

"I assure you, Vinnie, you let me walk out of here, you ain't
never gonna hear my name again. Your ex—"

"She ain't my ex."

"It might be best if you accept she's gonna *be* your ex," Barry
says. "That way, you both go on with your lives. You should find
yourself someone who makes you happy."

An exotic dancer, Barry thinks. *Diamond or Krystal or Amethyst. Have
fun, let her work out her daddy issues.*

Hauerback pushes himself upright and says, "Vinnie, please,
I—"

"Shut your mouth, asshole," Vinnie says. His face flushes red.
"I'm Mr. Andretti to you."

Hauerback collapses back onto the floor.

Vinnie goes to the couch where Alicia's school equipment is.
He picks up the field-hockey stick. Balances it, judging it.

"You doing coke?" Vinnie says to Barry.

"Yeah."

"Fucks up your dick." Pause. "You sure you didn't fuck my wife?"

"I swear," Barry says. *Not for lack of effort.*

"Fine, then. But you gotta know, this ain't a thing you just walk out of. You gotta have some skin in the game."

Vinnie hands Barry the stick. Barry feels the weight of it in his hand, and he understands.

"Get yourself a little dirty, then maybe we can talk some business," Vinnie says. He shrugs and sips his bourbon. "I got properties. I need a guy I can trust."

Hauerback's coiled on the floor, shaking like he's freezing. Barry thinks it must be shock.

It'll be the merciful thing. Quicker than Vinnie's goons.

The casualness of the thought stuns him.

Jesus Christ, are you really going to do this?

But what choice does he have? Hauerback is *not* walking out of here. If Barry does it, at least it'll be quick.

He grips the stick like a samurai sword and brings it up over his head.

Swing it hard, one fast blow, and it'll be done.

A long breath. Hauerback, eyes looking up like a puppy's, tears streaming down his cheeks.

Barry has never really liked Hauerback. His sales went down the day Hauerback started. With him gone, Barry can get back on his throne.

Especially with Vinnie in his corner.

"We work together," Vinnie says, at the bar, adding fresh ice to his glass, reading Barry's mind, "you gotta get off the coke."

Barry's already decided he's never doing coke again. Well, at the very least, he'll cut way back.

He hopes Vinnie never finds out about Alicia doing that line with him. Or the kiss.

One.

Hauerback's teeth chatter, his eyes roll back, nothing but white in the narrow slits.

Two.

The sound of bourbon being poured. "That's the thing about business," Vinnie says. "You gotta get your hands dirty."

Barry tells himself there's no turning back now. No reversals, no return trip. Welcome to No Man's Land.

Three.

This is what it takes to be the king, he tells himself, bringing the stick down hard onto Hauerback's skull.

Christ, but what this'll do to the carpet.

Return to Sender

FROM *Jukes & Tonks*

THE ST. LOUIS COUNTY Sheriff's deputy who'd come out to take the report was the one named Thorn, and Thorn was dubious, because who the hell wouldn't be? But he never gave Binny any trouble or made him feel foolish for calling it in. He was a total professional.

"Can you describe the stolen item, Mr. Binny?"

"Describe it? Come on, deputy, I just told you: it was a fucking jukebox. You know what a jukebox is, right?"

"Yessir, I do. Approximate size and weight?"

Lewis Binny was trying to contain himself. Some lowlife assholes had broken into his eponymously named bar off US 2 in Stoney Brook Township, Minnesota, and, along with several thousand dollars' worth of booze, had stolen his late father's jukebox, the one that had been sitting near the door off the parking lot, next to the candy machine, since the fall of 1961. It had been a birthday gift to the old man from Binny's mother Grace. Binny was angry enough now to chew nails.

"I'm going to take a guess, okay? About five feet tall, three feet across and three feet deep. Weight, two hundred and change. A lot of change. They would have needed a refrigerator dolly to get it out of here."

"They?"

"Well, assuming the Hulk only exists in comic books . . ."

Then Deputy Thorn nodded, Binny's point taken.

More questions followed. Jukebox manufacturer and model number (Seeburg HF100R-D), approximate value twenty-five hundred dollars, without records, three grand with), thieves' point of entry (the back door, through the storage room), etcetera, etcetera. Binny answered every inquiry, keeping his head but making plans to castrate somebody as soon as an arrest was made. Binny's wasn't much, in point of fact, it was a dump that barely kept him in corn flakes and cigarettes, but it was all Binny had to remember his parents by, and the jukebox was a huge part of the joint's musty, wood-paneled charm. Shaped like a cheap prop in a bad science-fiction movie, all curved plexiglass and chrome, the Seeburg was no fucking Wurlitzer, but you could drop a quarter in it every night and have it spill three singles of your choice in high-fidelity stereo, rain or shine. As long as "D6" wasn't one of your selections anyway, because that button combination had stopped working eight years ago. Binny had never bothered to find out why.

Most of the kids who came into the bar were wholly unimpressed, of course. There was no Taylor Swift 45 to load into the machine and who the hell under the age of fifty had ever heard of Bobby Vinton? But it wasn't the kids who were keeping the place alive, in any case—it was their parents and grandparents, and they fed the box nightly to stir the ghosts of Ray Charles or Johnny Cash as they drank up Binny's beer and ate his mediocre food, sometimes even moved to dance across the sawdust floor with whomever would accept the invite. So there was more to Binny's than the juke, but not a lot more. It was going to be missed, and no one was going to miss it more than Binny himself.

"I'm sorry, I didn't hear that." Binny's mind had wandered, eyes fixed on the dusty patch of checkered linoleum where the Seeburg had been sitting only nine hours before.

"I asked if you have any idea who might have done this," Thorn repeated.

It was a good question with no easy answer. Binny knew a lot of local Neanderthals brazen enough to break into his bar for the booze, but none stupid enough to take his father's jukebox on their way out the door. Because why? What the fuck was a thief going to do with a seventy-five-year-old jukebox filled with records by people long dead?

One name did come to Binny's mind, though.

"Beats the hell out of me," he told the deputy.

*

They dropped Binny's jukebox getting it off the truck. One of the two planks they were using as a ramp split right down the middle, and before Cyril or Nelson could catch it, the machine toppled sideways to the ground like a tranquilized elephant. Cyril thought Peoria would be furious, but she didn't seem to care.

"That's too bad," was all she said.

Cyril figured the juke had to be worth a couple grand, at least, in working condition, but it wasn't Binny's money Peoria had been after. It was blood. She'd sent Cyril and his baby brother out to rob her ex-husband's joint just to hurt him. They'd been divorced for more than eight years but Peoria was still getting over the job Binny's lawyer had done on her, using one lousy, five-month affair with a clerk at the local lumberyard to deny her any right to alimony. She got a four-figure lump sum and a 2002 Chevy Cruze out of the deal and that was it. The lump sum vanished in less than a year, the Cruze went belly up eighteen months after that, and Peoria had had her panties in a bunch ever since.

Opportunities for her to stick it to Binny were few and far between but she took every advantage whenever one presented itself. Important pieces of her ex-husband's mail that got mistakenly delivered to Peoria served as kindling in her fireplace; joint credit card accounts that should have been closed long ago stayed open just long enough to make a dumpster fire of Binny's credit rating. As Peoria's latest beau, Cyril had heard about it all, ad nauseam, fair warning that if things didn't work out between them, he ran the risk of being similarly abused.

But he was willing to take the chance. Peoria was a vindictive bitch, all right, but she filled a pair of jeans and a low-cut, sleeveless blouse like nobody's business, and she could ride Cyril's raging wild stallion as long as he needed her to stay in the saddle. In other words, she was special, and a man had to make certain accommodations for special ladies, like committing crimes that served more to injure the victim than enrich the perpetrator.

There was no way to make Nelson understand, however. Cyril's little brother looked upon Peoria as just another greedy, backstabbing whore with a killer bod, and robbing Binny's just to get a dozen cases of liquor and an ancient music box full of old records made no sense to him.

"This is stupid," he kept saying, from the moment they'd broken the lock off the bar's back door to when they started the truck's engine up to make their getaway. "This is just damn stupid!"

And now that it was all over and they were in the clear, everything having gone exactly as planned with the exception of dropping the goddamn jukebox off the truck while unloading it, Nelson's attitude hadn't changed one bit. Here he was in their mother's garage, he and Cyril drinking Binny's beer while admiring the brightly lit facade of Binny's broken-down Seeburg jukebox, complaining as loud as ever.

"Stupidest thing we've ever done."

"Jesus, man, are you ever gonna stop?"

"No. Why should I? You say let's do a job, I say let's go. We're brothers, we're a team. Always have been, always will be. But this? Putting our asses on the line for what? Five, six grand, tops? Just to fuck up some poor guy we barely know?"

"We *know* Binny. He's an asshole."

And that much was true. Binny's was a regular stop for them both; they'd been drinking there since before Binny and Peoria had even divorced, and the barkeep was no friend to either of them. In fact, Binny seemed to treat them like trailer trash, like that sorry highway rest stop of his was intended for a higher class of people.

"Yeah, he's an asshole," Nelson agreed, slamming back another swallow of Binny's Fulton 300. "But so what? I ain't never given a damn about Binny and neither have you. Only reason you care about him now is 'cause Peoria's still got a hard-on for him."

Cyril put a finger up, not wanting this conversation to go off the rails. "I think you'd better hold up right there, Little Brother."

"It's the truth, Cyril. She used us."

"Okay, so she used us. What of it? Six grand is still six grand, ain't it?"

"Except that it *ain't* six grand! It's four thousand dollars' worth of beer and whisky and a broken-down music box we could maybe get fifteen hundred for on eBay, if we're lucky."

"Fifteen hundred? That thing's vintage!" Cyril said, waving a hand at the Seeburg. "It's a one-of-a-kind collector's item."

"It's a piece of shit. It was a piece of shit before we dropped it off the truck and it's an even bigger one now." Nelson got up from his chair and dropped another quarter in the machine, his third of the night. Just as it had the first two times, the jukebox responded to his choice of three songs with a grinding wail, forty seconds of music from his last selection, and then silence.

"We could fix it," Cyril said.

"No. We couldn't."

"No, not *us*. I mean, maybe we could find somebody to fix it. Then we could sell it."

Nelson just shook his head, looking at Cyril like he'd lost what little of his mind he had left. "Stupid."

Handy White thought he had seen the Seeburg before. He didn't do much work on jukeboxes—slot machines and typewriters and old school arcade games were more his speed—but he was the only freelance repairman within a hundred-mile radius of Minneapolis–St. Paul who would touch the things, so he saw his share.

"Looks like somebody dropped this out of an airplane," he said.

The guy who'd called him out to this storage facility way up in Stoney Brook—a short, beefy white man with a ratty gray beard and lopsided gut—just shrugged.

"Never ask a woman to help you move something heavier than a breadbox."

Handy nodded and smiled, as if he didn't know bullshit when he heard it. "You had this thing long?"

"About ten years."

"How did you find me?" He kept his eyes on his work as he posed his questions to lend an air of innocence to his curiosity.

"Google, man, what else? Four-star rating on Yelp. Next closest repairman was in Rochester and he wanted seventy-five dollars just for a quote. Did I make a mistake?"

"No, no. Just wondered, that's all."

The damn thing *had* been dropped out of an airplane. The lower half of one side panel was crumpled and crushed, and loose shards of the juke's broken glass fascia were floating around its insides like kidney stones. The main load mechanism was off its rails, several records were badly scratched and one—having been jarred completely from its slot—was cracked nearly in half. And these were just the things Handy was able to determine in his first five minutes of poking around.

All the while, as he pressed on with his assessment, the Seeburg's owner, "Jay"—if that was his real name—watched him like a hawk, peering over his shoulder into the guts of the machine as if he might, at any moment, have some expertise to impart. Either that, or he feared Handy would clean out the coin drawer and flee the storage unit with seventeen dollars and twenty-five cents in cold, hard cash.

When Handy eventually buttoned the Seeburg back up and gave him his written quote, the white man's jaw dropped just as expected, but then he did something else that took Handy completely by surprise.

"All right," he said. "How soon can you do it?"

"Seven hundred and eighty dollars? You gotta be shittin' me," Nelson said.

"It's an investment," Cyril said.

"Investment my ass. How do you figure that?"

"One, because we're gonna end up with something we can sell for three times that much. And two, we ain't gonna pay no two-bit nigger repairman seven hundred and eighty dollars to do shit."

"We're not?"

"Hell, no. I gave him a two-hundred-dollar deposit and he's gonna have to be happy with that. If he's not, he can talk to our lawyer." Cyril laughed.

"After the work is done," Nelson said.

"After," Cyril agreed.

"How long did he say he was gonna have it?"

"Three weeks, maybe less. He's gotta order parts."

"Good. Should give us just enough time to find a buyer."

"Actually, I think I've already found one," Cyril said.

"Yeah? Who?" Nelson saw the grin on his big brother's face and started laughing. "Aw, hell."

Eight days after the robbery, Binny looked up to see Peoria sitting at her favorite booth, waiting for him to come around to take her order. He hadn't seen her come in and was in no fucking mood. Business was in the toilet, the Sheriff's Department was no closer to finding his father's jukebox than they were the remains of Jimmy Hoffa, and the last thing he needed was his ex-wife dropping in just to twist the knife. And he had no doubt that was the purpose of her visit, because the only time she ever came around anymore was to watch him squirm beneath the weight of her gaze and the foulness of her breath.

"Kinda slow in her tonight, ain't it, Bin?" She already had a Marlboro lit and she blew the smoke up and off to the right with exaggerated flair. She thought moves like that made her sexy, just like the streak of green in her auburn hair and the plunging neckline of the patterned blouse she was wearing, but it all just made her cheap and mildly amusing.

"And it just got a lot slower. What do you want, Peoria?"

"I want a drink and some time to relax. Is that a crime?"

"No, but murder is. And if you don't drink your drink and get the fuck out of here in fifteen minutes, I'm gonna strangle you."

She laughed as he walked away and was still laughing when he came back with her glass, a Vodka cranberry with crushed ice. Some things never changed.

"Thank you." She took a sip. "I heard what happened and I feel just awful. I had to come by just to see for myself if it was true." She turned her eyes to the other side of the room, where the discolored patch of linoleum flooring marked the old Seeburg's former resting place like a gravestone. "And it is, ain't it?"

"Yeah. It's true." By now, anyone who made Binny's a regular stop had spread the word about the robbery, and the most conspicuous part of its take, so it figured Peoria would have heard about the jukebox being gone. Still, Binny had to wonder, just as he had when Deputy Thorn of the St. Louis County Sheriff's Department had first planted the thought in his head: *You have any idea who might have done this?*

"It's a wacky world, ain't it?" Peoria asked, taking another draw from her glass. "I mean, who would think to steal a *jukebox*? Heavy as those things are? It just takes all kinds, don't it?"

"Eight dollars, Peoria."

"But I guess you could always buy another one, couldn't you. It wouldn't be the same one, not like the one your daddy gave you, exactly, but similar."

"You know, you could save yourself a lot of grief by just telling me where it is now," Binny said, done with his ex's fun and games.

"I what? I don't—"

"I'm just saying. If you know who's got my juke, the time to speak up is now. Because if anything bad happens to it before I get it back, and I find out you had something to do with it, I'm gonna put every power tool in my garage to work making you regret it. You understand?"

"You're crazy!" Peoria finished her drink, crushed her cigarette out in an ashtray like a bug. But she was shaking as she did it. "Why would I want to steal your old piece of shit jukebox?" She started to squirrel her way out of the booth but Binny blocked her exit.

"Eight dollars," he said, holding out his palm.

Handy had a full plate of work to do. A 1960s-era Philco entertainment center, an NCR cash register, a coin-operated motorcycle kiddie ride—but he kept going back to the Seeburg.

"I don't get it," Quincy Hardaway said, watching Handy work. "If you're thinkin' the man can't be trusted, why you doin' the job for him anyway?"

It was a question Handy would have asked himself, had their situations been reversed.

"I'm not really doing this for him. I'm doing it for the machine. For me and the machine, both. Does that make any sense?"

"No. That don't make any damn sense at all."

Quincy raised his mammoth body up from his chair and sauntered back over to his side of the shop. When Handy started waxing poetic about "machines," he often lost his audience, and Quincy was no exception.

The two black men shared a storefront building that Quincy owned outright in the Frogtown area of St. Paul, and each ran their own business on one half of the floor space. 'Ploitation Station, Quincy's video and memorabilia shop devoted to the cinema of the 1970s blaxploitation era, resided on the east side and Handy's antique repair business was conducted on the west. Twenty years his junior at forty-four, Quincy was Handy's best friend, and he never had a problem letting Handy know when he was acting a fool.

And what else could you call investing twelve days of labor and hundreds of dollars in parts on a service job for which you did not expect to get paid in full?

Handy didn't understand it himself. He just knew the Seeburg needed him. Sometimes, he took a job more for the owner than the old, mechanical object requiring repair, and sometimes it was for both. But every now and then, the only reason he said yes was the object alone. He didn't feel pity for it, exactly, but an obligation to correct a wrong, to undo whatever damage time, or neglect, or malice had done to it. If the work was challenging, that was all the better, but it wasn't about the work. It was about the outcome. It was about justice.

The Seeburg needed justice.

Tomorrow, Handy would be finished with his repairs. He would have to call the owner and return the machine to the Stoney Brook storage locker from which he'd taken it. Until then, he would run the jukebox through its paces, playing one 45 record in its 1960s-era honky-tonk collection after another—the Righteous Brothers, Roger Miller, Roy Orbison—and try to think of a way to avoid being played for an even bigger fool than he already was.

Binny had Peoria spooked.

"We've gotta give it back. He knows it was me!"

"Oh, we're gonna give it back, all right," Cyril said. "Soon as we see three thousand dollars in cash."

He didn't know why he hadn't thought of it sooner. Holding Binny's beloved jukebox for ransom would be a lot less work and a lot more profitable than trying to unload it on the open market. It would be a win-win for everybody. Binny would get his juke back and Cyril and Nelson would get three grand to split between them. Instant gratification, no eBay or craigslist hassle necessary.

"He'll never do it," Peoria said. "He's not gonna pay you to get somethin' back that already belongs to him."

"*Belonged* to him," Nelson said from across the room. He had another bottle of Binny's beer in his hand and the History Channel on the TV. "The juke belongs to us now."

"It don't matter. He won't pay."

"We'll see," Cyril said, taking a swig of Jack on ice, also courtesy of Binny. "That boy Handy called me an hour ago. He says our girl's good to go."

Early the next evening, Handy returned the Seeburg to the same storage facility from which he'd picked it up. He knew there'd be no electrical outlet in the unit so he'd brought a gas-powered generator with him.

"What the hell's that for?" the juke's owner asked, annoyed. There was a younger man with him he'd introduced as his brother "Vince" and together they painted a very unsettling picture.

"I thought you'd want to see it work. Or were you just going to take my word for it?"

There was nothing the guy who called himself "Jay" could say to that, so he simply nodded his head. Handy plugged the jukebox in and cranked up the generator. From all appearances, the three men were the only ones in the facility at this time of night and the generator's drone was like a dash of black ink against a white page of silence.

Handy told the two white men everything he'd done to the Seeburg to return it to working order, dropping a quarter in the slot as he spoke. He punched six selector buttons to choose three plays and said, "The record in D-six was too cracked to play so I replaced it with another I had laying around, rather than leave the slot blank. I can pull it if you want." The jukebox plattered the disk as they watched, smooth as silk, and out from the machine's speakers spilled the voice of Elvis Presley crooning "Return to Sender."

> I gave a letter to the postman
> He put it in his sack . . .

Handy waited for a reaction, saw the two alleged brothers share a look, followed by a smile.

"Elvis. That's cool," the younger one said. "Thanks."

Handy let the next two records play, finishing up his demo, and killed the generator. He handed an invoice over to Jay and said, "Total comes to just under what I quoted: seven-forty, even. Minus your two-hundred-dollar deposit, you owe me five-forty."

The white man gave the invoice a cursory glance, passed it over to his brother. "Well, I don't know. That seems kind of high."

Handy set his feet and suppressed a deep sigh. He hated being right about shit like this. "It's what we agreed upon. Less, even."

"Yeah, but . . ." Vince grinned. "Eight hundred bucks for an old piece of junk like this. How about you give us a break on the labor?"

"What kind of break?"

"Three hundred dollars," Jay said. "We give you two-forty now and call it even. I think that's fair, don't you?"

Handy studied the two men evenly, weighing them for bluster versus actual malice, and concluded the difference hardly mattered. They were his junior by fifteen years, at least, and would probably send him to the hospital just by putting a hand to his chest. This wasn't an argument he could win.

"Give me the two-forty."

The man named Jay counted it out in cash and slapped it into Handy's open hand. Hard.

"Pleasure doing business with you."

Quincy gave Handy a hard time all the next day.

"If you knew that was gonna happen—"

"I didn't know anything. I had a strong suspicion, that's all."

"You need to call the cops."

"And tell them what? That I got gypped out of three hundred dollars on a service call? It's a civil matter, Quincy, not a criminal one."

"So call your damn lawyer and sue the bastards."

"Right. Invest countless work hours and a hundred dollars or so in legal fees to get back three hundred. If I'm lucky. That what you mean?"

"What I mean is, you gotta do *somethin'*. You can't just let 'em do you like that, Handy."

"They didn't do anything to me I didn't let 'em do. I fucked up. It's a lesson learned. Next time I'll just say no."

Or take my Sig Sauer along with me on the return, Handy thought but left unsaid. He was no less enraged by the injustice that had been done to him the night before than Quincy, but hindsight was twenty-twenty and payback didn't seem to be in the offing. Had he been fifteen years younger, he might have been less willing to turn the other cheek, but everything it would take now for him to recover his money from Jay and his brother Vince added up to too much expense for not enough return. He had to let it go and move on.

It was small comfort, but experience had taught Handy that penny-ante hoods like the two white men who had just taken him for a ride never went unscathed for long. Eventually, one hair-brained scheme or another blew up in their faces and all the pain and suffering they had coming caught them right between the eyes.

Sadly, it was highly unlikely Handy would be there to see it when it happened to Jay and his little brother Vince.

Binny paid the ransom.

It caught in his throat like a chicken bone, like burning bile that had started its way up but could not be swallowed back down.

The submission, the *ad*mission that the thieves had put him in a spot from which there was no exit except through their demands would not give him rest. But Binny believed them when they said they would destroy the jukebox if he didn't buy it back, and the juke had been a prized possession of his late father. Before its theft, he would have thought himself too hard to care about such things, but he knew differently now. Binny's wasn't really Binny's without the Seeburg.

So the thieves had called to name their price and tell him how they wanted the three grand paid, and Binny had followed their instructions to the letter and got the jukebox back. He made the drop in one place and recovered the machine later in another—it had been left under a blue tarp in an alley off Marshall Road, bearing a fresh dent or two but otherwise looking none the worse for wear. Beforehand, he had given some thought to calling Deputy Thorn and even more to refusing to cooperate, keep his $3,000 and track the jukebox and the thieves down on his own if he could. But a cooler head had prevailed, and he'd paid the ransom instead, and it seemed his capitulation had been rewarded. Binny's had its music box back, the legacy of its original owner restored.

Still, Lewis Binny was not a man quick to forget an injury salted by both insult and expense. Weeks after he'd returned the Seeburg to its old spot on the bar's checkered floor, Binny continued to seethe, determined to find out who had robbed him and the limits of their threshold for pain. He remained as convinced as ever that his ex-wife Peoria had been the mastermind of the crime, and he believed her accomplices were patrons of his bar. Not friends, certainly, because Binny didn't really have any, but men who came in to drink his booze and eat his food at least two, three times a month or so. Smiling, laughing, tripping over their feet on their way out the door and back to their little lives of poverty and ignorance.

His list of suspects started with men he either knew or had heard were Peoria's fuck-buddies: Sandy Wells, Cyril Matthews, Jeff Sipes, Andy Butterworth . . . But this was like saying a bad apple was buried somewhere in a bushel of dozens. Binny didn't know any of these assholes well enough to assess their criminal potential or their disdain for him, beyond a calculated guess that they were all capable of the robbery and extortion he was trying to solve. He could put a gun to Peoria's head to speed things along, sure, but that approach would land him in jail for certain and, worse, could prove to be fruitless, should his ex-wife actually turn out to be innocent of the conspiracy of which he thought her guilty.

No, he'd have to find the bastards without Peoria's help. And it took him weeks to realize how he might do it.

A curiosity in the Seeburg's theft and return that Binny couldn't quite understand was that it had come back to him in better shape than it had been in before it was stolen. It bore the scars of having been dropped on its ass, and yet it remained fully functional, its inner workings running quieter and more precisely than Binny could ever remember them being. Somebody had worked on the juke while it was gone. That was the only possible explanation.

And it occurred to Binny that, if he could find out who this somebody was, he could also find out who had put them up to it.

Handy was replacing a striker on an old Remington typewriter when the phone rang. "Handy's Repairs."

"Yeah, hey. Tell me, you do any work on jukeboxes?"

The word "jukebox" caught Handy's immediate attention. The guy on the other end of the line sounded agitated, like he'd been making calls like this all day.

"Occasionally. What have you got?"

"I've got a Seeburg." Handy put down the screwdriver he'd been rolling around in his right hand. "You work on Seeburgs?"

"I have. May I have your name, sir?"

"Done any work on one recently? Like, say, about a month ago?"

"Yes. An HF-One Hundred series. Did you lose one?"

The caller was thrown by the question. He was silent for a long moment. "'Lose' ain't exactly the word I would use," he said.

"How about I tell you about my Seeburg and you tell me about yours," Handy suggested.

"Sounds like a good idea. Why don't you go first?"

They traded stories. The guy on the phone was careful to omit all names from his, including his own. When they were done, he said, "I don't know any Jay or Vince, but based on your description, I've got a general idea of who you might be talkin' about."

"And you think they're customers of yours?"

"The two I got in mind are, yeah."

"So what are you planning to do? If you don't mind my asking."

"Actually, I do mind your askin'. And you'll probably be better off not knowin', anyway."

There was no way to know over the phone, of course, but Handy's caller didn't sound like the kind of man who'd have any reluctance about doing serious injury to people who crossed him. Or worse.

"May I make a suggestion?" Handy asked.

"Like?"

"Like you'll want to be sure you've got the right two guys. Before you do anything rash, I mean. And I might know a way you could do that."

Another long pause. "I'm listenin'."

"Have you done anything to the machine since you got it back? Anything at all?"

"Besides plug it in? No."

"Good," Handy said.

Cyril no longer felt comfortable drinking at Binny's but Nelson insisted the occasional visit was necessary. Binny might find it odd if they stopped coming in altogether and the safe thing to do, if they wanted their luck to hold, was draw as little suspicion from him as possible.

"Besides. Where else we gonna go?" Nelson asked. This was Stoney Brook Township, after all.

What Nelson wasn't mentioning was the thrill he got out of being at Binny's these days, as the brothers were tonight. They'd ripped Binny off not once but twice, and here he was serving them hot wings and beer at their table in the back, forced to treat them like any other customer in the place because for all he knew, that's all they were. And in the background all the while, the barkeep's beloved jukebox played song after song, powerless to warn Binny that its former kidnappers were close enough to touch.

It was beautiful.

Not that Cyril cared. Nothing could improve his mood. By mutual consent, his fling with Peoria was over and the celibacy with which he'd been left to fill the void didn't suit him. Not even Sharon Anderson, the saucy little cashier at the local 7-Eleven, who had invited herself to their table, could bring a smile to Cyril's lips. And God knew, much to Nelson's amazement, she was trying.

"I've never done brothers before," she said at one point, three margaritas into the evening.

That was all Nelson needed to hear. He'd been trying to get a rise out of Sharon for months without success and, with or without Cyril, he wasn't going to let this chance pass him by.

"You want to get out of here?" Nelson asked, reaching for his wallet.

"Yeah, I do," Cyril said.

"I was askin' the lady, dumb-ass." Nelson looked to Sharon.

She smiled, swaying in her seat. "In a minute. After I've heard some Elvis."

"Some what?"

"You know, Elvis? The King? There's just something about his voice that really gets me hot."

Cyril looked at her like a toad that had just hopped onto their table. "Elvis Presley?"

"You think Binny's got any Elvis on that thing?"

Like his brother, Nelson found the sudden intrusion of Elvis Presley into their shapely companion's train of thought highly obnoxious, but getting laid always involved a certain amount of give-and-take. He started out of the booth, digging into the pocket of his jeans for a quarter.

Later, on their way out to the car in the parking lot, Sharon bolted. Just like that.

"I'm feeling sick. I better go home," she said, drifting out of Nelson's reach before he could stop her. She jumped into her Buick and was gone.

"What the fuck," Nelson said, pissed.

Cyril laughed and tossed his brother the keys to the truck. Binny didn't show himself in the back of the cab until Nelson had started the engine.

"You need to put an alarm in this old piece of shit," he said.

Cyril spun around after he got over the shock, froze like a marble statue when he saw the sawed-off Binny had trained in his general direction.

"Binny! What the hell?"

"Little Rick's closing up for me tonight, while you boys and me go for a ride."

"A ride where?" Nelson demanded.

"I'll tell you on the way." He tapped the front seat at Nelson's back with the snub-nose of the 10-gauge. "Start driving. Unless you like your chances against me and this old girl right here in the cab of this truck."

The brothers didn't. Nelson started driving.

"What the hell's this all about, Binny?" Cyril asked, his voice shaking.

"Three thousand dollars for my jukebox and twenty-five hundred in liquor, more or less. You two are the clowns that robbed my place five weeks ago."

Nelson was having trouble keeping his eyes on the road. "What? Who—"

"You told me. Just now, when you put that song on the box."

"What song? You're crazy!" Nelson said. But Cyril was strangely quiet.

"'Return to Sender.' Elvis Presley. Sharon sat with you boys tonight and asked to hear some Elvis as a little favor to me."

Nelson almost winced. Apparently, he was still waiting for Sharon Anderson to give him a second thought of her own accord. "So I played her an Elvis record. What's that supposed to prove?"

"Nelson!" Cyril shook his head in warning.

"Your brother gets it," Binny said. "There were no Elvis records in that jukebox before it was stolen, dumbass, so he's not on the playlist. But you knew he was in there tonight, and where to find him: D-six."

Now Nelson was as silent as his brother.

"D-six hasn't worked on that machine in eight years and the playlist says so. I marked it 'Out of Order' myself."

Nelson kept driving, trying to think of an explanation that might save them, only to face the sorry fact that no such explanation existed. He'd simply fucked up. *They* had fucked up. From robbing Binny at Peoria's behest to cheating that nigger repairman out of a lousy three hundred dollars, everything he and Cyril had done over the last six weeks had been stupid. Just plain stupid.

"Stupid," he said out loud.

*

One day not long after Binny took the Matthews brothers out for a ride, Handy White got a package in the mail. Somebody—he thought he could guess who—had sent his old Elvis Presley 45 back, no note included.

But a note hadn't really been necessary. The record's title was message enough.

Harriet Point

FROM *The Southern Review*

ABE AND I AGREED on no gifts for our fifth anniversary. Instead we took the treadmill and weights out of the basement, painted the walls white for reflectivity, drilled the ceiling to rig lights, charged a bunch of gardening supplies, and tucked our seeds between paper towels soaked with distilled water. The seeds were actually easy to buy online. They arrived in the mail, mixed in with a bag of coffee.

My name is Audrie McFadden. Back then, I was a thirty-three-year-old mother to a three-year-old and thriving as an account director at Anchorage's largest ad agency. Abe had a good job too, IT manager for Alaska Airlines. To most people, that might sound like enough. But my upbringing didn't instill the right temperament for the long slog of incremental gains. I pitched the idea to my husband on a sunny evening in the summer of 2010. We were drinking wine on the deck while our daughter chased cottonwood puffs across the lawn. "This'll sound crazy, but hear me out," I said. Working in systems administration, Abe was versed in threat assessment; he knew how to quantify risk. And the chance of us getting busted was so low he said yes almost right away—an immediate win for marital synergy. My vision, his pragmatism.

We had a good house for a grow, a two-story hulk with vinyl siding and a daylight basement, built in the 1980s on a gravel road in the Matanuska Valley, where the lots were separated by thick bands of spruce and birch. People have been growing pot in the Mat-Su since before I was born. After timber, it's long been Alaska's biggest cash crop. Alaskans kept voting down legalization, but the margins were narrowing. My dad (Joel McFadden) always says if you aren't early, you're late.

Dad provided the down payment on our house as his wedding present. He supported us starting our family outside the grit of Anchorage. Nevertheless, big houses have big costs. Property taxes. Energy. We spent seven grand replacing the furnace. Unforeseen expenses like that, plus our regular ones—family health insurance, two cars, Montessori preschool for our daughter (Joelle), midwinter Hawaii trips, ski weekends—had us locked into office servitude for the foreseeable future. I could've accepted that if a good-enough payday were on the horizon, but the economy up here is nothing like it used to be. When I thought about driving to Anchorage in the dark of winter for the next thirty years—the stale coffee smell in the break room, quarterly performance reviews with just enough manufactured "room for improvement" to counteract my raise requests—the back of my throat closed up. Leaving Alaska for a bigger agency was out of the question. My family was here. Plus, all the articles said Anchorage would be relatively safe when climate change really hits, and I have to think of Joelle.

Also, I'm not someone who can rely on the Bank of Dad. Nor would I want to. His oil checks stopped five years ago. He's doing fine—for now. With how he spends, who knows. I may have to take him in eventually. Abe hated Dad's long-shot investments and free spending (one plane, three boats, snow machines, four-wheelers, etc., etc.). He tried to make me talk to him about it. That would be like trying to tell water to stop being so wet.

By our anniversary (October 4), we had the grow all set up. I put Joelle to bed, and Abe brought two fold-out camp chairs and a bottle of Cook's to the basement. I was so tired; I put on my pajamas so I could go to bed as soon as we finished our toast.

When I came down, Abe offered me a champagne flute and a handsome smile that drew me back to our early dating days. Then he saw I was wearing my big, pink breast-cancer 5K shirt and his chin puckered. With his free hand, he pulled on the waist of his pants so I could see that he was wearing silk boxers. Oh well. I took my glass. And when it clinked against his, a lens of sparkly bubbles filtered over our starter pots.

"Can't wait to see some leaf," I said. Abe reached into the zip pocket on the side of his chair and pulled out a white envelope. Inside was a certificate for the downtown bistro Simon & Seafort's.

We agreed on no gifts, but, to his credit, Abe knew me pretty well. "Thank you! But who'll watch Joelle? I don't think we can have a sitter here with—"

"We'll figure it out." He squeezed my knee. My phone dinged. A picture text from Dad.

"Look at this ugly fish." I angled the phone so Abe could see Dad's hands holding a warty-looking Irish lord. "Help me think of something funny to write back."

"How about, 'I thought you were gonna let Callista go, question mark.'"

I chuckled. Callista was a salon manager Joel had dated—only six months older than me. I could only think of him as "Joel" when they were together, not *Dad*. He hasn't always been the most consistent father, so my mind wavers on what to call him. I tapped out Abe's dig, then deleted it. Too cutting. He already knew I hadn't approved. I would just be more comfortable if he found a financially independent lady friend his own age. I stared at the screen. Abe refilled his glass.

"If you spend even half as much time on growing as you do attending his ego," he said, "we'll have the best cannabis north of the Emerald Triangle."

In a week, our taproots turned into shoots. We liked to check first thing in the morning and also when we got home from work. Based on our square feet, wattage, and info gleaned from online forums, Abe estimated we'd yield a $50,000 annual crop just to start.

We started seeing leaves. Branches multiplied. I kept us up until two one night because I decided transplanting couldn't wait. We worried about the watering schedule. Abe wanted to up the nutrients and I was afraid he'd cook them to death with fertilizer. We compromised on the ratio. They kept growing. Soon, it was time to switch the light schedule from eighteen to twelve hours to bring on the buds. That's when they really started to look like pot plants. Fuzzy white pistils curled out of the bud sites, but with disturbing green pouches below them.

"These look swollen, right?" I nudged a pouch with my pinkie.

"Oh, I don't think so," Abe said breezily. A pause. He distracted me by offering to make the salad for dinner. We went upstairs and cooked while Joelle made a mountain out of Tupperware on the kitchen floor. Fridays were family movie night, so afterward we put on *Cars,* settled her between us on the couch, but after twenty minutes she wiggled down to play with her blocks. I couldn't blame her.

"We should find stuff with stronger female characters," I said when it was over.

Abe looked at me blankly. He got up to unload the DVD and stepped on one of Joelle's blocks and cursed. Then I knew he was checked out, and I just knew it was because of those swollen pouches. I leaped up, heading for the basement, but he grabbed my wrist. "Tomorrow."

"Why wait? You've been sitting here thinking about it all night!"

"And I didn't say anything because I knew you'd be like this."

He had me there.

I hardly slept. By five I was up, lying in the dark. I tried to go back to sleep, mostly for Joelle's sake. Her internal alarm went off whenever I got up. I held out until the digital clock showed 5:47 A.M.

"I'm gonna pop one open," I said.

"One more hour," Abe mumbled. I heard his arm drop onto my empty side of the mattress. I was already rummaging in my dresser for a safety pin. Abe lurched behind me, down to the basement.

I turned on the lights and brought my safety pin to a swollen pouch, the calyx, and when I poked it open, inside was a seed. Oh no. I poked another one, another seed. Each poke revealed a seed. All our plants were pollinated. We'd sexed during the preflower stage, removing all males, or thought we had. We must've missed one, maybe a hermaphrodite. Seedy bud is worthless. Kinda smokable, but not what you want to bring to market when you're trying to command a high price for potency.

I slumped into one of the canvas chairs, muttered "fuck" about ten times right as Joelle toddled down. Her little warm body came bumbling over in purple pajamas and a nighttime pull-up diaper; her black curls all matted by her pillow and sweat.

"Mommy sad?" She patted my knee. I couldn't even respond. Our electric bill the previous month had been $1,300. For nothing.

Abe brought down heavy-duty trash bags. Together we dug out the plants, all the way down to their woody root balls. We loaded them in the car and he left to dump them in a ditch along an empty stretch of back road. Our house abutted an undeveloped greenbelt, but we didn't want to take that chance. I told Joelle I'd make her waffles. That made her happy. Mixing the batter was meditative. The thickness of it reminded me of the slurry of oil when it first comes out of the ground. I smiled. What a thought to have on that morning. When Abe returned, I had the waffles warming in the oven. I said this was just like how it was for Dad before Harriet Point.

He grinned and nodded—game for the optimism. The amazing thing about my dad's success was he wasn't really an oilman. He spent the first half of my childhood in entrepreneurial scattershot. Ran through some nonstarters, like The Great Alaska Potato Chip Company, for instance. The bags were printed, the fryer system purchased before he found out the spuds grown in the Mat-Su were not ideal for chips. We moved a lot, sometimes surviving on my mother's optometrist-assistant paychecks while he regrouped.

When my grandmother died, Dad put half the proceeds from her house sale into a share of an oil lease in Cook Inlet. He had a geologist buddy who thought the tract showed promise but didn't have enough money to bid it himself, so he invited Dad to be one of his partners.

ARCO bought the prospect from the partnership, meaning ARCO would cover exploration costs, while the partnership retained an overriding royalty. It was promising such a big company was interested.

ARCO towed a jack-up rig up from Indonesia, the Green Eddie, and for eight months it sat anchored outside Seward Harbor. We took the three-hour drive to Seward every weekend for a whole summer, just to see if Green Eddie had moved. (ARCO wouldn't say when they planned to drill.) My mother refused these trips. But for me, Dad's excitement was contagious. He'd rub his hands together. His eyes gleamed, his pupils like shiny pools of crude. All day long, at every moment, he was always running the numbers. It became our bedtime incantation.

"How many barrels a day?" he'd ask when he tucked me in.

"Ten!"

"No, baby, ten thousand."

"Ten thousand!"

"And Daddy and his partners get five percent. Daddy's share of that is one half of one percent. Now the price of oil is sitting at a hundred a barrel, one half of one percent, that's fifty cents a barrel, and ten thousand barrels a day is how much? How much will Daddy get every day?"

"Five thousand!" (The math was beyond me; this much I'd memorized.)

"And what's he gonna buy you?"

"A pony!"

Either he'd score big or not at all. If the tract didn't produce that much, it wasn't worth ARCO's time to develop it. And as it turned out, it wasn't. I was watching *Teddy Ruxpin* when I heard my mother crying—Dad telling her ARCO spent $50 million to dig a dry hole. A year later, the state auctioned off another fifteen tracts, and my dad forked the last of his inheritance over to bid on offshore acreage on the westerly side of the inlet, Harriet Point. My mother was furious. I wanted to believe Joel knew what he was doing. I felt disloyal when I had doubts.

It took a long time to find a partner this time. Finally, some outfit out of Oklahoma, practically a mom-and-pop, bought the prospect. We were doing a lot of family dinners on the McDonald's Wednesday night hamburger special. My mother's hair clumped around the shower drain. But Dad's luck ran true. The well produced. Barrels and barrels bubbled up. Just before I started high school, he started drawing royalty checks—$40,000 a month. Those lasted a decade, until the well tapped out. We moved into a timber mansion in Bear Valley. I'd outgrown horses, but for my sixteenth birthday I got an Audi Quattro and my mother filed for divorce. Abe said he could understand wanting off the "Joellercoaster," but what I can't forgive is that she took me with her, back to North Pole, where she grew up. Not *the* North Pole, though it felt like it, but the suburb of Fairbanks, away from everyone I knew and Dad, who needed me. I wasted half of sophomore year up there. We fought every day until she let me return to Anchorage. Abe only met her a few times, once at our wedding. She wore this over-the-top necklace. "Did you see your mother's fuck-you rubies?" Dad asked me as we were waiting to walk down the aisle. She had no faith in Harriet Point, so it's hardly fair she left with half. I avoided her during the reception until she came to congratulate us. She must've had a few, because she used this exaggerated confidential tone with Abe. I think she even said, "Welcome to the club."

That seedy first run of cannabis was our dry hole at the bottom of Cook Inlet. But we'd learned a lot. We'd get it right the second time. Our Harriet Point.

I took the waffles out of the oven and we sat down to breakfast. Joelle sucked syrup off her fingers. I asked Abe if there were still seeds in the basement, and he said yeah, next to the fertilizer. I chewed without tasting. I didn't want to waste any time. The weather was turning, our energy costs would spike. I crumpled my napkin over my plate and headed for the basement.

"It's still dark out," Abe sighed.

"I coming!" Joelle squealed. I glanced back. Abe was struggling to run her hands through a wet washcloth as she pulled toward me.

This time around, Abe did many, many Google Images searches of male, female, and hermaphroditic cannabis plants. He was so diligent. I had vision. But Abe had details, that much was evident from the first time we met. It was a gray day in the Chugach Range, and I was on a solitary run down a gravel road flanked by mosquitoey alpine brush. I was trying to do two hundred miles that summer and mostly did the same trail since it had relatively low incline. I sensed him behind, pacing off me, but not in a creepy way. I stopped to catch my breath beside a teal pond of glacial runoff, and he caught up. Very nicely, he said he noticed by my gait that my shoes didn't fit properly. Our first date was to Skinny Raven, a boutique running shoe store. He kneeled before me on the showroom floor, feeling around the back of my heel, the inside of my arch. Tender and careful—I was reminded of that first delicate touch often in the early days of our growing experiment, when I'd come down to the basement and see him palming a leaf, scrutinizing a picture on his phone. He took so much care, so it must've disappointed him when I called Trevor to make sure we sexed right the second time.

"Audrie, I've got it, look I can show you—"

I held up my hand. "He's coming Saturday. I want to be a hundred percent."

Abe's shoulders sank. Then he went upstairs and came back down in fleece joggers—out the door for a winter run. He was gone over two hours.

*

Trevor went to my high school. The son of back-to-the-land types, he kept his parents' anti-authority bent but ditched their anti-capitalism, rolling up in our driveway in a Porsche Cayenne wearing crisp Patagonia. We'd agreed on $300 for the grow check.

Abe and I stood off to the side like nervous parents as he inspected each stalk. Turned out, Abe *had* sexed properly, but Trevor had useful things to say about expanding our light canopy, increasing ventilation. Better still, he knew a distributor who might be interested, something he was willing to share because he was pivoting out of pot, transitioning his grow space into a room for cryptocurrency-mining servers. In hindsight, I wish I'd asked more about *that*. Abe's jaw relaxed when Trevor mentioned the buyer. That had been a major blank in our plan.

"Audrie, you were the last I expected. You were so straight!" Trevor said.

I smiled tightly. "My dad used to smoke up a lot. So I was pretty anti." Trevor raised his eyebrows and shrugged. His folks probably smoked just enough to lend a chill, botanical aroma to their earth-parent vibes. Not Joel. Red-eyed and foul-smelling—he smoked every day after the divorce, pretended to listen when I talked at dinner, never remembered what I said. I'd worked so hard to get back to him. He couldn't even muster the energy to be an average parent. So I never even tried weed until I met Abe. On a lazy Sunday afternoon, he introduced me to his vaporizer. I took two hits and fifteen minutes later the fire hose of my thoughts—a worry train of work, dieting, money stuff, wondering if I've truly optimized my life—faded away. I felt so peaceful. I picked up the habit. Guess I really am my father's daughter.

Before he left, Trevor said we should look into increasing our ventilation. Joelle got up from her nap and tromped downstairs to give him toddler side eye. She answered his questions. Name, age, what she wants to be when she grows up. "Powerful," she said to that last one. It's a little something I'd coached her on. Abe rolled his eyes. Everyone else always laughed, including Trevor. He told her he'd come to look at the plants.

I thought I needed to warn him, "We don't say M-A-R-I-J—"
Trevor waved his hand at the obvious.

"Mommy plants? My mommy have so many plants. So big!" she told him, perking up.

"Does she now?" he laughed. When Joelle said "plants" it

sounded like "plans." We'd never told her they were mine, so it was interesting that's how she put it.

Next thing, Trevor ran out to his Porsche and came back with a little brass bowl and a mallet. "It's a Tibetan singing bowl," he told Joelle. He showed her how to strike the side and trace the mallet along the rim to make a ghostly ringing. "It has a special power when you play it, it will make you feel calm and happy." I guess his hippie side hadn't completely worn off.

"Thank you," she murmured. She clanged it again and again as soon as the door shut behind him. People never anticipate that part when they give noisy gifts. I wrapped my arms around Abe's waist as we watched Trevor pull out of the driveway. He kissed the top of my head.

Not long after that, I awoke to a vegetal aroma, green and pungent, with a trace of sourness. In the basement, the odor was overwhelming, the air like a curtain. I skimmed my fingers along the wall. Damp. Our former exercise room like a dank jungle. The plants drooped under the weight of the buds, glistening and sticky with resin. My spine tingled. They were ripe. "I think it's time," I said in a shallow breath. Abe slid his hand up my shirt, then down below the waist of my pajama pants. We went to the stairs. I knelt before him on the steps. We had to be quick; it was a workday.

The rest of the morning was a tornado. Joelle snuffled as I dressed her; I hoped it wasn't an allergic reaction. I dropped her off at preschool, and it snowed the whole drive to work, the heavy, wet kind. Flakes landed with momentarily discernible shapes on my windshield before dissolving under the wipers. Red taillights flashed ahead of me in the stop-and-go chain of valley commuters. Thoughts of checking the trichomes under the microscope, cutting fan leaves, and rearranging to make space for drying preoccupied me. I pulled into the employee parking lot, stepped into a bracing pile of slush. Usually I wear boots and change into my pumps, but I'd forgotten. I made my way gingerly across the lot. Elizabeth, not my favorite coworker, was also heading for the door. I wanted to get in ahead of her but the shoes were slowing me down. She was gaining, calling out "Good morning, Audrie!" then immediately diatribing on the new time-tracking software our company had adopted. I scrunched my face in the dark. There was no need to have such conversations this early. We came into the back hallway at the same time, a funnel of warm air and fluorescent light. She stopped to hang her jacket next to mine on the hooks. I unbuttoned my coat, vented it to shake off the snow.

"Whoa! What's tha—" Elizabeth cut herself off. She shook her head slightly, smirked, and walked off.

I lunged for the ladies' room, locked myself in a stall. Stuck my hand down my underwear and brought it to my nose. Could it be? No, I'd showered afterward. My legs jellied and I started to feel very hot. I collapsed on to the toilet and scrunched my blouse up to my nose, breathed in deep. A heady, sickly green smell traveled into my head. I sniffed my pants. More of the same.

I took the fire stairwell upstairs to my cubicle instead of the elevator, got on Outlook and rescheduled two meetings for the following day. My legs shook under my desk.

"I think I smell like it," I texted Abe.

"Yea Kyle and Ashok called me wake n bake lol," he replied.

I pressed my middle finger between my eyes. Of course it was lower stakes for him, sitting in some dark terminal with the computer nerds.

Two assistants shared the cubicle by mine. Nice girls, recent grads. I heard one snicker to the other, "Hey, do you smell weed?"

I grabbed the wastebasket under my desk and threw up.

Both heads sprang above the partition. "Oh my God! Audrie, are you all right!?"

"Yeah, I'm so sorry, can you guys take care of this? Tell everyone I went home sick."

I didn't wait for an affirmative on them cleaning up my vomit. I just left. Let one smell mask the other.

When I got home, I thought I might be sick again. The smell hit hard. I opened all the windows, never mind the outside temperature was thirty-four. My phone vibrated. It was Joelle's day care. Miss Karen said she was calling because Joelle smelled a little musty, so she was "checking in." I told her we were having a problem with our washing machine, that we'd thought we'd fixed it, but it looked like we were going to have to get a new one. She seemed to buy it.

I loaded all of our heavy-rotation clothing, mine, Abe's, and Joelle's, into my car and drove to a coin laundry where I could do multiple loads at once. When I got back home, I didn't take them inside. Instead I went into the detached shed on the east side of the house, where we kept the lawn mower and spare paint. I shoved what I could to the perimeter, cleared some space on the shelves, and with nails and picture wire jerry-rigged hanging lines. Our new walk-in closet. Then I went out for a haircut, traded my shoulder-length layers for a bob. Less for the smell to cling to.

"Jesus. Your hair," Abe said when he got home. He was upset I'd opened all the windows. The first floor's temperature was brisk, and he worried about damaging the plants, but the basement was still warm and moist. Neither of us wanted to cook. We went out for Chinese, and I asked the waitress to seat us in the back-corner booth. She said the section was closed, and I said not anymore it isn't. (We were regulars.) I hunkered over egg flower soup, casting dark glances at the other people in the restaurant. Could they tell what we smelled like? My phone buzzed, a text from Dad.

"Haven't seen you in a while! Come out to the house this weekend? I'll make chili."

I groaned. There was no way we'd have time.

"What?" Abe asked.

"Dad, about this weekend. We haven't seen him in forever."

Abe made a face. I didn't get a chance to ask what about because Joelle started beating on her singing bowl, which she'd somehow sneaked into the restaurant. I made a mental note to hide it after she went to bed.

The temperature dropped ten degrees the next morning. Abe and I trudged outside in our pajamas and snow boots, silently dressed under the weak light of the shed's bare bulb. Abe sniffed his shirt, grimaced, "This is not an improvement." I brought a pair of Elie Tahari wool trousers to my nose. They smelled cold and woody, faintly of diesel. My whole body shivered. There was no way we could dress Joelle out here. When it was time to go, I put her clothes under my butt in the car and turned up the seat heater. I pulled into a grocery store parking lot near her preschool, got in back, helped her out of her pajamas and into her outfit as fast as I could.

"I hate this," she said when I pulled the turtleneck down over her head. Her eyes shone in the dark. The world outside the car was an orange fog of exhaust and lamplight. It was one of those strange moments where, in her tone and manner, I glimpsed an adult self peeking out of her three-year-old form. I felt guilty. Then vaguely afraid. I gave her a quick kiss on the cheek and belted her back in.

This was the beginning of the workhorse period. Everything was unpleasant and hard. The weekend after the Big Smell, we purchased two window-mounted ventilation units, which helped—marginally. We still had to use the closet shed and our homelife was underscored by the tick and whir of machinery. When we cut down our plants, there wasn't enough space in the basement for drying. They needed more room. Hanging too tight causes rot. So we strung them along the walls of the stairwell leading to the first floor, above the kitchen bar, and on several lines in the living room. Dark, shriveled garlands—a kind of holiday house-of-horrors effect. I told Joelle they were boughs of holly because I had no energy to go buy a tree. "Fa la la la la," she said, twirling below them. She started watching more movies than she'd probably seen in her whole life combined. While we were drying, we were also getting new plants started. My heart stung every time I checked on her and she didn't notice me, eyes glazed in blue light. Dad kept texting, telling me he missed her. The guilt piled on both ends.

Trimming was the worst. Buds must be trimmed of leaves that don't have crystal. Otherwise your buyer will accuse you of padding out the weight when he inspects the bag. It's meticulous work, and Abe was bad at it. He took clumsy snips, crunched off too much. Then when I corrected him, he switched to a snail's pace, taking off one tiny leaf at a time. We argued. If I even glanced at a bud in his hand, he'd snap. He got so frustrated he declared he'd only do it for one hour each evening after work. He could barely clear an ounce a night. To compensate, I kept a trash bag of untrimmed branches by the bed and a plastic tub for finished buds. I trimmed before sleep, my nightly ritual, like other women darning socks. I also trimmed when I woke up. I started wearing wrist guards for tendinitis.

When we had five nicely trimmed pounds packed in clear turkey bags, I called Trevor. "Hey, Trev, we've got five pounds ready to go, think you could connect me to your b—"

"Whoawhoayayayaya . . . careful on the phone!"

*

The buyer came on a weeknight. I had on my work clothes, a J.Crew sheath and blazer. Abe wore jeans and flannel.

"Could you change into khakis at least?" I asked. "I think we should present a united front."

He gave me dead eyes. "We're selling *weed.*"

I rolled my eyes. I didn't have time to lecture him about presentation. He was petulant, I don't know why. But it annoyed me. His attitude drew on a chronic history of underestimation and implicit diminishment of my expertise as a marketing professional. I knew he thought it was a "soft skill," somehow less than. Maybe creativity isn't quantifiable, but I wanted to remind him it was *I* who'd devised this venture in the first place. The doorbell rang.

A short white guy with dark curls sprouting beneath a purple baseball cap, who was wearing jeans and a fleece-lined workman's jacket, stood on our stoop. A telepathic argument transpired, wherein Abe was saying *I told you so, he's dressed worse than me,* and I was snapping back about how that was not the point.

"Sam." He extended a hand. We shook, moved into the kitchen, where I had our pounds stacked on our kitchen bar next to the food scale. He picked up each bag, shook and examined them, set each one on the scale, then opened one and picked out a bud. I handed him our loupe magnifier for a closer look. "Twenty-three hundred a pound?"

Abe and I glanced at each other in veiled surprise. We'd spent the last week convincing ourselves it would be okay if they went for as low as eighteen. I nodded quickly.

Sam went out to his car, returned with a stack of hundred-dollar bills, wrapped in thousand-dollar increments, and a duffel bag. Abe and I reached for stacks. He flipped through his with his thumb. I flicked each bill with my index finger. The dirty residue of cash coated my hands and tickled my nose. Flustered, we both had to start over on the count more than once. Sam raised his eyebrow and smirked. He told us to get a bill counter. Then he was gone. The whole transaction was breathtakingly fast.

"We should've asked for twenty-five," I said. Abe's face deflated. There was $11,500 stacked before us, which would go a long way to recouping our investment, but now the negotiation was done. We'd have a tough time ever asking Sam for more, and the unrealized $1,000 of this transaction would grow to many more over time, unless we found a different buyer. Abe's nostrils flared. I knew what he was thinking. The negotiation was *my* responsibility. "If you would've just changed your clothes like I fucking asked I wouldn't have been so distracted," I snapped.

He gave me a hooded look. "Can you even hear yourself right now?" We left the money on the counter and went to bed, clinging to opposite sides of the mattress.

We moved past that night in a businesslike fashion. Our conversations were concise but polite. I found myself talking more to Joelle. She took an interest in the transformation of the house. I explained some of the things we were doing to make the plants grow. She wanted to help me trim, so I set her in her booster seat at the dining table with some Crayola scissors and discarded leaf. This lasted about five minutes before I worried about THC oil seeping into her fingers. (I'd accidentally got high a couple of times after hours of trimming.) She didn't want to give up her little project, so I gave back the singing bowl to avoid a meltdown.

Sam never gave any personal details, no last name, but I suspected he was a bush pilot. He had the look and had told us he didn't distribute in Anchorage. Add airplane fuel to the energy cost of grow lights—our plants had a mondo carbon footprint. Did it bother me? I'd taken an oceanography class in college where the professor made a convincing case for the factuality of global warming. After that, I decided not to pursue oil as a career. I'm a realist; we still need oil, and I don't look down on my friends in the industry, but because of Dad's bonanza, I've already benefited more than most. It was like a card I no longer wanted to charge on. But then I got out in the world and realized every job has its thing. At the ad agency, my coworkers and I laughed about contributing to statewide obesity when we rolled out a McDonald's campaign. We laughed less, opting instead for teeth-sucking grins and nervous shrugs, when we had to rebrand a mining company trying to develop Bristol Bay, home to the last great wild salmon run. What could we do? Refuse? Get fired? If everyone said no to such choices, the whole economy would collapse. There may be gradations of complicity, but no one comes out clean.

On Christmas Eve, we loaded Joelle and our gifts into the car and drove to Dad's house. Abe and I were frosty, having disagreed on what to get him. Abe didn't have any good ideas, so on my lunch break I went to the Fifth Avenue mall and spent $300 on Mephisto slippers, which Abe thought outrageous in light of the cannabis deficit we'd only begun to pay off. He could be so cheap. We put on Christmas carols. Joelle played her singing bowl like a jingle bell. The clanging reverberated in my neck, the base of my skull. It must've been bad for Abe too, but neither of us said stop—it was like an endurance contest for noise torture. When you reach a place in your marriage where you would rather prolong your spouse's suffering than alleviate your own—that is not good. But Joelle was happy.

She quit drumming when we pulled into Dad's neighborhood and gasped at the brilliant lights decorating the grand homes. Cast-iron post lamps glowed the length of Dad's driveway, and a big red-bowed wreath covered the front door. The curtains were open, offering a view of the bright living room, a Christmas tree towering over the leather sectional. I felt a stab of yearning, a longing to return to my childhood home, a pointless wish that was more like anguish. I'd turned my own home into an industrial farm.

Dad opened the door before we could knock. Joelle leaped into his arms. Warm air, spicy with cumin, washed over us.

"How's my best girl. Where've they been keeping you?" Dad kissed Joelle on both cheeks, nuzzling his seventies-relic mustache against her face. He's a head taller than both Abe and I. The charm he used to draw in so many investors is also present in his personal life. Gravity shifts when our family gets together. We are all drawn into his orbit.

Dad served his traditional Christmas Eve chili with hunks of sour store-bought garlic bread and glasses of red wine the size of soup bowls. I was too tired to be much conversation, but it wasn't a problem, he regaled us with boisterous hunting stories. After dinner, we did presents and Dad read *The Night Before Christmas.* Joelle fell asleep on his lap. He'd even made eggnog. We insisted on tiny glasses because of the long drive home.

"I shouldn't be making you guys drive all the way out here on Christmas Eve," Dad sighed. "Next year I could come there. I'll take the guest room, bring my chili and breakfast fixings—I could even play S-A-N-T-A."

A current of need threaded through his suggestion. I looked around. The house was clean, well decorated. The homemade eggnog. He'd tried so hard. I felt bad we'd seen so little of him of late, and that the secret of our enterprise put distance between us.

When it was time to go, Dad passed Joelle off to Abe who bundled her out to the car while I packed up our things. I put on my coat and Dad laid his hands on my shoulders. "Merry Christmas, sweetie. You work so hard. Your career. Joelle. Don't think I don't see it. I know I was a bum after your mother left. But I want to see more of you guys. If you or Joelle ever need anything, you can always come to me."

"I know, Dad." I drew him in for a hug so he wouldn't see the shine in my eyes. It was the nicest thing anyone had said to me in months.

"Is there a bottle of water in here? That chili was so salty," Abe said in the car. I pulled one out of the side compartment, but it was frozen hard. That's how cold the night was. The drive home was silent with Joelle asleep. The house was dark when we pulled up; we hadn't left on any lights. From the driveway, my stomach revolted, already dreading the dank smell within.

Abe shifted into park, shut off the engine. A peaceful quiet, crimped by how badly I did not want to go inside.

"We could go to a hotel," he suggested.

"Are you serious?"

He shrugged. It was all the reminder I needed. I was the strong one.

"If you put her to bed, I'll take care of the rest."

He sighed raggedly. We set about our tasks like silent assembly-line workers. He disappeared upstairs carrying Joelle. I breathed gently, halfway through my mouth, reacclimatizing to the fetid smell of home. It shamed me after an evening at Dad's. The lines of dark shriveled branches drying now canopied most of the living room. Bits of leaf and sticky crumble flecked the carpet. Some of these had defied previous attempts at vacuuming, smooshed by our feet and hardening to the fibers. I should have put down towels or a tarp. But to what end? There was no point on the foreseeable horizon where there wouldn't be cannabis drying in my living room.

I went to the closet below the stairs to the second floor to retrieve the presents I'd bought for Joelle. They still needed to be wrapped. My nose had adjusted to the pot smell, but now the closet burped up something different. Muddy. I pulled out the boxes and shined the light of my phone inside. At first I saw nothing. And then the far back corner—I recoiled. Traveling up the entire length of the wall, a brown plume of water stain, like some monstrous Rorschach blot. I touched it. Slippery, the paint clung and bubbled as I retracted my finger. Panic rushed me to the basement, where I pulled out the shelf with all our gardening supplies, directly below the closet—the brown bloomed larger down there. Then I went up to Joelle's room and shined my light in her closet. The rot was fainter, but present. The humidity from the basement had found a tunnel, winnowed a column of sludge through the center of our house. I needed a plumber, a drywaller, someone who knew about HVAC. But how? Untreated, the problem would spread—destroy our home from the inside out. What had I done? I was shaking—bereft. It was awful, but now I look back on this moment and think of a butterfly trembling out of its chrysalis. Destruction precedes greatness, especially in business. I knew who to call. From the hallway between the bedrooms, I used my cell phone to dial.

"Dad? Sorry, it's late. Can you come over tomorrow? I need your help."

Abe opened our bedroom door. He shook his head when I ended the call. I started to tell him, but he held up a hand. "It doesn't matter. You've decided to handle it." Which was true, but also a condemnation. I know some people think my first mistake was going into business with my husband, but between retirement savings, mortgages, negotiating child care against workload and respective salaries—aren't we all in business with our husbands? I won't be faulted for having the strength of my ambitions.

I wasn't ready to be in bed with him, so I went to the kitchen and sat down with a bag of untrimmed bud. The rhythmic swish of scissors had a calming effect. Whatever hurdles lay ahead, at least I was getting a bit of work done.

That was almost ten years ago. Of course, Dad was shocked when he arrived on Christmas Day. He wandered the rooms muttering, "Jesus Christ, Audrie. Jeee-zus *Christ.*" But he had to muster the disapproval. Amusement glittered behind it—somehow eager. I was finally realizing my entrepreneurial destiny. He *was* genuinely annoyed I hadn't come to him sooner, because he was sitting on a vacant warehouse ten miles from our house, a dicey commercial real estate investment—and the perfect place to move our grow.

It took a long time to repair the house for sale. Much of the work we did ourselves, only bringing in professionals when it seemed less obvious what had caused the problem. We sold it when the marriage ended, when I found out about Abe and Callista. *That Callista.* It still turns my stomach. I don't even want to know when it started. But Dad and I have a nickname for them. *The hangers-on.*

I worked with Sam for a couple of years, added outside distributors. In 2015, Alaska legalized. The following year I went legit, purchased a commercial grower's license from someone spooked out of the industry by the arrival of Vice President Mike Pence, fearing another big drug crackdown.

I left my day job. Now I have lab-tested strains selling in Anchorage dispensaries. I bought Abe out, which was only fair. He missed out on the real honeypot, something that started as my side hustle after the divorce: branded packaging for prerolls, edibles, and tinctures. With my marketing background, it was an obvious pivot. I have exclusive manufacturing contracts in China and commercial clients in Alaska, Washington, and Colorado. It's the thing that finally got me ahead-ahead. Like any gold rush, it's better to sell picks and shovels than go digging.

Dad is still my landlord. He's provided some bridge loans—a continuum between Harriet Point and my own venture that I can accept. There's really no such thing as bootstrapping. Anyone who thinks they've built something from nothing is probably just profiting off something stolen. I like to think of it as a positive evolution. My trade is one that lets people consume something to slow down, curb that persistent wheel of needing to achieve more and more. But I don't give myself too much credit. I own a vaporizer; my wheel still turns.

Joelle is thirteen. I get her every other week. That infernal dharma bowl sits on her dresser now, a receptacle for stud earrings. I wish she'd keep the expensive ones in their boxes. Like me, she's killing it at school. She's also a competitive swimmer. I sit in the bleachers during her practice. I have time to think then, about everything that's happened. I tell it to myself like I might if another team mom sat beside me, but the swim parents are rather frosty. The valley is full of Bible thumpers; Joelle has friends barred from sleepovers at our house because her mom is a "drug dealer." When I tire of my own company, I read news on my phone. Every day now it's something new. A strange bird flown up to the Arctic that no one has ever seen there, snow fences put up in Utqiagvik to withstand the mounting winter storms, cemeteries bubbling and swamped with permafrost melt. I wonder what career opportunities will be available to her in a changed world. Each time I glance up to check, her pace remains unchanged. She moves through the water like a piece of fluid machinery, strong strokes and very little wake. It braces the heart to see such determination in a daughter.

Stingers

FROM *Alfred Hitchcock's Mystery Magazine*

LIFE IS A CHEMICAL PROCESS. If the correct compounds are present, a chemical reaction will occur. This can happen by accident, or it can happen by design. I liked to think of mixology as chemical process, and with the right compounds I could create a delicious chemical reaction.

I added green minty liquid to the Hennessy and ice. After a good shake, I strained the mixture into four red Solo cups, each full of fresh ice. There were no trays or real dishes, so I carried the cups the best I could into the sitting room.

"Al," I said, stooping to hand him his drink. He took it without a word, freeing up a hand for the other three cups.

"Byron . . . Chris . . . Daiki," I said, as I continued to hand out drinks.

The quartet never took their eyes off the screen. They were entranced by the surprising comeback orchestrated by the Houston Rockets.

"These are called Stingers. Hennessy and crème de menthe."

"I taste the mint," said Al.

"Glad you like it. I'll get started on dinner."

The kitchen of the trailer was barely big enough to turn around in. It was also filthy. The flies buzzing around the overflowing trash sounded as steady as a microwave. The scent of a dead fish and rotten egg omelet was emanating from Styrofoam containers in the fridge and two of the cabinets were missing their doors.

The kitchen utensils were lacking, but there were enough to make the simple dinner I planned. I peeled potatoes with a rusty peeler I found in a junk drawer, and set them to boil in a stained pot that was missing a handle.

After delivering another round of Stingers to the sitting room, I opened a package of steaks. A quick rinse, a sprinkle of salt and pepper, and they were ready to be panfried.

Thirty minutes later, the brothers were eating steak with mashed potatoes and sipping fresh Stingers.

"This food is good, Artemis," said Byron.

"Thank you."

"You're going to have to keep her around," said Chris.

Al smacked me on the ass. "She's not going anywhere."

"No garlic in my mashed potatoes next time," said Daiki. "I hate garlic."

I kept my face neutral. It was a skill I had recently mastered. "I'll be back for the plates after I clean up. I made a bit of a mess."

"Put everything back the way you found it, Artemis," said Al.

I made a fresh round of Stingers and replaced their empty cups with full ones. They accepted without a word. I'd seen these guys drink half-gallons of grain alcohol while snorting or smoking all kinds of drugs. Yet I was still impressed by the volume of Stingers they'd managed to guzzle down.

I stood in the kitchen and listened. The decibel level had slowly been decreasing all night. It started with the brothers screaming at the referees, simmered down to murmurings about free throws, and now the only sounds I heard came from the TV.

I went back to the sitting room to find the four of them asleep. I wasn't going to wake them before I let myself out.

The hall closet was a mess. Broken hangers were strewn with tattered, dirty jackets and there was a heap of sour-smelling clothes on the floor. I had offered to clean, but Al had screamed at me to "stop going through his shit." But he was asleep now, so he wouldn't mind me tidying up.

There was acetone, paint thinner, and ether on the top shelf. I brought the bottles down to the floor of the closet. Their tops were disgusting. Grimy. Sticky. Black with grease. So I took them off.

There was a blanket folded over the back of the couch. I had allowed Al to do disgusting things to me under that blanket. It felt slimy to the touch. He couldn't even remember the last time it was washed. Yet he slept with it every night. I made a trail with the blanket, from where Al slept on the couch, to the chemicals on the closet floor.

Al didn't stir. None of the brothers did. They'd had twenty Stingers between the four of them. Those, combined with their very heavy meals, would make them rest through the entire night.

Stingers were a classic cocktail that were super easy to make. It was a shot of Hennessy and about half a shot of crème de menthe. But I had been so busy shopping for their dinner that I had forgotten to get the crème de menthe. The brothers drank straight Hennessy all the time. I wanted to give them something special. So I used the NyQuil they had in the trailer in lieu of the crème de menthe I had forgotten. They seemed to enjoy them, but an unfortunate side effect was extreme drowsiness.

I grabbed my jacket from the closet and put it on. Al had left his cigarettes on the two-person table near the kitchen. I borrowed one, lit it from the stove, and sucked air through it without inhaling. I pressed the lit end to the blanket until it caught fire. Then I walked out of the trailer, remembering to lock the door behind me.

Tonight was the first frost of winter. The air felt like a cold drink after spending hours inside that stuffy trailer. My apartment was a forty-five-minute walk through the metro bus lot. Technically this was trespassing, but I hadn't driven or brought my phone with me, so I had no choice but to hoof it.

Ruby was on the couch when I came in. She was drinking a soda and watching beautiful women live their lives on TV. It was a Friday night, and my beautiful little sister was at home, terrified to go out.

"Did you have fun on your date?" Ruby asked.

"No, he stood me up. I waited at the park for hours."

"That doesn't sound like him. There has to be a reasonable explanation."

She was right. It didn't sound like the guy I had told her about. I grabbed a soda from the fridge and joined her on the couch. "Who cares?" I said. "I'd much rather hang out with you anyway."

Thirty Days Before the Fire

My outfit was a bit much for a Saturday afternoon at the RiteAid. I was wearing a crop top, a miniskirt, fishnet stockings, over-the-knee boots, and a jacket to ward off the cool fall air.

He was at the register when I walked in, paying for a handful of bottles of NyQuil with limp damp bills.

"How much?" he sneered as I walked past.

It wasn't the opening I wanted, but it was the opening I got. "You mean you would actually pay me?" I said, with all the enthusiasm I could muster.

His face was pale and pockmarked. Greasy, mud-colored hair hung over his small eyes. He was taller than me, and when I looked up I could see his eyes under his hair. They seemed to be taking me in much faster than his brain could process. His pupils were huge and surrounded by clear gray irises.

For a second I wondered if smoke was going to come out of his ears. Then his thin lips parted. "How about dinner and a movie?"

"Sure, handsome," I replied. "But I think I should know your name first."

He stuck out his hand. "Al."

I shook it like it wasn't clammy and covered in germs. "Artemis."

"Double A," he said, and then he laughed like that was the funniest thing he'd ever heard.

I couldn't even remember the movie as I walked into my apartment a week later. Al had his hands all over me in the darkened theater and I was too busy fending him off to pay attention to the screen.

"How was your date?" asked Ruby. She was sitting on our living room sofa, wearing sweatpants and the crumbs from an empty tray of Oreos.

"He was a total gentleman. We're going out tomorrow."

"I'm glad you had fun."

"I want you to have fun too." I sat down next to her. "I want you to go out like you used to and stop staying in every night."

"I'm just fine staying here and keeping an eye on you," she said, then she pushed Play on the show she'd recorded.

I got up and walked to my room without another word. It would take her ten minutes to realize I wasn't there anymore.

I changed into pajamas and climbed into bed. Ruby wouldn't have to worry much longer. I was going to fix everything. I couldn't wait to see Al again.

Thirty-Seven Days Before the Fire

I had never seen a neighborhood with so many stray cats and dogs. They foraged for food in open trash cans and didn't seem particularly frightened of people. The trailer park was a domesticated animal jungle and the natives were even scarier.

When my parents were alive they had made it clear to Ruby and me that we weren't allowed to come here. And not because they looked down on the residents. Quite the contrary, Ruby and I both had friends who lived here. They visited our home often. And ate at our home, often. And slept over at our home, often.

We were told to stay away because most of the county's crimes happened here. Also because there had been several crystal meth busts in this area. Our Dad was a chemistry teacher, and he explained that most of the chemicals used to make the drug were explosive. He referred to the trailer park as "the bomb radius."

Luckily for me, my friends from the trailer park had moved on to less ferocious pastures. A few went away to college. Most of them went to the military.

I was over a hundred yards away, looking at the neighborhood with a pair of binoculars. I'd been waiting for hours to see him, and just when I was about to give up, I saw the owner of the trailer skitter out the front door. He was average height, and that was the only thing he had going for him. His hair was greasy and hung so far over his eyes that I couldn't believe he could actually see. His skin was pale, his movements were jerky. Everything about him said he was a tweaker, which is probably why he was committing petty crimes. He was trying to scratch up cash to cook for his habit.

A pair of men clamored out behind him. They had to be identical twins. They weren't as tall as their older brother but they were a great deal cleaner. Their skin tone reminded me of a chocolate malt milkshake.

A second later the screen door burst open behind them. The caboose was a tall, lanky teen. His skin, hair, and eyes were distinctly Asian. And staring into those eyes revealed the one thing the brothers shared: clear, gray eyes.

A picture was being painted in my head. The mother must have been Caucasian, and the genetic carrier of those eyes. Their fathers were all different. A family rainbow.

I lowered my binoculars and started my car. I didn't know where they were walking to and I wanted to find out without them seeing me.

We would all meet soon enough.

Thirty-Eight Days Before the Fire

Ruby was sleeping late, and I was grateful for it. It wasn't that I didn't enjoy her company, because I did. Ruby was full of energy and always seemed to know where the party was. But our parents had told me to look out for her, and I needed privacy to do that.

Ruby would have killed me, but I had downloaded a tracking app onto her phone. I happened to know that Ruby put all the apps that she didn't use—but couldn't delete—in a phone folder that she never opened. I hid the tracker there and only used it for emergencies. Luckily those didn't happen often.

It seemed a little excessive, but Ruby was the only family I had. Our parents, both teachers, were murdered during a school shooting two years ago. I couldn't lose Ruby.

Her phone was in the trailer park on the other side of town. The tracking app shared both where the phone was and where it had been. It hadn't been moved in hours.

Ruby would need me later, but at the moment I was looking up the address of her phone's location. An online search led me to a picture of the owner of the trailer. He had recently been released from prison and had a lengthy rap sheet. I wanted to see him in person.

Thirty-Nine Days Before the Fire

College was a lot harder than high school, so I, the college senior, was at home studying while my sister, the high school senior, was out partying with her friends.

My parents would have never let her stay out this late, but this was a safe neighborhood and I wanted her to have fun. She'd already lost so much.

Besides, those mumble rappers she blasted on the surround sound made it impossible for me to concentrate. The later she stayed out, the more I could get done, both tonight and tomorrow morning.

"Artemis! Artemis!" Ruby screamed.

It was four A.M. I must've fallen asleep.

"All right. You're home. You don't have to announce it to the whole neighborhood."

"I was robbed."

I leapt from the sofa to where she stood by the front door.

She smelled like Hennessy and mint. Her perfectly applied, smoky eye makeup was smudged, making her look like a raccoon. Her leather jacket was gone. The dress I had let her borrow was ripped, and she was holding it up to cover herself.

Ruby had obviously been out drinking, but this didn't seem like the right time to ask about it. Especially since I didn't care what she was doing before she was robbed.

"We have to call the police," I said.

Ruby collapsed to the floor. "No, we can't. They stole my ID. They know where we live. If I call the police they'll come back."

"They?"

"Four of them. Brothers."

"They told you they were brothers?"

"One of them said, 'Since we're already brothers we should become Eskimo brothers.'"

My entire body felt cold. Stale coffee began to make its way up my throat.

Ruby was crying in a heap at my feet. I swallowed coffee and bile, before kneeling to be eye level with her.

"Did they?"

"No, but they touched me. All over. I didn't know if I'd ever see you again. I thought . . ."

I wrapped my arms around my sister and listened silently as she told me what happened.

Ruby knew that I liked to wake up early to study. She parked far away from our apartment so she wouldn't wake me. She was alone in the parking lot, rushing to beat the fall chill when she heard footsteps.

Four men had swarmed her out of nowhere. Their hands were everywhere at once. Removing her jacket and her earrings. Groping her breasts and her behind.

She pleaded with them to stop. Offering them her purse and everything in it if they let her go. And they agreed, sort of. Her purse and all of its contents were indeed gone. But the leader had gone through it to find her ID. He recited our address to her and promised to visit if the police visited them. Then they walked her to our building, where she finally saw their faces in the light.

She said they were all different races. One white. One Asian. Two black. How could they be brothers?

It took Ruby a long time to tell me what happened between sobs. Emotions gripped me with each detail she revealed. Rage was directed toward the men who did this to her. Guilt radiated from me for letting her stay out so late. And terror enveloped me. What would happen if they came back?

When Ruby finished talking I walked her to her bedroom, and lay next to her until she cried herself to sleep. I didn't cry at all. Instead, I calmly went over my options.

I could tell the police what happened; depending on where the assault took place there should be camera footage. But how quickly would they apprehend them, and given how my sister was dressed, would they pursue justice for her, or would they just traumatize her further?

I could try to go on as if nothing had happened and hope they didn't come back. This offered the benefit of allowing me to do nothing, but I'd always worry about Ruby, and she'd always look over her shoulder.

We could move to a new apartment, but it would be expensive. Plus I didn't want to uproot Ruby in the middle of her senior year. She didn't do anything wrong: Why should she be punished?

The only thing I could do was go on the offensive. I had to find them before they came back to find us.

I watched over my little sister as she slept and came up with a plan. When the sun came up I felt oddly at peace, ready to get to work.

"Don't worry, Ruby." I climbed out of her bed slowly. I didn't want to disturb her much-needed rest.

God Bless America

FROM *Collectibles*

"SOMEBODY KEYED THE CAR!" Joe shouted as he came in the front door, slamming it behind him.

"What?" Connie yelled. She was in the kitchen. The water was running. She was filling the big pot to boil the eggs and you couldn't hear anything when the water was running, which she had told him countless times. "I can't hear you when you're in the hall talking to me and I'm in the kitchen, Joe."

"Goddamn it!" he shouted, throwing his car keys on the dining room table. They skidded across the polished wood like a pinball smashing into her Aunt Eleanor's blue-and-white platter.

"What was that?" she said and exhaled. She carried the pot of water and eggs to the stove, set it on the back burner, wiped her wet hands on the sides of her slacks and pushed her hair back from her face. It was probably 90 degrees already and it wasn't even noon.

"Both cars," he hollered, practically galloping into the kitchen, colliding with her in the doorway. "Jesus Christ, Connie!"

"What?" She gave him a look. "The water was running! What's going on?"

"Some bozo keyed the cars, both cars." He gave the refrigerator door a yank and took out a beer. He popped the tab at the top of the can and drank half of it.

"It's not even noon," she said, stepping in front of him and closing the fridge door. You could hear the soft sound of bottles hitting each other and various china dishes filled with condiments and covered with Saran Wrap that she had shoved into the packed shelves. She still hadn't decided on which coleslaw—the one with the mayonnaise or the one with the vinegar and sugar. Someone didn't like mayonnaise, but she couldn't remember who it was. Joe's Aunt Margaret? She sighed. You had to keep everyone happy. She looked at him. "What do you mean keyed?"

He backed up. "Keyed, you know, with a key!" He chugged the rest of the beer and threw the empty can into the trash.

"What do you mean?"

"For crissakes, Connie, I mean, you take a key and you hold it out in your hand and run it down the side of a car. Hard." He stepped around her, opened the fridge, took out another can of beer and popped the top. "From the goddamn front headlight, along the fender, across the doors and the back until you get to the taillights and the end of the car!" He took a gulp of beer. "Wah lah!" he said. "Keyed!" He looked at her. "Both cars."

She frowned, pushed at her hair. "Who would do that?"

"I don't know, my Uncle Max, your mother . . . some Dominican kid who doesn't have anything else to do. I don't know."

She shook her head. "There's no reason to think it's someone from the Dominican Republic."

He looked at her and burst out laughing.

The garage was his bone of contention. Or probably their bone of contention, which she had to look up after her girlfriend, Gloria, had pointed it out. *An ongoing argument on a certain topic or issue.* Well, you could say that again.

The boxes. The boxes stacked in the two-car garage where the cars should have been. "Rather than on the street where any fool can get to them," Joe could go on and on.

She could hear him now on the phone in the living room carrying on with the insurance guy about the key business. She still had to boil the eggs. She had slipped little notes detailing what she was going to put inside each bowl or platter so she wouldn't forget except, of course, on the deviled egg plate, which her mother-in-law had given her years ago. You couldn't put anything in that except deviled eggs. She ran her finger around the porcelain ovals.

"What the hell do we need all this stuff for?" Joe had said last week when she'd asked him to get the boxes of decorations for the Fourth of July out from under the boxes of Valentine's Day decor and the boxes of turkey things for Thanksgiving. Through the years she had collected several painted porcelain turkeys of various sizes along with little Pilgrims and Indians. Of course, the whole idea that we had taken the land away from the Indians was a terrible blemish on America and she'd thought about not using the little Pilgrims and Indians on the table last Thanksgiving, but she hated to give them up.

"You gotta get rid of all this crap, Connie," Joe had said, schlepping in the boxes. "If you think I'm going to park my new Tahoe on the street you've got another think coming." He had no idea that she knew the Tahoe he wanted to buy would not fit in the garage. She'd looked it up online and measured.

She decided on the coleslaw with the vinegar. She got up from the dining room table, pushed the chair back into place, went into the kitchen, and got the red and green cabbages out of the fridge. It's a wonder why no one makes red and green cabbage for Christmas. It would be so festive.

She turned the burner on under the pot of eggs.

"You didn't have all this stuff when we got married," he'd said, wiping his face with a dish towel after he'd carried up two boxes.

"Give me that," she said, reaching for the dish towel. "Don't you have a handkerchief?"

"Not on me," he said, smiling. "You want to check my pockets?"

"Don't start with me, Joe. I have things to do."

"Uh-huh," he said, taking her hand and dancing her around the kitchen.

It began with the first Christmas ornament, which is probably the way it begins in every family. You get married and then you get the first ornament for your first tree together and you put it on the tree, and it has meaning on top of the meaning of Christmas. And then after Christmas you wrap it carefully in tissue and put it in a box in the middle of wads of crumpled newspaper. A small box. The next year there's another ornament and it goes in the box. And before you know it there are two boxes. Even Jewish families, some of whom she knew personally, could have a box of something they put up at Christmas—nothing with Jesus, of course, or the wise men or anything that pertained to His birth—certainly not a crèche— but maybe a Santa or some plastic reindeer in flight across their front lawn. Her friend, Sherilyn Rubin, who was not only Jewish but worked chronicling historical documents in the library at Temple B'Nai Yehuda, told her that every Jewish person, even if they were Orthodox, secretly felt gypped out of Christmas. "After all," she said, "Hanukkah can't hold a candle to Christmas," and then she and Sherilyn had practically fallen over laughing because Hanukkah is all about candles—they light a candle every night until they have the whole candelabra ablaze with candles. Right? A menorah, it's called.

She got her big white bowl out of the cabinet and filled it with chopped cabbage.

And she was sure Jewish people probably felt the same way about their first Hanukkah together as she did about her first Christmas with Joe. Collecting memories was how she felt about the treasures in the boxes. She could look at the first ornament and remember that she had on her new winter coat and it was spitting sleet and Joe was holding her hand. The first ornament was a little French horn—just a little brass-colored French horn with a thin red ribbon to hang on a branch. They were in Little Italy walking through slushy snow and he saw it. "Look at that," he said, spying it through the window of a dusty antique shop. "Looks like the real thing," he said. And they bought it. It should have been a drum instead of a French horn since Joe was a drummer, but the first ornament was the little French horn.

The water was boiling; she checked the clock and set the timer on the stove for ten minutes. "No more, no less," she could hear her mother saying. Her mother, who was possibly clairvoyant or whatever it was when someone knew what you were doing when they weren't even in the same neighborhood, would probably call in ten minutes to tell her to turn off the eggs.

The second Christmas ornament was a little red drum. That was the year they did the tree in red—red bows and red plastic ornaments because the red glass ones were way too expensive, and red beads that they strung in loops on and off the branches. They were in a box she had labeled RED. That was the year she had the miscarriage. Joe was out of town. It wasn't like he was far away—he was only doing a club date in Philadelphia and she was going to go up on the train and then she wasn't. He'd just started playing with Louie Massimino then. He came home from Philly as soon as he heard and then he went right back—it was a five-night holiday gig

and there was no way he was going to lose it and she was too broken up to go with him—so there she was by herself on New Year's
Eve looking at the tree with the red lights.

She took the vinegar and sugar and oil out of the pantry. They
were still in the apartment then; the tiny one-bedroom Joe had in
Jackson Heights before they got married. If you walked too fast
when you came in the front door you went right out the back. Talk
about a lousy Christmas.

Seven minutes on the eggs. She mixed the sweet and sour dressing in a small bowl and tasted it on her finger.

"It might not be worth it to use the insurance," Joe said, striding
into the kitchen, "with the deductible." He opened the refrigerator
door and stood there looking inside. "Or it might be. I gotta see.
Marv says he's got a guy in Newark who can polish out scratches so
you'd never know. Says the guy's an artist. I'll believe it when I see
it," he said. "I'll get an estimate. What are you making?"

The timer on the stove binged. "Take the eggs off the stove, would
you, honey?" she said. "Sweet and sour dressing for the coleslaw."

He didn't move.

"Joe? What are you looking for in the fridge?"

"A cheeseburger," he said. He shut the fridge door, lifted the
pot off the stove, moved to the sink, poured off the hot water and
took handfuls of ice cubes out of the freezer and dumped them
into the pot on top of the eggs. "Wait a minute. You're not making
the coleslaw with the mayo dressing?"

"Nope," Connie said, smiling.

"What's so funny?"

She didn't answer.

"What are you doing with these little bitty flags on the toothpicks?"

"I'm putting them next to a bowl of olives. Then people can
stab an olive without putting their fingers in the bowl."

"I see," he said, looking at the plastic bag. "Toothpicks adorned
with American flags. Who would have thought such a thing existed?"

"Gloria found them. Somewhere in the city."

He shook his head. "The next thing you know they'll bring back
crepe paper."

She looked up, her lips slightly open. "They don't make crepe
paper anymore?"

"Oh, brother," he said, "I was kidding. Is Gloria coming?"

"Of course, she's coming."

"With that bonehead?"

"He's a perfectly nice man."

"Uh-huh. What time?"

"Four. Everyone's coming at four. You're being very grumpy."

"I am not."

"Yes, you are. Is it because of the cars?"

"Can I have an egg?"

"Absolutely not," she said.

He walked to the sink, took an egg out from under the ice cubes, cracked it and peeled it. He took the saltshaker out of the cabinet.

"Not too much salt, honey," she said.

He sprinkled it with salt and ate it. "I don't know . . . the cars, the goddamn garbage man . . ."

"What's the matter with the garbage man?"

"Does he have to throw the cans? What is it? His job to announce the dawn?" He moved behind her, his arms encircling her waist. "You want to take a nap with me?"

Connie laughed. "You must be kidding."

"If you change your mind, you know where to find me," Joe said and walked out of the kitchen.

They bought ornaments for the baby's first Christmas. They named her Catherine but Joe said she looked like a sax player he'd worked with in Toronto named Ching so he'd always called her Ching. The whole first year it made Connie crazy.

The Halloween boxes began when they bought the house. Catherine was five and Tony was three. The four of them had been stuffed into Joe's tiny apartment that whole time. Stepping around drums and sticks and cymbals and snares. Tripping on toy trucks and Barbies. And then there was the time the baby only wanted the cowbell from Joe's drums. "Bell, bell, bell," he would scream. Stepping around the high chair and the stroller and the changing table, the two of them sleeping on a pullout sofa bed with the kids stuffed into the one bedroom with a crib for Tony and a cot for Catherine—Joe called it a nun's bed. "You can't even turn over on this," he said when he was bolting it together. And they saved and scrimped and did what young couples do and bought this house and Connie thought it was a mansion. Twenty-three years ago.

She looked around her kitchen—some of the cabinets needed paint and especially the stain on the ceiling, which reappeared approximately six months after Joe painted it—every time—because the shower above the kitchen still leaked. How many times could you have that fixed? It was a brick house in East Elmhurst, which was a pretty classy neighborhood to her then. A brick with three floors—if you counted the basement which no one did—and a porch and three spacious bedrooms—well, two were nearly spacious—a front yard and back, and a two-car garage. A mansion. It didn't matter that the house was the mirror image of the house next door and every other house on the block. Whoever built up East Elmhurst had built the same house over and over, block after block. It didn't matter to Connie.

Catherine wanted to be a mummy that Halloween. The first Halloween they had the house. She was five. And she was stubborn. Connie's mother called her "Miss Stubb-Bore-Onn." "A mummy? What's the matter with her?" her mother said. From the time she was two Catherine never wanted to be anything pretty like a princess or a ballerina or any costume that had to do with tulle. Even when she was older her choices were crazy to Connie. Like the year she was twelve. "But Ophelia is so cool, Mom. The whole time she's drowning she sings! Can you imagine?" Her costume that year was at least pretty because women in Hamlet's time wore gowns, so Connie had cut up one of her old silky nightgowns and sewed on pieces of faded ribbon. The part that got to Connie was that Catherine not only wanted to look dead; chalk pale face—she had to take the train into the city to find that white powder the geishas wore—and charcoal hollows under her eyes, etc., but she wanted Connie to come up with something that looked like seaweed that was wrapped around her throat and choked her when she fell into the river. "Wouldn't you rather be Ophelia before she drowned?" Connie asked, and Catherine, giving Connie one of those eleven-year-old eye rolls, said, "Where's the drama in that, Mom?" and left the room, the nightgown dragging behind her.

The year they bought the house Tony wanted to be a fireman. That was easy—go to the store and buy a cheapo fireman costume for a three-year-old, including the red hat. That was in a box. Unfortunately, the mummy costume—which was strips of white sheets that Connie had cut and wound and partially sewed onto Catherine—had disintegrated.

She carefully peeled the eggs under a soft stream of water and cut them in halves lengthwise, scooping out the yellows.

It was Joe who was all about Halloween that year. "We'll make it haunted."

"What?"

"The house. We'll make it haunted. You know. Cobwebs and skeletons and stuff. Scare the crap out of the kids in the neighborhood. It'll be great."

He carved pumpkins with mean faces and even got a tape made with witches cackling. They didn't exactly sound like witches—Connie knew it was the guys who played with Joe. You could definitely tell one of the witches howling was Louie Massimino. And who had witches cackling accompanied by a piano, bass, and drums? Catherine loved it. Tony, on the other hand, was a mess. "It's okay, son," Joe said, "it's not real. See?" he said, holding Tony up to look face-to-face at the skeleton. Tony let out a shriek you could hear over the bridge.

"You've lost your mind, Joe," Connie said. The skeleton was in a box.

She mashed the yellows with mayo, dry mustard, and a little white wine vinegar, salt and pepper. Gloria's secret was a dollop of sweet pickle relish, she'd said, but Connie was sure that wouldn't go over with Joe. "What the hell is this?" he'd said, the time she'd tried a little relish in a tuna salad. "Pickles? No one puts pickles in tuna. Look at this, Ching," he'd said to Catherine, pointing out a speck of pickle. "Your mother's gone berserk."

She spooned the yolk mixture back into the white halves, taking care not to get any stray yellow on the whites. She fashioned the yellow into little mounds, placed each egg into the ovals in the porcelain dish, sprinkled them with paprika, covered the dish with Saran, and carefully slid it on top of several other things in the refrigerator.

Her dad had bought her the big blow-up leprechaun that they put on the front porch for Saint Patrick's Day. "Looks just like him," Joe said, which Catherine thought was hysterical. "It does, it does, it looks like Grampa," she whooped, running around the porch. "Where's Grampa?" Tony said.

She walked through the dining room and studied the platters and bowls and the slips of paper determining what would go

where. She had to go set the table. It was probably a scorcher outside. "It'll cool off by four, kid, and by five they'll all be drunk and
won't give a hoot. You worry about it every year," Joe said, giving
her butt a little pat. "Stop worrying." You could hear him snoring
upstairs. Like a faraway lawn mower. She pulled out a dining room
chair and sat down. *Take a load off, Fanny,* Connie thought and
smiled.

And what about all the Valentines? How could you not save
them? Joe went out of his way every year to find her the most
mushy corny large Valentine with long poems inside that would
make them both laugh. "Did you see the part about your eyes?"
he would say, looking at her. "I mean, I could have written that—
right?" She loved them. She set them on the hutch in the dining
room, opened like two-sided picture frames, where they stayed until probably the end of February. And the ones from the kids. Both
of her children, little heads bent, sitting at the dining room table,
cutting and pasting and the damn sparkles that you couldn't get
out of the rug until probably summer, and more red marker on
Tony's face than on the hearts he'd cut out of construction paper. "That's not a heart," Catherine taunting him. "Can it, Ching,"
Joe said, "be nice to your brother." His hearts did look more like
clouds than hearts. What was she supposed to do with all those
Valentines? Pitch them?

She wasn't sure what other mothers did—she'd never asked.
She was sure her mother had dumped the Valentines she'd made.
She hadn't even kept the little animal statues Connie had made in
art. Not even the giraffe.

She picked up the slip that said apple pie and the slip that said
cherry pie and switched them. Thank you, Jesus, that she wasn't
the one who was baking today. Even with the air conditioning you
didn't want to turn on the oven, and Sherilyn was really good with
pie. Her crust was perfect. Connie was never a baker. She gave that
up a long time ago. She baked a cake for Joe the first year they
were married. A disaster. Not only did it not want to come out of
the pan, but she had tried to fix it with icing. Like you fix a crack
in the wall with Spackle. Don't ask.

She ticked off the things she still had to do. You couldn't make
hamburgers and hot dogs until it was time to eat them. The beans
were in the big pot. She'd already arranged slices of tomatoes and
pickles and cheese on a plate. "Maybe we should make chicken

this year," she'd said to Joe. "You know, something different." He gave her such a look. "You don't have chicken on the Fourth of July, kid, that's like sacrilegious."

Her eyes drifted up and across the wall—framed photographs through the years. Taken by the same photographer. Looking in the same direction. The Queens Photo special. Framed photographs of the four of them. Framed photographs of the three of them. Connie exhaled.

"We can't take a photograph without him!" Catherine was screaming in the backseat of the car, sobbing and screaming. "I'm not doing it! I'm not, I'm not! Daddy, tell her." She had already been yelling at Connie—*she wasn't going to get dressed, she wasn't going with them, she wasn't going to sit still, she wasn't going to have her picture taken!* Connie looked straight ahead. Joe's fingers clenched on the steering wheel. "We still exist, Ching," he said softly to his daughter. "We're still here, kiddo. Tony isn't here, but we are." Joe's eyes intent on Catherine's in the rearview mirror. Connie put her hand on his knee. She didn't look at him. If she looked at him, she might have to throw herself out of the car.

And what about that box? The box with Tony's soldiers that she couldn't part with—after you give away the clothes and shoes to the church and change the drapes and bedspread from a boy's room navy plaid to a guest room's flowered comforter? What do you do with the little metal soldiers that he'd carefully painted? With special metallic enamel paint and special brushes. And all the research. The colors of the uniforms, the hats, the feathers. He loved that. "You see this guy, Mom? This guy was Michel Ney, one of Napoleon's eighteen original generals and they called him Le Rougeaud because he had red hair and was red-faced. *Ruddy*-faced they called it. Is that cool, Mom? *Le Rougeaud* is French."

"*Oui*," Connie said.

"Ha ha ha. Good one."

"It's very cool, honey."

"I need a light, Mom. You know? Like miners wear?" he'd asked, his head lifted but his eyes focused on the tiny soldier he was painting. "Like a helmet with a light in the front? You know. Can we get one?" The backs of his sneakers banging against the chair legs.

Connie's eyes moved from photograph to photograph.

He was a regular boy.

He didn't want to brush his teeth. He shot baskets in the backyard. He thought most green vegetables were poison. Was cucumber a vegetable? He had lots of friends. He told jokes. He said he was going to grow up and be a comic and study with Billy Crystal.

"Oh sure. How would you find Billy Crystal and why would he talk to you?" Catherine, always with a tone. "You're such a jerk, Tony."

"That's enough, Catherine," Connie said.

"Well really, Mom, he's going to *find Billy Crystal*!!"

A regular boy.

With big feet. And little shoulders.

"Hey, Dad, my heart did this really funny thing."

She was squeezing oranges at the kitchen sink. Trying to catch the seeds.

Joe turned a page of the *Daily News*, took a swig of his coffee. "What do you mean? What did it do?"

"I don't know; it like skipped a beat."

"You mean like a rhumba?" Joe said, smiling. "Come here, kid." He put down the paper and held out his arms.

Tony didn't make it across the kitchen floor.

She was in the ladies' room at St. Gabriel's when she'd heard them talking—right after the funeral mass—two women who'd come out of their stalls and were washing their hands and one said, "Well, at least it was fast, you know, they didn't have to watch him wither." Connie put her hand over her mouth. You could hear the rip of a paper towel out of the box on the wall. "I never heard of a child having a heart attack."

"Well, it happens, Mary," the other woman said. "You never know. You have to be grateful for every minute. Hand me a towel, would you?"

Connie couldn't believe the woman had said *wither*. Somehow it was wildly funny to her. But, of course, that year she was mostly hysterical. Laughing, crying, or both at once. Like a pressure gauge going off. Like a blowout on a tire.

She moved her eyes off the photographs, studied her hands. Her diamond needed cleaning. Was that egg? She could hear her father say: *Okay, missy, you better get on it. Enough with the dilly-dallying.*

Connie stood up, slid the dining room chair back in place, pushed her hair behind her ears, and headed outside.

Well, it was hot all right. Boy oh boy. She ran her hands across her cheeks. She looked across the yard. There was maybe a tiny breeze if you watched the leaves on the oak and there would be shade later where Joe had set up the big metal table. Her cell phone rang. It was in the pocket of her slacks and she'd forgotten she'd put it there and she nearly fell down the porch steps when it rang. "For crissakes," she said, pulling it out of her pocket, "Hello?"

"Hi, Mom," Catherine said.

"Oh, hi, sweetie. How are you?"

"Good, we're good. So, did you already do *everything*? Did you set the table two days ago? Are the drinks in the big bucket of ice?" Catherine had always been intent on teasing Connie about preparation. "Is Daddy taking a nap?"

"Yes. I didn't set the table yet."

"What? Are you all right? Do you have a fever?"

"Ha ha ha."

"Did you make the mayo coleslaw or the sweet and sour?"

Connie sat down on a porch step, slipped off her Keds. "Sweet and sour."

"Daddy likes the one with the mayo."

"I know."

"It's raining here. Raining in Southern California. On the Fourth of July!"

"Oh, that's a shame. What are you taking to Mary Lou's? Is she moving her barbecue inside?"

"I don't know. I'm taking the coleslaw with the mayo. I don't know if we'll even go. Stephen has a sore throat. So, I said, honey, if you have a sore throat we shouldn't go, and he says it's only a sore throat. And I said, well, why did you tell me if you didn't want me to react? He's so blasé about medical things."

"Probably because he's a doctor."

"Right. If it isn't about cancer, Stephen is not interested. I should have married a horn player."

Connie laughed.

"Well, I wish we were there."

"It's okay. I wouldn't want to get a sore throat."

"Ha ha. So, okay, I'll call you tomorrow for the gossip. Kiss Daddy."

"Okay."

"Bye, Mom."

Connie put her shoes on, picked up the box of Fourth of July stuff, and moved to the big table. She took the lid off the box, reached in for the red-white-and-blue tablecloth and napkins, and was face to face with the Christmas angel for the top of the tree.

She heard the toilet flush as she moved through the house. "Joe!" she yelled at the bottom of the stairs.

"Connie!" he yelled back.

"Very funny. You brought in the wrong box."

"What?" He was doing a semi-gallop down the stairs.

"Be careful. You'll fall."

"I haven't fallen since I was six years old. And that was the bike's fault."

"I don't see why you can't hold on to the banister."

"Oh, brother."

He followed her outside and into the alley to the garage. "What's going on?"

"I need the tablecloth. You brought up the wrong box."

"Am I allowed to wear shorts to this gala?"

"Which shorts?"

"I don't know, the beige ones."

"You mean khaki?"

"What's the difference between beige and khaki?"

They raised the garage door together. They'd never put in an electric garage door opener. It was another bone of contention. Connie said it was because *she* was the garage door opener and Joe said right; he was going to attach a remote to her cute butt.

And they pulled up the door. And they stood there.

Connie's hand flew to her chest. "Jesus Mary . . ."

"Holy shit," Joe said. He took a few steps forward and stopped. With arms raised, hands outstretched and mouth open, he turned in a circle like the ballerina in a children's jewelry box, staring at his empty garage.

The cops arrived right before Connie's mother who had driven Connie's Aunt Margaret and Margaret's neighbor lady because she didn't have anywhere to go on the Fourth of July because *her people were all dead.* That was how Connie's mother had wrangled the invitation. Aunt Margaret was cradling her famous lemon pie with the graham cracker crust and the neighbor lady was clutching a dusty bottle of some sweet liquor that she'd probably had in her kitchen since 1942. Sherilyn and her husband, Barry, were right behind them carrying the cherry pie and the apple. Barry had a can of whipped cream sticking out of each of his front pockets. Gloria and her new bonehead boyfriend, whose name was Bob, were right behind them. Bonehead Bob, who appeared to be in excellent shape, was carrying a case of Heinekens and Gloria had a bottle of Chianti in each hand.

They came right in; the front door was open. Connie and Joe were on the couch in the living room. Officer Lee and Officer Williams were in the La-Z-Boy chairs across from them.

"There's a police car in front of your house!" Connie's mother hollered, her hand on Aunt Margaret's arm, practically shoving her into the house. "Oh, dear," Margaret said, clutching her pie. "Hello, everyone," the neighbor lady said, practically twinkling. Both police officers stood.

"Ma'am," Officer Lee said to Connie's mother.

Officer Williams nodded at the people following her mother through the front door. He didn't say anything, and Connie thought, well, what could he say: Happy Fourth of July? She folded the wet Kleenexes in her hands.

"Hey," Joe said to all of them, "we have a little predicament here. Maybe you guys could all go in the back? Barry, maybe you could start the barbecue?"

"Sure, Joe."

"What's going on?" Connie's mother said.

"We'll take care of everything," Gloria said, giving Connie a nod and getting a grip on Connie's mother.

"Not to worry," Sherilyn said and Bonehead Bob gave a little positive gesture, kind of lifting the case of beer.

It was like a parade, Connie thought as they filed through.

"Sit down, guys," Joe said to the cops.

Officer Lee cleared his throat as he sat. He looked at her. "So, Mr. Caccavelli, as we were saying, it's a crime trend in the neighborhood. You're the fourth house . . . well, actually the fourth garage that's had a burglary."

"Oh my," Connie said. "Four robberies?"

Officer Williams leaned forward. "It's actually a burglary, ma'am.

A residential structural burglary. A robbery is when someone tries to take your property by force or fear."

"Oh my goodness," Connie said.

Officer Lee nodded.

"Yes, ma'am," Officer Williams said. "They got a Tabriz Persian rug worth like seven grand on Ninety-Fourth Street, and a Ducati Monster 1200, worth more than twenty-two thousand, maybe six blocks from here."

"You're kidding," Joe said.

"No, sir."

"A Ducati?" Connie said.

"It's a motorcycle, ma'am."

"Twenty-two thousand," Joe said.

"Yes, sir. Customized."

Connie shook her head.

Officer Lee smiled. "So, Mrs. Caccavelli, do you have any idea what your boxes were worth? I mean, considering what was inside the boxes? Their value?"

Well, how could you explain that? She opened her mouth and closed it.

"Nothing was insured?" Officer Williams asked.

"No," Joe said.

"No receipts? Nothing with a serial number? That someone could pawn?"

Connie shook her head, swallowed what was probably a sob.

Joe pulled her closer to him; he had his arm around her. "It was just . . ." he said and stopped, "you know . . . things . . ."

"That are irreplaceable," she said softly, tears moving down her face, "but not worth much. Does that make sense?" She looked at Officer Lee. He was clearly Asian. Maybe Japanese, maybe Korean. She didn't know. She ran the Kleenexes across her cheeks. "Officer Lee, does your mother keep things? I don't know what holidays you celebrate but does she keep things that she takes out . . . or maybe the drawings you made when you were little? Or the bear you slept with?"

"Yes, ma'am," he said. He blinked. "It was a lion."

"I didn't mean . . ."

"Of course not," he said, looking at her.

Nobody spoke for maybe a half a minute.

"Well, that's what we had," Connie said, her voice trailing off.

"I was born in Brooklyn, ma'am," Officer Lee finally said.

Joe smiled. "Well, there you go."

"I'm from Jersey," Officer Williams said, though no one had asked him. "Newark."

"Newark," Connie repeated.

Officer Williams sat back a little in the La-Z-Boy chair and it snapped back further, and the footrest zipped up, catching his big black boots and raising his legs out in front of him. His hat tilted over his forehead and he quickly pushed it back in place. "I'll be darned," Officer Williams said, giving a little laugh and struggling to get his legs back down.

"I was supposed to get that fixed," Joe said. "Sorry." Joe extended his hand to the big black cop, pulling him forward in the chair, the footrest lowering.

Officer Williams cleared his throat, adjusted his hat, and set his boots on the rug firmly in front of him. "So, Mr. Caccavelli, did you hear anything?"

"No," Joe said, frowning. "You mean last night? No. Just the garbage truck this morning—the guy barrels up the alley and throws the cans. I mean, *throws* them. He must have wanted to be a ballplayer."

"Mr. Caccavelli, it's the Fourth of July," Officer Lee said.

"Right?"

"There's no garbage pickup on holidays."

It took a minute. "Oh, dear," Connie said, her eyes wide.

Joe shook his head. "Well, I'll be damned."

Officer Lee nodded. "So, you know, we have to wait for the detectives to get here to make a report, see if there are prints and everything."

Nobody moved.

"Oh, don't be silly," Connie said, wiping her nose. She stuffed the wet Kleenexes into her pocket and stood up. "Everything is probably over the border by now," she said, giving a little laugh, "you know, like in the movies." She took a breath, gave the two officers a long look. "Nobody is ever going to find those things. Really. You shouldn't waste your time." She lifted her hands and shrugged. "We just have to let it go." She raised her shoulders. "And think how upset the robbers must be. If this was a movie you would see them, right? Taking the lids off the boxes. Hysterical!" She smiled at Joe. "What do you think they did when they saw the skeleton?" She turned to the police officers. "Gentlemen, if you would excuse me," Connie said, pushing at the wave in her hair and moving toward the kitchen. "I have things to do."

The three men sat there a minute.

Joe shook his head. "Well. Isn't she something?"

Officer Williams struggled out of the chair. The three of them stood facing each other. "We'll be out front, sir," Officer Williams said as he and Officer Lee turned to the front door.

"Wait a minute, guys," Joe said. "Why don't you come out back and have a burger?"

"Well, that would be good," Officer Williams said.

"Yeah, we've only had coffee."

Williams gave Lee a look. "One of us had a doughnut."

Joe laughed. He took the lead as the men followed him through the dining room and into the kitchen, batons clanking, boots hitting the linoleum.

Connie was moving wrapped dishes out of the refrigerator and onto a tray.

"The officers are going to have a burger."

"Oh, that's good," she said.

"You know, Mr. Caccavelli," Officer Williams said, "I saw you once. Well, saw you and heard you."

Joe turned. "You did?"

"Yeah, at Small's." The three men stopped in the middle of the kitchen.

"Small's in the city," Connie said.

"Yes, ma'am. Must have been in the nineties." He shook his head. "Hell of a jam. Probably two, three in the morning. You played, Jimmy Betts played. Then you played again. Everybody who'd done a show uptown . . ."

"Ended up at Small's," Joe said, grinning. "Yeah, man, well, those were the days."

"You play a mean set of drums, sir."

Joe shrugged and smiled. "Thank you very much. You guys can't have a beer, I guess."

"No, sir," Officer Williams said, laughing.

"So, Mr. Caccavelli," Officer Lee said, leaning against the kitchen counter, "you're gonna put your cars in the garage from now on, huh?"

"Oh, yeah," Joe said, "I'm getting a new Tahoe."

"Good car," Officer Williams said, nodding.

Officer Lee looked at Joe intently. "You know, Mr. Caccavelli, you better measure—I don't think a Tahoe is gonna fit in your garage."

"I was going to tell him that," Connie said, smiling.

Joe looked at her.

"Take these outside, will you, honey?" she said, and handed him the big pot of beans.

A Bostonian (in Cambridge)

FROM *Collectibles*

THE MAN WHO brought the letter to Nathaniel was stooped with age. Yellowed of teeth, of nails, of skin. He extended the piece of paper over the counter and asked, "How much do you pay for something like this?"

Nathaniel put on his glasses. "Well, I'd have to see what's here."

The old man handed it across the counter. "What's here is his kiss-off to me."

Dear Johnny Jr.,

The most important thing a boy can learn in this world is to buck up. Because life can be quite the thing! (Why sure it can.) So I need you to buck up. For yourself, for me, and also for your Ma. She's going to need you, son. Need you to be the man around the place, to give her a strong shoulder to cry on when she has one of her sob sessions. Someday, I'll come back and check in. I expect to find a strong feller where I left a fearful boy. You wait for that day, son, and we'll throw a ball around, catch up on a few things why sure.

Respectfully,

Your father, John Sr.

"So, you're Johnny Junior?"

"Well, 'a course," the old man said with a hint of indignation. "No one's born old. I was just a kid when I got that."

Nathaniel considered him. "How old?"

"Six? Seven, tops."

The bell above the door jingled as a woman in a large winter coat and oversized dark glasses entered the store. The cold came with her. She shut the door and passed the counter on the way to the stacks behind Nathaniel. She kept her head down and the dark glasses on, but he noticed the skin along the side of her left eye was purple. The sound of her footsteps came to a stop somewhere between Ancient History and Literary Theory.

Nathaniel returned his focus to the old man.

"Did he ever," he held up the letter, "'come back and check in?'"

Johnny Junior shook his head.

Nathaniel read the man's furtive eyes. "But you know what happened to him."

Johnny Junior nodded.

"And that was?"

"He was bit in the head by a tiger at the circus. It was in all the papers at the time."

Nathaniel used the old Dell to Google it. Took all of thirty seconds. It checked out.

He bought the letter.

As he wrote Johnny Junior the check, the woman with the large glasses walked quickly to the door and let herself back out into the cold. He wondered what she'd been looking for and, given the limited profit margin associated with most of the books in the store, if it would have been worth his time to ask.

He said to the old man, "Did he ever write you again?"

The old man nodded. "But it was after he was bit in the head by the tiger, so it was a bunch of gobbly gook."

"Even so, I'd like to see the letter if you still have it."

"It doesn't make any sense." Johnny Junior took the check. "He was missing a bunch of his head."

"Let me be the judge of that."

"I'll look around for it," the old man said, "but I make no promises."

The bell over the door jingled as Johnny Junior let himself out onto Mount Auburn Street, the bell as much a nod to an imagined past as the rest of the store. Larchmont Antique Bookshop had stood in this spot, a few blocks east of Harvard Square, since the first year of the Lincoln Presidency. Some books, not terribly valuable necessarily, had sat on its shelves almost as long. Others, not so much old as simply used, bent the description of "antique," though those were the ones—trashy bestsellers mostly with wobbly spines and pages that often smelled of sand and sunscreen—that sold most reliably. And then there were the few books of actual value that Nathaniel kept behind lock and key in a nineteenth-century Henri II bookcase at the rear of the store. One book, the rarest of them all, he kept tucked away in a lockbox under the floorboards beneath that very bookcase. Few of the books, rare or otherwise, had sold in some time. But it didn't matter much; Nathaniel owned the building, which housed the store and the three-story townhouse above it, and the property taxes were paid by trust.

Truth be told, Nathaniel wasn't as interested in books these days as he was in his ever-growing collection of letters. Rejection letters, in the truest sense. Goodbye letters, stay-away letters, I-don't-love-you-anymore letters. He added Johnny Junior's to the file he'd been building this year. It contained a letter to a woman from the husband who left her the day their fourth child was born, another from a woman whose fiancé left her at the airport as they were about to board a flight to meet her parents. (He said he was go-ing to get some magazines; instead he hopped a cab, went back to their apartment, packed up his stuff, and showed back up for work on Monday at the company where they'd met. Like nothing had ever happened, she told Nathaniel. As if their love had been something you tried out—like Pilates, like kale—before abandon-ing it without either prejudice or regret.) The file also contained emails—from jilting lovers, jilting parents, jilting children—as well as a photocopied screenshot of a text that a groom-to-be received while standing at the altar: *On second thought, no.*

Nathaniel had read that text at least a hundred times in the first few days after he purchased it. So succinct! So lacking in any room for misinterpretation. The groom-to-be told Nathaniel he'd come to admire the clarity of it, the steely, no-bullshit thrust. Which, he admitted, only made him love her all the more.

Nathaniel put the file away, locked up, and walked along Mount Auburn Street toward Harvard Square. It was a frigid windless night and his shoes snapped sharply against the cold pavement. The lack of wind could delude one into suspecting it wasn't as cold as one feared, until the chill crept under every stitch of clothing and went to work on the bones. Ankles, knees, hips, elbows, nothing was immune. They were locked in that heartless stretch of winter when the holidays and their festivities hung in the rearview but the promise of low skies, bitter winds, and icy sidewalks still stretched ahead for a few months more. He looked at the windows along Mount Auburn and remembered a time when, on winter nights just like this one, they'd all be yellowed with lamplight and one could easily envision a collective of disparate readers, here in the intellectual capital of the Northern Hemisphere, as they consumed the knowledge of centuries. Now the light behind those windows was blue or white and small and flickering, like a match flame, as the devices—the smartphones, the tablets, the laptops—held dominion over their willing supplicants.

Nathaniel kept a computer, the old Dell, to deal with inventory. He did not own one at home. His cell phone was a flip phone, nothing "smart" about it except for its consistent ability to make and receive calls. He still looked every inch a young man, but he was an old soul.

He had a bite to eat and a single martini at his usual haunt, Ripley's on Brattle. His mind wandered to the woman who'd come into his store at the end of the evening, of the purple that fringed her left eye. He wondered where she was now and how she had come to his store in the first place and why she had stayed for such a short time before venturing back out into the cold. Nathaniel hadn't dated a woman in over a year—that curator from the Fogg who left him for a boxer who wrote free verse in Spanglish—and hadn't realized he missed it until now, in the way he was picturing the woman's cheekbones and half-imagining a life she led . . . somewhere. When the bill came, the bartender asked, "How goes the hunt, Nathaniel?"

Her name was Chloe and she'd worked there for years, long enough certainly to know the very few micro-facts there were to know about Nathaniel Dodson, the bookstore owner who never talked about himself.

"Which hunt?"

"Any of them." She looked around the empty bar. "It's a quiet night."

Nathaniel left cash on the small tray she'd delivered, plus his customary tip of 18 percent. "Not that quiet," he said and shot her a small smile as he shrugged on his coat and headed for the door.

He let himself out and walked back home along the same frigid empty streets.

Despite all attempts to remain as private an individual as one could manage in the current age, three pertinent facts about Nathaniel Dodson always slipped out. The first was that he was a twin who'd been separated from his sister at birth. The second (less a fact than an inference) was that his odd interest in collecting letters of abandonment stemmed from never having received one of his own. And the third pertinent fact (more rumor than fact, but ever-persistent) was that he owned the first and most pristine copy of *Tamerlane and Other Poems* by A Bostonian. Fifty copies of this rather pedestrian collection of poems had been published in 1827. Most of these fifty copies failed to survive the next decade. Only five made it out of the century. Of this remaining five, a few popped their heads up over the next 120 years and sold for substantial sums, the last known such sale garnering $800,000 back in 2005. And that copy had been dog-eared, wrinkled, several letters smudged within the text.

That comprised what was known. What was not was that Nathaniel Dodson did, in fact, own a copy of *Tamerlane and Other Poems*. But his copy looked to have just arrived from the bindery. It was also the only one to have been numbered in the upper right corner of the title page—*1*—and initialed by the author himself.

The initials were EAP, which was of little surprise to those who had, over 150 years ago, ascertained that "A Bostonian" was, in fact, Edgar Allan Poe.

Though Poe had been born in Boston, he'd lost both parents before he was a toddler, and spent the rest of his childhood in Baltimore. Yet, in his first clumsy stab at a pen name, he'd identified as "A Bostonian," as if to say who we become to the world matters less than who we remain in our hearts.

Nathaniel reached the bookstore to find the woman waiting outside. With her dark hair, dark glasses, skin marbled white with the cold.

Somehow, he wasn't surprised.

"Mr. Dodson?"

"Nathaniel." He shook her gloved hand.

"My name is Caris."

He peered back at her, at a loss.

"Caris Jones," she said. "I believe you knew my mother?"

For a moment—maybe several moments, who knew how long exactly—Nathaniel couldn't speak. He stood on the cold street with a closed-off throat and considered this woman in her mid-thirties (or well-preserved early forties) standing before him. A gust moved through the center of his chest, and it seemed possible for a moment that all he'd ever known (and ever wished to know) of heartbreak drizzled through his soul.

"Why don't we step out of the cold?" he suggested.

Inside the bookstore, he turned on a couple of lights, and they sat in the two armchairs by the European History Pre-20th Century section. He offered her tea, which she took him up on. He made it in the back room and brought the cups back out to discover she'd removed her coat, scarf, and gloves and lain them across the radiator under the stained glass window. Her skin, which had been so white in the cold, was now mottled red and pink in the warmth of the store.

She removed her glasses and as he'd suspected, the flesh around her left eye formed a mostly unbroken circle of deep purple. Black eye, some called them, though in Nathaniel's limited exposure to them, they usually came in shades of purple or brown.

"Did you fall?" he asked.

She cocked her head at the idea. Then: "Let's go with that for a bit."

He nodded in a way he suspected looked uncertain.

"My mother," she said after a few sips of the tea, "always said you'd be a smart one." She met his eyes over the cup. "She said even as a baby your eyes 'blazed.'"

"And that was a sign of intelligence to her?"

She nodded.

"You're speaking of her in the past tense," he said carefully.

"You don't," she stuttered, "you don't know."

Oh God.

"Know what?" he said.

"She passed. Died."

He went very still. "How?"

"A blood disorder," she said.

"What kind?"

"The plasma in her bone marrow overproduced protein. It killed her. That's what the doctors told us anyway."

"Amyloidosis."

Her big brown eyes grew bigger. The purple stretched around the left one. "That was it. How did you know?"

He sat back across from her and sipped his tea, holding the cup in both hands.

He rolled his eyes at the store. "I read."

"Everything?"

He thought about it.

"Yes," he said.

"She talked about you a lot near the end." She looked over her teacup at him. "Never before. Only once she knew she'd seen her last birthday, last New Year's, that sort of thing."

"What did she say?"

"It's all in the letter."

It's all in the letter. His whole life he'd waited to hear those words. He worked fluid back into his mouth before he dared speak. "She left a letter?"

"Of course. That's why I'm here."

"How do you mean?"

"If a person gets on a laptop anywhere in the world and enters 'twins separated at birth' or 'twins divided' and add our birth date, you come up. The articles about you, this store, your search for the letter you hoped your mother wrote about the day she gave you up for adoption but . . ." She trailed off.

"No, no," he said, "finish your thought. The day she gave her son up for adoption, *but* . . ."

"Kept her daughter."

"Did you read the letter?"

A nod.

"What does it say?"

"It says why."

"Why what?"

"Why she left you."

Well there it was. There it was. The thing he lived for. The need to know. To hear. To find proof that while he was discarded, he had not been discarded *thoughtlessly.* Not if someone wrote a letter to him, decades later, to explain.

"May I see it?"

"I don't have it at the moment."

"Where is it?"

"Back at my motel."

He put his teacup aside. "Well, let's go get it."

"I can't right now."

"Why?"

"I just tried," she said, "but he's still in the room."

"Who is?"

"Gerhardt."

"Who's Gerhardt?"

"My husband."

He gestured in the direction of her bruised eye. "That looks recent."

She nodded. "He gave it to me a few hours ago."

"Why?"

"I tried to leave with the letter."

"And he took it from you?"

"Yes."

"Why?"

"He wants you to pay for it."

"How much?"

"Fifty thousand dollars."

"For a *letter*?"

"Yes."

"Why does he think I'd pay it?"

"Because you want it so badly."

"Even if I did, why would he think I have that kind of money?"

Her eyes roamed the bookstore. "You know why."

"I don't."

"Because you have the book."

"What book?"

"*The* book. Everyone in the book world knows you do."

"And how would you know the book world?"

"I don't. I know the auction world. I used to work for Jardín House in San Francisco. That's where I met Gerhardt. He used to seem nice but he's grown violent. Drinks too much." She shrugged. When she looked him in the eyes, hers were moist. "I never thought this would be my life."

"Leave him."

"When I think I can leave him without him finding me and killing me for it, I will. Until then, I bide my time and mind my manners."

"What will he do if I don't pay?"

"Burn the letter."

"Take me to the motel now."

She shook her head. For a very long time she said nothing and for the same amount of time he watched her.

She raised her head and met his eyes. "Not until you tell me about my father."

Well, of course, he thought.

Nathaniel Dodson's biological father had not been named Dodson. His name was Moss, Arthur Moss, and when he'd discovered his girlfriend of a few months, Mary Jones of Gilmore, Pennsylvania, was pregnant with twins, he took the news poorly. So poorly he left Gilmore, left Pennsylvania, and took no part in his offspring's life. Arthur was indigent at this point, not a nickel in his pocket, but that would change five years later when he invented the Wet Weasel, a handheld dry-wet vac' with a canister shaped like a weasel's face. Via *TV Guide* and infomercials, it became a sensation in the mid-'80s, and Arthur Moss sold the company and the patent for an obscene amount of money, most of which he invested in cryogenics research and real estate. The former pecked away at the original fortune but the real estate holdings boomed. Mary, on the other hand, had remained destitute and, with no family to speak of, was soon overwhelmed trying to take care of two babies. So, she put one up for adoption.

Nathaniel.

For the next two years, Nathaniel grew up in an orphanage. This led to attachment issues, particularly with women, and a lifelong fascination with those who left. And those they left behind. He'd eventually been adopted and raised by the Dodsons—Nan' and Barry—for whom he always felt fondness, though never love. They were the opposite—they bathed him in love, showered him with it, baked it into his daily bread. They reminded him often that he was unique, as was his story. But he saw through that. Everyone thought his life story was unique, but it wasn't. That it had inherent value, but it didn't. The lives of the abandoned were not much different than the lives of the abandoners in that regard— they lived, and few outside their immediate circle noticed or cared; they died, and were quickly repurposed into anecdotes, cautionary tales, sentimental reveries only half felt, at best, if one were being honest with oneself.

It was the Dodsons who told him the story of his mother, scant as it was. And it would grow scanter. Mary Jones left Pennsylvania while Nathaniel was still in the orphanage; she was never heard from again. If she'd been named Philomena Pinkovich perhaps, or Claudia Benninger, say, she may have been easier to find. But her name was Mary Jones, and when a Mary Jones decides to hide, she can stay hidden.

Even from Arthur Moss. Who'd hired a half-dozen private detectives over the dwindling years of his life to find her and his daughter. He found Nathaniel, who was a high school junior at the time in Portsmouth, New Hampshire, quite quickly. He arranged with the Dodsons to have the boy picked up one fine autumn Saturday and driven to Arthur's home in Dover, Massachusetts. In that home, Arthur asked Nathaniel about his interests (books, reading, reading, and books) and informed him that he was both dying and determined to make amends for his past failings. He told Nathaniel that while it was too late to become a proper father, he hoped to prove himself an adequate benefactor.

When he died, he left the house, among other things, to Nathaniel. Nathaniel quickly sold it and purchased the bookstore and the building in which it was housed. As for the rest of Arthur's estate, what didn't sit in Nathaniel's bank account remained in trust.

"Why a trust?" his sister—sister!—asked him now. "You're over the age of twenty-five."

"It's not for me," he said. "It's for you."

Nathaniel had never owned a car. Hadn't driven one since college. She drove, taking them west out of Cambridge toward Route 2. The tires would fail to catch here and there on patches of ice on the road; for a tenth of a second it would feel as if the car might fly off into the trees or slide into someone's front yard. It took a bit for the heat to circulate through the car, and in that time, their teeth chattered when they spoke.

"How m-m-much did he luh-leave me?"

"S-s-s-several million dollars."

"Oh, my."

They drove in silence for a bit and when she spoke again the car was warmer. Not warm exactly but they could no longer see their breath as it left their mouths. "Did he mention me? Wonder what became of me?"

"All the time." He looked at her in the car and searched for a resemblance. In the chin, maybe, and the slope of the forehead. "He searched for you."

"Not hard enough," she said with a sudden bitterness, her teeth clenched against more than just the cold.

"What about her?"

She looked over at him, and empathy flooded her face. "I'm sorry, Nathaniel. She told me at the end that it had hurt so much to give you up once, that she couldn't revisit it. She imagined you were happy, well cared for. And then . . ."

"What?"

"She shut you out of her mind."

A girlfriend, a nurse, had once elaborately taken Nathaniel's pulse, sighing through her nostrils the whole time. When he asked her why, she said she was checking to see if he had one. He had cultivated his existence on a removal from messy emotions, not because he was afraid of them but because he suspected he might not have any. But at the mention of his mother and her lack of interest in him, he could feel his heart. He could feel it perfectly. As it clenched. Contracted. A muscle suspended in blood. Screaming and screaming. Unheard, unnoticed, unwanted.

To turn his heart back away from the things that made it scream, he changed the subject. "It's about ten million."

"What he left me?" her eyes grew wide in the car.

He nodded. "Not counting real estate. You could get away from Gerhardt. Hire attorneys, get a restraining order."

They stopped at a red light hung by cable above the country road. It swayed in a sudden gust that whistled as it moved through the surrounding hills.

It finally sank in.

Caris turned in her seat. "I could just leave right now. I could turn the car around." She looked back the way they'd come. "Why not?"

"The letter."

Her mouth formed an "O." She continued to stare back down the empty road as the traffic light washed the windshield in a green glow. But they stayed put. "Maybe we could negotiate with him."

Nathaniel gave it some thought. "He'll be furious you left him. Irrational. He'll burn it." He looked at her for confirmation. "Won't he?"

She didn't have to nod. Or speak. The answer lived in her eyes.

She pulled the car over on the soft shoulder, old snow crunching beneath the tires. She looked across the seat at him. "Can you live without it?"

Could he?

If they turned the car around right now, he could go back to his life. But now with a sister. She could tell him more than any letter ever could. Yet . . .

It wouldn't be his mother's penmanship and it wouldn't be a permanent artifact. Just an oral history, prone to gaps of memory. No direct one-to-one connection with the woman who'd carried him in her body for nine months.

So, no, he couldn't live without it.

Except . . .

Caris could turn around and drive right into a whole new life. A life of comfort, free from worry, with, as he'd mentioned, access to attorneys who could make her problematic husband go away.

For the price of one letter from a woman he'd never met, he could buy his sister a whole new fate.

"Yes," he said and his stomach eddied. "I'll live without it."

She didn't seem ready for that answer. "Why? You barely know me."

"I don't know her at all," he said.

She sat very still for some time. Long enough that the heat overtook the car and grew stuffy and they had to turn it down.

When she spoke, there was new steel in her voice. "I know what it's like to spend my life with a question that might never be answered, a need that might never be met." She took his gloved hands in hers. "It's unbearable. You've given me our father tonight. You've given me our father plus a future. More than I could have ever hoped." She squeezed his fingers, her eyes glistening in the dark. "Let me give you our mother."

He could hear them both breathing. As close together in that car as they would have been in the womb.

"You want to go get the letter," he said.

"I want to go get the letter," she said.

His eyes had fully adjusted to the dark of her car. And her face loomed from that darkness in distinct colors—the white of her flesh, the red of her lips, the great warm brown of her yearning eyes.

"Then let's go," he said.

They turned into the parking lot of the Redcoat Inn in Acton, a one-story, U-shaped compound of utilitarian motel rooms, each with a faded red door. Nathaniel guessed it housed about fifty units but there were only a dozen cars in the parking lot. Once the fall foliage season was over, few travelers came to Acton, a sleepy bedroom community for people priced out of Concord and Lincoln. However, the motel (calling it an inn was far too charitable) sat along a main industrial strip that appeared to have been cut out of the surrounding forests by a pack of drunks wielding scythes or driving backhoes. Across the road from the motel was a grain store and a shack that repaired lawn mowers and down the road a bit was an office park. None of it, save the motel, was lit up. The motel itself gave off the air of a place where people went to quench illicit desires and fell asleep smoking in bed. The door to unit 112, in fact, was scorched black and boarded up as if to bear out Nathaniel's suspicions.

Gerhardt and Caris had rented unit 127, first floor, in the back, facing the woods. Caris and Nathaniel parked in front of unit 123. Someone had discarded a truck trailer back there long enough ago for it to sprout weeds, but otherwise there were only four cars around back and one of them was the one they were sitting in.

"His car's not here."

"You brought two cars?"

She nodded. "In case."

"In case of what?"

"That what I asked Gerhardt. He said, 'In case of things you need an in-case for.'"

"Where could he be?"

"There's a bar about two miles down the road," she said.

He looked at the clock on the dashboard and was surprised to discover it was only 9:30. A common deception of the dead of winter, he'd long found, was that it always felt so much later than it actually was.

She removed a door key from her purse. Not a key, per se, but a white plastic card with a magnetic strip. Her hands shook, and it wasn't cold in the car. She unbuckled her seat belt and reached for the door handle.

"What are you doing?" he asked.

"I'm going in before he gets back."

He snatched the card out of her hand. "You can't. What if he comes back? He's hurt you once."

"I know he's hurt me. And it's a lot more than once." She chewed her lower lip for a moment, then turned to him with a look in her eyes that was a bizarre combination of ferocity and terror. "It's our one chance. I run in and run right back out."

"I'll do it," he said.

"You don't know where it is," she said.

"So, tell me."

She stared at him long enough that he knew what she was thinking—was he up to the task? Nathaniel was not a physically formidable man. He had no tales of bravery or wild pluck in his biography. He was a bookstore owner; he wore comfortable loafers, wool sweaters, and corduroy pants.

"Nathaniel," she said carefully.

"Just tell me where it is. Come on. He could come back any second."

Her eyes scurried back and forth. Then settled. "It's under the nightstand on the far side of the bed."

"Why did you hide it there?"

"I didn't. Gerhardt ripped the envelope out of my hand and threw it across the room. When I looked around for it later—with him never taking his eyes off me—I saw it peeking out from under the nightstand."

He looked down the line of red doors until he reached 127. He swallowed several times. "Does Gerhardt have a gun?"

"I don't think so."

That wasn't exactly a definitive answer.

"Have you ever seen him with a gun? Known him to have a gun? Entered a gun store together?"

"No."

"To which question?"

"All of them."

He could picture Gerhardt—a big blocky German, he assumed, with a blocky crewcut and a big square head and shoulders like I-beams—sitting at a bar up the road. Downing a shot and the rest

of his beer as he tossed bills on the bar top and reached for his
coat . . .

He reached for the door handle. "Be right back."

And before he could stop himself, he stepped out of the car
into the bracing cold. It had dropped at least ten degrees since
they left Cambridge. It found the small bones in his ears first, in-
vaded his nostrils, and froze the interior walls. As for his feet, he
should have worn boots.

His hand shook when he tried to swipe the key in the door lock.
Shook enough that it took him three tries, but on the third one
the red light above the door handle went from red to green and
he opened the door and stepped inside. The moment he was inside, he marveled at the fact that he'd done it, he'd actually done
it—entered a stranger's room with a borrowed key. To steal something.

He kept his gloves on.

The room smelled of fast food and a recent shower and the
faint chemical smell of ritually applied cleaning solvents used in
cheap motels countrywide. (He assumed they all purchased in
bulk from the same company.) Nathaniel again got an image of
big blocky Gerhardt pushing off from the bar, and the thought
got him moving around the bed to the nightstand. He dropped
to his knees and slipped his finger under the nightstand and felt
only rug. He tilted the piece back with one hand and slid his whole
hand under. And felt nothing.

A shadow fell across his body.

A thought—*This is not good*—crossed his mind as he turned his
head to see a somewhat slight man standing over him. The man
had a face too chubby for the rest of his body, as if he stored nuts
in his cheeks for the winter. He also had a stick of some kind in his
left hand, which he swung down onto the side of Nathaniel's head.

It's not like in the movies, Nathaniel would have told a friend later
(if he had any friends)—when you get knocked out, you don't just
go to sleep and wake up with a headache. In reality, it was more
like a temporary liftoff from your everyday consciousness. Your *full*
awakeness. The man hit Nathaniel twice—the first blow a bit hes-
itant, the second more assured. The first blow landed on Nathaniel's ear and the second just above it. The room *did* spin—movies
got that much right—and the walls and bed lurched as if they were
being uprooted. Nathaniel felt instantly nauseous. The lights were

suddenly far too bright. The man with the stick (or club, whatever it was) pulled Nathaniel to his feet by the back of his hair and Nathaniel was propelled backward, stumbling, until he landed, half-in/half-out of a chair. After a few moments, his right buttock came off the chair arm and settled into the chair with the rest of him. The man stood before him, swaying with the room, and Nathaniel worried he might throw up. He blinked several times, clenched his eyes for several seconds in which he feared he *might* pass out, and then his eyes cleared even as a pins-'n'-needles sensation in his face grew worse.

"Are you gonna puke?" The man seemed genuinely curious.

"I don't know," Nathaniel admitted.

The man brandished a nightstick, the kind police carried. It was wet near the tip. *With my blood,* Nathaniel realized, and a bit of bile found the back of his throat at the thought. Still, he didn't puke.

The man lifted his chin with the end of the nightstick. "What's your name?"

"Nathaniel. What's yours?"

"Gerhardt."

He didn't look like a "Gerhardt" at all. He looked like a "Cooper" or an "Aaron." He looked WASPY and a tad schlubby. Fine blond hair thinning rapidly at thirty, dad bod on its way under a plain white hoodie and charcoal sweatpants. He looked like he was hanging around the ski lodge for one more cup of hard cider before retiring.

"What are you doing in my room, Nathaniel?"

"Is this your room?" Nathaniel tried.

Gerhardt stabbed him in the abdomen with the nightstick. "Let's not be rude."

It took Nathaniel a minute to get his breath back.

Gerhardt watched him. "You came for your letter from Mommy." He poked him in the abdomen again with the nightstick, but it was much lighter than the stab. "Right?"

Nathaniel nodded.

"Did you bring my money?" Gerhardt asked.

"I don't have fifty thousand dollars on me."

Gerhardt squatted down in front of Nathaniel. "But you could get it."

Nathaniel said, "When my bank opens."

Gerhardt laughed at that. Laughed hard. When the laughs

eventually trailed off, he said, "It's not the nineties for god's sakes. You can access your bank account from anywhere and wire me the money."

"Right now?"

"Right now."

"I don't have a computer."

"I do."

"Was she in on it?"

"Hmm?"

"Caris. Is she part of this?"

A strange smile. "She's not part of *this*, I can assure you."

"But of something else? Some other part?"

Another strange smile. "Let me get my laptop."

They never checked for a gun. It was quite amazing. Time after time, Nathaniel would have assumed these grifters, these hustlers, these stickup men and women, these cut-rate liars and thieves would consider the possibility—at least *one of them* over the years—that even meek and mild-looking men who read Trollope by the fireplace and could quote Yeats might own a firearm.

Or several of them.

When Gerhardt turned back with the laptop open in one hand and the nightstick in the other, Nathaniel was pointing the small .22 at him. It was Gerhardt's turn to grow pale and sickly-looking. His mouth opened to say something and Nathaniel fired the bullet straight into it. Gerhardt barely made a sound. He landed on the double bed along with the laptop. Much of his brain matter, pink as tonsils and tongue, ended up on the print over the bed, a wholly unimaginative painting of Walden Pond in the autumn. So unimaginative, in fact, that the addition of blood and bone and brain matter arguably improved it.

Nathaniel stayed where he was for a minute or so, waiting to hear any movement from adjoining rooms. There would be some kind of to-do if someone thought they heard a gunshot, the sounds of scrambling and scrabbling. But nothing. Just silence and the drips from the print above the bed.

He opened the door and looked out on the mostly empty parking lot. Caris's car was gone, as he'd expected it would be. He closed the door again and returned to the corpse on the bed. He fished in Gerhardt's sweatpants and came back with a rental car key and fob. He pressed the fob and heard a satisfying *beep-beep* from the parking lot.

He found it in a dresser drawer. It was addressed to him in a typescript that was designed to look ritzy, he supposed. He opened it and pulled out the single sheet of paper inside. Even now, some part of him hoped against all evidence to the contrary that it would be the thing he sought, dreamed of, yearned for.

It was blank.

"But don't you feel stupid?" he asked the corpse before he let himself out of the room.

Over the years, a few enterprising grifters had come to the conclusion—independent of one another, it bore noting—that the best way to separate Nathaniel from his copy of *Tamerlane* was to lure him away from the bookshop where it was rumored to be hidden with the promise of a letter from his mother.

Which is to say, Nathaniel had picked up a bit of an antenna when it came to grifters.

He'd had the first two arrested. But the third, a slippery sociopath named Harris Euclid, had forced Nathaniel's hand, which is to say his heart, which was a cold, cold organ, when one got right down to it. For while his heart knew much of—and highly valued—civility, courtesy, basic decency, and even sympathy for those less fortunate, it knew nothing of empathy or love.

He could have sold *Tamerlane* and put an end to it. But he realized the grifters saw it all as a game, and so did he. He loved games. The orderly nature at the heart of them. How, in the most serious games, nothing less than fate hung in the balance. And if some of these grifters hadn't understood they were playing for mortal stakes, that wasn't Nathaniel's concern. Ignorance of the stakes was no absolution for poor game play.

Nathaniel found a classical station on Gerhardt's rental car and drove the rest of the way to Cambridge with the music playing softly. He parked the rental car on Mass Ave., alongside the red brick wall that encircled Harvard Yard, and walked toward the river and his building. He bypassed the store and entered the building through the front door. He was unsurprised to find his home ransacked—drawers open in every room, cushions removed or flipped up, the mattress half off the box spring in the bedroom. Which is where she would have found the key. Just frantic enough by that point to fail to consider why it had been relatively easy to discover.

He took the back stairs down to the bookstore.

She'd moved the nineteenth-century Henri II bookcase (easy enough to do; it was on wheels), and removed the loose floorboards to get to the lockbox beneath. It was cemented in place so moving it wasn't an option. But she'd had the key, which still dangled from the open door.

Tamerlane and Other Poems by A Bostonian was kept in a clamshell box, the kind so commonly used to protect rare books that to find one without it would be suspicious.

Caris had dropped it after sitting down. It lay at her feet, the top corner of *Tamerlane* edging out from inside. Nathaniel nudged it back in with a gloved finger.

He was surprised to hear the tiniest wisps of breath leaving Caris's mouth and nostrils. Some part of her still struggled for life.

"Ironically," he told her, in case she could still hear, "the box is arguably worth more than the book. Not that one could legally sell such a thing." He placed a chair across from her and sat in it. "I had it made in Australia many years ago. The man who made it charged me four hundred thousand dollars. One could hardly blame him. His life was at risk from the first stage of creation to the last. He used the pulp of a stinging plant with the ridiculous name of gympie gympie, native to the region. In the smallest quantities, the gympie gympie can make a victim feel like they're being electrocuted. Sometimes the sensation lasts for months. Months! Of feeling you're being electrocuted. I can barely imagine. But, of course, you weren't exposed to a small quantity. You suffered a maximum dose." He watched twin rivulets of blood leave her nostrils. "Still hanging in there," he said and whistled.

He peered into her eyes but they were blank. Whatever piece of her still fought for breath did so like a germ or a virus. It had no conscious will, just innate selfishness.

"When I was very, very young," he told her, "my mother threw me away. I have no memories of my two years in an orphanage. People would always assure me that was a good thing. But what they don't realize is that lack of memory of facts doesn't mean lack of memory of feeling. I can remember *feeling* afraid. And discarded. And unworthy of love. And by the time someone came along to wipe those feelings away, well, it was too late. You see, those who leave take the power of those who are left. They take it with them. Somewhere, I assume, are people who care about you. But you're gone now and they'll never know what happened to you. You can trust me on that one. They'll wonder. They'll search for answers where there are none. Invent fantasies of what happened. Some of them, like your Bostonian here—" he indicated the book on the floor in front of her—"become great storytellers because of this."

Sometime in the last minute, she had stopped breathing. He removed his winter gloves so as not to ruin them and went to the small bathroom in back, where he retrieved the gloves of vulcanized rubber he used on such occasions. He returned to the room and lifted the clamshell box off the floor. She stared at him with empty eyes, her mouth open, jaw askew.

"You know," he said to her, "Poe's father left him when he was a baby. And then a year later, his mother died. He was adopted very quickly thereafter, but I suspect he always thought of himself as an orphan." He returned the book to the lockbox. He washed the gloves in the sink for a full five minutes, then left them to dry on the side of the sink. He returned to the lockbox and closed it, moved the floorboards and bookcase back into place.

He had a long night ahead of him—there would be cars to move and bodies to dispose of, and all of it on a heartlessly cold night— but he sat with her one last time. And he spoke to her about Edgar Allan Poe and orphans and the conflicted inheritances of those the world rejects. He recited a poem to her from *Tamerlane,* one he'd always been fond of, about a cat that lived forever and never ran out of mice.

Remediation

FROM *This Time for Sure*

IT HAPPENED BECAUSE Carter got a job working for the Radon King. A sign caught her eye while she waited for the bus at Broad and Wilson—HAND OUT FLYERS GET PAID DAILY SIGNING BONUS EASY!!!!, written in a clumsy scrawl with capital letters randomly thrown in like the human resources version of a ransom note. The situation was this: ten cents per flyer, uniform provided, a location-tracking app that must be downloaded to Carter's phone to prevent funny business. "So if you just dump the flyers in the trash, I'll know." The Radon King handed over a heinous lime-green polo shirt with a logo embroidered on the chest along with the signing bonus—twenty dollars, cash. "Use it to get a normal haircut," he said. "I don't know what that is, but I don't even know where to look."

Carter took the money and smoothed over the long side of her asymmetrical shag, which covered her one eye a bit too much. "So is it a bonus, or?"

The Radon King flapped a hand. "Do you want the job or not?"

After leaving the Radon King's office with instructions to return in the morning in the polo shirt to collect flyers for her route, Carter went to the Mobil station to see what twenty bucks could get today. One pack of Turkish Golds with enough change for a soda, half a ticket to New York on the Chinatown bus, or ten tablets of tramadol, the weakest, cheapest opiate available. She went home and gave her roommate three of them in exchange for a haircut with a pair of sewing scissors.

Her roommate couldn't stop laughing while she did it. "This

haircut is legit terrible," she said, "I mean, no wonder you grew it out. Your ears are like side mirrors. And the shirt is not helping matters, no, it is not."

Carter studied her reflection in the window above their sink. Without her bangs in her face, she looked like her father, if her father had been a semi-recovered junkie flyer-deliverer instead of an abusive carpet salesman. The color of the shirt gave her skin a nuclear glow. She said, "But the question is, would you take a flyer from me?"

Carter's roommate snipped a last little bit off the crown of her head and frowned. "Maybe you could get a hat too."

Steve Simons was not a quitter. He had never quit a damn thing in his life, except his first marriage, though that wasn't so much about quitting a relationship as it was restarting a life. He didn't quit the restaurant business despite a couple very bad years in the nineties; he didn't quit pursuing young waitresses even though they were less and less interested these days; he didn't even quit smoking despite knowing better, because smoking was fucking fantastic and, also, because Steve Simons was not a quitter.

"They can put it on my tombstone, okay, *Here lies Steven J. Simons, who was not a quitter,*" he said to the guy at the third-rate bank, aware that his eyebrows were beginning to sweat, "that's how true it is. This is nothing but a momentary setback. If you see me through this, I'll tell you, you will have my business forever."

The guy at the bank did not seem impressed. "I'm sorry, Mr. Simons," he said, again. "We're unable to extend your credit line any further, as I've said a number of times now. I do wish you the best of luck with the project. Now, if you'll excuse me but . . ."

Which was a polite way of saying *get out of my face, you sweaty, broke loser.* Simons swallowed carefully and mopped off his forehead. So this was it. The end of an empire. He had no choice now. He could sell, but he'd never recoup what he had already put into the building. It should have been the easiest money of his life— twenty brand-new condos on the edge of the next hot neighborhood, where rents had easily doubled in the last couple years. The fringes of downtown were perfect for the influx of New Yorkers who'd chased fashion-industry jobs out to the Midwest, for suburbanites who woke up one day determined to become interesting. After two decades of helping the local economy with a string of highly successful Olde Towne East restaurants, he was finally going to get his payday. He'd gotten a no-brainer good deal on the land itself, and all Simons had to do then was build.

But the project had been cursed from the beginning. Protests from the neighborhood groups, who didn't want another high-occupancy building on Parsons, decrying him as a money-grubbing gentrifier—him! Longtime resident of Bryden Road, the Near East Side Restaurant King!; a string of mysterious thefts; two fires; a site foreman who had an actual nervous breakdown in the middle of laying brick for the elevator shaft and had to be replaced, at the last minute and at great cost. Everything went wrong, expensively. Dramatically. He had to sell some of his stake in the restaurants, then a little more, he remortgaged his own house, then re-remortgaged it, and by the latest estimate, Simons still needed eight hundred grand to get the building into livable condition. But these units would pay for themselves nearly right away, if he could just get them finished. Except now, even the third-rate bank, which at one time would have been happy to throw money at him, was saying *if you'll excuse me but* and getting up from the desk, actually leaving him sitting there alone, because that was how little he mattered.

He drew himself up to all of his five-eight-and-a-half height and strode out to the lobby, where Deirdra was waiting. She barely looked up from her phone when he walked in. She said nothing. She didn't even make a sympathetic expression. This woman, his *wife* for chrissakes, whom he hated in this moment even more than the third-rate banker, could not be bothered to acknowledge him.

He said, "Let's go."

She pressed her mouth into a thin line and kept typing away. The sound of her opal nails tap-tap-tapping was enough to make him want to strangle her right then and there.

He suddenly got a terrible, wonderful idea.

The green polo shirt was like a cloak of invisibility. Carter quickly learned that there was no better way to make people ignore you than walking around a residential neighborhood in a uniform with a stack of flyers. Nobody answered her jaunty knock. A few times, front door curtains ruffled in response and once, an eye looked out, took in the sight, and disappeared like Carter wasn't even standing there. But every twenty houses equaled one trama-dol from the guy behind the Mobil station. So Carter kept an eye on the prize. The sun was out, and the homes in this part of Olde Towne were mansions, really, grand Victorian dames with widow's walks and solariums and retaining walls and carriage houses and other features with fancy names. Carter's grandmother had lived in one of them long ago. She remembered a pond in the backyard with fat orange koi, a framed-in patio with this ornate iron trellis that had a pattern like lilies. *Fleur des lis.* She had some family memories from that time that weren't total shit, so she was in a pretty good mood as she walked around and got into a rhythm.

She was almost up to four tramadols when she happened to look across the street: that floral trellis. It had been painted white, and the rest of the house looked newer somehow, but that was the place. She hadn't seen it in, what, thirty years? But there it was. She knocked on the door but didn't get an answer, so she nipped over an ivy-covered garden bed and into the backyard.

The pond she remembered had been replaced with a small, bean-shaped pool surrounded with plush chaise lounges, and as she squinted into the sunlight, she realized the pool was occupied: a woman, topless, floating on a raft.

Carter froze.

The woman's eyes were hidden behind huge sunglasses with white plastic frames. When she didn't react to Carter's presence, she assumed the woman's eyes were closed. She gingerly stepped back into the ivy, hoping to leave before the woman realized she was there. As she backed away, the woman, still without moving, said, "Who the hell are you?"

"Um, I'm, so sorry, ma'am, I'm just . . ." Carter waved her satchel of flyers. "Have you had your radon levels checked recently?"

The woman slid her sunglasses halfway down her nose. She had long, opalescent fingernails and was beautiful in an artificial way, but one that made you want to believe, like Vegas. "Radon?"

"It's an odorless, colorless gas found in central Ohio soil," Carter recited from memory. "And it's the second leading cause of lung cancer—"

"Why are you in my backyard?"

Carter couldn't tell how old she was. Maybe a rough thirty-five or a well-preserved fifty. Nothing surprised her anymore. But the woman's eyes were bright blue and looked at her with something like curiosity, so she told her the truth. "I was walking by, delivering flyers. And I saw this house. My grandmother used to live here."

Now she smiled. "Really."

"Years ago. There was a pond. With fish. I just wanted to see if it was still here."

"My husband took it out," the woman said. "He said the fish were disgusting. Which they were, honestly."

"What happened to them?"

She took her sunglasses off. Her hair was dark and wavy, snaking in damp tendrils around her bare shoulders. "You know, I'm not sure. The construction people handled the demolition."

"Maybe they set them free. In the wild."

"What, like *Free Willy*?"

She still hadn't moved to cover up her chest. Carter liked that about her, that she didn't give a fuck about much. She could relate. As such, she made a point of not ogling the woman's breasts. "Or rehomed somewhere. Taken in by a backyard goldfish rescue organization."

She laughed, and then she looked surprised, like she had forgotten the sound of her own laugh. "Come over here and keep me company."

She took a few steps into the backyard. Once she crossed into a stripe of shade, she could make out fine lines around the woman's eyes.

She said, "That shirt can probably be seen from the International Space Station."

Carter sat down cross-legged on the smooth, cool concrete. "I know. It's bad."

The woman looked her over, those bright eyes lingering at the crook of her left arm, the ropy mess of pink and white scar tissue that, apparently, might never go away. She said, "What's that like?"

There were a lot of ways to answer a question like that. She could tell her that a heroin high was like floating on your back in Horseshoe Bay and masturbating while all your exes say they forgive you. Or she could say that addiction was like being chained to a radiator in a building that you set on fire yourself, or that it's damn expensive for something so desperate and ugly and small, that if you keep it up, you die, and if you stop, you die anyway. That the last time she got arrested, dopesick and shoplifting from the CVS on High Street by the Ohio Theatre, she got tramadol in the infirmary to stave off withdrawal symptoms, which almost kind of half worked, so there she was, the poor man's rehab. Instead, she said, "I don't really remember."

"Good for you." She snaked out a hand and grasped at a tumbler of something fruity on the edge of the pool. It became clear that she was quite drunk. "Take it off. Your shirt. It's hurting my eyes. I hate it."

"Not on the first date," Carter said, and the woman laughed and laughed and then started crying. Carter pulled herself into a crouch next to the pool. "Maybe you'd like to lay down in the shade for a little bit."

"Lie," she said thickly as Carter helped her off of the raft. "Lie down."

Once the woman was upright, she tottered past the chaises and into the carriage house at the back of the property. There was a small sofa against one exposed-brick wall, and the woman collapsed onto it. "Sorry," she mumbled. "About the fish."

She began to snore, softly. Carter found a blanket and draped it over her. She couldn't ever tell anyone this story. She had no idea what had just happened. She turned to leave, then paused to pull out a flyer, which she tucked into the doorjamb.

The following week, Carter stopped by the Radon King's office to pick up a new batch of flyers. "A lady called. Mrs. Deirdra Simons on Bryden Road," the Radon King said. "Scheduled an appointment to get an estimate, so good job. She said she was very impressed with your knowledge of local architecture."

"Excuse me?"

"Something about the prevalence of goldfish ponds. I don't know."

One benefit of being the Near East Side Restaurant King was that you always knew a guy who knew a guy. It was the nature of the business. Need to buy cocaine? Ask a waiter. Need to murder your wife for the life insurance money? Delicately inquire to the sketchy linen delivery guy if he knew anyone looking for work of the messy varietal. That was how Simons wound up in touch with Earl.

Their first and only meeting was in the produce department of the Main Street Kroger. As instructed by the sketchy linen delivery guy, Simons walked up to Earl with a shopping basket in the crook of his elbow and said, "Can you tell me if you have any blood oranges?" It sounded so stupid—*blood oranges*? What was he doing?—

that Simons felt a deep rush of shame, not a guilty shame, but the embarrassed kind, and he started to retreat, but Earl's head snapped towards him in a vaguely reptilian way that indicated calling off the arrangement was not an option.

Earl said, "Blood oranges are expensive."

That was code for *give me the money*. Simons had an envelope of cash in his back pocket. Five grand, with another five upon completion. Simons took the packet and dropped it into his shopping basket, then covered it with a bunch of wet carrots. He set the basket on the floor and pretended to examine the radishes. "The address is in there," he said. "She's home most afternoons. Make it look like a robbery."

Earl deftly used a foot to slide the basket behind his stocking cart. Then suddenly the basket was empty. He'd had some practice at this. Clearly, the blood orange business was good. Earl cleared his throat and Simons realized he'd just been standing there, staring.

He said, "Um, is that it?"

Earl scowled deeply and pushed his cart towards the lettuces.

Simons swallowed a lump in his throat and went outside into the sharp sunlight. He felt a little sick. Was that really all it took? Shouldn't someone have tried to talk him out of it? He supposed he was that someone.

This was the only way out, he told himself on the drive home. Only one of them could prosper, and it was damn well going to be him. He'd already tried everything else, and if he let the project fail, or if he tried cutting his losses and walking away, there was no doubt that she'd tie him up in divorce proceedings for the rest of his natural life, or at least until he murdered her anyway, so really, he didn't *have* a choice, did he? The generous life insurance policy had been purchased years ago, shortly after they got married—one for each of them, his and hers—long before any money trouble or relationship trouble materialized. She had been a waitress in one of his restaurants when they met, a dark-haired spitfire who initiated a conversation with him out of the blue to tell him that the menu had a typo on it. "*Restauranteur*," she said. "It's not actually a word."

His initial response was a spike of anger. "What are you talking about? Of course it is."

But Deirdra had been adamant. "That's a common misconception. The word is actually *restaurateur*. Technically. No *n*. Look it up."

He ignored her and went about his day, but the idea needled at him—not that she might have been right, but that she had the guts to imply that he was wrong in the first place. When he eventually looked it up and realized she was correct, he found himself inexplicably aroused. Her nervy little mouth! He had to have her.

A brief seduction, a few trysts in the wine cellar, the jettisoning of his wicked first wife, and then Deirdra was his. The happiness this gave him was profoundly short-lived. She was beautiful and impossible, a perfectly plated but prickly dish at the finest restaurant. After years of trying to get out of his first marriage, Simons felt a bit like the mad priest in *The Count of Monte Cristo*—all that time, he thought he was digging to freedom, but here he was, in another cell. Instead of being enthusiastic about Pilates and patronage of the arts like other housewives in their tax bracket, she was interested only in astrology, succulents, and in spending his money on impractical furniture. She was big into *textures*. Anything vinyl-slick, or hairy, or covered with tiny sharp beads. She rejected all wifely duties and spent her time correcting his grammar or complaining loudly about him on the phone or moving around the end tables. A footstool with black and white yak like fur and a sickly tangled fringe had recently appeared in the living room. She left the price tag on it, like she was daring him to say something. Six hundred bucks! She was fully aware of the current cash-flow situation. He nearly had a stroke. He told her to return it, and she bought a second one instead.

This was what he was dealing with.

When he got home, Deirdra was on the sofa, flipping through a magazine, a sheer kaftan slipping off one shoulder in a way that made Simons feel almost tender towards her. Then she turned her head and said, "I made some appointments today. Radon remediation. And a landscaper, for the backyard. I miss the goldfish."

"Radon," Simons repeated. For the love of Christ, the woman's eyes were dollar signs.

"It's an odorless, colorless gas," she said. She pointed to a lime-green flyer on the coffee table. "It can cause lung cancer. And central Ohio buildings are rife with it."

Simons felt pinpoints of rage sweat along his brow. "I know what radon is! I've been dealing with buildings since before you were born, you miserable shrew. Why are you making *appointments*? *Remediation,* Jesus Christ."

Calmly, looking back down at her magazine, Deirdra said, "It means the act of remedying something, specifically of reversing damage."

Simons kicked over the yak stool. Oh, he had zero regrets.

Most days Carter enjoyed walking around Columbus with the horrible shirt and satchel of flyers. The work agreed with her too—she was tan and strong for the first time in a while. But the job was also deeply boring. Her shitty cell phone would run out of charge if she used it to listen to music while she walked, and she only got paid if the Radon King's app was transmitting the entire time. So she thought about things. About her dead father, about basketball, about the limp trajectory of her life so far: high school point guard with decent college prospects, torn ACL, Vicodin during recovery, Vicodin recreationally, Vicodin cost-prohibitively, the switch to heroin because it was cheaper, at first, until her tolerance was sky high and getting enough to just maintain required some low-key thuggery, jail, rehab, eviction, homelessness, days—weeks—months she couldn't remember much of at all, shelter, jail, shelter, jail, freewheeling through the system finally, what appeared to be rock-bottom, the dopesick trip to the county jail's infirmary and the nurse who told her, flat-out, "You'll be dead in less than six months if you keep going on this way. Probably less than three. Get high on something else."

And sometimes, she thought about the woman with the lovely, lonely eyes and the bean-shaped pool that had once been a goldfish pond. Deirdra. She imagined having a conversation in a restaurant with her, exchanging witticisms over glasses of jammy red wine and thick slices of bread slathered with miso butter. It seemed to her that butter flavored with something other than itself was the pinnacle of luxury. On the opposite end of the spectrum, you had the artifice of margarine, an oily nothing with a fake buttery flavor. That was where she had spent most of her time, letting herself be swindled by something that was almost good enough but never quite would be.

She wasn't sure if Deirdra's life was any different. She'd seemed just as unhappy despite having what appeared to be a nice life, or at least a comfortable one. On a hot Tuesday in August, breathing humid air that felt like the inside of a plastic bag, Carter let her thoughts linger on that slice of shade next to Deirdra's pool. She had a momentary vision of swimming in it, though it was hard to imagine what series of events would allow that to transpire. Maybe she could show up. Maybe she'd be happy to see her, even. Maybe she still wanted Carter to take off her lime green shirt, and maybe she was in the mood to do it. So after she was done with the flyers, she got off the bus at Wilson and walked over to Deirdra's section of Bryden Road.

She could tell something was wrong as soon as she turned up the narrow sidewalk. The sun reflected unevenly off the windows that flanked the front door; one of the panes had been punched out, a jagged, flat hole in its place. Carter peered through, her view suddenly occluded by the appearance of a silent figure inside the house. Then another sound—the hard metallic click of a handgun's safety flicking off. "Don't fucking move," Deirdra hissed. Then she stepped backwards, leaned down to look her in the face, sighed softly, almost contentedly. "It's you."

"What," Carter said, "the hell is going on? Are you all right?"

"I almost shot you just now," she said. With peculiar emphasis, on *you*. Not on *shot*. "You picked quite a day to finally come back here." She stepped aside, pointed behind her. There was a man on the floor, splayed across a smeary bloody ooze on the tile.

Carter started, "Is he—"

"Dead? Yeah. He is."

"No, I was going to say, is he your husband?"

Deirdra stared at her for a second, then began to laugh and laugh and not stop. It was like the crying from last time, except more disturbing, because there was now a gun and a murderous intent in the mix. Finally she got a hold on herself and opened the door and let Carter inside. "No," she said, "but my husband is next."

Earl had a system. He would call the restaurant and relay a message to Simons via code. If he asked if they served peach pie, it meant the job was done. If he asked about key lime, it meant there had been an issue and the deed had to be postponed. If he asked about blackberry, it meant there had been a serious issue and Simons needed to get his ass over to the produce department immediately.

But on the day that it was supposed to go down, Simons didn't get any calls. The phone didn't even ring once. It was actually bordering on suspicious, telephonically. Simons kept checking for a dial tone—always present, infuriatingly reliable—before he realized that this could interfere with Earl getting through.

By three o'clock, he was getting antsy. By four, he was downright panicked. What did no call mean? This hadn't been part of the code. He worried that it meant Earl had been caught in the act, arrested, had sung like a canary, and now there'd be cops on the street waiting for him when he went home. He considered the possible solution of not going home, but that required complete confidence that something had gone wrong. If Earl had simply flaked, or died of natural causes in the night, then Simons not coming home on time would be its own kind of suspicious and would alert Deirdra that something was up.

The late afternoon sun was hot through the windshield as he parked on Bryden Road in front of his house. He'd driven past once, looking for cops, seeing none, but he noticed a broken pane of glass in the front door. Make it look like a robbery, he'd instructed Earl. So maybe there had been something wrong with the phones all along. Maybe everything had gone off without a hitch. Simons realized he had spent more time reflecting on the pie-related code words instead of what he would actually do in any of the three cases—he was now wholly unprepared. Should he call the police and say that he thought an intruder might be in the house? Rush in, concerned for the safety of his darling wife? Probably that.

He tried to make up for lost time and quickly map out his next steps. How did a person normally get out of a car and walk into a house? He tried to picture it. Lock the doors with the clicker. Stride up the sidewalk, squinting in the sunlight, whistling—no, stop whistling, Steve Simons was not a whistler. It would be impossible to see the broken window on foot until he'd entered the patch of shade cast by the porch's overhang, at which point he would gasp. No, his jaw would harden. His grip on his keys would tighten. He would say, desperately, urgently, "Deirdra. Oh my God," in case anyone happened to be walking by at just that moment. Then he'd rush up the steps and open the door, shouting her name as he bustled into the house, looking handsome and distraught and brave. He'd grab the first weapon he could see—there was a golf umbrella in the stand just inside the front door, with a savage metal point on one end—and charge forth, ready to defend his wife's life or seek instant vengeance for her death.

Simons was in the process of enacting this plan, his beloved wife's name on his tongue as he threw open the door, shards of glass crunching beneath his shoes, when he noticed the gun on the polished tile floor of the entryway. A Ruger 380, black and silver, that looked an awful lot like his Ruger 380, the one he kept in his study at the back of the house. He froze. The visualization exercise had not accounted for this at all. He looked around the sitting room but nothing appeared out of the ordinary. The yak stool was on its side, but it had been that way for a month.

He picked up the gun, and that was when Deirdra stepped out of the kitchen and into the doorway.

"Steven, Steven," she said. She was wearing the slinky robe and holding a gun he'd never seen before. "A divorce would have been so much less painful for you."

"I don't know what you think—"

She shot him in the thigh, without a hint of hesitation. Simons was on the ground before he even realized the bullet had left her gun, before the pain exploded through his body. Blood spurted from his leg, hot and wild.

"I think you're an idiot for assuming you're the only one to know about Earl and his blood oranges," Deirdra said. She took a few steps closer, the big gun still trained on him. "Remember, I worked in the restaurant business too."

"Let's talk about this—"

"No," she said.

The Radon King was shaken by the news, which was everywhere for the next few months. He brought it up every time Carter came in, marveling in the near miss of it all. "Just think—I could've been caught in the middle of that. If I'd scheduled that appointment at her house a few weeks later, I could've walked right in on it all."

"Yeah, wow," Carter said. Again. People loved to co-opt a tragedy, as if the only way anything could be understood. Through the risk to one's own self. Her father the carpet salesman had once been inside a bank two days before it was robbed at gunpoint, and over the years his telling of the story had shifted so that it had been only one day, then a few hours, then a few minutes. By the time he died he practically had himself convinced that he'd been in the bank when it happened. Probably the Radon King would do the same thing, but Carter would not be in his employ when that happened. She handed over the green polo shirt and shook the Radon King's hand. "Thanks for the opportunity, sir."

"Sir!" The Radon King loved that. "You take care, kid."

Carter walked out of the cramped office and down the sidewalk. It was November now, the air cool and crisp through the sleeves of her jacket, which was leather, actual leather, as she headed up the block and over to the building that she now called home. A building with a buzzer and a name—The Fleur Des Lis—which was at least as fancy as miso butter. The building wasn't 100 percent finished yet, but every unit was sold already.

She just happened to know the developer and got to move in early.

Deirdra was on the phone in her office on the first floor when she got there. "Dormant? What do you mean, dormant? Like, dead?" Her bright blue eyes flashed at Carter as she talked, leaning back in her chair, legs parted. "I don't want them to look dead. Let's just do it inside then. That solves the problem, right?"

Carter sat on the edge of the desk and watched her. Deirdra was terrifying, certainly. It would be a long time before she got over the calm clip to her words as Deirdra had requested her help in the house that day—move the dead guy outside, into the pool, like he staggered outside and fell there. Help her clean up the blood on the black-and-white tile. Then leave.

"It was self-defense, wasn't it?"

"Yes, of course."

"Then you could just call the police—tell the truth—"

"No, this isn't just some guy, some robber. I know exactly who this is and why he's here."

"Who is he?"

"I'll tell you someday."

Carter had done exactly what she asked her to do, buoyed by the idea of a someday. A few days later, she read about what had happened in a newspaper that someone left in the bus shelter at High and Long. *Local restaurateur and real estate developer killed in apparent home invasion,* the headline said. It appeared that Deirdra's husband had interrupted said invasion, shot the robber, who then fled out the back but succumbed to his injuries in the backyard. Ballistics confirmed it all—bullets from Steve Simons's gun had killed the robber, and bullets from the robber's gun had killed Steve Simons.

Funny, the way things worked out sometimes.

Now, Deirdra said on the phone, "I want a koi pond in this lobby, and I want it now. I don't care how much it costs. You know I can afford it."

She hung up and looked at Carter. "I told you I was going to do it."

"You said you thought the koi were gross."

Deirdra shrugged. "I hear the residents might like them."

They stared at each other. It was only eye contact but felt like a full-body collision. Carter said, "Are we ever going to talk about, you know, everything?"

"Yes," Deirdra said, "but not today."

Long Live the Girl Detective

FROM *Electric Literature*

THE GIRL DETECTIVE reads about her death on Twitter. She is surprised. She doesn't remember much from the night before—a bar with Bess and George. A man. A drink. A struggle. A stumble home in the dark—but she is The Girl Detective. She can't be dead. She has hamburgers already pattied for dinner tonight. She has a case to solve after putting the kids to bed. The Girl Detective holds up her hand. She can see right through it, just like Marty McFly could see through his own hand on that stage at Hill Valley High School. She wiggles her fingers.

Do dead people still drink coffee? she wonders.

The Girl Detective listens to the radio talk show hosts murmur about the rumors of her death while she drives the kids to school.

Her boy says, *Mama, is that you they're talking about?*

The Girl Detective says, *shhhh, love, there are lots of Girl Detectives.*
Her girl says, *Mama that's not true. You know there's only one.*

The Girl Detective catches the eyes of her children in the rearview mirror.

Do I look dead to you? she says.

You look the same as always, says the girl. *Mostly.*

Yeah, says the boy. *That's what worries us.*

Back home, The Girl Detective examines her face in the bathroom mirror. She is ninety, but somehow her face is unwrinkled, her skin as supple and dewy as if she is still eighteen. What will she look like in the coffin? Will they write the truth of it in her obituary? Will they say she lived long and stayed young because of coffee and Chinese food and bourbon at strip clubs and illicit sex in the back of her ancient blue roadster? Will they say she aged in reverse after her divorce?

In the mirror, the wallpaper is just visible through the skin of her cheek. She puts her fingers to her cheek, presses. How long before she is a character in the Gilman story, blending into the wallpaper itself, circling the room repeatedly on her hands and knees, invisible? How long before she disappears completely?

A partial list of The Girl Detective's talents:

- The Girl Detective is a skillful oarsman.
- The Girl Detective speaks fluent French.
- The Girl Detective runs a bakery out of her kitchen and a chop shop out of her garage.
- The Girl Detective has summited Mount Everest twice, once while pregnant, once blindfolded.
- The Girl Detective is a crackerjack shot.
- The Girl Detective fucks like Grace Kelly and dances like Fred Astaire.

The Girl Detective pulls up WebMD. There is no medical advice, unfortunately, about what to do when you've been murdered. There are no helpful tips on how to bring yourself back. She contemplates her bookmarks, as a little treat. She begins with a ghost story by Maggie Smith. When she gets to the part about how the death of a marriage turns the spouse into a ghost, about how Maggie floated, invisible, through room after room of her house, The Girl Detective whispers *yes oh yes:* it happened to her too.

Last year, right before she threw her husband's belongings onto the lawn and set them all ablaze, she felt herself ripping seam by seam away from her body. She haunted her neighborhood for three solid months before she returned to find her body where she'd left it, sitting on the couch with her hands folded in her lap. She remembers cracking open her jaw and forcing her way back in. She remembers it was as hard as birthing her children, as hard as being born, but after a while, the pain was worth it, after a while, she came back into her body and into the world, screaming, sweating, panting with rage, her fingernails digging into the palms of her hands like shovels into the earth.

She remembers.

She forced herself back to life once.
She can do it again.

From *Variety:*

POLL: WHO SHOULD BE CAST AS THE GIRL DETECTIVE IN HER
   BIOPIC?
A. Scarlett Johannson
B. Emma Stone
C. Scarlett Johannson as Regina King as The Girl Detective
D. Regina King
E. Sofia Vergara

The Girl Detective gives The Boy Detectives a little ring-a-ling.
I know you've got my body, she says. *But I'm not dead yet.*

Half an hour later, they show up on her doorstep. She opens
her screen door to them, pushes her hair out of her face, leaving
a small comma of flour on her translucent cheek. They are, to be
honest, a little starry-eyed. Until now, she has only been a name
that's a constant ripple in the fan threads online and a shining set
of features: The Girl Detective with the Satin Hair, The Girl Detective with the Silken Grin. She is smaller than they imagined in real
life, but she is bigger too. She is baking something; they catch the
warm smell of cinnamon, nutmeg, a hint of banana. Her mother's
secret recipe. In the background, the low hum of a voice on the
television. She welcomes them inside.

Boy Detective Number 1 isn't surprised that The Girl Detective is in front of him, a bit pale, but still intact. Somehow, that
seems like a thing she's capable of. But she looks so much like his
mother/the woman across the hall with the abusive husband/the
lady they found dead in the alley last week. *Funny how they all look
alike,* he thinks as he takes a seat.

In the background, someone is murmuring that The Girl Detective has been murdered.

We're so sorry this happened to you, says Boy Detective Number 2,
and he takes her hand in his. How pale her skin is, how cold,
how much it feels like the hands of all the other dead girls in the
morgue. But when he looks at her hand, he realizes she isn't pale
at all. In fact, he can see his own skin shimmering just beneath the
surface of hers, as if she can take on any cast. He thinks of all the

pictures of her projected on the sides of buildings, all the sketches and the stickers, all the wholesome pinup posters they've made— our heroine, the gumshoe white girl, blond-haired, eyes as blue as the car she drives—and how his mind filled in that likeness as if it was for real, the same way he always fills in the end of his wife's sentences. The coldness of her hand has sunk beneath his skin, slid along an icy thread into the pit of his stomach. He takes his hand away. He shivers. *Funny how on top of it all, she's also a master of disguise. Funny how she could look like anyone.*

In the background, a voice, incredulous: *The Girl Detective did not go gentle into that good night. She raged, raged, raged, against the dying of the light.*

What can you tell us about your attacker? he says.

I remember nothing, says The Girl Detective. *But I'll find out.* The lamp behind her shines through her face like light through a fog.

Be careful, he says. *This is dangerous business.*

I promise to be as careful as a pussycat walking up a slippery roof, she says.

In the background, a voice mocking: *The Girl Detective thinks there's no teacher like experience, Player, and you'll know that when you've logged a little more.*

What can we do to help? he says.

You can tell me where my body is.

City morgue. Drawer B5.

Boy Detective Number 2 will not meet her eyes.

You looked at me naked, didn't you? In the morgue.

He pulls at his collar.

I remember nothing.

The Girl Detective sighs. Things might have been different if she had been killed in the Pacific Northwest, left on a riverbank, wrapped in plastic like some delicate-crumbed pastry. But her body was shoved behind a dumpster in Illinois, so she is left with these two delicate-crumbed pastries of men. She crooks a finger at the first one, leans in, pushes a lock of nearly invisible hair from his cheek and whispers into the pale pink whorl of his ear: *Go on home now. I've got a handle on this.*

In the background, a voice enraged: *The Girl Detective knows that the ability to tell your own story, in words or images, is already a victory, already a revolt.*

What are you going to do? says Boy Detective Number 1.

The Girl Detective leans back and wipes her hands on her apron. She traces her finger along the creep of ivy that sprawls across the fabric and remembers how her mother used to trace her finger exactly the same way. The leaves spiral away from their vine like a dozen different possibilities, like a dozen different lives. She remembers how she looked at herself in the mirror in the bathroom at the church just moments before she married, a woman in white like a million women before her, and the words rose up in her: *we are a legion of ghosts.* For a moment, she looked past herself and saw the ghost of her mother there too, standing just behind her, wearing this apron, tracing her finger along the thin line of vine that runs through the center. She used to think all of it began that day she was married, that finger on the vine, the fragment of skin that kept her there. But gradually they crept in: the moments before the marriage, the big ones and the little ones that led her there.

There was no neat little fix for a death like this.

She will have to reach back and back and back to the moment when she became a person in order to truly become a person again. This time, she will have to rupture something to animate herself. And again, the memory, like a vine stretching itself toward the sunlight: the mirror, that moment before her marriage when she thinks the ghost of her mother is mouthing something, but the ghost isn't there. It is only The Girl Detective, whispering to herself in the mirror, alone: *Chaos killed the dinosaurs, darling. Everything that rises must converge.*

The Girl Detective smiles a smile that says something, if you're the kind of person who can read it.

I'm going back to the beginning of the story.

From reddit.com/r/book/thegirldetective/legends-and-rumors:

Pinned by Moderators
Posted by thelegitcarolynkeene 206 points • 1 day ago
Who is The Girl Detective?
Everybody knows her face, but I keep hearing all these rumors about her real identity and idk, it all feels like speculation but does anybody know what her actual name is? Like who she is and where she lives? Cause I would really just like to take her out for coffee and like pick her brain, you know?

morale666 42 points • 8 hr. ago
You know she's just one of those women with a true crime obsession who sits around eating full fat ice cream.

Booyakasha 655 points • 7 hr. ago
Somebody told me she runs a podcast and likes to wear caftans.

Vertical inverter 134 points • 7 hr. ago
Aw, sweetie, no. She's the one who took down the woman who wrote that shitty romance thriller about the Mexican cartels. She wears a mask like a fucking superhero.

Souperstarsfastcars 83 points • 7 hr. ago
Naw, she writes a Black Panther spinoff for Marvel.

ElectricYouth7753 65 points • 6 hr. ago
My sister met her. She lives in Florida with her girlfriend. Eats at Olive Garden constantly.

Bebeboi 533 points • 6 hr. ago
I think she's probably just a divorcee with a couple of kids.

Tinymurmur22 74 points • 5 hr. ago
Isn't she the one who caught The Golden State Killer?

To travel back in time, you don't need a flux capacitor or a De-Lorean. You don't need a door in a cave underneath a nuclear power plant in Germany or a portal in the back of a diner's pantry in Maine. All you need to do is crack the spine of the right book.

In the library, here they are: all the books of her life, a hundred little doorways into the past. The Girl Detective ties an arm's length of black ribbon to her wrist and runs her hands along their spines—Carmen, Kelly, Octavia, Ursula—until she comes to the one where everything started. She opens it. She places her finger on the first words in the first chapter—*The Rescue.*

Like crawling through a sewer shaft of shit and emerging into the thunder and the rain, she is there again: in the crisp, cold air of River Heights, 1930, in the deep green grass on the side of the road. She closes the book around her hand and ties the length of black ribbon around it, because once she removes her finger from the page, she'll be sucked back into the library. Thank God for the little fragment of skin still solid enough to keep her here, thank God for the loaf of banana bread, still warm, under her arm, because now she feels fully like a specter, now she feels so faint that without these things, she is sure that she would just float away, and at that moment, she needs something to remind her that some part of her somewhere is still alive.

But careful now, duck, because look, there she is, The Girl Detective at Eighteen, driving along in her ancient blue roadster, distracted by the little girl running into the road and the van that nearly clips her, and The Girl Detective Who Is Dead but Not knows she has just enough time to complete her task before her younger self makes it home. Quiet now, through the soft shush of the grass, through the chattering cloud of insects that dip and dart all around her in the evening light, she makes her way homeward, her coat striking her ankles like the clapper of a bell and ringing something deep down inside her again and again, and then, up on the hill, the house of her childhood, its one lone porch light beaming out into the gathering dark.

From the-girl-detective-slaps-blog.tumblr.com:

THE DEFINITIVE QUIZ ON OUR FAVORITE FEMALE
SLEUTH! SEE HOW YOU STACK UP!

FILL IN THE BLANK: THE GIRL DETECTIVE IS

A. good, clean fun
B. dying of dysentery
C. as cool as Mata Hari and as sweet as Betty Crocker
D. in danger, girl

The Girl Detective Who Is Dead but Not climbs the stairs of her childhood home quietly, quietly. A breeze drifts down from somewhere above her, a breeze that she knows is from the window she left open at eighteen, the very morning her life first became a story, and she creeps toward that slow seep of air.

Opening the door is like opening a locket with a photo of her mother inside. There is something precious about every placket on every shirt in her closet, every particle of dust. She wants to swallow it the way a snake swallows its own tail. But there isn't time.

Out the window, the buildings of River Heights are scattered across the hillside like stones, and that glimmer of blue there, that one traveling like a beetle along the arching gray branch of the road is The Girl Detective at Eighteen, her car just minutes away. The Girl Detective Who Is Dead but Not takes the banana bread from under her arm, unwraps it, places it on the desk. She picks up a sheet of paper and pen, and using the handwriting she memorized years ago so she could forge her mother's signature on every school permission slip and report card, she writes:

> Dear one,
>   Stay alive.

And just as she hears the key in the door, just as The Girl Detective at Eighteen makes her way into the house and drops her bag and coat and calls for her father, The Girl Detective Who Is Dead but Not unties the ribbon—she opens the book—she lifts her finger—and she is back in her library again.

From graffiti on the side of Los Arricros Restaurant, Roosevelt Ave. and 76th, Jackson Heights:

> The Girl Detective can mimic any bird call.
> She can bring forth the flocks of ravens and
> crows and seagulls and sparrows
> faster and with more force than
> Hitchcock on Bodega Bay

For a moment, it is as if she can almost see it, the new memories rewriting the old. Each image, each thought, each word she knew is scratched out and a new one carved in its place: The Girl Detective now remembers walking into her bedroom at eighteen and finding the note, the banana bread, still warm, on her desk. She remembers she could feel it in the very roots of her teeth: her mother had been there. *Stay alive.* And it was as if her mother had reached inside her and turned up a dial: the world became brighter and sharper and slightly more terrifying. From that moment on, every man she'd walked past, every dark alley, every honk of a horn was a warning.

Now she knows that memory is faulty. There was no mother. She's been her own mother all along. And in the moments it takes for history to rewrite itself—for it doesn't happen in an instant, as she had assumed it would, it is instead like the long, slow pull of a rubber band before it is released to snap back into place—while the world shimmers and quakes in the gap between the before and the now, she can hear it: the creak and slide of the morgue drawer. Her body, loose-limbed, pale as a corn husk, drawing itself up off the metal. Her naked corpse with its dark, dead eyes, its limp limbs, marionetting its way up the stairs and out the door and across the city toward her, one plodding step at a time.

She waits, thin as a reflection in the glass, in the dark of the library, for her body to come back to her. She can feel each step as it gets closer, the way you can feel it in your feet when a door slams somewhere in the depths of your house. As it grows near, she can still feel the letters of her story being rewritten, the memories retooled, until she comes to last night, sitting at the table in the bar with Bess and George and their round of drinks.

Bess, with her typical sweet cheer, Bess drinking her Cherry Coke without a hint of remorse, and George, all angles, all snark, all bourbon neat as always. The Girl Detective steps away from the table for a moment, laughing, to get another drink at the bar. A man is there, a drink before him, pushing one toward her. He is tall and slender. He is wearing a sweater vest like her father's. (She can hear the dragging of her corpse's feet across the concrete, the screams of the passersby as they clear the street in front of it.) His smile is infectious, and she takes the drink from him absently and thinks *how lovely you are* but before she touches it to her lips, she remembers: *stay alive.*

Would you mind, she says, *buying drinks for my girlfriends too?* She points over his shoulder, and he turns to look at Bess, who waves at him, and George, who rolls her eyes, and while he's looking at them (she can hear the manufactured shutter click of the phones as people snap photos, stream video, the gasps and whispers as they recognize her face), she switches their drinks. He turns back.

Sure, he says. He waves his fingers at the bartender, *two more,* and when the bartender brings them over, she takes them, and she smiles at the man, balances all three drinks in her hands. She returns to the table and (already the first video is up on YouTube— *HoLy ShIt THE GIRL DETECTIVE IS A ZOMBIE!*—and now she cannot just feel, but see it: her slack-skinned body is here, it is staggering across the concrete walkway and up the stairs to her house and somehow, it is herself but even she is scared) she tells Bess and George what she suspects.

If you're wrong, says George.

Then nothing will happen, says The Girl Detective.

But in half an hour, he is nodding, sliding off the stool. She and Bess and George look at each other. They get up off their stools. They walk across the room and slide his arms around their shoulders.

We're going to get him a Lyft, The Girl Detective says to the bartender.

Outside, Bess puts her head in her hands.

What do we do now with two hundred pounds of self-roofied white guy? says George.

The Girl Detective is about to say, *fuck him*. The Girl Detective is about to say, *let him sleep it off in a pool of someone else's piss*. But then the guy moans and grabs her wrist (and there is a knock at her door, and she walks over slowly and opens it, and there she is, looking at herself, her eyes hooded, drool dripping down her chin, and she feels sorry for this thing, this body, because all it has are its urges, its desires, and she feels the sudden need to love it) and it is as if the memory of what happened in the other time-line was so terrible that it is still imprinted somewhere in her skin. She has nothing but vague impressions—an arm around her waist, dragging her behind a building, a momentary flutter of surprise and desire as the man cups her breast, the quick liquid rush of terror as he takes her by the neck and begins to squeeze—and this is where she leaves that memory, because she refuses to be the audience to her own death—but then it comes to her: just before she blacked out, just before he was about to squeeze her life away, she pulled herself away (and so she reaches out and cracks her jaw open just like last time, but instead of forcing herself back inside like she did before, she whispers *let me love you back to life* and she can feel her body jump under her touch as if her fingertips are electric). But instead of pulling her neck from his hands, she'd ripped *herself* away from *herself* again just like after the divorce, seam by seam, and then she'd been standing there all of a sudden next to her slack body, marveling. It wasn't him who had killed her. It was her who had saved herself. She'd taught herself a glorious trick, and now it was sheer willpower that was keeping her here. She can feel her body open itself to her, and she slides down inside and saturates every space and suddenly, she is home and staring out of her own eyes again.

She wonders if the memory of her death will be erased, but she thinks not. The timeline is too strong. There will be too many videos, too many photos, too many stories to erase them all. Something will survive that erasure just like she did. Something will persist.

The Girl Detective remembers. *Go ahead,* she says to Bess and George. *I'll see him home.* And once they are gone, she takes out his wallet, and she tucks them both into a Lyft. They go to his apartment. She draws him a bath. She strips him of his clothes and she helps him into the water. And then she presses his groggy head under the surface, gently, gently. He doesn't struggle much. When he stops sputtering, when he is still, she lifts her hand away.

It is this—the sound of the man taking water into his lungs, like water passing a slow drain—that will for The Girl Detective forever be the sound of time correcting itself, the sound of the two timelines of her life seaming themselves together again into one.

The Girl Detective picks her kids up at school. The girl throws herself into her arms.

You look better, she says. *More solid somehow.*

I feel better, says The Girl Detective. *What do you think?* she says to the boy.

He hugs her around the waist. *You're all right.*

The Girl Detective helps her children with their homework. She makes them hamburgers for dinner. She draws them a bath. She strips them of their clothes and she helps them into the water. She presses their giggling heads under the surface, gently, gently, and after a moment, they pop back up again. While they're splashing in the tub, she goes downstairs to the kitchen to pour herself a glass of wine. There, on the counter, is a loaf of banana bread, still warm, and a note in her mother's handwriting. It says:

Dear one,
    Keep safe.

The Girl Detective pours her wine. She cuts herself a slice of bread and eats it. This time, at least, she understands what it means.

Once the children are settled in bed, surrounded by stuffed animals, she asks them what story they want. *Make one up,* they say, patting their blankets the way the men at the cemeteries pat the dirt down on top of newly filled graves.

The Girl Detective is silent for a moment. Then she says, *Once upon a time, in a great dark room lit only by candlelight, a man wrote the final words in the very first book. And he sent the book out into the world under the cover of darkness to another great, dark room, where it was copied by another man twice. And this went on and on and on in more great dark rooms and in some small ones, with more men, and with women, and with more books.*

Sometimes, people wrote new stories alongside the old ones. Sometimes those stories were long enough that they spilled over into books of their own. And after a while, there were millions and millions and millions of books, and it was good.

Once upon a time, in a small, bright room, someone began to write a story, and I was born. I pondered. I hunted. I loved my parents. I listened to my friends. I poked around in tunnels and old houses and in the innards of clocks. And slowly, slowly, all the stories about me began to fill a book, and then another, and then another, until there was a collection and then a shelf and then an entire library. And I knew all the secrets. And I was the mystery and the resolution. And I was The Girl Detective, and it was good.

And once upon a time, on a night like this one, a woman went into a bookstore and found the first of my stories on the shelf. She took it home. She stuck it under the covers with her child, and in the low light of the nightlight, under the beam of the flashlight, in the pale yellow light peeking in from the hall through the cracked bedroom door, the child opened the book and was behind the wheel of my ancient blue roadster, driving toward River Heights, 1930, rushing to save a girl, and it was good.

The Girl Detective smooths the hair of her children. They are still and silent in their beds.

And what, my loves, do you make of this? she says.

There is no death, says the boy.

There will always be a Girl Detective, says the girl.

From the two-story billboards in Times Square.

From the ticker at the New York Stock Exchange.

From the script scrawled on the chests of all the steel-eyed girls on TikTok.

From a hundred thousand flyers thrown out of a thousand different planes.

THE GIRL DETECTIVE IS RISEN

THE GIRL DETECTIVE LIVES

MAYBE NOW

WE CAN SAY HER NAME

RAQUEL V. REYES

Mata Hambre

FROM *Midnight Hour*

SOMEBODY KILLS BUT NOBODY WINS *at a Miami late-night food competition.*

"Meet me at la cafeteria."

"I'm not hungry."

"We're not going there to eat."

Pugi was the most *chonga* of the chongas and still chonga-ing at the old age of twenty-five. With black marker eyebrows, hair pulled back so tight it looked like guitar strings about to pop, big gold hoops, and a push-up bra on display from the low scooped neck of a tight tank top, my cousin was sex and intimidation stuffed into a pair of butt-lift skinny jeans. Her exaggeration of gender was one-eighty to my uniform of chinos and guayaberas.

"What time?"

"Eleven thirty."

"It's too late. I need my sleep."

"Too late? When did you turn *viejo?* Dee, it's not about food or sleep. Okay?"

"What is it about, then?"

"Thirst."

Pugi, always on the prowl, liked to drag me on her hunts. I wasn't competition. She took the men and I took the women, much to Mami y Tia's embarrassment and shame. And on the rare occasion she got into something she couldn't handle, my right hook was there to get her out of it.

"Fine. What's it this time?"

"The Medianoche at Medianoche contest."

The parking lot of Tres Palmas Latin American Café de Hialeah was alive and vibrating like it was the Calle Ocho Festival. The streets around it were blocked off. Ritmo 95.7, the Cubaton radio station, had a flatbed stage with ten-foot-high speakers blasting Cuban-accented reggaeton. A large white event tent twice as big as the actual restaurant stood monolithically in the center of it all. Despite all the chaos, I found Pugi easily. I followed the direction all the phones were pointed. She was doing her thing, gyrating and twerking like a Cardi B doppelganger. By the time the song ended, she'd be WhatsApp famous in Miami-Dade.

"You made it."

"You didn't give me much choice, *mi querida* ball and chain."

"Shut up. You love me."

"It's not like I could divorce you even if I wanted to. We're family."

"*Hablando de familia,* Mami saved us seats."

"Tia is here?"

"Your mom and my mom *y* Tio *y* Lenita *y* Ruben, *y*—"

"*Coño.* For real? The whole family is here?"

"Not the whole family. Just like eight of us."

"I thought this was a thirst mission."

"It is."

"Then where is he?"

"He's number five."

She took a folded, sweat-damp paper from her back pocket and waved it for me to grab. I read it as we walked to the tent. The program listed the sponsors. In addition to the restaurant and the radio station, there was Cruz Toyota, donor of the grand prize, a red RAV4; Bembe Botanica; and Sedano's Supermarket. Twelve contestants were listed, most of them local celebrities. Number five was former Hialeah High quarterback and current Univision weatherman Alex Perez.

"Super."

"I know, right?"

Pugi hadn't gleaned the sarcasm of my superlative. Nothing good was going to come from Pugi lusting for her ex-boyfriend. Alex and Pugi had dated their junior and senior years of high school. Tia had heard wedding bells. But when Alex came home from UF that first Christmas, the sweethearts broke up in grand Pugi fashion.

"You keyed his car."

"That was forever ago."

"You spray-painted a *pinga* on his front door."

"Oh my God, that was so funny."

"His mother did not think it was funny. A huge dick in dripping black paint was on her house."

Every plastic-wedding-rental-chair seat in the tent held a body, except for the two in the front row right that were occupied by my mother's and aunt's purses. Pugi squeezed past drowsy *abuelitos* and kids jacked up on Jupiña to claim our saved seat. She waved for me to follow. I did against my better judgment. Mami gave me a kiss and a reprimand for dressing like a man. Tia did the same, except instead of chastising me for my appearance, she asked me why I couldn't do something about the way Pugi dressed. I'm not saying Tia used the word *puta* to describe her own daughter, but the way she said *fulana* was vicious.

"Why are we here?"

"Duh. Alex."

"The guy you were never going to forgive?"

"Ancient history, bro."

Pugi adjusted her boobs, crossed her legs, and puckered her lips. An air kiss flew in the direction of weatherman Perez as he and the other contestants pulled on aprons embroidered with the Tres Palmas logo. Alex flashed his above-market-salary smile. The Univision camera trained on him followed his gaze into the audience. It found a blonde in a Cruz Toyota T-shirt. The woman grinned, flipped her hair off her shoulder, then clapped her hands together like she was sending a prayer to La Caridad del Cobre. Alex gave the woman a thumbs-up. His focus shifted from her to his workstation. The camera panned the audience and missed what I saw—Alex winked at Pugi. I lip-read the single-word message that accompanied it. *Later.*

"Who is that?"

"Who?"

"The blonde across the aisle. The one *primo* Ruben is drooling over."

"Oh, that bitch? That's Cristina. Alex's girlfriend."

"Excuse me?"

"She's fake. I'm real."

The music died. Standing viewers pushed in from the open

sides of the tent. The contest's MC tapped the mic. Feedback squealed. Once the levels were balanced, he welcomed everyone and explained the rules. There would be three rounds with a different sandwich in each. If a contestant touched the food with his fingers or any meats fell out of the sandwich, they'd be eliminated. At the end of each ten-minute round, there should be five finished sandwiches on the serving tray. Otherwise you didn't pass to the next round. Tres Palmas's *lonchero*, a lanky clean-shaven senior, was introduced to demonstrate the perfect sandwich-making technique. A butcher cart on wheels was pushed in front of him. With a long-tined fork in one hand and a sharp knife in the other, the lonchero deftly sliced a baton of Cuban bread into three equal parts, cut each lengthwise, and began the assembly of meats and cheese. His movements were swift, with no wasted effort. A smear of mustard and two pickle chips followed by slices of Swiss cheese, roast pork, and sweet ham piled tight and neat. It was a ballet of fork and knife. The audience applauded. When the lonchero bowed, his red-and-black *eleke* rolled from his collar. The Santeria bead necklace was for the orisha Eleggua. Not a good sign for the night. Pugi was mischievous and troublesome enough without any supernatural trickster help.

"What does that mean?"

"*Mira*. It's like . . . It's like part of his job."

"What?"

"She's like some rich bitch socialite that wants to have the handsome news guy as a boyfriend. So, papi and papi's money put the pressure on the station. It's not for real."

"Hold up. You're telling me Canal Veintitres told him to date her?"

"Shhh. It's starting."

I looked at the fiancé, Cristina, who was looking at Alex, who was looking at Pugi. Alex turned his attention quickly to Cristina. In that split second, it felt like a laser bounced from her to him to Pugi and made a neon-bright triangle. The two women whipped their heads toward each other following the path of the dangerous beam. I sat forward and disrupted their metal-melting stares before a real fire started.

"What the fuck is going on?"

"Nothing. She's nothing to worry about."

A bell rang and the contest started. Twelve pairs of knives and forks clinked and clanked. Each row of four had a judge watching for violations. Someone in the back row let their pyramid of bread roll off the cutting board and onto the floor. She was out. Next out was a big guy wearing a thick Cuban link bracelet. The meats in his sandwich had sloppy layers that fell apart during transfer from board to plate. The audience reacted with a collective "Ay." Before the end bell rang, two others were out. One for lack of mustard. The other for touching the bread with his finger when his fork got stuck in it.

"How long have you been back with Alex?"

"I'm not back with Alex. I'm fucking Alex. Big difference."

"You didn't answer my question. And I think the girlfriend won't see a difference."

"A couple, three weeks, *más o menos*."

"Does she know?"

"No."

"Are you sure?"

"She knows we dated in high school, that's all."

"The look she gave you said she knew something was up."

"She's the jealous type."

"Watch yourself. I don't want to have to break up a fight."

While the set was condensed, a spokesperson from Sedano's was thanked for supplying the bread and food. The woman was very Latina corporate. Her heels were high and her makeup perfect. She told the audience not to miss getting their $5-off coupon from the Sedano's clerks walking around the tent. Bembe Botanica's support was acknowledged. The store owner reminded everyone that all *despojos y limpiezas* were on special until the end of the month. The MC asked the crowd if they were hungry. They replied with a loud "*Sí.*" Tres Palmas servers appeared with trays of mini-sandwiches fresh from the press. Cuban link bracelet dude, dejected and deflated, took a fistful. He stepped over the low barrier separating the audience from the participants. He stood in front of Cristina like a kid who had lost at kickball. The man next to Cristina rose, patted him on the back, and gave the Cuban link his seat.

"Who's that guy?"

"A loser."

"Not him, the older guy?"

A plea was made for everyone to settle down. Round two was

about to start. The remaining eight filed in from offstage. When
Alex Perez passed in front of us, Pugi sprang from her seat and
wrapped her arms around him like she was a giant squid and he
was a sperm whale. Mami and Tia covered their mouths in shock.
The Univision camera caught it, as did a few phones. I checked for
a reaction from Cristina and saw what I'd expected. The hatred ra-
diating from her was atomic level. What I hadn't expected was the
shock wave of anger from Mr. Cuban Link. He was looking at Cristina the way she was looking at Pugi. Was this a love quadrangle?

"Who is the guy that got eliminated?"

"I don't know. I don't care."

I fingered my shirt pocket and found Pugi's folded program.
Contestant number eight. DJ Peli, as in Peligroso. He and his
homeboy Puñeta had a YouTube channel that was getting noticed.

The crowd was shushed again. Round two was the Elena Ruz
challenge. The piles of pork and Swiss had been swapped for turkey. Made with *medianoche* sweet egg bread, the Elena Ruz had
cream cheese, jam, and turkey. The trick to winning this round
was not to rip the bread when spreading the cream cheese. The
bell sounded. Ten minutes began to tick. Contestant number
nine, the owner of several quince-dress stores, staked a bun to his
cutting board and plopped a mess of cream cheese onto it. He
tore two buns before frustration overcame him. He pinned the
yellow bread in his thumb and index finger to spread the cream
smoothly. Skin contact with the food meant instant elimination.
Alex, in contrast, was calm and cool. Three sandwiches lined his
tray, with plenty of time to finish numbers four and five. Alex set
down his utensils, pumped his hands to relieve the tension, then
rolled up his shirt sleeves. Pugi licked her lips.

"I thought you were thirsty, not hungry."

"*Je, je, je.*"

Four more contestants were dismissed. One minute remained
in the round. Tia's phone beeped, as did several other phones
in the immediate area. I looked left. She stared at the phone in
her lap. The WhatsApp *chisme* grapevine was alive. The text read
Chanel 23 weatherman Alex Perez tiene una enamorada. The video was
more like a GIF of Pugi hugging Alex on endless repeat. A big red
heart had been drawn over her ass. It was kind of funny. And others around us thought the same, if their giggles were any gauge.

Tia looked to my mom for support, and they both sighed. The bell chimed. Applause boomed. The contest was down to three.

"You've made the gossip pages again."

"What are you talking about?"

"There's a video of you hugging Alex."

"Let me see."

"Ask your mom."

"I don't think so. Did they get my good side?"

"If you mean your ass, then yes."

Pugi laughed. Whoever had filmed and sent it had to be on our side of the room. And they were close to the front, judging by the angle. Curious, I scanned the rows behind me.

Who cared who'd done it? Obviously not Pugi. I noticed a few people pointing in Pugi's direction, then returning to their phones for a second viewing. The man who'd given his seat to DJ Peli stood behind the announcer. He tapped the screen of his phone, grimaced, then narrowed his eyes at Alex as he walked off-stage. The MC cranked the crowd up with promises of *cafecitos*. The Tres Palmas servers passed through the audience with trays of thimble-sized cups of espresso. Once most of the seated patrons had been served, he introduced the owner of Cruz Toyota and donor of the grand prize. It was that man, the seat-giver man. He twisted the cord off the mic stand and began speaking. His voice was practiced and performative. I realized he did the voice-overs for the dealership's ads.

"Alex better win that car like he's supposed to."

"I'm sure he can afford a new car with his new job."

"Duh. The RAV4's for me. He promised. Plus, he's been practicing for a month."

"Practicing?"

"With the lonchero. Alex has some deal with Cruz."

"That Cruz? The Toyota guy?"

"*Sí.*"

"Isn't that cheating?"

"It's advertising. Like Alex is gonna talk about Cruz Toyota on the weather. Whatever."

Mr. Cruz finished his soft-sell sales pitch and invited the audience to stop by the showroom soon. I thought that was the end of it, but he kept talking. He waved into the front row, and both DJ Peli and Cristina stood. They bookended him onstage and were introduced as his daughter and the star of his soon-to-be-released new theme song. There was a burst of applause. Mr. Cruz and his daughter returned to their seats. DJ Peli took the mic to debut "Cruzin' in a Cruz Toyota." He unzipped his black hoodie to reveal a Cuban link necklace fatter than his bracelet on which hung a diamond-encrusted Toyota emblem. When he hunched and postured to swagger with the Cubaton beat of the song, the pendant swung from pec to pec.

"*Tengo sed.*"

"You can't be serious. You called him a loser like two minutes ago."

"No, I didn't. He's kinda sexy."

"Chill your thirst, cousin."

The lyrics to the song were the standard get a big car, be a big man, party on the beach, and get a pretty girl. When DJ Peli rapped the lines about the pretty girl, he pointed to Cristina. Cristina made a fake smile and cut her eyes to her father. He ignored her. He watched DJ Peli like Gollum looking at the gold ring. The song ended. Mr. Cruz stood and clapped with vigor, which got twenty or so others on their feet. Pugi and I kept our butts in our chairs. The MC asked the three remaining contestants to return for the final stage of the contest. All the vacant work areas had been removed during the rap performance. The three stations left were placed center stage. The sandwich to be prepared was the famous Medianoche, similar to the Cubano sandwich but made on tender egg bread. The lights in the tent dimmed as the spotlights on the stage came up brighter. First to walk to their station was the ex-superintendent of Miami schools. Second was a distant member of the Julio Iglesias family.

"Stay in your seat. No more hugs."

"I'm not taking you out with me anymore if you're going to be *pesada* and no fun."

"Promise."

Our jesting halted—a streak of red and blond vaulted over the partition and onto the stage. Cristina kissed Alex on the mouth. All cameras, Univision and cell phone, recorded the action. My arm instinctively went out to bar Pugi from starting a fight, but I was too slow. Pugi pried Cristina off Alex and pushed her away. Cristina recovered and lunged at Pugi. Alex told the women to calm down. Pugi never liked to be told to calm down. Soon she was throwing roasted pork and *jamón dulce* at Alex. Cristina came to Alex's aid and blocked the flying meats from hitting him. Words were exchanged. *Whore. Cheap. Basic. Daddy's girl.*

Alex told the women there was enough of him to go around. The women weren't listening to him. Pugi's pointed acrylic nails dug into Cristina's scalp. Cristina yelped like an injured dog. Pugi held tight to a fist of blond hair. The women fell to the floor, with Pugi on top and with the advantage.

DJ Peli entered the ring. He cussed at Alex. Called him a *pedazo de mierda* who dated Cristina only for the money. Alex faded into the shadows and away from the heat. DJ Peli encircled Pugi's waist with his husky arms and wrenched her off Cristina. Tia asked if I was going to help Pugi. I replied that Pugi appeared to be fine. She waved a ball of blond strands, validating my assessment. As Pugi kicked and screamed to free herself from DJ Peli's shackle, Peli professed his true love to Cristina. When Cristina rebuked his love, he set Pugi on a butcher block and fell to his knees. He wailed and begged. Why? Why Alex Perez? Why not him? He loved her, not Alex. All eyes and cameras were on the melodrama. It was like a live telenovela.

Cristina ignored the man groveling at her feet and insulted Pugi instead. She called her a chonga bitch. Pugi stood on the rolling table as she balanced herself, bread and pickles tumbling this way and that. She prepared to jump like a *lucha libre* wrestler from the top rope. A guttural scream silenced the entire tent, followed by an equally primal, "You ruined everything!"

Alex Perez staggered from the dark part of the stage and fell onto the center workbench. Blood gurgled from a wound in his back. I watched the Univision camera zoom into the shadowy background beyond him. Someone brought up the tent lights, and the audience gasped. Mr. Cruz had a bloody fork in one hand and a knife dripping blood in the other. He repeated the same two lines over and over. "You ruined everything. You ruined my business."

A chorus of sirens closed in on the tent. I yanked Pugi off the stage and into the seat next to me. Her black eyebrows and eyeliner were still crisp, but her face had gone from the color of a coconut shell to the color of coconut milk.

"Are you still thirsting and hungry?"

"I think I've lost my appetite."

Turning Heart

FROM *This Time for Sure*

I PARKED MY TRUCK in the lot at Turtle Creek, the Rosebud Reservation's supermarket, and looked around for dogs. A pack of them had attacked a woman on the street last month and nearly killed her. They'd gone blood crazy, biting her repeatedly and ripping the skin off her face and arms. We had an animal control officer, but he couldn't keep up with all the escaped and abandoned canines. People in the border towns outside of the rez dumped their mutts here if they wanted to get rid of them. Some of the dogs were picked up immediately but others adapted quickly, turning feral and joining packs. Those were the ones you had to watch for.

I didn't see any, so I walked inside. I headed to the freezer cases at the back of the store, underneath the hanging sign that said WOYUTE TASAGYAPI. I'd pick up some pizza rolls, a couple of frozen macaroni and cheese dinners, a six-pack of Shasta Cola, and maybe a few Tanka bars for later. I was reaching for the frozen food when my cell phone started vibrating. A number I didn't recognize flashed on the screen.

"Is this Virgil?" A woman's voice.

"Yeah, who's this?"

"Janeen. Remember me? Rob's sister."

Janeen Turning Heart. My buddy's little sis. Rob and I had been tight back in high school—classmates, best friends, comrades. We'd taken the same classes, hung out after school together, and cruised up and down Main Street endlessly on the weekends, hoping that someone would notice us. When my mom died, the first place I went was to Rob's house, where they gave me food, burned some sage, and helped me through the roughest days. In our last year of high school, we'd talked about getting some money and opening up an auto body shop on the rez. But I'd started drinking and listening to heavy metal music. Rob joined the army instead, got shipped out to fight in the war, and came home in a body bag. I'd always felt guilty over his death, thought it was my fault, somehow. I hadn't gone to the funeral. Instead, I'd hopped on my motorcycle and rode flat out to the Black Hills, pushing the bike to its limit, the road just a blur beneath me, riding until I couldn't see anything, stopping only when I ran out of gas.

"Hey, Janeen, been a long time," I said. "How's it going?"

"Not so good, actually. Wondering if I can talk to you?"

"Sure. What's up?"

"Well, are you still, you know, helping people out? If they have a problem?"

Damn, she wanted me to kick the shit out of someone. I was the reservation's enforcer, the guy you hired when the police wouldn't take action. The person who'd make sure justice was served when the feds released a child molester or rapist. No set fee—I got paid according to the number of bones I broke, teeth I knocked out, and black eyes I gave. Now my dead friend's sister needed my help. How could I let her know that I was trying to quit beating people up?

"What's going on?" I asked.

"Kind of complicated. Rather tell you in person. If that's cool."

I put the pizza rolls back in the freezer. "Yeah, no worries. Where you at now?"

"Living out by Parmelee. Just past the elementary school."

Twenty miles away. "You going to be in Mission anytime soon?"

"No, that's sort of the problem. Any way you could come out here?"

Images of Rob Turning Heart flashed in my head. The goofy way he'd smiled, the ratty ball cap he always wore. The last time I'd seen him before he shipped out, both of us too embarrassed to say anything meaningful, instead just giving each other an exploding fist bump.

"Yeah, I'll head over now."

Half an hour later, I pulled up in front of a little trailer off Highway 18. The yard was neat, the little patch of grass mowed and free of weeds. I tried to remember the last time I'd seen Janeen.

I vaguely recalled speaking to her a few years ago—maybe at the Rosebud Wacipi, but I wasn't sure. I rang the doorbell and waited.

"Virgil!" She smiled as she opened the door. "Come in."

I stepped inside the tiny living room. A small couch, an old television, and, off in the corner, a crib. She noticed me looking at it.

"Six months old," she said. "He's asleep, for now. Go ahead and sit down. You want some pop?"

"Yeah, sure." I hadn't heard about Janeen being pregnant, but that was no surprise. I'd quit drinking and didn't go to the bars anymore, so I didn't hear a lot of the rez gossip. I had no idea what her situation was now.

"Cherry cola or grape?" she said from the kitchen.

"Grape sounds good." While she was pouring the sodas, I took a look at her. Long dark hair, tall, blue jeans and a red T-shirt. I could see some of the little kid I'd known back in the day, but she was her own person now.

"Thanks for coming over." She handed me an old jelly jar filled with purple liquid and sat down.

"Yeah, good to see you." I noticed there was a framed photo of Rob in his army gear hanging on the wall. I didn't see any other pictures.

"You too." She looked me over, up and down. "Dang, you're even bigger than before. You lifting weights?"

"Naw, just working, gettin' by." I drank some of the soda. "So, how you been? Don't know the last time I saw you."

She looked at me with a strange expression on her face. "You don't remember? We ran into each other at the Depot a while back. We stayed there a long time, talked about Rob. You started crying."

I didn't remember, which wasn't surprising. If we'd talked at the Depot, then it was back in my heavy drinking days. I'd put all that behind me, although it was hard to avoid the ghosts of old conversations and past incidents.

"I'd probably had a few. Sorry."

"Yeah, you were pretty smashed, but whatever. It was all good. We were just missing Rob. Drowning our sorrows, I guess. You told me some stories about him I never heard before, had me laughing."

Yeah, I missed him. He was another one of my ghosts—more than just a friend, he had been like a brother. I still heard him in my head sometimes, cracking jokes or telling me to get off my ass and do some work.

"Seems like only yesterday he was here," I said.

She got up and threw the empty soda can in the trash. "Yeah, it does. I named the baby after him, you know. That's little Robbie."

"That's . . . really great." I turned away and pretended to take a drink so she couldn't see my face. I took a few seconds, then walked over to the baby. He was starting to wake up, blinking his eyes and looking around.

"Hi, Robbie, how you doing, little guy?" He grinned, his tiny face lighting up. "Hey, he smiled at me!"

"He might be pooping," Janeen said. "He makes a weird face when he goes."

She came over and picked the baby up, then smelled his bottom. "No, he's okay." She put the baby back down in the crib. I could hear him making little noises. It sounded like a forest after a rainstorm, crows and jays returning to the nests, talking among themselves.

"Listen, I appreciate you coming out here," she said. "It's hard for me to get around now. That's what I wanted to talk to you about. You know, with a baby, I got to be able to buy formula, diapers, all that stuff."

I nodded, not sure where she was going with this.

She went on. "Here's the thing. Last month, I wake up, Robbie's screaming his head off. I don't got enough formula for the whole day, so I need to run to the store. I feed him, get him dressed, and we head out. Except my car's gone. Missing."

She looked at me like I knew who'd done it. "Well, it's not a car, I guess. It's a minivan. A crappy old Dodge Caravan, but it runs. I'm like, shit, somebody stole my ride."

"You sure it was stolen?" I said. "It wasn't repo'd?"

"No, it was paid off. Bought it in cash. Someone took it."

"Okay. Anyone else have the keys?"

"Yeah. My shitty ex-boyfriend. Robbie's dad. He's gotta be the one who did it." She went to the kitchen and put some water on the stove. "Hold on, I need to get some formula ready."

I watched her scoop some powder into a baby bottle. "Who's this guy?" I asked. "The ex-boyfriend."

"Just some asshole I met at the bar. You know, we hooked up, I let him stay here, then I got pregnant. My fault, but I'm not sorry.

Only thing I'm sorry about is being with that jerk. Turns out he was messing around with some skank. I told him to pack up his shit and get out."

"Why do you think he took your minivan?"

She scowled. "Because he's a lazy dick! And he's got my spare set of keys. Who else could it be?"

"It's not that hard to steal a car, you know, especially the older models. You don't need keys, just a slim jim and some wire cutters. Could have been anyone."

"Who's going to come all the way out here to steal a '95 Caravan?"

This was compelling logic. "Okay, so what do you want me to do?"

"Well, I just need my ride. Can you go see him and get it back? Hey, you gotta rough him up, that's cool with me."

I hadn't laid down a beating on anyone for a while. I'd decided to change my ways, do things the right way. Wolakota, the Lakota path. Restorative justice and all that, not leaving some guy by the side of the road with a broken arm and a bloody face. But I looked at Janeen. She had Rob's eyes, his mouth. Rob, the friend I'd let down. The guy who'd always stood by me. Some debts can't be forgiven so easily. This was my second chance to do right by Rob.

"I'll help you out, okay? See what I can do."

"Oh jeez, thank you so much!" she said. She came over and hugged me, which I wasn't expecting. "You don't know how hard it's been without a car. Look, I don't got much money, but there's sixty dollars—"

I held my hand up. "Don't want your money. Save it, buy some baby food. Just give me the key to the van, in case I find it. And what color is it?"

She smiled. "Silver. Used to be anyway. Kinda rusted out now. Oh, there's a sticker on the back window—you can't miss it. It's that Calvin cartoon kid taking a pee. The asshole stuck that on."

I finished the last swallow of grape soda and put the glass down. "Hey, you haven't told me who this guy is, where he lives."

"Oh, right," she said. "His name's Gil. He's out in Norris, last I heard."

"Gil? What's his last name?"

"Uh, White Eyes. Gil White Eyes. But most people call him Chunky."

Chunky White Eyes. My cousin.

As I drove home, I tried to remember when I'd last seen Chunky. He was my second or third or tenth cousin—tough to say on the rez, given that we were all related. He was about five years younger than me and had been a goofy, gangly kid who always smelled like dog food. We used to play together when we were little; I remembered one day when we were climbing on wrecked cars at the junkyard. We'd been having a fine time until he pushed me off an old Duster and I hurt my arm. He'd laughed like a hyena until I hit him in the neck. Then he ran home and told his mother.

He moved away to the Pine Ridge Reservation with his mom when he was a teenager, so we lost touch. I'd heard that he dropped out of high school and was a wannabe gang member, but that was all I knew. We'd simply drifted apart—the fifty miles separating the Rosebud and Pine Ridge Reservations might as well have been an ocean.

And now he was back, and living in Norris, of all places. A small, isolated community on the rez, people who lived in Norris didn't take kindly to outsiders. Most of the people there only spoke Lakota, and they lived in the old Sioux 400 and transitional houses. Cheap, shoddy homes built in the 1970s, with split floors and cracked foundations. Some of the houses had been used as meth labs and were permanently boarded up.

I decided to head out to Norris right away. If I found the minivan, I'd drive it back and leave my truck there and hope no one messed with it. But the bigger issue was Chunky. If he had the minivan, would he hand it over or would I have to take it? I had no idea if he was still affiliated with a gang. It was hard to imagine Chunky as a hard guy, but maybe he was a different person now.

As I drove, I thought about him. Was he the same person, sometimes annoying and sometimes funny, or had he changed over the years? I wondered if it was possible for a person to alter their basic nature, or if some part remained fixed and absolute. I'd been filled with anger for so long, but I'd tried to let that go and become calmer, peaceful. Part of that meant giving up vigilante jobs, but people still came to me with their problems. Problems that

could only be resolved with violence, which I was trying to quit.
And now I was right back in it.

I slowed down and made the turn on Route 63 into town. There
were only a few hundred people living in Norris, so I'd be able to
find the place pretty easily. I drove around slowly for a while, keeping my eyes open for a silver Caravan.

A kid rode by on a yellow bicycle. I motioned to him.

"Hey, you seen Gil around?"

"Who?"

"Chunky."

"No, not today." He started moving his front wheel from side to
side, so he didn't fall over.

"You know where he lives?"

"Uh, over there." He pointed off to the north. "About two
blocks down. Big dog in front."

The place wasn't hard to find. A huge mutt was tied up in the
front yard with a metal chain. It looked like a Rottweiler or pit bull
or maybe something else. Heinz 57. When I got closer, the dog
noticed me and started barking ferociously. I kept my distance and
looked around the place. Weeds and trash in the yard. No minivan, but a beat-up Toyota Tercel parked in front, one window gone
and replaced with a piece of plastic sheeting.

"Hey, anyone here?" I shouted. The dog barked even more
loudly, growling and straining at its chain.

I saw some movement through the window. After a minute,
the front door opened, and a man stepped out on the small front
porch. He was tall and skinny, had long black hair, and was wearing sweatpants and an old T-shirt that said RED CLOUD WARRIORS.
He didn't look like the Chunky I remembered.

He grabbed the dog's chain and pulled it back. "Diesel, shut
up."

When I heard the voice, I knew it was him.

"Chunky?" I said.

"Yeah?" He stared but didn't recognize me.

"Hey, it's Virgil. Your cousin. Virgil Wounded Horse."

He looked at me closely, top to bottom, and his face slowly
changed.

"Shit, Virgil? That really you? Damn, you look different. Bigger. It's been, like, I don't know, maybe twenty years since I saw
you."

I kept my eye on the dog, who was quiet now, but still watching me. "I know. Long time."

He stayed on the porch and didn't ask me inside. "So, uh, what are you doing here? I mean, how'd you know where I lived?"

"Don't mean to bother you," I said. "Thing is, I was talking to Janeen Turning Heart today."

His face darkened. "That bitch."

I felt my anger start to rise up like a red wave. "Hey, I know you two had a thing. Not my business. But she tells me that you got her minivan. That true?"

He looked down the block, both directions. "She here?"

"No," I said. "It's just me."

"Huh. So, where is she?"

I moved closer to the house. "That's not important. I just want to get her ride back."

He took a step back. "It's my goddamn car. I bought and paid for it. Don't know what horseshit she told you, but it's mine."

I figured he'd say something like this. "I don't want to get involved in any beef between you two. She tells me it's hers and I got to believe her. How about I just take the minivan back and you guys can work it out on your own?"

He bent down and unhooked the dog's chain, then looped it around his hand. "Yo, that skooch did nothing but whine and complain for three months. I figure she owes me about a grand for the shit I put up with. You talk to her, tell her she can kiss my ass. How 'bout that?"

So it was going to be like this. "Chunky, where's the minivan? Tell me now or we're gonna have a problem. I get the Caravan back, it's all good. Best offer I can give you."

"Here's my offer," he said, smirking. "Get the fuck out of here or I'll sic Diesel on you. You don't want to mess with this guy. Tear you up."

He yanked the dog's chain, tapped it in the face, and pointed at me. The dog was at full attention now, staring and growling. Its short tail was rigid and sticking straight up. I could see that the dog's face was scarred, and its ears were mangled. Diesel was a fighting dog.

Chunky must be one of the shitbags who entered their dogs in these matches. I'd never been to one, but I'd heard about them. The fact that Diesel was still alive meant that he'd won in his fights, because they'd shoot the loser, if it managed to survive. This crap sickened me. In the past, the Lakota people valued the sunka, using them to serve as guards against intruders and even assist in ceremonies. Now, assholes like Chunky used dogs for sport.

I didn't want to harm the animal, but I knew it could hurt me badly, even kill me. I looked at the dog, still growling. The animal wasn't snarling or showing its teeth—it was in fighting mode.

"What's it gonna be?" Chunky said.

Stupidly, I'd come unarmed. Given that I wasn't beating people up anymore, I didn't feel the need to carry. I had a baseball bat in my truck, but it was parked two blocks down.

The only play I had was to walk away.

"All right, you win," I said, and took off my jean jacket. "Just let me grab a smoke."

"That's what I thought." He sneered at me. "Take off, homes."

I fumbled in the pockets of my jacket, looking for my cigarettes. "You got a light?"

"Eat shit," he said, and turned away.

"One more thing."

He turned back and looked at me. "What?"

"Fuck you and your goddamn dog." I opened my jacket, leaned over, and quickly wrapped it around the dog's head so he couldn't see, and then I lifted its hind legs in the air so it couldn't move. He started squirming and I fell on him, using all of my 275 pounds on the dog's torso to break its ribs. It started whimpering and yelping, and I moved away quickly in case he got up, but the dog stayed on its side.

"What the fuck, man! What'd you do to him?" Chunky started moving over to the dog, but I got behind him and pushed him face down. I grabbed his right arm and twisted it, then put my knee on his back.

"Get off!" he shouted.

I increased the pressure until he stopped moving.

"All right, dude," I said. "You gonna give me any shit if I let you up?"

He grunted and mumbled something.

"I'll ask you again. You gonna be cool?" I ground my knee into his shoulder blade.

"Yes!" he shouted.

I let go of his arm, slowly stood up and moved back a step. I glanced over at Diesel. The dog watched me but was no longer in attack mode—it was lying on its side and trembling. Chunky sat up and stretched his arms and his neck.

"You'll be all right," I said. "But you better take that dog to the vet—the one in Valentine. That Toyota yours?"

He nodded.

"Take him today. If I find out you put that dog down, I'll kick your ass for real. You hear me?"

He stayed quiet then nodded again.

"Okay, let's get back to it. You got Janeen's minivan?"

He glared at me. "Yeah, but I paid for half of it. She gonna give me my paper back?"

"I told you, you guys work that out. I don't give a damn who paid what—she needs that ride for baby stuff."

He turned his head to the side. "Wait, what?"

"I said, she needs her car for baby stuff—you know, diapers, formula, all that."

His mouth dropped open in surprise. "Baby?"

No, it couldn't be. He didn't know about little Robbie?

"Uh, have you been out to Janeen's place in a while?"

He shook his head. "Not since early last year. I mean, I went out there to take the Dodge, but I didn't go inside, you know?"

I stood still for a minute, trying to figure out what to do. This dipshit had stolen Janeen's car, then threatened me with his dog. I didn't owe him anything, right?

But then a memory flashed into my head. When I was just eight years old, Rob Turning Heart was already my best friend, and he got sick. Really sick. He was coughing up blood and unable to get out of bed for over a month. I'd talked to him on the phone, and he'd asked me to come over to his house because he was lonely. But I didn't go. I was scared. Scared that I'd get sick too, and scared that I wouldn't know what to say or how to act around him. I never did go to visit him when he was ill. He got better, slowly, and finally came back to school. When he first returned, I was embarrassed and tried to pretend like nothing had happened. But after school, Rob walked home with me and told me it was okay I hadn't come over. He said he understood. And I started crying then. Crying for my cowardice and for Rob's compassion. And I was happy I hadn't lost my friend, my blood brother.

I looked over at Chunky White Eyes. He looked scared, like he'd entered some new, unfamiliar territory, a land where he didn't speak the language or know the customs.

I sighed. "Come on. Let's take a ride out to Janeen's place. You can put the dog in the back of my truck—we'll go to the vet afterwards."

Lycia

FROM *The Colorado Review*

FOR NEARLY THE ENTIRETY OF MY LIFE, my father was the Turkish ambassador to the Russian Federation. It was a position that gave him access to certain luxuries, most of which I, my siblings, and my mother enjoyed immensely. We moved with the seasons of his assignment between three houses, each of which had no fewer than nine cats and two servants. He bought my mother beautiful clothes, fine jewelry, the highest-caliber arak for their anniversaries. My siblings and I attended international schools where the ripple effects of my father's political decisions had no bearing on our existences and where we were certain never to interact with the class of people upon which they did. I never once thought of my father, who was kind and intelligent and not like the coked-up, egotistical, hypocritical new-money fathers of my schoolmates, as a man who would exploit his status. And perhaps it's not fair to say he did. I suppose it's more accurate to say that he exploited his privileges as a veteran when, four days after my brother's death, he went to the military morgue and stole my brother's corpse.

"How? How possibly?" My mother in her mourning clothes on the phone.

"Mechanical failure, Mom." My sister from the dining room, her infant son and my mother's oldest cat in her lap. "It happens all the time. They just don't release the documents." My sister, who couldn't see the newness of the shock on my mother's face, believed her to still be asking about the details of my brother Berat's death.

"That's impossible." My mother, again, one hand gripping the phone so tightly the screen threatened to crack, one hand waving *shush shush* as she approached all of us in the living room. "My husband is in his seventies!"

He was seventy-six, a number of no significance except to explain how preposterous it was that he had, as my mother, an army functionary, and several morgue attendants would soon explain, simply picked up my brother's corpse, walked out the door, and buckled them both into his new Mercedes—a retirement gift from the president the year before—before driving away into the dawn.

"Look, here," an attendant with a CCTV feed on a tablet said when we arrived at the morgue, showing us the crime once, twice, three times. "It's undeniable."

My mother, sister, and I did not deny. We watched the loop. My generous, hardworking father walked with his head high. Before he had been a diplomat, he had been a soldier. He was a credit to our nation, a credit to our army. Why shouldn't he have walked so proudly through that empty hallway? Simply because he was supporting my dead brother, whose disfigured head lolled on his shoulders and whose bare feet, not yet cleaned, dragged?

"Where did he go?" the attendant asked. And then, in the stilted way of men who are not usually tasked with being polite and must abruptly be so, "Why would he do this?"

If we had had any answers, we would have given them. If we had had any answers, we would not still have questions.

It was perhaps less surprising upon reflection. After retiring, our father became odd. He fretted, he stopped eating meat, he shaved his head and began dressing only in traditional clothes—as though he intended to make each visit to the grocers a cultural exchange. He forced my sister to join him on an excursion to his former outpost in Moscow, where he simply informed his successor that he would be taking all the cats, thank you. He drove the full twenty-five hours back to our permanent residence—stopping only when the car was forced to, sleeping on the ferry across the Black Sea while my sister remained awake, as she tells it, trying to soothe twelve anxious animals who my father insisted not be caged and who all urinated at least once in the backseat during the journey.

My mother was unconcerned. He was adjusting, she explained. Men who work for all their lives struggle in retirement, even when that retirement is comfortable. She assured me that he was normal, otherwise. Yes, yes, he had collected several additional strays, but cats had always been important to our family, and my sister, a veterinarian, lived at the family home with her surgeon husband and their baby.

Perhaps, my mother suggested, I ought to mind my business or move back home and find a nice husband of my own, if I was so worried. I told her, as I always did, that she ought to pray that I stay busy in New York instead. When she suggested that my father would pray with her, I told her I found that strange, that my father had never been overtly religious before. She brushed me aside. "Men become religious in their old age," she said. "They see themselves in the Prophet."

I remained unconvinced, apparently the only one concerned. Weekly, I called my father on his office line, which he had always kept separate from the rest of the house. I would pace around the gated basketball courts across the street from my office, hoping for clarity and receiving only increasingly cryptic suggestions of a newfound spirituality, a new appreciation for life, a new commitment to repentance. Repentance for what, I would press, and my father would say that dinner was on the table and part of his appreciation for life was appreciation for my mother's cooking. Repentance for what? Our family's was a show-faith. My mother, sister, and I covered our hair for the same reason my father kept a prayer rug in his office. Merely a professional obligation to the idea of God. For what did any of us have to repent?

Many parts of my father's career were classified, and much of his early life was unknown even to us, his children. What, then, could he repent for, I wondered. I rode the train each morning, imagining him as a boy. I could see him, his dark hair and dark eyes, his studious expression as he wrote Arabic, Cyrillic, Latin in a tidy child's script. He wore a school uniform, carried his books in a leather bag, deferred. He was incapable of evil, free of malice. He was simply my father, but small. Were these visions the truth? I don't know. They bore elements of truth, or some truth, surely, and I was forced to subsist on those. My sister refused to help me search, and my brother was away at Special Forces training and then he was dead.

*

How did my father find God? After years of personal atheism and public devotion, did he simply turn over the pillow on which he kneeled and discover God, resting amidst the fabric—a coin, a whisker, a surprise to delight? Did he comb my mother's hair and see God in the strands she kept covered in public? Did he receive his retirement medals and, upon opening the box, discover God was there too, nestled in the fabric keeping the awards for his dedication safe? Or was it perhaps the opposite? Had my father simply given in, as my mother suggested, to his old age? Was he nothing more than a hare in the mouth of God-fox? Did he kick, kick, kick until giving up, until he was carried away?

While he was struggling, the jaws of God unbreakable, did my father think of me? Of my sister? Of my brother? Did he lie awake at night and watch the moon through the window in the bedroom of our house while my mother slept beside him, her hair as silver as the light, and contemplate my life as I contemplated his when I watched the moon over the skyline of Queens, knowing the sun was beginning to rise over the strait halfway across the world? Did he sense the future, the way that I did, that it was a year destined to end in tragedy? Why else would God have shown himself?

My engagement had collapsed. My position as a documents translator at the UN seemed futile, and the UN itself seemed nothing more than a global hallucination for all the good it could do on the ground. Turkey was back at war. My roommate had announced her intention of returning to France to avoid enduring another nuclear summer in New York. My father had become possessed.

The odder my father became, the less I slept, the more I drafted emails to my supervisor that always began *Dear Sir* with the highest level of politeness and did not send them. *Dear Sir, my father has had an accident. Dear Sir, my father has become unwell. Dear Sir, my most respected father, Elazig Bayraktar, whom you may know as a statesman, has begun to experience the ill effects of his old age.* Nothing explained. Each draft deleted, I despaired. It was too much for an email. There was no magic combination of words, no code that could be unlocked.

Ultimately my email was simple. *Dear Sir, my brother has been killed in Turkey, and I need to take two weeks to attend the funeral.* I was granted three. I was so grateful, I wept.

*

We had no recourse, no explanation, no leads. I had been back in Turkey for seventy-two hours, my brother had been dead for ninety-six, and we had no clues as to how long my father had been planning his heist. Upon returning from the morgue, we tore apart my father's office. What were we expecting to find? A note? My mother seemed to expect a written statement, a draft of a speech worked over in the meticulous way my father left all drafts—highlighted in neon blue, checkmarked in green felt-tip ink until it could be spoken in a way that mirrored song. My sister, more practical, opening the phone he'd left on his desk, the laptop abandoned in his reading chair, found nothing. He had pushed everything back to factory settings, and while my brother-in-law insisted there could be a fix, that he could call a friend who worked at a start-up and who knew everything there is to know about this cloud storage shit, I knew the futility before the suggestion was even made. Had my father been awarded medals in espionage for incompetence?

My mother fell to tears in my father's reading chair. Her sobs were enough to inspire curiosity, and within minutes of draping herself in her despair, my mother was also draped in cats. They came from every open angle: through the doorway that led to the main hall, through the doorway that led to the en suite bathroom, through the doorway just their size built into the sliding glass that separated us from the plaza where they had their own house, which my brother and father had built for them together.

When I looked away, ashamed that I hadn't been the first to try comforting my mother, I saw our first and only clue—on the back of a grocery receipt that had been upended from the garbage—a series of gaping darknesses, a winged figure, a mountain range. My father's art, unmistakable. Beside his drawings, he had written the date of my brother's death, made a clean line to the date of his disappearance.

For all his skills, his seven languages, his adaptable analyses, his charm and cunning, my father couldn't draw. Unbound by sense of proportion or perspective, his fantastical sketches were rabbit-ducks, a source of comedy for my sister and me. *Papa is drawing cats again. No, no, he's drawing elephants. No, no, he's drawing antelope. No, no, he's drawing you! That's what you look like, ugly!* We mocked, carried discarded sheets of public policy through houses protected from their impacts, while our father protested. *What is the greatest art in the world? You think it's Mona Lisa? You fools, you children! The greatest art in the world is a handprint on a cave wall, a handprint!* Was he thinking of those handprints, those lasting impacts, I wondered, careful not to tear the receipt, when he drew the mountains?

I brought the receipt to my sister, who reviewed the evidence, and then grasped my arm, pulling me from my mother. I thought of the tetanus shot I'd been given before returning, the uninterested cruelty of a woman in scrubs. "Why are you showing me these— what are these? *Pussies?* That our father drew?" She stressed the vulgarity between her teeth. We looked uncannily similar. I saw myself in her crooked nose, her uneven brows, her low cheekbones.

We looked nothing like our father, a man whom I couldn't imagine drawing a pussy on a grocery receipt, much less five, much less one beside an angel.

"It's a door, I think. A door in a mountain," I protested, though my sister's words had indeed revealed the shapes as yonic.

My mother languished, holding my nephew and her cats. My sister stepped out into the plaza to have her first cigarette in three years. My brother-in-law called the military police and asked, again, if anyone had seen my father's Mercedes leaving the city, perhaps in one of the commuter lanes, perhaps with a passenger. I took a photograph of the drawing and sent it to a group chat of UN friends comprising my favorite coworker, a friend of a friend I had added out of politeness, a university roommate, and my ex-boyfriend, who had been spared the humiliation of the blocklist only because my brother's death had prevented me from attending to my own needs. Anyone who could place these mountains in the real world, I promised, would get free wine and a very long story when I returned. Immediately a flood of suggestions. None were as crude as my sister's. One was our starting point: *Myra?*

When my mother was asleep, watched over by my brother-in-law, my sister rolled her eyes at my questions. "There was time for you to bond with him before all this, if you had wanted. Stop treating our father like some kind of dementia-ridden freak simply because you didn't care to know him."

She had no answers, only condemnation of my failure as a daughter. It didn't matter to her that we didn't know, with any certainty: where my father was born, if he had siblings, if he had another family somewhere, if he had ever been truly religious before, if he had a favorite café, if he had friends outside of work, why he had never told us any of this.

It was meaningless to my sister that we had nothing but a Wikipedia page that cleanly informed us our father was from Istanbul, attended university in Ankara, served for ten years in Special Forces, and then took the ambassadorship, where he worked until his retirement. We had only the false, the superficial, and my sister was satisfied by this because my sister never needed to think beyond the superficial. She was a girl who had gotten a husband simply by sitting so demurely at a bench in the park between the colleges of Human and Animal Medicine, waiting until a handsome man with a good name came to ask my father for her hand.

"So tell me what you know," I countered. She was silent. She looked at her hands, at her clean nails and shining wedding ring, at the coffee table we sat across, and then up across that birch expanse to the window behind my shoulder, to the wall that surrounded our home, which kept the eyes of outsiders from us. She looked at me and her lips were sealed. I asked, "What did your bond with our father look like? What did you learn because you cared to know?"

"He was responsible for a great deal of suffering. Of course he became religious. You, you're the one in politics. You should know." She put a candied lemon peel into her tea. "Such as, Berat wouldn't have been at training if our father hadn't started a war on his way out of office."

What I knew about politics that I did not tell my sister, then, was that nobody was ever responsible for anything. Blame came and went, bounced from man to man and back again, unsettled and ever-shifting. People suffered and people died and there was no tidy order to it, no finger could stay pointed in one direction for too long. And what I knew about our father's politics that I did not tell my sister, then, was that the however many hundred or thousand or unknown uncounted who died from the petty trade arguments or the immigration squabbles or as a result of his successful request for Russian intervention in the turf war in the East would have died anyway by his estimation because our father was a diplomat, and if his conscience hadn't been strong enough to bear the death of individuals, he wouldn't have represented the nation.

So I told my sister what I knew about politics that I could tell her, which was "It's more complicated than that."

"It's not, Aladet."

"It is. You don't understand international relations."

"So you're a politician of our father's caliber, huh?" My sister shook her head. "You don't understand that Dad was fallible."

Her easy explanations and self-assured tone were an insult. "This wasn't Dad's fault."

As children, my sister and I were so close we were assumed to be twins. So close that we held hands walking to school, so close that we spoke our own language, so close that we were doomed to fall apart. As adults we referred to each other only in formal registers, but my sister became familiar, suddenly, to say, "No. Not entirely, was it? Berat died because our father pushed the army into the mountains. He had the good sense to feel sorry for it. You've been gone long enough, but you might consider your role, here."

Her accusation burned. I had nothing to consider. I knew instinctively, automatically, where I had failed. My brother had failed to enter a foreign university and so, despite his name, despite being so handsome that he had fifteen possible wives at the age of twenty-four, despite our status, he was dead. If he hadn't been a soldier, he might have been anything else. I sat silent as my sister stared me down. It was a moment that I felt, myself, an impulse toward God. The wonderment of my guilt, the fervent wish to have it removed.

My brother was killed due to equipment failure. Equipment failure is a term nonspecific enough to conjure the phantoms of the Soma mine or the Vrasta dam. Equipment failure suggests my brother burst into flame reentering the brilliant blue atmosphere, or melted down into a collection of irradiated particles in the middle of a dark forest. Equipment failure leads to a period of mourning or a series of reforms or, at the very least, an investigation. Equipment failure glamorizes, glorifies, grants freedom from. Equipment failure sees my brother a martyr, his dark eyes so much like my father's, steeled against the inevitability of his death, his soul made good with God before being shown a door made of pure light. A door that leads to a penthouse suite in heaven that we, who will not die so tremendously, will never be granted the keys to.

It says nothing of the mundane. It does not make clear that my brother's neck was broken in one swift collision when the emergency brake of a repurposed Gulf War–era piece of shit Humvee snapped under tension and thousands of pounds rolled backward down a dusty hill where my brother was kneeling to relace his boot. When he heard the noise, he looked up. He began to rise and got only as far as the height of the bumper, which cracked his head open before twisting his C2 vertebrae away from the C3 the way one twists open a particularly sticky container of cranberry juice. The medicinal, unfiltered kind that comes in heavy glass bottles, so bitter it erases every other taste.

"What does *Myra* mean?" My brother-in-law wondered at the message from my ex after my sister and nephew had gone to bed. I was stranded alone in the living room with my sister's husband, a man from the UK who was nothing more than halva. Plain, sweet, soft. "Is it a name?"

Seated on the Anatolian rug, on which I had kissed my first boyfriend (who was also my sister's first boyfriend), I was too aware of the photos of the family. On the bookshelves, between biographies and poetry collections, were the photographs of my sister, Berat, me, and my mother from the time we had entered my father's life until he left ours. "It's an archaeological site." I took my phone back and made the decision not to engage with the message that had followed it: *when are you coming back btw? let's get coffee?*

"So what does it mean?" My brother-in-law had a lisp, a concerned expression. I imagined how it would be, married to him. Did he fuck as gently and stupidly as he spoke, or was he another man when my mother and I weren't looking, one whom my sister liked better? "Did your father have a connection to it?"

Yes, of course, and no, not at all. My father had a connection to every archaeological site in the country. To every building in the country. To every person, to every object, to everything. He was all of us, to some. "I'm not sure."

"He always seemed so together." My brother-in-law reclined on the patched calfskin sofa, stroked the trio of cats who rotated under his hand. "Where could he have gone? Back to Azerbaijan?"

"What the fuck are you talking about?"

My brother-in-law blinked, then his lips twitched into shapes before settling into words. "Wasn't that where he was from? I got the impression . . . He talked about it once. I don't know. It might have been a mission he was talking about. I don't know. I just . . ." He faltered, his tongue limp in his mouth, his eyes wide. "I'm sorry."

Our living room faced the walls, which faced the street, and in the gap between the window and the top of the wall, I could see the haze of the city's night sky. My brother-in-law continued to speak nonsense. I had been afraid that he had somehow learned something, that my father had somehow confided in him, that I had been left out again. But my brother-in-law knew nothing but the geographical details of my father's diplomatic duties, the things my mother knew. Places where my father had been stationed, places where my father had killed, places where my father had been somebody else to somebody else.

"You can drive?" My brother at seventeen, my charge for a holiday, his features midway between the boy with whom I had played trivia games and a man for whom I would mourn. In America, where he cared very little about my graduate program and less still about my boyfriends, where he spoke English with an accent specifically crafted to sound British for fear that a vowel would see him mistaken for foreign in that way that the Brits were not in America, where he evaded passersby on the sidewalk with the posture of a frightened animal and not a wealthy young man considering the prospects of an international university education. "Can we see the big red bridge? What's it called, the Gate? The one from *Pacific Rim.*"

It was fall, the Hudson Valley brilliant in gold and red and reeking of cider and fully accessible by train, and there was my brother, looking out the window of the studio I was so proud to live alone in, watching the neighbor's dog shit on the courtyard square ten stories below us, longing for a vista at least two days away.

"Do you know where California is in relation to us right now, Berat?"

"Sure I know, but can we? You can drive, right?"

A dozen reasons to say no, a schedule I could have reminded him of, the carefully constructed college tours I was to ensure he attended, the handpicked selection of pick-your-own orchards, the reservations I'd made for a series of dinners he had so far eaten with neither complaint nor enthusiasm.

At that point, I had been in America for six years. The way my father had been taken in by Moscow, I was taken in by New York.

My father would sometimes visit, often for work, but it was understood, to me at least, that I was like him. That I was doing important work, that I was the next in the family to take up the mantle of cosmopolitan and international, and that I was not expected to return to Turkey until I was offered a job that made it worthwhile. My brother had been eleven years old when I left, and until that winter when he visited, I had been only peripherally asked to attend to him. Mostly to check his English projects.

So I said, "Yes, I can drive. Can you get Dad to send you around $500? For renting a car." I knew he could. The money appeared in my brother's account ten minutes later. I made the arrangements; my brother made the playlist.

At each stop, each monument, each park, all the way until the Golden Gate itself, my brother would laugh and ask, "So, really just like you see in the movies, huh?" I had to admit yes. And so America, in the end, failed to impress him. I failed to make it impressive. My brother had already seen the best of the country from thousands of miles away; what could his distant older sister do to supplement its majesty?

The only time my father had ever raised his voice to me, over the phone while I sat numbly in Grand Central Station waiting for the next train to Westchester to visit the sweet family of a boy who would soon after dump me via text, was to say, "What do you think your brother is going to do now? Go to school in England? In Moscow? You stupid girl, only an American school would take him, the way his marks stand now, and you didn't try at all."

"Send him back." A train pulled into the platform, a beam of light swallowed into the whispering, crackling fluorescents under which I could see my skin had become dry again, my knuckles bloodied. "Send him back and I'll explain. I'm sorry, Papa."

"He has a schedule, I have a schedule, you, I assume, have a schedule as well. There's going to be no doing this over, Aladet. I'll handle your brother." He hung up, leaving me to fight my way to the center of a northbound MTA, unsure if I had been consoled or threatened.

The rental car had been a hideous green, the traffic nightmarish, the hotels suspicious of our IDs, the music a three-hour, hand-curated soundtrack full of our favorite bands—the Smiths, the Pretenders, David Bowie—that played on shuffle fourteen and a half times over thousands of miles, the fact of my brother's curated American experience forgotten, replaced with his hand out the open window at eighty miles an hour across the flat, dry expanse of the plains, the swell and crest of the mountains, and his face an impassive smile that I know now had not revealed anything about his true feelings, which would remain forever a mystery to me, too far away in time to know him as anything but my little brother, but which I thought of as I crossed the Osmangazi Bridge, east out of Istanbul in my mother's car, which I had borrowed without her knowledge after the rest of my family had gone to bed, desperate to find his corpse.

The Myra necropolis at noon, every darkened door a missing tooth in the yawning face of the mountains. Tourists posing for panoramic photos, guides smoking in ruin shadow not minding the ropes. Ancient ground on which I parked my mother's car and placed my feet, unsteady with adrenaline. "Tell me, does this look familiar?" I asked the first man in a uniform I could reach.

Wild eyebrows touching, lips turning down, his hand nearly touched my shoulder before he stopped himself. "Are you all right, Miss?"

"Does this look familiar?" My father's art was somehow more grotesquely amateur in daylight. Lines began and ended with no clear pattern, edges wobbled outward, inward, upward, away. The angel warped, wings wounded by imprecision.

"Umm . . ." He looked from me to my father's message. "I think this is more likely to be in Fethiye. You see the stairs in this one?"

Did I? I looked at the illustration again and they appeared. No longer did the angel stand on a simple series of lines but rather on stairs that propelled it toward the door. "Thank you." Fethiye was more than an hour away. I folded the receipt up once more and met the eyes of the man whose eyes searched me. "By the way, have you or any of your colleagues seen a man in a Mercedes recently? He would be wearing an army uniform, shaved head, around eighty years old."

"No. I haven't heard anything of the sort. Why?"

I left him and headed back up the coast around each twist in the scrubby hills that tumbled lazily to the sea, another now with only mystery. In Fethiye, I passed between the ceramic-tile-roofed houses that hunkered warmly into the ground and the elevated ancient sarcophagi around which low fences and tall flowers proudly announced their historic value. The sun was skewed, afternoon announcing itself. Abandoning the car out front of the McDonald's on the boulevard, I hiked in the house slippers I hadn't thought to change out of when I began my journey. Feral cats sunned themselves on the embankment, families laughed together, a young couple kissed for the back camera of the latest iPhone, and above them all, in the hills on which olive trees grew twisted and wild, the tombs were visible.

Four columns supported the intricate facade, the cliff chiseled in clean lines, the sun falling on the faded stone; I stood where the angel stood on the stairs that would carry me to the enormous door. There was a world around me, I knew, but as I began to climb, that world peeled away. Layer by layer, I was stripped. Fethiye fell to silence, the wind snatched the lingering scent of my mother's perfume, my body became nothing. I moved independent of myself, my thirst forgotten, my burning hunger burnt out, my exhaustion nothing more than a gentle rocking in my vision as I climbed and climbed and climbed, hand over hand, foot over foot, foot over hand, hand over foot, up up up to the doorway that made me a child again, listening anxiously for the sound of my father's laughter on the other side. In this door was a mousehole for a mouse of my size. One inch at a time, I reached through. Nail, finger, hand, arm, shoulder, foot, shin, thigh, until the rest of me could no longer linger in the safety of the light.

Had I imagined I would see them, truly? Had I imagined they would be serene? Had I imagined I would find my father washing my brother's corpse, laying the shroud on his beautiful, broken face? Had I imagined there would be another door, a darker door, a blacker blackness, through which they had passed and I might follow? Had I imagined that they would be waiting for me, sitting on the cerulean cushions of my favorite café, drinking coffee from a gold glass carafe, laughing at a joke I had just missed, ready to embrace me, to forgive me? *Aladet, you've made it, just in time.*

I had. I had. I had.

And when my eyes adjusted to the tomb's interior, to the graffiti that marred the marble stretching up to the ceiling, where a nest of swallows chirped in surprise at my intrusion, when my body pulled back into itself and saw that it was alone in a vacant, ancient grave, I wept. I wept until I could no longer stand, no longer kneel, no longer breathe, no longer think. I wept until a woman of nondescript middle age in a black headscarf appeared, and then I stopped weeping, only to marvel, thinking, for one blissful moment, that my tears had turned to prayers and that those prayers had been answered, that I had been sent a messenger and could apologize.

"Miss, you need to go home now." The woman brandished a flashlight as though she were a gangster with a baseball bat. "The Amyntas Tomb closed at 19:30."

"I was supposed to meet someone. Have you by chance seen two men, one old, one young, in a Mercedes here recently?"

"No. How would a Mercedes get up here anyway?" She laughed, amused at her own joke, willfully oblivious to my pain. She closed her eyes, pointed to the door as though to say, *You know the way out,* and I wanted to say I didn't, I couldn't, I never had.

And in the end, what happened to my brother? What happened to my father? None of us ever heard. The military police searched for three weeks through traffic footage, looking for my father's plate, and then called the hunt off. The condolence cards came in waves from Ankara, Baku, Damascus, Moscow, Saint Petersburg, New York City, Paris, Geneva, until the ocean of my father's old friends dried up and there were no more letters to be sent to my mother, who passed away the next year in her sleep and became the first body to fill the family plot.

My father likely died, of course. Whether he drove his car off a cliff somewhere along the Riviera or crashed it into a boulder in an uninhabited corner of Anatolia, whether he drank poison in the wilderness, where he had laid my brother to rest, whether he shot himself with the ceremonial pistol given to my brother's corpse, whether his body simply gave out as he carried another—I am under no illusions of a positive outcome for a septuagenarian suffering a psychotic episode, nor for a dead man.

But I kept the illustration, the angel, the doors. I returned to New York. I returned to my apartment and my roommate and my friends and my ex. I returned to my useless work translating reports on transnational drug trade and sex slavery and murder and every other imaginable, unsolvable violence that generated forms and figures and hinted only distantly at the human beings left miserable, wondering, or worse, and that kept me secure in my job the same way it had kept my father.

I woke up each morning and rode across Queens into Manhattan, where I imagined my father, where I imagine him still, standing with my brother in the mouth of that great tomb, waiting. I see them, tiny similar silhouettes in a towering blackness lit in violent white as though by a train emerging from a dark tunnel as the angel ascends—a lightness that makes everything else light, that lifts first my brother's limp body, birdlike in grace, and rights his head on his shoulders, turns his face to God, then takes my father's outstretched hand and clasps it tightly in the greeting of a politician: *An honor to meet you, Ambassador Byraktar.* I see them levitating, leaving. I see the faintest traces of them shimmering in the air—the sound of my brother's easy laughter, the feeling of my father's proudest hug—and then the angel raises its fist, and the sun burns all evidence of them away and I arrive too late.

MATTHEW WILSON

Thank You for Your Service

FROM *Alfred Hitchcock's Mystery Magazine*

ODELL SAID, "At the Home Depot. Out there in Salinas. A little
Mexican fella. I said, 'You see that sign right there.' I'm pointing
at it. I said, 'You see, right there. Says FOR U.S. ARMY VETERAN.'
This was in the parking lot, you know, reserved spots. There was
another one right next to it said FOR U.S. NAVY VETERAN."

"I bet that one was painted battleship gray."

Odell said, "One more down from it was one said FOR U.S. AIR
FORCE VETERAN."

"I bet that one had carpeting."

"Wall to wall . . . and cable, and a La-Z-Boy recliner."

"Air Force. Bunch of candy-asses."

Odell said, "Anyway, I said, 'You don't look like no army veteran
to me. What rank was you? What was your MOS?' The fella said,
'*No inglés. No inglés.*'"

"You should have filmed him. Like they do on the TV."

"What do you mean?"

"Saw it on one of them morning shows. Real veterans catching
fakes on camera. A fella says he's a veteran, and he's getting special treatment. Tickets to ball games, free drinks, upgrades, and
discounts. That sort of thing. The real vets catch the imposters and
put them to shame right there on TV in front of a million people."

Kyle, the young guy, said, "It's called 'stolen valor.' They got it
all over YouTube. Whole channels of it."

They all turned to look at Kyle. He didn't talk much, and when
he did, he didn't make a lot of sense.

Odell said, "How am I gonna go around filming this guy. I don't walk around carrying a video camera."

Kyle said, "Right there on your phone. You didn't know you had a camera on your phone?"

Odell pulled out his Motorola flip phone. He opened it up and said, "I don't see no button for a camera." The icons too small for Odell's old eyes.

"Here, let me see it."

Odell handed the phone to Kyle. Kyle, shoulder to shoulder with Odell, held the camera out in front of them, pushed the tiny button with the camera icon, navigated the menu to turn the camera around, and then pushed the big square button and a flash went off. Odell had to wait for his eyes to go back to normal, but then he looked and there on the little screen was his mug right next to that young fella's, the one called Kyle, the one not quite right in his head.

"Selfie," Kyle said. "That's what they call it."

Kyle began hanging around the VFW about the time his girlfriend started talking about taking a break. A little blue building with a flagpole out front in Marina, California, ten miles north of Monterey. Marina was full of retired guys like Odell, Vietnam-era men who bought up cheap tract homes, three-bedroom snout houses with ice plants and rock gardens. Marina, it hugged up against Fort Ord, so it made sense the place was full of retired military. Even after Fort Ord shut down in the drawdown of the nineties, Marina was still full of these men, except now besides military pensions, they drew Social Security and Medicare too. And at their age they were all equity. Houses they bought for thirty grand in the seventies listed now for six hundred. But getting their hands on that money was another thing. They had to die first, and then their widows would outlast them by five, ten years.

Young guys like Kyle, not so many of them at the little blue VFW. Kyle had done two tours in Iraq and now worked security at the Walmart Supercenter, down there off of Reservation Road, right before you get to the Coast Highway. He rented a one-bedroom in a complex that looked like a motel, two stories of doors facing a parking lot, a fog-rusted railing stretching across the second. He used to share the one-bedroom with Brittany, but she moved out for "a break." She said it like that, "a break," like they weren't quite together, weren't quite broken up. Both of them born in the eighties and not getting any younger. Now he paid the whole rent, not just half, and money was tight.

Odell's story about the Mexican in Salinas, that gave Kyle the idea of how he could pick up a little extra in his spare time. He read online how you could make money posting videos on YouTube. Some said a dollar for every thousand views, some said five. Ten thousand views, well that was at least a hundred bucks, and he saw plenty of videos with twenty, thirty, fifty thousand views—he could do that. And maybe Brittany would come back home. With the extra money he could take her out to nice places down in Monterey, seafood on the wharf, maybe shopping in Carmel.

After he heard Odell's story at the VFW, Kyle went back to his apartment and watched a bunch of videos on his laptop. The connection was slow, but what could he do? He wanted to complain, but he piggybacked his Internet off a neighbor, so complaining about something that was free wasn't an option. He typed "stolen valor" into the search box and stayed up half the night watching one after the other. Losing sleep, that's what he was doing, but ever since Iraq he didn't sleep much at night anyway.

He watched a bald-headed fifty-something in Marine dress blues attending a high school graduation. Haphazard ribbons scattered all over his chest like pin the tail on the donkey. No way this guy was a Marine. Behind the camera a voice berates him, telling him he is going to be big star now, but not in a good way. A million and a half views. Kyle did the math and liked the numbers.

In other videos, there were out-of-shape young men wearing Ranger and Airborne tabs on the wrong sleeves. Easy giveaways. The real men who had earned these tabs would never make this mistake. Not after hard landing from low-altitude jumps out of C-130s, the static line snapping like a dog chain. Not after humping hundred-pound rucks in the Fort Benning summer haze. Men who could bust out a hundred perfect push-ups in two minutes, run two miles in eleven minutes—these were the kinds of men who earned these tabs, and they knew which sleeve they belonged on. The guys in the videos, they looked like they couldn't make a recreational badminton team. Kyle watched as the sane ones turned tail once confronted, scurrying away from the camera in panic, while the less stable insisted on their authenticity, spouting

off three, four, seven deployments, the names of phony dead comrades, pulling up shirts to display appendix scars as war wounds.
Each of these videos, Kyle imagined, was worth something, view
after view, after view. Eleven thousand views for one, twenty-two
grand for another. Kyle added up the money in his head.

Many of the fakes stumbled on the first question: "What was
your MOS?" Military Occupational Status. In the service, every job
had a code and no one ever forgot their code. An infantryman
was 11B, called out with pride like this: *Eleven-Bravo*. A cavalry
scout was 19-Delta. An air traffic controller was 15-Quebec. An in-
terpreter was 9-Lima. Kyle watched a man on a street in Florida
wearing a full combat uniform. Where his name should appear
in bold capital letters he has VETERAN instead. He is selling tiny
U.S. flags for $5 donations to some bogus charity. The camera ap-
proaches him, the voice behind the camera saying, "Thank you
for your service." But then the question comes straight after: "So
what was your MOS?" And the fraud answers, "Staff Sergeant." The
voice says, "No, no, that's your rank, dude. What's your MOS? You
know what an MOS is, don't you?" And it is already too late for the
fake. But Kyle likes the video. There are 65,000 views, and Kyle is
thinking, that's a lot of $5 flags.

These are ambush interviews of men who never had to face a
real ambush. Old men who never walked a single trail in the Me-
kong or the Iron Triangle, never stalked by Charlie Cong in his
tire sandals. Younger men who never rode Humvees down rutted
Iraqi lanes, the RPG or IED never out there waiting to take them.

Three in the morning and Kyle was still up clicking on videos.
He closed his laptop and lay down, hoping for three hours of
sleep. He was due for his shift at Walmart at seven A.M. Three
hours, that would be a nice stretch, more than what he was used
to. And maybe he would have good dreams, of the money he was
going to make, and of Brittany, and the good times they would
have once the dollars rolled in.

First he drove around to all the corners where men with cardboard
signs lingered. Signs saying, PLEASE HELP. HOMELESS VET. GOD
BLESS. Men with sun-weathered faces and gaps where teeth used
to be. They carried little dirty rucksacks, some had mangy dogs by
their sides, some small collections of granola bars or cans of Prin-
gles potato chips drivers had offered instead of money. Kyle had

heard the chatter among the Walmart crew, about how these men were all scams, probably making more dollar by dollar on the corner than they all did at minimum wage. And paying no taxes, not like them, with the FICA and the Social Security, and before long what was left to take home for the rent and the ramen noodles.

Kyle picked a man just down the Coast Highway in Seaside for his first video. Had to give him credit for his choice of location, a big four-way stop on Fremont Boulevard feeding cars from the Edgewater Shopping Center back onto the highway going both ways. People who had just loaded up at Costco or Target, maybe lunched at Chipotle or Panera, stopped for a beverage at Starbucks or Jamba Juice, these were people with singles and coins at the ready, moving past in their Hondas and Toyotas like an infusion of chump change.

The man with the sign, he wore a Woodland camo field jacket, a scruffy Giants cap, jeans faded dirt gray, a pair of old leather hightops, one toe sporting wraparound duct tape. Kyle circled around him and then parked two blocks away. He pulled out his phone, checked the battery life before hitting Record a block before he reached the guy. He began narrating the way he'd seen it done on so many of the videos on YouTube.

"Just minded my own business coming back from the Starbucks and I spot this dude on the corner. I'm thinking something's fishy about this so-called vet. Me, I did two tours in Iraq, and damned if I'm gonna have anybody disrespecting the uniform on my block."

That was good, he thought, like the vet who confronted the fake in Florida with the $5 flags. Sell it with indignation, that's what you had to do. Coming up to the man now, Kyle could see the salt-and-pepper whiskers on him, the man looking up to Kyle, not used to someone on foot at this busy intersection.

Kyle said, "Afternoon, mister. Just want to say thank you for your service."

The man not sure what to do, looking at the phone in Kyle's hand hanging between them. "Well . . . you're welcome."

Kyle paused, taking a moment to look at the field jacket. There were unit insignia on each sleeve, on the left the 1st CAV, a triangle pointing down with a black band running diagonal and a horse's head in the corner. Left sleeve, that was reserved for former wartime units, a way for a soldier to show he had been to war, that he hadn't been sitting in some office stateside the whole time.

"You were with the 1st CAV?"

"That's right."

"Out of where?"

"Out of where? Out of Fort Hood."

"And you fought in what, Vietnam?"

A Ford Explorer pulled up. The window buzzed down and an arm shot out dangling a dollar bill. The man in the field jacket took it and said thanks. A voice from the vehicle said "God Bless" before the window buzzed back up and the Ford accelerated toward the on-ramp.

"Vietnam? No, I ain't that old. Gulf War. Desert Storm."

Kyle looked at the name tape, there stitched over the right breast pocket. CONWAY. Kyle said, "That your name there?"

The man looked down at himself and then said, "That's right."

"I don't see no rank insignia. What rank were you?"

"E-five."

"So it's Sergeant Conway?"

"That's right."

This video, it wasn't going the way Kyle had planned it. All the ones with thousands of views, they had drama, confrontation, unbelievable lies and denials. This guy wasn't giving Kyle any of that.

Kyle said, "What was your MOS?"

"I was 19-Kilo. Armor crewman. I loaded shells on an M1 Abrams."

"How come you're wearing Woodland? Desert Storm, that was Desert cammies, wasn't it?"

"Yeah, I had those. Ugly things, had them little chocolate chips all over them. But you know how quick that war was. We got back to Hood and it was back to Woodland. This is what I was wearing when I got out."

"And when was that?" Kyle desperate now to trip him up in a lie, something he could use to ratchet up the drama, make his video go viral.

"Ninety-four. During the big drawdown. Back when they closed this place up." He was pointing his thumb over his shoulder in the direction of Fort Ord. "Back then they'd find any excuse to discharge a man. I got a DUI and that was all she wrote."

Nowhere to go, Kyle took one last crack at catching a lie. "So you were at Hood with 1st CAV. How come you're here on the coast? Fort Ord, that was what? Infantry, wasn't it?"

"I came back here. I lived here as a kid. My old man was army. We lived right over there in family housing, Hayes Park, on Okinawa Road. Had some friends back then in Seaside, thought I'd check them out, that's why I came out. But they're long gone now."

As a teenager, Kyle had made friends at school with kids from Hayes Park, and he had cruised through it a few times in his old Datsun. Hayes was one of three family housing areas, two of them closed now, but Hayes still opened for personnel attending the Defense Language Institute, DLI, in Monterey. Hayes was built after the Second World War, and Kyle remembered how most of the streets were named after great battles. Okinawa, Luzon, Anzio, Normandy. Maybe in the future, Kyle thought, there would be streets named Fallujah, Mosul, Ramadi.

Kyle lowered his camera but forgot to stop recording, so the last half-minute of this first attempt was only audio of him talking, with a crooked image of the sidewalk. Kyle reached into his pocket and pulled some bills he kept there scrunched up in a mess. He peeled a five out of the mess and handed it to the man with the sign.

On the video you can hear Kyle's voice. "Here you go, buddy. I hope you meet some better times."

And the man responding. "Thank you and God Bless."

The first attempt and Kyle was moving backwards. Five dollars down. That wasn't how it was supposed to be. He was supposed to be making money. But he got better at it.

He went back and watched more of the most popular stolen valor videos. He noticed how quick talking the men behind the cameras were, how the fakes got tripped up on barrages of questions. Kyle, he couldn't talk that fast on his feet. He once thought of himself as a rapid-fire thinker, but since coming home he found his tongue often tied, the words not coming out right away, his brain processing language like slow-loading video stream, the little spinner in the middle turning and turning and testing his patience. To compensate, Kyle put a list of the best questions on an index card he could pull out when his mouth failed to follow his brain's orders.

There were more vets idling on corners and by overpasses, and about half of them didn't know the difference between an MOS and a CO, between a Battalion and a Brigade. They were your everyday hobos who put VET on their signs to drum up sympathy.

The other half were more like the Desert Storm vet in Seaside—the real things with hard luck stories. For these, Kyle began carrying a roll of single dollar bills because he couldn't afford the five every time.

He got the idea to hit up tourist spots, so he went to Fisherman's Wharf in Monterey and shot one of his better videos there. In the video you see the camera come up on a skinny Asian guy. He's maybe thirty and he's styled up with a ponytail, goatee whiskers coming off his chin. A bandana wraps around his head and over a T-shirt he's wearing a black leather vest. Emblazoned on the back across the shoulders you can see the block letters: SEMPER FI. Under that the Marine Corps seal—a bird on a globe, an anchor, and a rope. Kyle turns the camera around and you can see an American flag and U.S. MARINE CORPS over the left breast pocket. Kyle shoots off his index card questions and the man stumbles on every one, more in shock it seems than ignorance. You can see tourists with ice cream cones and cotton candy walking by in the background, turning their heads at the spectacle but still moving along. The video ends with the fake Marine pushing at the camera, the picture rattling, and Kyle's voice saying, "Don't you touch my phone, dude! Don't you touch my phone!"

At Cannery Row, Kyle filmed a grandpa in a red golf shirt, the shirt straining at his enormous beer belly. In the video the grandpa is wearing a baseball cap with U.S. ARMY arching across the front. Under that you can see a silver eagle resting on a branch, wings spread, a crest centered at the chest. This is the insignia for what Kyle learned to call a "full bird." The camera approaches and you can hear Kyle's voice, saying, "Excuse me, sir. I was in the service too."

The grandpa looks surprised and then seems to realize it is his hat that has set off this encounter. There are two young teens with him and they seem confused by Kyle holding his phone up to their grandpa. "You mind if I call you colonel," Kyle says, and the grandpa says, "What?" touching a finger to his ear. "Colonel," Kyle says, "Should I call you colonel, sir?" The grandpa shrugs, not comprehending, and says, "If you want to, I guess." And now Kyle is on him, like a man at a pole who's got the bite, tugging and reeling at the catch. He barks at the grandpa, about sporting the full bird, and doesn't he know what the bird means, the full bird *colonel?* And why wouldn't he like to be called colonel? Even in retirement it's a habit of the men of such rank. The grandpa shrugs some more and one of the kids, the granddaughter, tugs at his sleeve, trying to move him along. Kyle throws out the MOS question, the rank question—"You're a full bird colonel, don't you know that's an O-six?"—the unit question, the deployment question. The grandpa mumbles inaudible answers as his shoulder turns away, both of the grandchildren now—a boy and a girl—are helping him along. We hear Kyle's voice, he is calling out—about valor and disgrace and buddies who died—and then the image streaks to the sky and abruptly ends.

Once at the 7-Eleven off of Reservation Road, Kyle happened on a man wearing ACUs. This is the Army Combat Uniform, with camouflage like digitized pixels—it became the standard issue not long before Kyle's discharge. This man, he wasn't quite right, his face scruffy and out of compliance with army grooming standards. Kyle pulled out his phone, this time discreetly. In the video, the man holds a bag of Spicy Cheetos and a can of Monster Energy drink. His hands look beaten up, dirt under the nails, and Kyle seems to have caught him as a fake. The man has a tattoo on his neck, some kind of dragon or snake, the tattoo a bit too large for his collar to hide, and Kyle interrogates him about it. It is an army regulation Kyle knows. The army will tolerate tattoos on arms and legs and torsos because they can be covered. But a neck tattoo, that is a problem. This video is short. The man throws bills on the counter, almost forgets his change, and makes a quick exit from the store. You can hear Kyle's voice as the camera moves to the door. We see Kyle's arm push the door open, we hear Kyle shouting, "That's *my* uniform! Take off my uniform! You don't deserve to wear it!" He had rehearsed these lines in his apartment, copied them from the stolen valor videos he'd seen on YouTube.

Kyle learned to go where men could be seen—the mall and the airport—and where braggarts could be heard—the bars and taverns. Malls and airports were good places for vets and active duty because airlines granted perks like first seating privileges, and food court restaurants in malls offered free beverages and desserts. Kyle hunted frauds along baggage carousels, and in the seating areas between frozen yogurt joints and express teriyakis. In the bars and taverns, men boasted of Special Forces and Navy Seals, and of other impressive occupational specialties—snipers and gunners and Airborne Rangers. They narrated dangers they had survived and celebrated the big *cajones* they carried. Kyle knew the drill, of how the real thing stayed quiet about such matters, and any man talking loud in a bar was either a lifelong civilian or some kind of pogue MOS—92-Golf, food service specialist, or 56-Mike, chaplain's assistant. The results of Kyle's efforts here were mixed. The airports were heavy with security, and the best hunting grounds—the lounge areas—were out of reach for a man with a camera but no ticket for a flight. The bars and taverns were ripe for catching fakes, but they were dark, and low-lit footage played poorly on YouTube.

Back at the VFW, Kyle sat at the bar between Odell and another vet he only knew by his nickname, Skeeter. Skeeter was Air Force, so he always got razzed by the army vets. Skeeter wore a bad rug too, so in a way he deserved the scorn, the rug an invitation for derision. Still, he was a vet, even if it was just Air Force, so he got the privilege to drink at the VFW just like all the other men there.

Kyle pulled out his phone to show Odell and Skeeter his videos.

"You remember that Mexican out in Salinas? One stole your reserved parking spot at the Home Depot?"

Odell nodded.

"Remember me telling you about stolen valor? And videos of these fakes all over YouTube?"

Skeeter said, "Yeah, YouTube, I heard of that. Like TV on the computer. My granddaughter watches it."

"Have a look," Kyle said, and he held up his phone. Odell and Skeeter leaned in. Skeeter titled his head up so he could watch through the lower half of his bifocals. Kyle played them a video of a homeless man trying to catch tourists coming out of the Monterey Bay Aquarium.

"What's going on?" Odell said.

"This guy's telling people he's a vet. See the sign. Right there. It says VIETNAM VET."

"Yeah, so what? He's sitting there, I can see that."

"No, listen to him. He can't answer any of my questions right. Doesn't know his rank, where he did basic, year he was in Vietnam, MOS, none of them. He's a fake for sure."

Odell and Skeeter leaned in more, but the tiny speakers on Kyle's phone just sounded like a tin can to them. They couldn't make out any of Kyle's interrogation. When it was over, Odell shrugged his shoulders and picked up his bottle of Bud Light.

Skeeter said, "I don't get it. You got a vagrant with a sign. Why would anyone want to watch that?"

"No, no," Kyle said. "It's the audio. Did you hear him? Straight up caught in a big-ass lie. And it's a crime, you know."

"I couldn't hear a thing," Odell said.

"Seems kind of boring to me." This was Skeeter. "Now that fella, what's his name, with the show catching child molesters, now that's something to watch."

Kyle put his phone away and called out for a shot of bourbon with a beer back.

Skeeter said, "You're right, though. There are a lot of fellas out there lying. Real vets even. Fellas who were in the service but want to make it out bigger than it was."

Kyle wanted to reach for his phone and pull up a video of one of the braggarts in a bar, but Odell said to Skeeter, "You would know about that, Air Force."

Skeeter let it slide off of him, and Odell got up to go take a leak. Skeeter said, "Kyle, that's your name, isn't it?"

Kyle nodded.

"After I got out, I got a job down at the VA. Almost got twenty in there too. I can't tell you how many benefits claims I've turned down over the years. How many men claiming tabs and awards that were nowhere to be found on their service records. Wounds too. PTSD. There's a lot of money to be made in disability checks, let me tell you."

Kyle let that sink in. Maybe he could make more money on disability. Then he wouldn't have to go out hunting down fake vets for his YouTube channel. He could claim PTSD, say he couldn't work, collect a disability check every month. But then he'd be a bigger fake than the men he'd been out stalking with his phone.

He turned to Skeeter. "You send those frauds my way and I'll make them stars on YouTube. The kind of stars no one wants to be."

Lately, Kyle would get headaches, and he thought it was from caffeine withdrawal, the time between cups of coffee stretching too long. It gave him a good excuse to drop in the Starbucks. Brittany worked at the only Starbucks in Marina, over there on Del Monte Boulevard. It was a big deal when Marina got a Starbucks, and it would be nice to sit there on the patio and sip a vanilla latte. But Marina was a place known for two kinds of weather— fog and wind—so most people sat inside, and the drive-through stayed busy.

Kyle strolled in on Brittany's Wednesday shift, told her he had another headache, something she had heard too many times before. Was it really another of his frequent headaches, or just an excuse to see her? Kyle ordered drip coffee in a house cup—not the paper—so that he could sit for as long as he wanted, getting refills at fifty cents a pop. He knew that if he lingered long enough Brittany would get a shift break, and then he could find her outside by the garbage cans taking a smoke.

When she removed her apron, that's when her break happened. He watched her do it and walk out the doors. He waited a few minutes and then followed her to the spot by the cans. She was there sitting on her haunches, her back leaned up against the wall, her cigarette arm up like a mailbox flag.

"Hey," Kyle said, and Brittany said "hey" back. Small talk at first. *How's work? Same old, same old. Still staying at your mom's? Yeah. Still got that job at Walmart? Yeah. Been up to Santa Cruz lately, beach and boardwalk? No, not lately. How about you? No, not much fun all by myself.* That right there, that's when the small talk wasn't small anymore. *By myself.* It was an unhealed wound.

"I got this idea to make some extra cash," Kyle said. "Starting my own YouTube channel. You heard of stolen valor?"

Brittany said, "YouTube?"

"They pay if your videos are popular. I got a plan, gonna make my videos go viral."

"What's stolen valor?"

Kyle explained it, and how videos of stolen valor were getting millions of views and that was money in the bank. Brittany kept smoking, not giving him any particular reaction.

Brittany said, "Kyle, they don't pay you for the videos. They pay you for the ads. You got to attract ads. That's what they pay you for."

"I know that. I'm not stupid. But ads don't pay squat for videos getting a hundred hits. First you've gotta have the good videos, and that's what I've been doing."

Brittany pulled out her phone to check the time, her break dwindling away. She said, "Are you sure about this? You know how you get confused sometimes? Mix things up?"

"Like the time I warmed up my coffee in the toaster oven?"

"And put the toast in the microwave."

They both chuckled at this. A good memory of them still together up in that second-floor apartment with the rusty rail.

Brittany said, "What happened with MPC?" This was the community college down in Monterey.

Kyle shrugged his shoulders. "College, it just wasn't for me."

"But you got all that money with the GI Bill. Free school. It sounded like a good deal."

"I would sit there in those classes and my mind would drift. I couldn't focus. Psychology, sociology. Maybe I just got too old to be a college boy. I don't know."

Brittany checked her phone again and then pushed her cigarette down onto the asphalt. "Time for me to get back to work."

Kyle said, "Brittany, when I get my payment on those videos, you and me, let's go out? What do you say? A big crab dinner? Or we could go do something fun. They got the races coming up at Laguna Seca. That would be fun. What do you say?"

"I don't know," Brittany said. "My schedule here. You know how it is. They change shifts. It's hard for me to make plans. She looked at him long, saw his tired eyes, his insomniac life written all over him. She jerked her thumb toward the wall. "Anyway . . . I gotta get back in there."

When she was gone, back inside the Starbucks, Kyle thought, *she didn't say yes, but she didn't say no either.*

Over the next few days Kyle uploaded his videos to YouTube in the early morning hours before heading to his job at Walmart. Hopeful, that's how he felt. Maybe Brittany was going to come back. He'd show her a good time. She'd see the money flowing free and easy. She'd see that he was making something of himself.

Kyle would spend the day patrolling the aisles of Walmart, mostly making people think twice about shoplifting. Loss prevention, that's what they called it. You didn't need a gun and a badge, just a warm body in a blue vest to warn people off. After work he would come home and check his view counts. Ten, twenty, maybe a hundred views here and there. Going viral was going slowly. Most days he would get so down that he'd want to escape the apartment, so lonely it felt without Brittany there.

He'd think about maybe going out and trying some more, maybe shoot that one gold-mine video. So he'd cruise around with his phone to the street corners and to the malls in Salinas and Monterey, but just as often he'd go to the Marina Club, a cardhouse down there off of Carmel Avenue. It was a hole in the wall that was grandfathered, the only legal gambling on the whole bay. Asian women dealt cards to retired military Kyle knew from the VFW. And others too. Artichoke pickers from Castroville, short brown men with just enough English to get by. Filipinos, Koreans, Vietnamese. Black guys from Seaside. Old GI brides, Germans mostly. All of them just looking for an angle for more cash, like Kyle. There was the lottery, and then there was the cardhouse. Kyle would go in with forty bucks, play blackjack, and lose most times, occasionally coming out ahead, but not by much, maybe doubling his money.

When he did come out ahead, he'd go drink a few beers at the VFW, his mood up again, his hopes—all tied up into his YouTube channel—renewed. The last time he felt so good he bought a round for the five men at the bar. There was Odell again, and Skeeter too, plus a couple of the other regulars and a new young guy down at the end who didn't say much. Skeeter asked Kyle about the videos, and Kyle pulled up YouTube on his phone and showed him the channel. He scrolled through the dozen or so videos, pointed out the view counts of the more popular ones. The grandpa down on Cannery Row had 375 views.

"And how much money you make on something like that?" The number 375 not sounding very big to Skeeter.

"Nothing much yet. Gotta give it time. Big things sometimes start slow."

Skeeter said nothing, and his silence wasn't the kind of encouragement Kyle was hoping for.

"You ask me," Odell said, "this TV on the computer thing, it's a fad. You seen how big TVs have gotten lately? I mean, who in his right mind wants to watch TV on a little ol' dinky thing when you could be sitting there in your living room with the seventy-five inches?" He put his hands out wide to indicate.

"You ought to see my granddaughter," Skeeter said. "She'll curl up in her bed half the day watching TV on her phone. It's a different world."

"Different world? Sounds lazy to me. But coming from you, Skeeter, I guess I should expect that."

Skeeter rolled his eyes like he knew what was coming.

"Air Force. Never spent a day in the field. You know how many times I slept on the ground? Mosquitos buzzing all night in my face in Vietnam. Nearly froze to death in Germany."

"Yeah, I know. You're real hard, Odell."

Odell didn't catch the sarcasm. He said, "Tell you what, you pull guard duty on my beer while I hit the latrine."

Once Odell was out of earshot, Skeeter turned to Kyle and said, "Gotta be his prostate. He takes more leaks than a dog walking a street full of fire hydrants."

The regulars broke into a murmur of laughter, all except Kyle and the new guy down at the end.

Skeeter said, "Show me your channel again."

Kyle pulled out his phone and Skeeter read out each video title in a low voice. After a minute, Skeeter looked around over his shoulders and then turned back to Kyle. "You want to, what is it? Go viral? What you need is a bigger fish. You know what I'm saying? A real *big* fake. The kind that gets people mad. What you've got there isn't big enough. You got idiots playing dress up. Old men wearing the wrong hat. What you need is a genuine first-rate fake. Criminal fake. The kind that's been riding his lie for a long time and in a big way, making everyone think he's Rambo or something. I saw one like that on TV. Not the computer, but real TV. On *Dateline*. Anyway, you remember me telling you about my job at the VA? Well, I've got one for you. A big-time pogue going around like he's Audie Murphy."

Kyle didn't know who Audie Murphy was, but he sure knew what a pogue was. P-O-G, but pronounced *pogue*. People Other than Grunts. Never pulled a trigger other than qualifying at the rifle range. Clerks and mechanics, nurses and paralegals. All the jobs outside of combat arms. *Pogue* was an insult infantry riflemen and cavalry scouts hurled at men who never saw combat, never even really trained for it. Audie Murphy, Kyle had to google that. The most decorated combat soldier of World War II, that was the first line on Wikipedia.

A big fish. Maybe that's what Kyle needed. A big, fake, criminal, pogue fish.

*

Brittany used to take care of paying all of Kyle's bills. Kyle had direct deposit for his Walmart paycheck, and Brittany had his passwords, so she would handle the transfers from his checking to rent, the phone, Netflix, electricity. She had taken it all over after watching him screw it up a couple of times, getting confused about when his paycheck was in there, or when a bill was due. Now that Kyle was on his own, he twice nearly got evicted after forgetting the rent. This last time it was the weekend and he got locked out until Monday morning. He drove out to what used to be called CDEC Hill over there on Fort Ord. It was a hill with lines of decomposing wooden barracks, the roads between them nearly overtaken by weeds and ice plant. More than twenty years of abandonment and the place looked like the apocalypse had hit it. Kyle had heard about teenagers from Marina partying in some of the broken-down buildings, and of homeless people squatting in others. Kyle parked his car under an overgrown cypress at the top of the hill and spent two nights in one of the old barracks. The first night lying there unable to sleep, he pulled out his phone and scrolled through his channel again. Not much had changed in the views counts since the last time he'd shown them to Skeeter at the VFW. By the light of the screen he could see a draft of dust move past his face. He thought about Odell and all his pride, all his toughness. Lying in the dirt and the mud, fighting off mosquitos and Charlie Cong in Vietnam, and the cold of Germany, in places like Grafenwöhr and Hohenfels. He thought of what it was like to sleep in his own bed, or not sleep, really, but at least it was soft and comfortable. And back when Brittany was still there. In the bed next to him, asleep like a baby with him there wide awake half the night. But still, she was there and that was nice, and he wanted that back.

On Monday, Kyle straightened out his rent and got back into his apartment, the landlord warning him this was the last time. He checked his mailbox and there were the photocopies of the VA file Skeeter had promised him. It was just as Skeeter had said, a pogue who'd barely carried a rifle after basic training, a 91-Bravo, wheeled vehicle mechanic. There was a note attached where Skeeter had written *Free Veterans Day lunch down at the senior center. He will be there. Bring your camera.*

Looking through the file, Kyle thought this could be the gold mine he'd been waiting for. If what Skeeter said was true, that this 91-Bravo had been lying for years with his Purple Hearts and Vietcong body counts, when all he really did was twenty years of changing oil filters and rotating tires, then a video of him parading around in his great big lie could pay something good.

Kyle looked up at his calendar. November tenth. The free lunch was tomorrow. He went out to his car and drove over to the Starbucks. Brittany was on her shift behind the counter tamping down espresso grounds. This time Kyle didn't bother to wait for her break.

"What're you doing Friday night?"

Brittany only glanced up. "Kyle, I'm at work right now."

"You like that Grotto place over on the wharf, don't you? Remember the last time we were there, right after the tax return came in? The linguini with the shrimp and clams? You said that was the best meal you ever had. How about Friday we go there again?"

Brittany had seen this before. Kyle off the earth happy. She had also seen the crash back down.

"Kyle, aren't you supposed to be at work or something?"

He didn't hear her. He said, "Pick you up at your mom's. Seven o'clock. I'll make reservations."

He was out the door before she could say no.

At the senior center a couple dozen men showed up for the free lunch. There were three women too, and that surprised some of the men. A lot of the men wore ball caps with logos like U.S. ARMY RETIRED emblazoned on the front. Two guys shuffled around with walkers, and one man was in a wheelchair. His hat said KOREAN WAR VETERAN, and Kyle noticed his old arthritic hands folded on his lap. There was one active duty there in ACUs. He'd come from the recruiting center over there in Seaside, and he was talking up the teenage Boy Scouts who'd volunteered to help serve the meal. A few of the men made a show of it, dressing up in their class A's. These were the old army-green dress uniforms, not the new fancy blue ones. The uniforms looked like they'd hung well preserved in closets with mothballs, but the bodies of the men had changed over time. Paunches strained at buttons, and shoulder seams sagged where once there was more muscle mass to fill them.

The mayor of Marina was there, and when he got up to give a speech that's when Kyle pulled out his phone. Shooting the speech was a good excuse to film something, and while the mayor went on too long, Kyle panned the room until landing on the 91-Bravo pogue across the room. He zoomed in and held it there. It was him all right, and he was one of the men in Class A's. He was resting his forearms on the table, but Kyle could still see the service bars on the lower sleeves. On the left sleeve the bars ran diagonally, one for every three years of service, and the man had a bunch of those. He'd done his twenty to collect his pension, and the bars were proof of that. But it was the bars on the right sleeve Kyle was after. They were smaller and ran a perfect horizontal line four inches above the edge of the sleeve. The man had only two of these, but that was where his big lie marked him. These were bars for service in a combat zone, one bar for every six months. Here was the year in Vietnam the fraud had never served.

The mayor finally wrapped it up with the same old phrases civilians kept canned and ready when they didn't know what else to say to vets. There was "we honor your sacrifice," and "thank you for your service."

There was clapping and when that died down and all the vets went back to their forks and knives, Kyle got up and carried the phone in front of him over to where the 91-Bravo fraud was sitting. He got to the edge of the table and then the fraud looked up, surprised at Kyle's phone sticking out at him.

Kyle said, "Happy Veterans Day, Odell."

Odell didn't say anything at first, not sure how to respond to Kyle's awkward greeting or that damn phone of his. Then he said, "What the hell kind of thing is that to say? '*Happy* Veterans Day.' Boy, this ain't nobody's birthday. And get that thing out of my face, why don't you."

Kyle zoomed in on the ribbons on Odell's chest, a patchwork of rectangles in various colors. There on his little screen he could see the two more lies that would make his video go viral. The distinct green-yellow-red rectangle of the Vietnam service ribbon, and the other one white and purple—mostly purple—for wounds suffered in combat.

Kyle said, "Odell, you're looking good in those Class A's. Can you tell me about your ribbons there?"

Odell put his knife and fork down and stared into Kyle's phone. He stuck a finger out like that Uncle Sam poster. "Listen you, I ain't got time for your shenanigans." He stood up and Kyle followed his upward movement with the phone. Then Odell said, "I got to hit the latrine."

He was moving, fast for an old man, and all Kyle could get was the back of Odell's uniform. Kyle remembered to pull out his index card with the list of questions. Odell entered the men's room and Kyle followed him through the swinging door. Odell looked over his shoulder, said, "The hell's wrong with you, following a man into the toilet," and then entered a stall and closed the door. Kyle started firing off his questions, but the only video he was getting was Odell's spit-shined dress shoes poking out from under the stall. And Odell wasn't answering any of his questions.

Out in the parking lot, Kyle sat in his car and reviewed the footage he'd shot. He was worried it wasn't good enough, like he'd missed his one chance at the big time. There was a knock on the passenger window and there was Skeeter. He opened the door and took a seat.

"So, did you get it?"

Kyle tilted the phone Skeeter's way. Skeeter watched it through, and then said, "Listen, don't put it on that YouTube just yet. I got a better idea."

They waited until the evening and then drove over to King Circle, off of Reindollar Avenue. King Circle was a dead-end cul-de-sac of snout-house tract homes, the floor plans flipped every other one, garage on the left next to garage on the right, and so on.

When they knocked on the door, Odell's wife answered. Her name was Helga. Skeeter said hi and they talked like they knew each other and Kyle could hear Helga's accent. It was like in the movies, the German characters, and always the villains, like in *Indiana Jones*. Skeeter asked if Odell was in, and Helga swung the door open more and called out Odell's name. He was over there in the corner in a recliner with the remote in his hand, the TV on with some old movie, a Western. Odell looked over at Skeeter and Kyle, got up out of his chair, and told Helga he was going out to the garage to have some beers. Kyle and Skeeter followed him out around the corner and watched Odell open the big door, the sound of the electric motor pulling it up the only thing breaking the silence.

There were old lawn chairs in there, plaid nylon webbed around aluminum frames. Odell told them to take a seat. He went over to a green refrigerator that looked like it had been around since the seventies and pulled out three bottles of Bud Light. He passed out the beers and they small-talked for five minutes until Skeeter broke it off and said, "Odell, you know why we're here."

He told Kyle to show Odell the video. Kyle pulled out his phone and turned the screen toward Odell. He played a couple of minutes until Skeeter said, "That's plenty," and then Kyle turned it off and put the phone away. Odell sipped his beer and didn't say a word.

"So this is how it's gonna go," Skeeter said. "The boy here is gonna put that up on YouTube and make you famous, and not in a good way. And that's gonna follow you around so as you won't want to show your face. Not at the VFW, American Legion, the free meals at the senior center. That church your wife drags you to. The cardhouse down there on Carmel Avenue. Everybody will know you're nothing but a lying pogue. See, I got your service records. We can take pictures of them, add them pictures to the video. Can we do that, kid?"

Kyle nodded.

"Vietnam . . . Purple Hearts. Hell, you were in Germany most of those years. Fixing carburetors and eating sauerkraut. You never even stepped into Vietnam, not even as a 91-Bravo pogue."

Odell gulped at his beer, still saying nothing.

Skeeter said, "We can put that video up for all to see . . . or . . ."

"Or what?" Odell said.

"Or you can pay us a thousand dollars and we'll call it good. And no more crap about me being Air Force."

"And where am I supposed to get that kind of money?"

"You got it. This house alone's got to be worth, what, a whole hell of a lot?"

Odell chugged the rest of his beer, looked at the empty in his hand, and made a move to the fridge for another. Skeeter glanced over at Kyle, and Kyle could see the confidence on Skeeter's face. Odell had his back turned. With one hand on the fridge door he reached with the other into a dark space between the fridge and a stack of boxes. When he turned around it wasn't a Bud Light he was holding, but a shotgun. Skeeter had his bottle to his mouth and had to pull it away when he saw the barrel coming at him.

"Now, Odell," he said. "Let's just calm down."

"Calm down?" I'll shoot that dead squirrel right off your head. Then I'll put the next one in your chest." He swung the barrel over to Kyle. "Give me that phone."

"It's no use," Skeeter said. "We made copies. We're not dumb enough to bring the only one here. Tell him, kid."

"I uploaded it, but I haven't posted it yet."

"See, he uploaded it. That means it's saved out there in . . . What's it called?"

"Cyberspace," Kyle said.

Odell swung the barrel back over to Skeeter. "I'm not paying."

Skeeter made a slow move to set his beer down and then he stood up. He walked backwards to the big opening of the garage. "You'll pay," he said. "And no more crap about me being Air Force." He looked at Kyle, still sitting there with the beer in his hand. "Come on, kid, let's go."

Kyle looked up at the calendar behind the bar. It was two days before Friday.

Skeeter was there and a couple of the regulars, men used to laughing at Odell's jokes. Odell, he wasn't there, but the new young guy was, down there at the end and quiet again.

Almost Friday and Kyle had the money in his pocket to take Brittany out to the Grotto on Fisherman's Wharf. But he wasn't feeling quite right about it.

"Maybe," Kyle said, "maybe we shouldn't have done it that way."

"Of course we should've." This was Skeeter.

Stolen valor. It was a crime. Put the videos up on YouTube, that was a public service, and if YouTube paid you money when you hit a million views, well, nothing wrong with that. But taking Odell's money, that was something different.

"It feels like stealing," Kyle said.

"Stealing from a thief. Oldest trick in the book. You shouldn't feel bad about it. Odell's getting what's coming to him. Besides, you got cash in your pocket. Five hundred dollars and no tax-man. Take your girl out, have a good time. You'll feel better after that."

Kyle looked at the mirror behind the bar, catching the reflection of him and Skeeter sitting there, longneck bottles standing in front of them. He looked close at Skeeter and thought, *that rug really does look awful.* Maybe Skeeter could get him a better one with his five hundred.

He found himself tiring of Skeeter's company, so he swung out of his bar chair and crossed over to where there was a dartboard. He pulled the darts out, stepped back, and threw them a couple of times without much interest. Then he took a seat at a table nearby and stared up at the wall. There were beer signs mixed in with military decorations: COORS stretching out in cursive over a mountain panorama, a black POW-MIA banner, MILLER LITE in neon, and then an American flag.

The new guy, the quiet one at the end of the bar, got up and walked over to the dartboard, pulled the darts out and started throwing. He went like that for a few rounds before he turned to Kyle. "I've seen you in here a couple of times, and I didn't say anything before because I wasn't sure. But now I think I am. We know each other."

He was still holding a dart. He threw it and then picked up his beer, walked over, and sat across from Kyle.

Kyle said, "My memory isn't so good anymore. What was it, high school?"

"No. Iraq. I wasn't sure it was you. Your hair's all grown out. So's mine. Sure look different once you take off the cammies, let your hair grow, and stop shaving every day."

Kyle hesitated to respond. "Like I said, my memory isn't so good."

The quiet guy took a chug of his beer. "I'll bet. Then again, there's things you don't want to remember. Last time I saw you, they were evacuating you out to Landstuhl. You don't remember that? Of course you don't."

"Why wouldn't I remember?"

"You kidding me? They had you so drugged up. Brain swelling. They kept you in a coma to keep you from dying. Only thing you probably remember from that day is the dreams you had on the flight to Germany."

"No," Kyle said. "I think I do remember."

There in his head Kyle was recalling the view out the window. Iraq. Dust on the bullet-resistant glass. The sky a red haze. Utility poles and palm trees ticking past. A pile of cinder blocks, a skinny dog, a wrecked car. And then dark.

"That day, man, when we hit that IED. It was the most action we saw the whole deployment." The quiet guy began peeling at the label of his bottle, a nervous habit. "Couple of 35-Novembers. Who would have thought a 35-November would be getting a Purple Heart? I'm just glad none of us was killed. Broke my femur, and that dude up front lost his foot, and you . . . well, you got your brains scrambled pretty good."

35-November. Kyle remembered. Signals Intelligence Analyst.

"Yeah, we always said we were too smart to be trigger-pullers. But you can't spend the whole deployment behind concrete walls. It's when you get out on the road, that's when they'd get you, and they got us. But like I said, at least we didn't die."

It was coming back now. The two tours. Long days on the FOB—the Forward Operating Base. Hardly ever leaving it other than to move to another FOB. It wasn't soldiering, it was technical work, the kind brainy kids did who scored high on the aptitude test, signed up for pogue MOS's, and got out still young enough to cash in the college money and start a nice civilian life. There was *some* danger. A random mortar round might get lucky inside the concrete walls and hit you while you walked back from the chow hall. And when you had to drive from one FOB to the next, the roads could get hairy. Snipers, RPGs, IEDs. It was the IED that got Kyle.

The quiet new guy said, "Man, it's good to see you. Tell you what, let me buy you a beer."

Kyle watched him walk over to the bar. He was thinking of Brittany and the Grotto and the five hundred he had in his pocket. It would be a good time Friday night. It would be like old times.

But he didn't like the way they had done Odell. And now it was as if all three of them—Odell, Skeeter, and Kyle—were all just frauds like the rest of the pogues going around playing dress-up, or talking loud and lying.

Kyle pulled out his phone and navigated to the Odell video. There it was frozen on the first frame, Odell across the room in his class A's at the senior center, the Play triangle waiting for a touch. It was like that IED under the road that day, just waiting for a chance to blow up a man's life. Kyle glanced up at Skeeter there at the bar now telling some kind of joke, the regulars laughing at it.

He never did upload the video like he'd told Odell in the garage. That was just him playing it cool with the shotgun sticking in his face. No, he only had the one copy on his phone the whole time. He glanced down at the little trash can icon in the corner and touched it with his thumb, and Odell's stolen valor video went away for good.

Contributors' Notes

Other Distinguished Mystery and Suspense of 2021

Contributors' Notes

HECTOR ACOSTA is the Edgar Award and Anthony Award–nominated author of the wrestling inspired novella *Hardway*. His short fiction has appeared in *Mystery Tribune, Shotgun Honey, Thuglit,* and other publications. He resides in Texas with his wife, dog, and, inexplicably, two cats. He's still waiting for The Rock to follow him back on Twitter.

• A lot of my fiction involves wrestling, in some way or another. I'm not only a fan of the sport (and yes, it's a sport), but I'm also fascinated by so many of the aspects which come with it. For a long time I've had this image of a wall covered with masks in my head, but never had the right story to go along with it. When Colin Conway invited me to participate in his *Eviction of Hope* anthology, I had a heck of a time finding an angle until I came across an article about video-game streamers. The article detailed how so many of them had a persona they put on for their audience, and I began to see parallels between them and wrestlers, with their larger-than-life gimmicks. La Chingona—and Veronica—came out of that realization. Her personality, her attempt to persevere even as the odds were stacked against her, came from all the strong women I have been fortunate to know in my life, my mom, my aunts, and my wife. And Trevor was born from all the people who tried to stand in their way.

TRACY CLARK, a native Chicagoan, is the author of the Cass Raines Chicago Mystery series, featuring ex-cop turned PI Cassandra Raines. A multi-nominated Anthony, Lefty, Edgar, and Shamus Award finalist, Tracy is also the 2020 winner of the G. P. Putnam's Sons Sue Grafton Memorial Award and was shortlisted for the Grafton Award again in 2022. She was also nominated for the Edgar Award for Best Short Story for "Lucky Thirteen," which was included in the crime fiction anthology *Midnight Hour*. She is a proud member of Crime Writers of Color, Mystery Writers of America, and

Sisters in Crime and serves on the boards of Bouchercon National and the Midwest Mystery Conference. Her debut novel, *Broken Places,* was recently optioned by Sony Pictures Television. Her latest book, *Runner,* was released in 2021, and her next book, *Hide,* featuring Detective Harriet Foster, will be published in 2022.

• I'm not a short story writer. I consider those writers who can tell a story in five thousand words or less to be geniuses. This is a genius I do *not* possess. So, when Abby Vandiver approached me to ask if I could contribute a short story to a crime fiction anthology she was putting together, my initial response was pure panic . . . then I said yes. I am nothing if not a glutton for punishment. As a diehard pantser (a writer who flies by the seat of her pants), I had no plan, of course, so I fished around for an idea, a hook, a theme . . . anything. And then it hit me. Perception. Mistakes made at a glance. Turned tables. An old man. A young one. One fatal night. I wrote the story. I made the deadline. I'm still not a short story writer, though. I'm a panic writer, a writer who accepts a challenge, then regrets it until the ideas come. I think "Lucky Thirteen" turned out okay in the end, but, boy, how I sweated over every one of those five thousand words.

s. a. cosby is a bestselling, award-winning author from southeastern Virginia. His work has appeared in numerous anthologies and magazines. His novel *Blacktop Wasteland* won multiple awards and was on more than a dozen best-of-the-year lists. His novel *Razorblade Tears* was a *New York Times* bestseller.

• "An Ache So Divine" started out as a story about unrequited love, but somewhere along the way it became a story about how hurt people tend to hurt people. In many ways it was a challenging story to write, but in other ways it allowed me to indulge in a bit of nostalgia. I grew up behind a shot house bar and I spent some time as a bouncer, and in both instances I saw broken hearts and broken teeth scattered across the scarred dance floor.

alex espinoza was born in Tijuana, Mexico, to parents from the state of Michoacán. He graduated from the University of California–Riverside, then went on to earn an M.F.A. from UC Irvine's Program in Writing. His first novel, *Still Water Saints,* was published in 2007, and his second novel, *The Five Acts of Diego León,* in 2013. Alex's work has appeared in several anthologies and journals, including the *Virginia Quarterly Review,* the *Los Angeles Times,* the *New York Times Sunday Magazine,* and *Lit Hub,* as well as on NPR's *All Things Considered.* His awards include a 2009 Margaret Bridgeman Fellowship in Fiction to the Bread Loaf Writers' Conference, a 2014 Fellowship in Prose from the National Endowment for the Arts, a 2014 American Book Award from the Before Columbus Foundation for *The Five Acts of Diego León,* and a fellowship to MacDowell. His latest book is

Cruising: An Intimate History of a Radical Pastime (2019). Alex teaches at UC Riverside, where he serves as the Tomás Rivera Endowed Chair of Creative Writing.

• I wrote "Detainment" during the height of the Trump administration's barbaric and inept handling of the influx of migrants from Central America. My social media feeds were full of horrific accounts of families separated at the border and children being held in cages for months. I read an account of a father reunited with his son who claimed the boy was exhibiting aggressive behavior upon his return. He said it was as though his son was returned "wrong." I thought about the psychological trauma these families must have gone through, and the ways in which inhumane immigration policies negatively shape the lives of migrants for generations to come.

In 1995, JACQUELINE FREIMOR won first prize in the unpublished writers category of Mystery Writers of America's Fiftieth Anniversary Short Story Competition, and she has been writing ever since. Her stories have been published in *Ellery Queen Mystery Magazine, Alfred Hitchcock Mystery Magazine, Rock and a Hard Place,* and *Mystery Magazine,* among others, as well as in the e-zine *Blue Murder* and at akashicbooks.com. Her Derringer Award–nominated story "That Which Is True" was reprinted in *The Best Mystery Stories of the Year: 2021,* edited by Lee Child, and the story in this volume, "Here's to New Friends," originally appeared in the anthology *When a Stranger Comes to Town,* edited by Michael Koryta. Jacqueline is a music teacher and freelance editor and lives in Westchester County, New York, with her husband, daughter, and annoying Yorkshire Terrier.

• "Here's to New Friends" was the synthesis of three incidents that have disturbed me for years. The first happened long ago, while I was in graduate school, when I was assaulted in my own apartment; the second happened a quarter of a century later, when a local girl went missing from her college campus and her parents posted flyers all over town that stayed up for months and then years, their edges curling and ink fading until they were unreadable and people had to take them down. The third and most recent was a fight with my then high school–aged daughter when she blithely announced she was going to start jogging in the early mornings on the path by the river near our home—wearing headphones. "Absolutely not," I said, and when she wouldn't let it go, I finally yelled, "Listen to me! I know you think you're a person, but some men think you're *prey*." I won that one, if you can call it winning. Anyway. Not long after, while I was researching sexual predators, these three incidents fused themselves into a story I could actually tell.

It's been eleven years, and the missing college girl is still missing. Her body has never been found.

TOD GOLDBERG is a *New York Times* bestselling author of over a dozen books, including *The Low Desert,* a Southwest Book of the Year; *Gangsterland,* a finalist for the Hammett Prize; *Gangster Nation,*; *The House of Secrets,* which he coauthored with Brad Meltzer; and *Living Dead Girl,* a finalist for the *Los Angeles Times* Book Prize. His nonfiction appears regularly in the *Los Angeles Times, USA Today,* and *Alta* and has been anthologized in *Best American Essays.* He is the cohost of the popular podcast *Literary Disco,* along with Rider Strong and Julia Pistell, and a professor of creative writing at the University of California–Riverside, where he founded and directs the Low Residency M.F.A. in Creative Writing and Writing for the Performing Arts. Tod lives in Indio, California, with his wife, Wendy Duren, and any number of Cocker Spaniels.

• Nothing in this story is true, except for this: there's a man who dresses up like a clown and hangs out at various bars and restaurants in and around Palm Springs. Like in the story, he's a silent clown, which is disconcerting, but the truly crazy thing—apart from, obviously, *everything*—is that he's been doing it for at least forty years. When I was a kid, for instance, my mom was the society columnist for the local paper and would run into the creepy-ass clown at different events, enough so that they got to know each other a bit. Or as much as one can get to know a silent clown, I suppose. This was in the 1980s. Now here it is 2022 and the clown still makes the rounds—The Nest on Friday nights, Kitchen 86 on Thursday, etc.—and my mom has been dead for over a decade. I'm not saying the clown did it, of course.

JULIET GRAMES is senior vice president and associate publisher at Soho Press, where she curates the critically acclaimed Soho Crime imprint. She is the 2022 recipient of the Mystery Writers of America Ellery Queen Award for her editorial work in the crime fiction genre. Her debut novel, *The Seven or Eight Deaths of Stella Fortuna* (2019), a national and international bestseller, was shortlisted for the New England Book Award and the Connecticut Book Award, received Italy's Premio Cetraro for its contribution to southern Italian literature, and has been translated into nine languages. Her second novel, *The Lost Boy of Santa Chionia,* is forthcoming. Juliet's essays and short fiction have appeared in *Ellery Queen Mystery Magazine, Real Simple, Parade,* and the *Boston Globe,* among other venues. She lives in New England.

• In New England, where I grew up, springtime is marked by the popping up of crocuses—and tag sales. My mother, a tag sale addict, would stop at every single one we passed, "just to look." It was while I was sitting in her car in some stranger's driveway waiting for her to finish rummaging through their cast-offs that the question occurred to me: Had tag sale-ing ever driven someone to murder?

LAUREN GROFF is the author of six books, including *Fates and Furies, Florida,* and *Matrix,* all of which were finalists for the National Book Award. Her work has been translated into thirty-five languages. She lives in Gainesville, Florida.

• Some stories live with you for years before they allow you to tell them. This is the case with "The Wind," which has two sources: someone beloved to me who will remain anonymous, and a drunk stranger in a Philadelphia bar when I was very young, a person who told me a harrowing story that time, memory, many failed attempts to tell the story, and the exigencies of the current moment morphed beyond the original. I wrote this story suffocating from domesticity in the early part of the COVID-19 pandemic, painfully aware that no matter how dark my situation was, I was fortunate to live in peace and plenty and love; that, equally, in the larger world, there were others to whom the world's sudden domestic tightening meant actual horror and immediate fear for their lives. It was while watching the brave people out in the streets protesting police brutality that summer that the story came together and let me write it the way it wanted to be written.

JAMES D. F. HANNAH is the author of the Henry Malone series; his novel *Behind the Wall of Sleep* won the 2020 Shamus Award for Best Paperback Original. His short fiction has appeared in *Rock and a Hard Place, Crossed Genres, Shotgun Honey, Anthology of Appalachian Writers, Trouble No More, Under the Thumb: Stories of Police Oppression,* and *Playing Games,* edited by Lawrence Block. When he was younger, he was rightfully mocked for claiming his favorite Billy Joel song was "You're Only Human." He's still attempting to outlive that shame in Louisville, Kentucky.

• When editor Josh Pachter invited me to contribute a story to *Only the Good Die Young,* I couldn't say no. As a diehard Billy Joel fan (allhailthe-BardofLongIsland), the chance to spin one of his tunes into a crime yarn was too good to pass up. That euphoria turned into panic when I tried to pick a song. Rather than choose one of Joel's myriad hits, I opted instead for a deeper cut. The opening track to his *River of Dreams* album, "No Man's Land," was Joel's last swing at being "an angry young man"—a screed against big business, suburban sprawl, and the changing face of Long Island. After giving the song about 150 listens, I knew the resulting story would be set in 1992 (the year the song was recorded), and it would involve real estate (the film version of *Glengarry Glen Ross* was released that year), the Amy Fisher story (referenced in the song's lyrics), and that year's presidential election between Bill Clinton and George H. W. Bush. "No Man's Land" gave me an opportunity to step away from Appalachia, where my novels are set, and explore an old-school mob tale, as well as to play with two of my favorite fictional themes: Faustian bargains—how far will you go to be the man you thought you were—and murder via sporting goods.

GAR ANTHONY HAYWOOD, a winner of both the Shamus Award and the Anthony Award, is the author of fourteen novels and dozens of short stories. His crime fiction includes the Aaron Gunner Mystery series and the Joe and Dottie Loudermilk Mysteries. His short fiction has been included in the *Best American Mystery and Suspense* series, and *Booklist* has called him "a writer who has always belonged in the upper echelon of American crime fiction." His most recent novel, *In Things Unseen,* was published in 2021 and would best be described as a thriller for fans of nontraditional Christian fiction.

• In an anthology entitled *Jukes & Tonks,* somebody had to write a story that centered on a jukebox, and I figured it might as well be me. Usually, I have a short story's ending in hand before I even start in, because the ending, for me, is always the point of the exercise. But in this case, I just began writing to see what would develop. What developed was a stolen jukebox that gets dropped from a truck by the knuckleheads who stole it, and once that happened—once I had a broken jukebox on my hands—I suddenly knew what would come next. Because I've been looking for a way to revisit Handy White, the repairer of all ancient things protagonist of my favorite stand-alone, *Cemetery Road,* for years, and this was it. Eureka! A Handy White short story.

LESLIE JONES is a writer from Anchorage, Alaska, whose fiction has appeared in publications such as the *Hopkins Review, Southern Review,* and *Narrative.* She has worked as a city magazine editor in China, an English teacher in Taiwan, and a freelance journalist in Texas and New York. Leslie lives in Brooklyn with her family.

• In 2014, I camped on a pot farm in Humboldt County, California, for a magazine assignment. I was fascinated by the extralegal wealth of America's top cannabis-producing region, but also by its family-centric culture: one grower told me how cute it was during harvest when the kiddos showed up to preschool with leaf stuck to their clothes. I drew on those impressions when I started imagining a marital marijuana venture.

The other animator was family history: in the 1980s, my dad held an oil lease with partners at Harriet Point, but nobody found anything. Decades after "ARCO spent $50 million to dig a dry hole," he still talks about the time he spent hoping and wishing the exploratory well would produce oil. His yearning is infectious. It makes me feel like we're waiting together, that something might still bubble up. For better or worse, that appetite drives so much American activity, past and present, on both sides of the law—it's good story fodder.

LATOYA JOVENA was born in Prince George's County, Maryland, and simply decided not to leave. She still lives there with her husband and two daughters. She's most definitely in the middle of a writing project or two. Find her @LaToyaJovena on Twitter or Instagram to say hi.

• "Stingers" actually started as a fantasy story, more specifically my fantasy.

Someone I love very much was robbed at gunpoint in the early evening, in what was considered a safe neighborhood. It was nothing like what happened in the story. An empty wallet and a cell phone were stolen. Mean words were spoken, but no one was touched. The victim in this incident got over it almost immediately.

I didn't. I was enraged. I plotted a plot and planned a plan. Then I wrote it all down as a means of catharsis.

I had written several stories, submitted them everywhere, and been rejected all over the place. Before "Stingers," I'd only had two acceptances. Rejections were friends, and one can never have too many friends. When *Alfred Hitchcock Mystery Magazine* decided to publish "Stingers," I was dumbfounded, but grateful. But acceptances weren't friends, just mere acquaintances. So I submitted to *Best American Mystery and Suspense*.

And here I am, living proof that one can find acceptance by looking for friends in all the wrong places.

ELAINE KAGAN is the author of five published novels as well as several pieces for *Los Angeles Magazine*, the *Los Angeles Times*, and the *Kansas City Star*, her hometown paper. Her short stories have appeared in Lawrence Block's collections, and her essays have been published in *The Normal School*. She is working on an anthology of short stories that will accompany a novella about the extraordinary people who make the movies, called "The Picture Business." Elaine worked for many years in film production and still works occasionally as an actress. She lives in Los Angeles.

• Larry Block asked me if I would write a story for his collection called *Collectibles*. My original thought was to do a story about a woman who collects men. Well, that didn't work out.

So what do people collect? Stamps? Baseball hats? Red shoes? Nothing appealed. And then it occurred to me that practically everyone you know has a collection of boxes filled with holiday stuff—cardboard boxes labeled in bold black ink: tangled lights for the Christmas tree, flags for the Fourth of July and Memorial Day, pink and blue straw baskets for Easter . . . you name a holiday and they have a box for it, probably stacked in their garage. Or stuffed in an upstairs closet with Aunt Margaret's winter coats. And envisioning these lovely people and their collections of boxes was the beginning of the story "God Bless America."

DENNIS LEHANE is the author of thirteen novels, including *Mystic River* and *Shutter Island*. His fourteenth novel, *Small Mercies*, will be published in

2023. *Black Bird,* a limited TV series he wrote and produced, can be found on Apple TV+. He lives in Los Angeles with his family.

• When I was a kid, my mother forced me to take piano lessons with a nun whose office was in Harvard Square. The lessons didn't take, but the wandering I would do around Harvard Square before and after the lessons made a huge impression on me. There were twenty bookstores within a square mile in the area back then, and I would wander from one to the next, not just shopping for books but soaking up the atmosphere, which felt, in many cases, like London (or how I imagined London at eleven years old). Antiquarian and somewhat antiquated, very much out of time. I felt in touch with a much older Cambridge and, by extension, a much older Boston. So when I sat down to write this story, I was paying tribute to that world, which has, in the years since, been rolled up and stashed away on a high shelf.

KRISTEN LEPIONKA, the author of the Roxane Weary Mystery series, has won the Shamus and Goldie Awards and been nominated for the Anthony and Macavity Awards. She grew up mostly in her local public library, where she could be found with a big stack of adult mysteries before she was out of middle school. She is a cofounder of the feminist podcast *Unlikeable Female Characters,* and lives in Columbus, Ohio, with her partner and two cats.

• I'll tell anyone who asks that writing a short story is so much harder than writing a novel. As a writer, I tend to revel in backstory and character development, for which there is plenty of space in a novel. You have to be so much more concise in a short story, and this poses an interesting challenge. I like to play with multiple points of view in a short story, setting two people on a collision course with each other, as this seems to be an effective way to jump in and get down to business. The wider the gap between these two people's lives, the better. In "Remediation," I wanted to explore gentrification in the Olde Town East neighborhood of Columbus (where my novels are also set) through the perspectives of someone who seems to have everything and someone who seems to have nothing. But before I got to that point, I had a humbling experience during the copyediting process on one of my books when I learned that I'd mistakenly thought "restauranteur" was a word for my entire life, when it's actually "restaurateur"—no *n*. From then on I found myself wanting to correct anyone else who said or wrote the word incorrectly, though I managed to refrain from being such an insufferable know-it-all. It got me thinking about the type of person who wouldn't hesitate to be an insufferable know-it-all on this particular point. Although the "restaurateur" line is a minor element of the story, it somehow set the stage in my mind for the rest of the story.

MEGAN PILLOW is a graduate of the University of Iowa Writers' Workshop in fiction and holds a Ph.D. in English from the University of Kentucky. She is project manager for the writer Roxane Gay and coeditor of *The Audacity*, Dr. Gay's newsletter. Her work has appeared, or is forthcoming, in *Electric Literature, Guernica, The Believer, TriQuarterly,* and *Gay Magazine*, among other publications, and has been featured in *Longreads*. Megan's stories have been featured on the *Wigleaf* Top 50 Longlist, an essay was honored as a notable essay of 2018 in *The Best American Essays 2019,* and a story honored as a distinguished story of 2019 in *The Best American Short Stories 2020*. More information about her can be found at www.meganpillow.com or on Twitter at @megpillow. Megan lives in Louisville, Kentucky, with her two children.

• I've loved Nancy Drew since I was eleven years old. My aunt, just thirty-seven years old, died that year of breast cancer, and I inherited a collection of about thirty of the mysteries from her. I read every single one. Those books helped me navigate my grief, and they cemented Nancy as one of my guides through difficult times. So when I read *Polygon*'s January 2020 announcement that Dynamite Comics would be publishing a comic for Nancy's ninetieth anniversary about her murder, and that The Hardy Boys would be sent to solve it, I got angry. Nancy Drew didn't deserve to get fridged, I thought. And Nancy was better at solving mysteries than The Hardy Boys any day. So I used that anger as the impetus for my story: The Girl Detective reads about her own murder on Twitter, and she decides to tell The Hardy Boys to get lost, because even dead, her detective skills are better than theirs, and even dead, she knows she can do a better job of solving her murder. While I was writing it, however, the story evolved past anger: it became about honoring Nancy's legacy and my aunt's, about coping with my divorce and my own sexual assault, about reckoning with my grief and joy over how to begin a new life as a divorced woman over forty, to force myself alive again. It became one of the best things I've ever written, a story I'm really proud of, and one I hope helps other people navigate difficult times the way the Nancy Drew books helped me.

RAQUEL V. REYES writes the Caribbean Kitchen Mystery series. Her stories celebrate Latina protagonists and Spanglish. She lives in Miami. Find Raquel across social media platforms as @LatinaSleuths.

• The call was for crime stories that happened at midnight. As a Cuban-American, I couldn't resist having a little fun with the translation. Midnight in Spanish is *medianoche*, and it is also the name of a sandwich. Once I had the location and setting, my main characters came quickly. Dee is a character from a PI series I have in a drawer. And Pugi came to me in this sentence. "Pugi was the most *chonga* of the chonga and still chongaing at the old age of twenty-five." Chonga, once an insult, has become a subculture in South Florida. A chonga is a young woman with agency. She fully embraces a hypersexual and "alpha aggressive" persona in speech and dress. I loved the idea of celebrating that sexual hunger.

DAVID HESKA WANBLI WEIDEN, an enrolled citizen of the Sicangu Lakota Nation, is the author of *Winter Counts,* nominated for an Edgar Award, and a winner of the Anthony, Thriller, Lefty, Barry, Macavity, Spur, High Plains, Electa Quinney, Tillie Olsen, and Crime Fiction Lover Awards. The novel was a *New York Times* Editors' Choice, an Indie Next pick, a main selection of the Book of the Month Club, and it was named a best book of the year by NPR, Amazon, *Publishers Weekly, Library Journal,* the *Guardian,* and other publications. He has short stories in the anthologies *Denver Noir, Midnight Hour, Never Whistle at Night,* and *The Perfect Crime,* and his nonfiction has appeared in the *New York Times, Shenandoah,* and *Writer's Digest.* David received the PEN America Writing for Justice Fellowship and is the recipient of residencies and fellowships from MacDowell, Ucross, Ragdale, and Tin House. He is professor of Native American studies and political science at Metropolitan State University of Denver and lives in Colorado with his family.

• Virgil Wounded Horse, the main character in "Turning Heart," is also the protagonist in my novel *Winter Counts,* and the story takes place after the events in that book. I'd been trying to work out what Virgil would do in the next novel, and this story provided an ideal opportunity to begin sketching out some new obstacles for him. I knew that his goal would be to stop working as a hired vigilante, but that the transition would not be so easy, as is shown in the story. I'd also had a hazy idea that Virgil would help to retrieve a stolen car, but I wasn't clear on the details. Once I started writing it, the story went in a different direction than I'd intended, but I was delighted to bring in some backstory for Virgil regarding his childhood and close friendship with Rob Turning Heart, and how that relationship continues to influence him.

Another topic I wanted to explore was the role of dogs on the reservation. There's a deep and long-standing love for dogs in the Lakota culture, but problems with packs of stray canines have become an issue recently, and several people have been attacked. Virgil has to balance his own affection for dogs with the awareness that Diesel, a former fighting dog, could kill or maim him. It was important to me that Virgil insists Diesel receive veterinary care after the incident.

I'm grateful to Hank Phillippi Ryan for the invitation to contribute a story for the 2021 Bouchercon anthology, *This Time for Sure.* Of course, the Bouchercon conference was canceled because of the pandemic, although the anthology was printed and distributed by Down & Out Books. I'm thrilled that "Turning Heart" will appear in this volume, giving readers another chance to read about Virgil and his world.

BRENDAN WILLIAMS-CHILDS is a fiction writer and zine maker from Wyoming who lives elsewhere. His work has appeared in *Catapult, Nat. Brut,* the *Colorado Review,* and several Lambda-nominated anthologies. See more at williamschilds.com/fiction.

• I had previously written about the character of Elazig in passing, and I found myself asking, "What would it look like if the serious consequences of this man's work finally reached him in some form?" By pure luck and chance, while I was thinking about it, I stumbled on a photo series of the Lycian rock tombs. Almost all of my fiction is written with two things in mind: the ending and a central image. These two were easily married in "Lycia."

MATTHEW WILSON is a teacher from Portland, Oregon. His stories have appeared in *Ellery Queen Mystery Magazine* and *Alfred Hitchcock Mystery Magazine.* He has been twice shortlisted in the *Best American Mystery and Suspense* series and was once a finalist for a Derringer Award.

• I keep a list of story ideas, and a lot of these are just weird little phrases like "wheelchair fight," "the shoplifting river," and "tree killer." These ideas come from all over—what I'm reading, a memory, something I see out the car window—and they often never go anywhere, while others eventually grow into characters and plots. That is the case with "Thank You for Your Service."

I had written "stolen valor vigilante" on my list after reading about ambush videos of fraudulent veterans. I had also read Sebastian Junger's book *Tribe: On Homecoming and Belonging* and was thinking about the challenges of returning to civilian life for recent veterans. I knew I wanted to have a wounded Iraq veteran at the center of a story about these topics, but I couldn't quite find a plot. I was stuck for a while until I decided to set the story on the Monterey Bay, a place I knew from my childhood as an army brat, where many retired veterans live in the communities surrounding the now-defunct Fort Ord. From there the voices of those old veterans came out of my memory, and I wrote that first scene set in the VFW. Once I could establish the personal rivalries among the older vets and the contrasting life experiences between them and the more recent and much younger vets, I could see where this thing was going.

I would like to thank Linda Landrigan at *Alfred Hitchcock Mystery Magazine* for giving my story a place for readers.

Other Distinguished Mystery and Suspense of 2021

Frankie Bailey
  Nighthawks. *Midnight Hour*
Travis Wade Beaty
  A Bad-Hearted Man. *Rock and a Hard Place*, vol. 1, no. 5, Winter/Spring
Avery Bishop
  Dear Seraphina. *Audible Original*
Ken Brosky
  Mile 4. *Tough,* November
Brenda Buchanan
  Means, Motive, and Opportunity. *Bloodroot*
Alafair Burke
  Seat 2C. *When a Stranger Comes to Town*
Hilary Davidson
  Weed Man. *Ellery Queen Mystery Magazine,* September/October
O'Neil De Noux
  Ticking of the Big Clock. *Alfred Hitchcock Mystery Magazine,* January/February
Will Ejzak
  Savages. *Pembroke Magazine,* no. 53
Eve Fisher
  The Sweet Life. *Alfred Hitchcock Mystery Magazine,* July/August
Jim Fusilli
  Loogy. *Alfred Hitchcock Mystery Magazine,* November/December

Paul J. Garth
  Aperture. *Vautrin,* Winter
Nils Gilbertson
  Washed Up. *Mickey Finn,* vol. 2
Barb Goffman
  A Tale of Two Sisters. *Murder on the Beach*
Rob Hart
  Bar Wall Panda. *Collectibles*
Talia Klebenov Jacobs
  Perfect Strangers. *When a Stranger Comes to Town*
Serena Jayne
  The Six of Me. *Rock and a Hard Place,* vol. 1, no. 6, Summer
Scott Kikkawa
  Joe Sukiyaki. *A Bag of Dick's*
Kari Kilgore
  What Breaks a Man. *Fiction River,* no. 36
John Lantigua
  Death and the Coyote. *Ellery Queen Mystery Magazine,* November/December
Ken Linn
  Stray. *Ellery Queen Mystery Magazine,* January/February
Mike McClelland
  Devil's Island. *Pank,* 1.1
  Environmental Futures

Gwen Mullins
    Violent Devotion. *New Ohio Review,*
    Spring
Richie Narvaez
    Courtesy. Professionalism. Respect.
    Under the Thumb
Delia C. Pitts
    Midnight Confidential. *Midnight
    Hour*
Ellen Rhudy
    The Mystery of the Mislaid Girls.
    Uncharted Mag, August 9

Lori Robbins
    Leading Ladies. *Justice for All*
Eduardo Santiago
    The Ankle of Anza. *Palm Springs
    Noir*
Frank Zafiro
    The Rumor in 411. *The Eviction of
    Hope*
Désirée Zamorano
    Caperucita Roja. *Chicana/Latina
    Studies,* vol. 20, no. 2,
    Spring

EXPLORE THE REST OF THE SERIES!

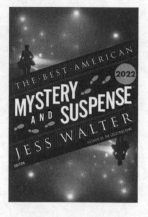

On sale 11/1/22
$17.99

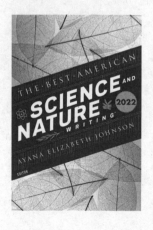

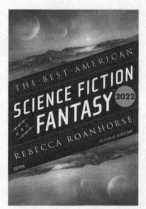

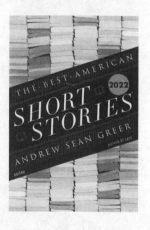